AS THE RAINS BREAK

By L.R. Claude

To all of the men and woman that have served and sacrificed in order to protect the lives and livelihoods of others, I wish there were words to truly express the gratitude I hold within me. For the members of all military branches around the world I shall bow my head to honor those whom put others before themselves.

-L.R. Claude

As the Rains Break

Underneath everyone is a raw, untamed, unapologetic animal. When you back someone into a corner, pile on the stress and take away everything they might be proud of, take away hope, rob him of his faith and that man will deal with the situation. Do that to a man's family and there are no ends to what he will do to give his family a tomorrow. Destiny, fate, these are terms people use to cope with the way things turn out. When there is absolutely nothing left for someone to do, they settle and call it fate. Man can often accept their destiny. The last few moments before death is most often when people accept their fate, the way things are, they finally give up fighting. Few fight all the way to the end. When the shadows reach from the unlit corners of the dark, what will your mind reveal? When you find yourself at that moment, when the shadows come for you, will you fight or simply surrender your last breath and call it fate?

The history of man is full of struggle, the struggle to survive as Neanderthals foraged and migrated, struggled to breed and find mates to secure their lineage. It had been the experience of man to fight for the success of themselves since man shed their tails and left the trees to take up walking among fields. As man evolved, so did the need to become better at locating, searching, hunting and mating. Each of us is the result of such successes, proof of the shear will our forefathers had.

There are moments in time where everyone remembers specifically where they were and what they were doing when a historical moment happens. Many people remember the declaration by President Wilson that the United States would be joining the World War in Europe after the assassination of Archduke Ferdinand. Everyone remembers hovering around the radio when the official resonance came across the speakers when the cease of the same World War was reported. Obadiah Withers was finishing household chores at the family farm as a young lad when his father had expressed interest and gratitude for the return of soldiers from across the Atlantic.

Obadiah met a young girl named Mary Sue at a local dance in Charleston. They wed in June on a hot Sunday with loving friends and family gathered around. Obadiah and Mary Sue had both saved all the money they could when they were first starting out as a couple and decided to move to Oklahoma. The lands were overflowing with promises of fertility. The gasoline tractor made tilling and plowing of the prairie lands ever more prominent and available to plant crops. The thick tall buffalo grass that covered the plains became less of a threat after tractors were able to chop through the thick tangle of root systems that fought back the farmers as they had tried in the early nineteen hundreds and merely survived. Farmers in the Oklahoma-Texas area fared better as cattle farmers as the Buffalo grass was hearty, plentiful, and created a vast sea of waving green for cattle to feast upon.

Obadiah read farmer's reports with his father as a young boy and learned ways to till and plant crops in order to maximize the plant density. Obadiah was raised as a cotton farmer. Word spread that wheat prices were sky rocketing and that there was a fortune to be made in the mid-west in the form of golden wheat. Farmers fled to the mid-west to fight off the prairie grasses to make room for their own wheat farms.The Withers had begun their family with a beautiful little girl shortly after their wedding. Obadiah worked hard at a local cotton mill as well as on his family cotton farm. Cotton was a huge money crop in the Carolina's and has propagated the Withers family since the Civil War.

Obadiah and Mary Sue welcomed Elizabeth in the fall of 1927. She was a beautiful healthy little girl that shared beautiful brown eyes with her mother. Mary Sue was a slender bride in the summer of '26. She and Obadiah had become acquainted in the previous year and learned to get along as they walked the dirt roads that crossed their town. In the winters they hitched up horses to buggies and still spent time together before they were married. After the wedding they moved into the Withers farm where his father Norman had made ample room for them. Mary Sue loved being pregnant. She was of smaller, slender frame, had shoulder length brown hair that she kept curled and tied up, Obadiah fought often to keep his knees from buckling whenever she grasped his hand to kiss him. Their love was immense and it was beginning to blossom into children.

After Elizabeth arrived they spent their first winter as parents planning out a future for themselves. Once they had enough money saved to buy a house and a tractor to use to plow land, they headed west. Little Elizabeth was a giggling bundle of rosy cheeks and Norman was proud of the family his son was starting. As the cold South Carolina winter came and went, the small family hunkered down to work together in the farmhouse. The young proud couple set forth to navigate their future together. The country was still wobbly economically but there were strengths in the country and farming was one of them. After the World War ended, there were thousands of young men who hadn't returned.

With the holes in families and workforces, young men that had a harder time finding some factory work, had better luck as the workforce still needed able bodies. The mines in the Virginias were still turning out black gold and the cotton mills were still pumping out textiles for the world. The southern states didn't feel as distraught as the rest of the country seemed to in the newspapers. Obadiah worked hard to provide for his new young family. With a medium build he felt resilient against the wear and tear of the grueling long shifts of the mill and still made the time and energy to take part in rearing his daughter, with pride.

The notion to move westward with his family came from the newspapers printing articles about thousands moving to the plains to reap the rewards of fertile grounds and plentiful land for all. Obadiah was slightly hesitant on his move. He had spent his entire life in Charleston farming with his father. Obadiah was a spitting image of his Poppa, Norman. Both men were of darker hair and medium complexion, dark brown eyes and wore their hair short so they would sweat less under the harsh South Carolina sun when it came time to plow or harvest. When you farm land and also spend ample time working the machines in a cotton mill, you build up coarse hands, Obadiah's hands were padded thickly with calluses and they resembled baseball mitts, his upper body rippled in the summers from bailing and bundling cotton. Norman grew up a cotton farmer and found great pride in working his land, Norman instilled a sense of duty and hard work in his son and that seed took. Obadiah was muscular from his hard work, Mary Sue felt blessed to have a husband that made her hands shake when they

5

were together and she wanted to bear more of his children and raise them with him.

Obadiah had a strong jaw from gritting his teeth while working. His genes form Norman had really shown through in good sturdy posture, broad shoulders and a good muscle tone. Obadiah had a mahogany tone to his hair and Mary Sue adored his strength in physique and also in his faith and character. Obadiah and Mary Sue wanted several children to carry on their name and to help around the farm in the next few years. They desperately wanted a farm of their own and it was becoming closer within reach. When little Elizabeth began to walk it was the third winter that Obadiah and Mary Sue had been through as husband and wife. This was the winter that secured them in the dream of moving west. Obadiah and Mary Sue made arrangements with some of the local farmers to purchase a trailer to load up, as well as a used tractor to haul with them to begin their own life. It was the Spring of '29 when Obadiah secured the loan and a deed for a remote parcel of land in the western end of the Oklahoma panhandle. The young couple and their daughter loaded up everything they needed in order to prosper on their own in a new town.

With the help of Norman, Obadiah loaded up his newer 1927 Farmall tractor onto a trailer and the Withers then began to make their way across the Appalachian Mountains and through Oklahoma by way of Arkansas. The small family and their 1928 Dodge hay-burner chugged along the roads and learned their ways of husband and wife, along with learning about their new home state. Mary Sue took great confidence in their abilities to get through small struggles of disagreements all while raising a toddler. Little Elizabeth was anxious to walk and run through most of the trip and hardly sat still on the lap of her mother as the scenery lay out before them once through the mountains. The Withers raced along the often two tracked roads and left a long trail of road dust behind them. Obadiah was anxious to see what his property would grow as well as how it was laid out just outside of Indian Gulch.

Indian Gulch was a small town. It was pretty removed from some of the medium cities too. It left its' residents to rely more on themselves and each other. The new Withers were familiar with relying on others as they had leaned pretty heavily on Norman and some of their church family to gather supplies before their westward adventure.

The Withers camped roadside for two airy crisp nights during their travel as caution was a necessity when driving with a loaded trailer and his two most important worldly possessions riding in the passenger seat right next to him. On the second day of their drive, Mary Sue bounced the seventeen month old toddler on her lap as her husband drove. March was warming and the married twosome spoke about the coming chores and preparation their new farm might need once they arrive at their new residence. Mary Sue kept bouncing her young daughter and turned her eyes to her husband; "Darling, when would you be ready for another child?" she asked her driver. "We have the makings of a great family, the promise of fertile grounds to raise both crops and family. The Lord has blessed us to do both in a new state." Mary Sue took the pause in Obadiah's' speaking to interject her news. She had patiently tried to save it for their arrival at their own farm; she had planned to tell her husband the wonderful news of yet another great life blossoming inside of her.

Mary Sue was so overjoyed with the news, new farm, great promise of the future ahead that she just blurted it out " how about later this summer?" Obadiah kept his focus on the road ahead and nodded along with the bumps in the dirt road that they jostled down. After a minute of long awkward silence and dread beginning to fill his young bride, it finally clicked in the mind of the grateful father what his young wife was speaking of and his thick black eyebrows seemed to race towards his hairline in joyous glee.

Fumbling and trying to safely pull over to embrace his wife and the mother of his first and soon second child. Obadiah and Mary Sue raced one another to exit their car doors with Elizabeth in tow; they held each other tightly in excitement and tried not to squish the now big sister while doing so. After a few moments the elation dulled enough for the man to reclaim his throne behind the wheel of the hardtop car and finish his final ascent to their final destination. The grand news lifted the heart and spirit of Obadiah and made the last few hours of their drive much less grueling than the previous two days had been, the weather continued to warm up more and more and the air continued to smell of promise under the slight smell of dirt and wildflower buds.

The drive had left them with sore bums and short tempers at times but together was the only way they were going to survive and when tempers got strained and harsh words crossed to each other, they learned to quickly apologize and make amends. Mary Sue apologized sincerely to her husband for having to keep her secret but she wanted to make the beginning of their life in their new home that much better and also, only being a month or two along, she wasn't entirely certain. The young husband and wife had even more reason to prosper with their newly purchased land and as each day was anew, so was the desire to quickly establish themselves.

The days became warmer; Obadiah rolled his shirt sleeves up higher and higher as the days of March passed on. With a bundle of money in the left pocket of his overalls, Obadiah stopped to fill up the gas tanks of his motor vehicle and of the tractor when they drove into the new city of Indian Gulch. There was a tall slim man at the gas station that came out to crank the gas station pump when they pulled up and turned the engine off. After the few days of driving it was nice to have a few more frequent stops to stretch and let their beautiful young daughter run in a nearby patch of grass while the girls' father purchased the necessary petroleum products.

The tall gas station owner was named Johnson Franks, he was in his late forties, had a thick bushy salt and pepper beard and his overalls hung on him as if on a clothesline, over a worn through gray button up shirt. Franks' shirt had holes worn in it from frequent use as well as some stains soiled from motor oil or grease. Mr. Franks and Mr. Withers exchanged pleasantries as well as general information about where to purchase goods, groceries and any other supplies to propagate their new home.

Johnson gave final directions to the Withers so they could make their last hour drive to their new farm. The farm was purchased from a couple that decided to move to California and start a fruit farm, leaving behind a flat span of luscious once prairie land that had been tilled under and mixed in with the tall grasses that once covered everything as far as the eye could see. The dirt was rich with nutrients, the topsoil was dark black and each handful smelled of compost and the thick aroma of life. The Oklahoma winds whirled around the dust covered burgundy Dodge that had three passengers, and one on the way. The Withers took deep life reassuring breathes that settled any worries of insecurity they may have had. With their eyes tuned west and the twist of the ignition, Obadiah navigated the last bit of drive towards their land. The engine hummed as the driver kept constant

8

pressure against the accelerator and the trailer behind them squeaked as they turned down Saginaw Way which ended at their driveway.

There were three farms between town and the end of Saginaw Way, each home was simple and dotted the large fields of dark brown earth just waiting to produce a rich bountiful harvest. The dusty Dodge made the last of its' drive down the worn reddish brown driveway with hardened mud slots worn into it as it neared the house. The house had a dark brown tin roof, and faded brown wood walls. The windows were dirty and the one out building looked like it needed some of the faded grayish-brown wood boards replaced. The brakes made a high pitched squeal as the car came to its final stop of the trip.

The couple took a moment to survey their surroundings and both smiled at the vision of golden wheat under their fingertips as they walked along in the fields. It was the middle of the afternoon and the sun had already peaked and begun its decent towards the California valleys. Mary Sue unloaded her little daughter with curly brown ringlets and let the wee one run and play in the dirt as her parents began to untie and unload the trailer and put away furniture into their home. The unpacking didn't take all that long for the two but the need for cleaning was a much longer task.

With broom in hand Mary Sue swept and made many piles of light gray powder during their first day while Obadiah played with his daughter in the front yard and tried his best to keep himself and young daughter out of the house while his wife toiled away. Much of the first day was spent arranging dressers and making rooms livable. The rocking chair sat specifically near the front window for when Mary Sue was further along in her pregnancy so she could rock for her own comfort while taking in the view.

The day warmed up and the family made a trip into town to get better acquainted with Indian Gulch. Mary Sue wanted to find a new church as well as a market to buy some supplies for the icebox. The Withers journeyed down the dirt roads back to town and took stock of all the fields that surrounded them. Many of the fields still glinted green with the grass, while others were just dirt ready to be sowed. The couple was overwhelmed with the promises of home and the new land around them. Their small town had polite and courteous people who smiled and waved at one another as they passed.

The town tack and hardware was run by a man named Theodore Carvell; he was a shorter, tanned and stocky man with three young kids and an Indian wife. There was little diversity in town. There was a laundry and tailoring shop run by a Chinese family. You could hardly understand them, but they were nice nonetheless. There were two simple rows of buildings that lined the main street of town. Towards the end was the food market that had a weekly truck delivery of goods and produce. Indian Gulch was over a hundred miles from any other medium sized city. Gulch swelled then shrunk again as people stopped along their routes to California. But most only stayed long enough to refuel or replenish supplies along their path.

Their smiles gleaned as they explored their new town. Their eyes were bright with potential and it gave a silver glimmer to the horizon of Indian Gulch. The windows in town were brushed with dust from the warming spring winds that gusted about. Bright eyed and filled with hope the young couple set back towards their home to end their first day in their new home, new town.

The townsfolk spoke about new citizens, cattle ranchers moving herds, and auctioneers keeping up cattle auctions for the butcher, and walking up and down main making salutations with fellow Gulches during their stroll, while the boards under their feet creaked and offered up small puffs of dust from between the cracks. Little Elizabeth held the hands of her parents and wobbled bow-legged down the boardwalks, along with many of the nicely dressed ladies in various sized hats. Some hats had big fluffy feathers while some had different kinds of lace adorning them.

The market had shelves stacked with glass jars filled with carrots, peas, and beans with small hunks of bacon inside for flavoring. There was an ordering desk inside. It was stacked with catalogs from which you can order various furniture or tools from different companies and have freight shipped in on big trucks. The nearest train station was three hours away, so costs to have things trucked in were a bit pricey, still, it offered the chance to provide for the citizens of Indian Gulch.

Indian Gulch was a small quaint town but the people seemed to have large visions of what it might become. The ladies dressed fashionably in their finest dresses and bonnets with different laces or tie designs. Many of the farmers wore dirty or faded overalls, but, there were several gentlemen who stood around beating their gums in bowler hats, or, in vests while speaking of business.

10

There was sharp dressed man in spectacles and he shot a "howdo" towards the couple sauntering with their little girl in tow, on their new main street. The gentleman peered over his eyeglasses at the folks walking by. He wore a white dress shirt with black stripes running down it, over the white dress shirt was a dark gray vest with a gold chain hanging out of the pocket watch pocket. The sharply dressed man was the town doctor, a well-educated man named Joseph Martinez, he had been educated in the northeast and saw the opportunity to establish his own practice in the mid-west as larger groups traveled in hopes of better prospects. Tens of thousands of people continued to leave the east coast to stake their claim all over the rest of the country, the spiffy Dr. Martinez had himself a young wife and was settling in to begin a family alongside with his practice, the town was full of newcomers so everyone was more than willing to be accommodating and welcoming.

The air still smelled of rich fertile land, the trees were beginning to produce pollen and some of the light brown dust covering windows began to take on a yellow hue. The bank in town was run by a stingy Jew named Hirsch Morgenstern. He was a man of little stature, kept short salt and pepper graying hair. He had an abrasive attitude towards people. The sour facial expression he wore was almost branded upon his face, much like the sun wrinkles that come from long summers of working outside. Hirsch carried a piss poor attitude towards everyone outside of himself and almost grumbled when his bank gave out a loan, whether it was for housing or new equipment, as the local farms continued to grow.

Hirsch was from New York and came from a lineage of "tight fisted money hungry Jews" and he embraced it. He did not hide his tendency to hoard or be tight fisted when it came to finances, He held most of the control in town when it came to tax money used to keep street lamps lit or pays the sheriffs salary. Hirsch had a tough line of work but having one of the larger houses in town, he had very little reason to complain. Anytime Hirsch got to turn down a loan it was almost the only time he might express any form of joy. Anytime any of the residents in town had a disagreement about why they had been turned down for a loan from Morgenstern bank, they questioned the man whose name was emblazoned across the top of the building. He was quick to quell any anger with "I'm a Jew..... What do you expect?" He hid behind his beliefs but also knew that if he was first to use the slanderous terms so that it wouldn't be used against him. It was a smart ploy on his behalf and gave him the higher standing.

Johnson owned and ran the gas station. It had two pumps that needed to be hand cranked. His store was meekly stocked, but it also had one large bay to pull in cars to jack them up. He would repair parts of vehicles or tractors when the owner couldn't. Most of the farmers from town fixed many of their own things, be it motorized or architectural, like board repairs or replacing windows. Johnson was one of the few town members that had Hirschs' favor. Not only did he pay in full when he needed to, he also gave Hirsch the priority he thought he deserved, the secret was, it was simply because Johnson had the time and made the priority for each of his patrons when they needed his expertise. Johnson lived next to a clothing store owner, Pauline Curtiss.

Pauline was a heavier set lady in her mid-forties. She had auburn hair that she kept in tight curls tucked under various hats, trying to keep up with the latest fashions, Pauline had a heavy gate when she walked and she seemed to struggle to keep her heavy frame balanced over small heels or as she tried to keep a parasol overhead with her uptight classy posture whenever she walked outside. Mrs. Curtiss kept herself bundled, wedged into different corsets and dresses that seemed to heave her bosom closer to her chin than her collar, Johnson said that even in the hells heat in the summer, she is still a "Mrs. Grundy." Pauline considered herself a Bluenose but most of the town considered her just an odd bird.

There was a keen little joint that served piping hot joe in the mornings, the kind that put your ass in the john on cold winter mornings. They served sandwiches throughout the day. The little eatery was a counter inside the butcher shop run by a hardboiled Murry Ponsen, and his wife Katherine, they worked side by side. They cured hams in September, and processed many other meats year round, and when some of the hams were ripe, they would thinly shave piles of it to keep in an icebox for Katherine to serve on bread slices for lunch and sandwiches in the mid-days.

Murry was an older gentleman and made his livelihood in the Virginia mines in his youth. He and his bride raised two children that dispersed to other cities back east. Murry had a dark gray Vandyke and longer slicked back hair. His bushy eyebrows gave him a weather worn look and his medium height was offset by his thin upper body that rested upon his rotund abdomen from eating

12

so much of his own salted meats. Katherine had dark red hair that she kept tied back under a simple white bonnet to keep it hidden during the work days. Katherine had nimble coarse hands from years of bean picking and working with her hands. Together the Ponsens helped to serve their small community and it also gave them ample gab time with different affluent citizens as they made time for lunch in one of their four small tables in the deli.

As the young couple continued to stroll through town, they were reassured over and over that they made a great choice is moving to Indian Gulch. This town was the bee's knees and everyone seemed too willing to reach out and embrace each other as community members. Everything continued to look on the up and up as the two slowly sauntered down the boardwalks that lined the main street of town. Mary Sue had a glint in her eyes as she peered back and forth at the shops and the people that scurried about. Obadiah clenched his jaw as his impatience got the best of his having to walk at one-third the pace as his little smiling daughter grabbed his hand. He took it as Gods way of telling him to slow down and enjoy life, as a few cars raced through town.

Elizabeth wore a pastel yellow sundress with a white sweater over the top, Mary Sue kept feeling the small left hand of her daughter to keep an eye on her internal temperature. She had concern of overheating as the afternoon warmed up. The Withers shared loving looks, having only found out yesterday that his wife was carrying the second child in the making of their family. Some of the sharp dressed men and very tidy up kept, women that trotted by all smiled and nodded with gratitude towards the young miss and her adoring parents. The Withers finished up their hour long adventurous stroll through town, they liked all they had seen.

Obadiah spoke with his wife about the need to stop at the tack shop for a pound of penny nails. He wanted to begin fixing many of the boards that had fallen to disrepair on the outbuilding back at their new farm. Mary Sue responded with a list of her own. She needed things of a hardware nature as well as many items from the grocery market. She needed items such as flour and other baking essentials. Mary Sue loved a warm oven on chilly mornings with fresh bread or muffins to feast on for breakfast at home.

Little Elizabeth was an early to rise child. In the past few months she has taken to waking up not long after sunrise. She did not give her parents a choice but to wake with her. She shook her sleeping basket by kicking her feet and making a rapid thumping that echoed through the floor while laughing from her jiggling belly. Elizabeth was a happy child; anyone who met the bright eyed wee-one could see the bright mind and loving joy in her. Mary Sue loaded her daughter into the backseat of the family Dodge; she shot a comforting smile to her husband as Obadiah closed the door behind her when she tucked her legs into the passenger side.

Obadiah carried himself with an even greater pride for his choice in location. He felt God had blessed him with the good sense of purpose and direction for his family. As he walked past the front of his car he swiped his hand across the front light bulb lenses to remove a thick layer of road dirt, he glanced at his bride through the windshield wiper streaks of the windshield. The rest of the dirt was piling up enough to almost obscure any viewing other than where the wipers had landscaped the glass. The burgundy car had almost lost all of its' color to the dirt that shrouded it. Upon slamming the driver door shut a thin top layer of dirt fell from the door and left a small plume from falling to the ground, causing a small smirk in the left corner of his mouth and a hearty exhale of dry breath.

The previous few days had crossed through the mind of the stoic driver. It had taken a long slow two days to drive from South Carolina, over the mountains and through Oklahoma to Indian Gulch. The three had made semi frequent stops for gas and time to play with little Elizabeth in the various roadsides. It was a pleasant drive as the spring air brought different smells of promise and wild flowers preparing to bloom. One of the first stops they decided to picnic for lunch was in a bungalow of tall Jack Pines. The squirrels were waking from their winter slumber and still foraging for the long buried nuts. Elizabeth murmured and pointed as the furry creatures scampered around them. They sat upon a blanket that provided a padded barrier between them and the mounds of pine needles layering the floor of the dark green canopy above.

Theodore Carvell was reading through a new spring catalog of available equipment behind his counter as Obadiah entered the tack store, Carvell was a stocky man with broad shoulders and a gut than hung over his black leather belt. He spoke with a slow drawl when he greeted people; "How do ta-day suh?" The pleasantry fell upon deaf ears until his one customer made it six feet in the door. The skewed greeting clicked inside the mind of Obadiah and he proceeded to respond in kind: "Sir, Obadiah

Withers, pleased to meet you." After asking the man behind the counter to assist with a small brown bag of penny nails for his farm, Obadiah promptly paid and thanked the man for his help. He reassured him that he would probably return multiple times in the near future as his new home had a long list of required updates. After shaking hands good bye, the store owner wiped his moist brow with his handkerchief then returned it to his rear pocket. He leaned back against the counter and resumed searching the printed catalog.

The young family made a fast trip of their stop at the market. They bought a few cases of jars filled with various vegetables, bags of flour and grains as well as jams and marmalade. The orange marmalade was Mary Sues' favorite. The car headed down the main road bound west towards their home. It was midafternoon at this point and the sun hung just over its zenith in the sky, Obadiah had to lean back against his seat to keep the edge of the windshield below the sun to keep its rays out of his eyes, while he followed it west.

The drive from town took almost an hour as they bumbled down the road. There was still plenty of home organizing to be done, and many boxes on the trailer that had been backed into the small barn like building. They had spent their first night in their new home atop a few blankets sleeping on the floor. They had the cot like bed set up for their daughter and did their best prioritizing for what they would need to unpack in their first afternoon. The couple jostled ideas for how to arrange the remainder of their furnishings. Do they place their bed under their west facing window in the back of their home or towards a northern wall? They didn't have all of the riches of the world but they had one another and in that they felt like a queen and a king in their castle. No one could take that away.

The couple dated for over a year before deciding to exchange vows. They had been to grammar school together, they grew up on opposite sides of town and each had cotton farms, cotton was the staple crop in the south, the weather was ideal for such plantations and for fifty years on each side of the civil war, cotton was of high demand. Mary Sue was the youngest daughter of three girls, her oldest sister Gertrude had passed away when Mary Sue was six, Gertie had a bad case of pneumonia that had started with the first snowfall of January and worsened until her passing in late February. The other remaining Kelsonovich daughter was Mary

15

Sues sister Charlotte, whom was fourteen months older and hadn't married yet.

Charlotte was a well-educated young lady, had blond hair and an affinity for dancing. Charlotte felt destined to be her father's caretaker now that Mary Sue had become a Wither and moved into the house with Obadiah, thus leaving behind her family home. Charlotte made her lone sister promise to write when they first got into their new home, Mary Sue had purchased the necessary stationary to correspond with her family and friends back east. Mary Sue looked very forward to helping her husband continue to arrange her new living arrangements with her husband Obadiah, the house seemed quiet and empty after the rambunctious toddler finally fell asleep, Obadiah's mother left the world after an accident on the farm just a few years ago, leaving the home to just Obadiah and Norman, Obadiah had grave concerns about leaving Norman behind but knew his father was bent on ensuring his son had the necessary strength and skills to make it all on his own, far from home.

After loading up the trailer for their journey west, the Withers spent most of the day with Charlotte and the rest of the Kelsonovich's, Mary Sue parents Margarete and Melvin were going to miss their only grandchild as well as their youngest daughter, Margarete and Melvin were hearty southern cotton farmers much like Norman and Obadiah was, they did their best to educate their daughters and even after Gertie passed on, they tried to keep from preventing their daughters from living their own lives. Charlotte expressed much more concern about the almost two-thousand mile drive that the new family would undertake upon themselves, Charlotte cried and hugged her only sister ever so tightly, she tried her best to smile off her tears to keep from upsetting her young niece but was still at the whim of her emotions.

The invitation to come visit was offered to the elder sibling, Mary Sue knew that offering housing at any time Charlotte had interest to come visit would lessen the feeling of new found solitude. The last day back in Charleston was spent with mostly goodbyes, Charlotte wore a pleasant light blue dress that flowed behind her as she walked, she had a white choker around her neck that matched the fluffy lace that ribbed the dress around her corseted bosom, she also kept her blonde hair in thick spiral coils that bounced behind her with each step, the light pink makeup made her cheekbones stick out and shortly after her first tears fell from her eyes, her cheek makeup began to smear onto her cotton napkin she used to wipe away the sadness.

Margarete and Melvin both hugged little Elizabeth and spoke in higher tones about wanting to keep her forever. The Kelsonovichs' were supportive in the idea for their baby daughter to join her husband at the Withers home but were much more open about the concern to move several states away. Melvin had lost his younger brother at the end of the World War in some god forsaken country in Europe, his loss had only shortly proceeded the death of his oldest Daughter, he had taken to sipping whiskey and increased his pipe smoking, leaving his voice raspy and deep, almost matching his barrel chest and thick haunches, giving him a much older appearance.

The Kelsonovich's kept their front hedges adorned with multiple blue blossoms, Margarete called them her Benson hedges, the postal stand seemed to have some of the same Benson hedges out front of it and the slight touch of home had appealed to Mary Sue. "I already miss Charlotte" Mary Sue began a late afternoon conversation, "I know Mare, now that you have your stationary you can write each night and once a week we'll take the letters to the post to have them mailed out" Obadiah kindly responded, hoping to comfort his wife. Melvin bestowed some simple yet intimate advice to his only son in-law; "Keep her close and stay open, and also talk a lot" Obadiah had spent a few days discussing said advice with his life passenger as they made their way to their farm, to the best they could muster, they figured Melvin meant to hold one another dearly and wanted to rock in tandem side by side to wind down each night after any sort of day that might fill the years until they've grown old together.

The afternoon supper consisted of hard tack biscuits with a marmalade spread, water steeped with flavoring leaves like a citrus tea and a bit of a lamb shank, the couple donned their rocking chairs that sat adjacent to the bigger window in the main room, Elizabeth succumbed to sleep with her full tummy while sitting sideways in the swaying lap of her mother. Obadiah looked upon his two best ladies in the chair by his side and took stock of how lovely they were and how blessed his life had become. Obadiah had wallowed in sadness as his father had tried to drink away the pains as they both did their best to heal from the loss of the first Mrs. Withers; Victoria.

It was already a stupendous year, with everything that had already transpired and come to fruition, finally getting enough then buying their house, loading up his small family and then wagon-training westward and for the first semi nervous time, they were a family and all on their own having finally cut the emergency ropes from Norman. Obadiah and his bride Mary Sue have spoken often about how important it is for a couple to stake out on their own, be in a situation by themselves in which they only have one another to rely on to strengthen their bonds as husband and wife, they looked forward to the day when it was just the two of them, and in their own home.

The last few days had been chaotic onslaught of changes, the magnitude of those changes was exhausting, one week ago the young couple was only mere minutes from everyone they had ever known, minutes form emergency relief, minutes from a safe hiding place if they as a couple ran into a disagreeable topic they could part ways for a night to blow off steam and then to later work out their problems and grow closer together. All out and on their own, they had to dig deep, grit their teeth and work through any problems they may have. Both halves of the couple had their fears, had worries for the future, also had the added pressure of rearing the life of the sweet precious young Elizabeth.

The delicate little life was a bright eyed girl with medium brown curly hair, she adored any sort of critter she could come across, ants, grasshoppers, frogs, anything that moved she just wanted to cuddle and hold, this tiny two-legged ball of love was a spark of energy and ran around the rooms of their new abode. Elizabeth often woke from her afternoon nap shouting "*MAAAAAAAMMAAAAAAA*" even if Mary Sue was within reach, she often fumbled and clumsily made messes while eating but kept working further and further towards independence as she learned to feed herself.

Mary Sue best guessed she was probably between two and three months pregnant with family member number four. There was so much to do and the list continued to expand as the pair just sat and rocked in unison in their rocking chairs as the end of their first full day in their new home tapered off. The Withers just let exhaustion overtake their minds and bodies into the late hours, the Oklahoma sky to the south was pitch black and dotted with bright stars to the left as the bright orange of the horizon to the right left a trail of darkening crimson behind that faded to black. Their home smelled of dust and dirt with a tiny hint of the supper biscuits still hung in the air. The smell, and view both were wrought with such potential the side corners of Obadiah's mouth just seemed to curl up without having to try. The spring crickets sang their lullaby and the chorus helped to shuffle in the sweet slumber of the evening. Obadiah had a few muscles in his shoulders twitch after the day of lugging, hauling and unpacking. Mary Sue's head began to fall to her left as her eyelids grew heavy and the breathing of her daughter joined the cricket chorus, the small breaths of the toddler soothed her mother alongside the gentle rocking of the loving and soft caring Mary Sue.

Obadiah fought with the last ounces of energy he could muster to heave his worn out hide off of his chair, his backside tingled as blood began to rush to it, he scuffled quietly to the side of his wife and used his sore left hand to gently brush the hair across the forehead of his beautiful wife and tuck it behind her ear as he reassured her it was just him. The slightly startled whole body twitch of his bride made her pop her eyes open widely at first, it only took a split second for the comforting sight of her husband standing vigilantly by her side that brought a smile to her face as she moved her right hand to offer access for Obadiah to lift the tiny half drooling Elizabeth from her lap before he carried the little girl to her bed for the night.

Mary Sue turned to her left a bit to and crossed her arms to keep her chest warm where her daughter was, without her baby nestled against her, the warmth began to feel cold and left her with a subtle shiver that further enticed her to want to go to sleep. Obadiah looked at the peaceful dreaming face of his baby girl as he cradled her safely in his arms, he saw the future with her, he was afraid to admit she was almost two already, he was scared that he would have a second child before the end of the year and he felt the pressure upon his spirit that this year's harvest had to be a great one as he needed to set a solid base for his crops and get a solid footing in establishing himself as a farmer in the area. The small body breathed her shallow breaths, he could feel her small ribs push against his fingers and she made a small squeak as he laid her in her bed and covered her with a modest sheet.

Obadiah brushed the thin hair of his daughter out of her face and while resting his right hand upon her forehead, he lowered himself to her height and kissed her on her cheek to help ensure a good night's sleep. With left hand upon his left knee, he used his arm to push his upper body away from the floor to stand as erect as possible, his body was sore from the work but he deeply felt accomplished, a good hard day's work is always the key to success, as a farmer he was well versed in hard work and had often reaped the rewards of a hard days labor. His lower back felt swollen and the muscles bulged when he tried to straighten out his posture, he turned and headed back to his wife whom was nuzzled into the wooden backing of her slightly smaller rocking chair, her head was resting against her left shoulder and her arms were crossed, she was his angel and she looked like it too.

Mary Sue was at peace, her breaths were free of burden, her eyes were still behind her eyelids, not frantically pacing side to side from dreams of worry, and she appeared to be at peace as she slept, in her own home and with her husband nearby. Obadiah extended his left hand again, he kept his left hand half curled and brushed her right cheek with the backside of his fingers as he shushed her with comfort to wake her gently and escort her to bed. Mary Sue was devoid of energy, she rested her weary head upon his shoulder as his much larger arm embraced her to help guide his tired love to their bedroom.

With their room almost completely pitch black, Obadiah sort of fumbled as he unbuttoned the shirt of his wife, he laid her down and ran his left hand down her row of buttons to ease them undone and work the shirt off, Obadiah ran his fingertips down the center of her chest, she let out an ever so slight moan in a lightly enticing manner , they were still young in their marriage and found themselves in the throes of passion at every chance they could, it was sometimes a juggle with the having lived with his father for the past two years, and also with Elizabeth often nearby.

The urges to make love to his wife was at the cusp of his desires, he ran his left hand from her collarbone and down her right breast while beginning to kiss her cheek, Mary Sue remained silent, no go ahead murmur or sounds of approval so he finished undressing his wife and enjoying a few copious gropes while getting her night shirt on. Obadiah un-clicked the buckles that held his overalls to hang on his body, his fingers were swollen from the days' work and it took a moment to get them to work together to get himself undressed the rest of the way before his tired body fell to the bed.

The mattress was supporting and cradled Obadiah and the pressure from his lower back seemed to disperse down his legs and up his spine, his body throbbed and ached from various parts, his hands throbbed from all of the lifting, his head ached from being tired and the beating of his heart seemed to pound in his chest and ears alongside the crickets that were just outside of his window. The soothing orchestra of crickets, all trying to woo their mates and search for love in the bug world, seemed to fade and all of the heart beats seemed to fade in force as his head swirled and the pillow in which he rested his weary head seemed to engulf him.

Morning light broke; the light orange from the eastern sunrise entered their window. Mary Sue's hair seemed to glow as the sun sparkled within the strands. Her heavy eyelids, that were slightly encrusted, were hard to open, Obadiah had to lurch his eyelids apart in order to accept the fact he had to wake up. He glanced towards the silhouette of his wife, she was so heavenly and he was assured yet again, that she was his own personal angel.

Obadiah crept over to kiss his young bride on the cheek, hoping to make her swoon for him early this warming morning. He elbowed into the mattress to get a better angle on her. He reached his left hand towards her stomach to embrace her in his one armed manner, and kissed from her earlobe, it was a specialty that she liked, down her jaw line to her chin then back across her cheek. As he kissed her upon her cheek he could feel the muscles under the skin tense and he could feel her cheek puff up as she smiled. She gave out a slight moan and he smiled largely knowing that he woke up his wife in one of the most romantic ways he could offer.

Mary Sue turned to kiss her husband she opened her stance to hug on her big brawny husband and their embrace turned their passion into a fiery love making. Obadiah kissed and handled the body of his wife as they tried to remain quiet as not to wake their daughter, they tried to express their love physically as often as they could but also took great comfort in the simple things like muscle rubs, hand holding, and sly loving smiles that they passed to one another as frequently as possible. Mary Sue straddle upon Obadiah, her breasts glistened with a slight perspiration.

Obadiah kissed the small goose bumps that encircled her nipples and when doing so, she writhed upon him and ran her fingers through his hair. They embraced ever so tightly, their bodies entwined as if they had become one soul in their lovemaking; they volleyed turns kissing one another when breathing got heavy or the thrills of passion got to them in the midst of intimacy. It wasn't as often as their bodies desired one another but their yearning for intimacy kept them lusting for each other. This was their first time sharing their bed intimately in *their* home, it was ever so much more exciting and they were much freer to give themselves to each other as a married couple should.

After their fiery session of private husband and wife time, they laid beside each other, her breasts heaving into the air as she fought to catch her breath, he laid there and admired the body of his wife, it brought their child into this world, it had within its' womb, their second child, it was also still in firm slender shape and he enjoyed it thoroughly. They often giggled together about many things, they often ducked into the barn back at their farm in South Carolina, like teenage kids with wild hormones and deep desires for one another. Mary Sue would sometimes wear a bosom lifting corset that would ignite the loins of her husband and he would simply ravish her when he had the chance.

The love that blossomed from simple eye contact when they were a little younger had lead them to this moment, laying naked in the brisk Oklahoma air, their bodies still damp with sweat and light sprouts of steam that seemed to cascade from them. The passionate writhing has left the couple breathing heavily but trying to control it to keep the noise level from reaching a level that might wake the wee one in the next room. They began to exchange whispers as to what needs to be done around their domain, boards of the porch need to be secured, Obadiah wanted to finally go and walk the property line, his plot of land had been tilled in the years past but without having been planted last year after the previous owners moved across the country, the boundaries were fairly clear, Obadiah also wanted to take his old rifle and maybe find a rabbit or something of that nature to make a few meals of.

The shelves were stocked with many canned goods, the icebox could hold a few pounds and could help to keep meat or fresh foods that way for a few days, it was hard to keep lights from flickering as the power had surges and draws but the icebox was fairly new and reliable. Mary Sue learned to cook from her mother and was wonderful at making each meal a feast. One rabbit could make three or four meals for the growing family, the meat was also a rather important staple for the pregnant woman in the house, Obadiah also wanted to walk their property lines to see if the grassy land borders contained rabbit holes or trails or what else the land held that might help to sustain the family in their future.

Obadiah twirled his left forefinger around the right nipple of his wife as she ran her fingers across the back muscles of his neck, they enjoyed the touch and comfort of one another, and they shared light and gentle touches while they could.

"MAAAAAMAAAAAA" rang out from the other room; the couple chuckled at the bellowing holler coming from the tiny lungs of the girl they brought into the world. The couple heaved themselves into a seated position, took turns listening to bones creak and pop with movement, Mary Sue eyed the rippling muscles of her husband and desired to feel him inside her again already, she truly desired him every chance she could and he felt the same way. Their love had been so strong and passionate that there were many nights that were spent wrapped up with one another rather than sleep and some of the weary days were dealt with sans rest, both viewed the dog tired days spent longing for one another, as absolutely necessary to quench their thirst for each other.

Obadiah lustfully eyed the smooth contours of his wife's backside as she dressed, he admired that she was fit, she was so loving and he longed to spend every night with her for the rest of his life, and even if they spent every waking moment in passionate, lustful love making, for the rest of their lives, it still wouldn't be enough for either of them. The slowly moving couple, sore from the previous days' moving, dragged themselves to their posts, Mary Sue grabbed her daughter and began breakfast, Obadiah stepped into the restroom and began to froth some shaving cream and dragged his straight razor across the leather strap in order to ensure a nice clean shave from a very sharp blade.

Obadiah spent the few necessary moments to drag the cold blade across the stubble that had accumulated on his rugged face; the splashing of some cold water upon his face helped to clear up his sinuses and tuned his nose to the smell of his coffee brewing in the kitchen. As he sauntered out of the bathroom, he placed his hands against the back of his pelvis and tried to shove his pelvis forward while arching his spine backwards to bend stretch the best he could, a few snaps and pops from his backbone announced his arrival to his girls awaiting him in the next room.

Elizabeth offered up some fists squeezes to her poppa, this was her "come hither" motion for him, he picked up is pace to rush to her side and give her a big kiss good morning on the cheek, she returned the favor with a chin covered with the glaze from syrup, Mary Sue smirked and let out a momentary huff in the humor that her husband was just slimed by the wee lass. Mary Sue set her husband's mug on the table as the lava hot mud colored liquid inside steamed and let its' aroma out into the room, she blew across the opening of her mug and tried to hide her loving smile behind it, she was truly happy with her life and in every way, she found ways to become more and more happy each and every day that went by. The young couple had truly been handpicked to be so blessed and the happiness and love they had among them just exuded in many ways.

Mary Sue often had a loving twinkle in her eyes, the glint so rarely seen it was almost unheard of now a days and Obadiah knew it was his doing and he took great joy in it. Mary Sue and Obadiah fell asleep holding hands each night and awoke freshly in love each morning with each other over and over again. Obadiah propped his heavy head upon his left hand as he sat at the table to finish sipping his brew, Mary Sue tried to ramble through her list of things she needed to accomplish around the house, things such as finish unpacking the rooms and linens while adorning each of the windows with trimmings and drapes.

There was ample work that required the attention of the couple outside in the yard also, the two shade offering trees near the front of the house needed pruning as they spent the previous year in neglect. The weeds sat tall against the house, sand, dust and spider webs had piled against different corners of the home and barn, high weeds and places for bugs to conjure also made for suggesting places for rodents and snakes to be found also, all of which weren't safe for the curious and mobile child.

Obadiah focused most of his energy on the home and child that they already brought to this world, the small makings of the child within the womb of his wife sat just behind the forefront of his mind, Obadiah was excited about becoming a father again, Elizabeth required most of his attention and energy but the thought about giving her a sibling was another step towards the family of his dreams. Mary Sue finished her coffee before her husband, and just to rouse him, she tugged at the left strap of his overalls to tease him to get up and on with his day.

Obadiah took a large swallow of the rest of his coffee, Elizabeth was shaking her head to the left and right as she was done with her breakfast and growing inpatient. After lacing up the dusty work boots, the slow going father hoisted his daughter out of her high chair and headed outdoors to give her mother some much needed alone time and some desired father-daughter time. The two inspected the land, they swung the weed sickle toppling down the

26

tall grasses and looked into many of the small holes trying to determine what might have been residing within it.

The little lady picked at most of the dirt or many other weeds trying to help her father, they made their way towards the fields overrun with tall rough weeds, for the walk Obadiah set his daughter up on his shoulders to keep her out of the weeds, and away from any possible snake that might be curled in hiding. After the first hour of pacing back and forth in the fields checking for any large rocks that might damage the tilling tines when it comes time to turn over the land to plant his first wheat crop of their futures. Elizabeth spent a fair amount of her time whacking her father with sticks, from her perch on high. With a growing pain in his lower back from the long drive, followed by a lot of heavy lifting and now the transporting of the bright smiling girl on his shoulders, he wasn't given much of a choice but to set her down to fight some of the weeds on her own. Obadiah tried to stand tall to correct his posture but with a sharp pain traveling down his left leg, his pace had slowed a bit.

Elizabeth began to lose her cheerful playfulness, her having to fight the get through the coarse grasses began to wear down her energy and nerves as she struggled to keep up with her father. The twosome wandered from one edge of their field to the other, they managed to kick up a few rabbits as well as many of the bugs waking from the the previous winter still. Some of the grass spots were damp from the previous nights' dew, the bottoms of his pant legs were soaked and the water traveled upwards, the poor little girl was wet from the shoulders down as her stature put her whole body in the depth of the weeds.

The sun wasn't at its peak yet, the day wasn't even half over and the young father was already worn out from the constant struggle to fight his way through the entangling weeds, not to mention having carried his daughter for the first hour or so. They started their adventure towards the most northern border of the field then zig zagged back towards the house, The adjacent fields spanned as far as his sun beaten eyes could gaze, some of the swaying grasses that made for land boundaries waved in the breeze, the trees were scarce as many of the farmers cleared them out to make room for more crops and improved profits. Some of the boundaries were marked with simple wire fencing, unrolled and staked up with wood posts, most of the posts held but a few were half rotten or eaten away at by bugs.

27

Near the house, Obadiah scooped up his daughter whom seemed to be yawning more and more as their late morning wore on, the girl became cranky and tired from wearily fighting to keep up with her father during their survey of the surrounding lands. Obadiah football carried the girl, the crook of his right elbow sat between her knees as she straddled his forearm and rested her face in the large comforting palm of her father. Obadiah tried his best to sway his daughter and comfort her, trying to persuade her into an early nap. Elizabeth quickly lost the energy to fight and struggle and just became a whimpering little brunette.

Obadiah struggled to drag his wet and heavy boots as headed down through his final few steps up the porch to check in with his wife. Obadiah swung the screen door open to find his beautiful bride having just finished her list of house chores, she turned a frown laden face towards the door right after he entered and she caught how wet his boots and legs were, her frown and quick temper promptly turned lighthearted with an adorning smile and "awwww" as she saw the sleeping face of her deep sleeping daughter, so delicately cradled within the safe bounds of her big strong father's arms.

Obadiah handed off his little girl to her mother as the soaking wet pant legs from his clothes, clung to his legs and made for treacherous walking. Obadiah unsnapped the clasps on his overalls and the releasing of the heavy water strewn pants seemed to release several pounds of weight, the freeing from the clothes was a giant relief, he fought the overwhelming urge to yawn as his mind had taken its focus off of the tired daughter and realized how exhausted he now was. Obadiah's young body held up to many chores and days of hard work but occasionally he exhausted all of his energy running his daughter, as a good parent should.

With dry clothes and a second cup of wake up juice, Obadiah sat on the front porch and doodled in the dirt, he sketched out a rough design of the land and mentally did the work so as to efficiently till and plow then plant his land, Mary Sue sat in her rocking chair patiently awaiting the waking of her daughter from her nap, she watched her husband draw in the dirt, reminiscent of a little boy. Watching the inner youth of her husband had sparked her desires for him again, she quietly stepped through the screen door and began to rub her hands across his bulging back muscles, he rippled through his shirt, the muscles at the base of his neck were still swollen from carrying Elizabeth on them, she found

28

herself more and more attracted to him because of how great of a father he was, the attentiveness to be caring was one of his greatest attributes and she lusted for him.

With her hands gripping his neck muscles in a massaging fashion, he leaned is head to the left to pin her hand between his shoulder and his cheek, he felt deeply reassured that she was there with him, she began to play with the hair on the back of his head and lightly started to kiss the right sides of his neck, she leaned in and kissed around the right side of his face, he was slow to start but took the obvious hint that she was intending relations between them again. Obadiah grabbed the right arm of his wife and swung her around and onto his lap, she smiled at his playfulness and her medium length hair fell behind her as she leaned up to kiss her husband. With is left arm cradling her and his right hand grasping her left side, she rested her body on his thighs and she began to unfasten his shirt.

Obadiah moved his hand up her left side, starting at her left knee, he slid up her light flower patterned dress and caressed her left leg under her dress. Her breath became heavy, as she became more excited she began to randomly hold her breath, Obadiah took the cues from her breath holds that he was on the right path to pleasing his wife, the sun was high in the sky and the silence of the area was a reassuring sign that they were plenty isolated and had all the privacy to play around all they wanted. Seated on the front porch, Obadiah slid his wife's body down as she backed onto him, both of them facing the front yard of a home they called their own.

Her cold posterior was a welcome relief against his bare stomach, his right arm held tightly around the waist of her petite frame while his left hand ran up and through her hair, pulling her head to the left so he could kiss on her neck, her bosom was bare in the sun as the top of her dress hung down off of her on the sides. Together they danced in passion together, seductively, the private time together was a smile inducing, heart pumping fling of heated passion, they were young in love and now that they had much more privacy, they looked forward to many times of being able to duck away in many ways to partake in husband and wife time.

After their second jaunt of the day, Mary Sue sat upon the lap of her strong attractive husband, her right arm slung around the back of his neck, they sat together breathing heavily as Obadiah still suckled the exposed breast of his wife, they kissed passionately and sat with one another, half nude in the late spring sun as the breeze cooled them off and made the grass in the front yard look like it was rolling along.

Obadiah ran his right hand under the dress of his wife, grasping her bare milky white thighs, pressing his hands into her inner thighs as the hot and steamy afternoon love making session wound back down, both were still heightened in their sensitivity and with the gentle nipple kisses and squeezes to her rear and thighs still gave her goose bumps in pleasure and her right hand clenched into his right shoulder, her fingers fit into the large divots created by the tendons in his shoulders, her kisses to the left side of his face were strong with passion and love. After twenty minutes of grabbing, touching, kissing and light tongue flicks shared back and forth, their breathing was back under control, the exasperation and bewilderment was fuel for their passion, it was unheard of and taboo to make love anywhere other than a bedroom.

The lovers suspected that everyone had their thrills of passion in other places, it was an exciting turn on to have shared their front porch in this way, laying down and face to face was supposed to be the one way to make love, the few times love making was ever mentioned it was always mentioned to be face to face lying down, all other ways were considered a sin. Deeply, everyone was at the mercy to their human nature, the only difference between heaven and hell is either a clear conscience or a guilty one, feeling guilty is the only real hell there is, a husband and wife have only each other to answer to and at the end of their lives together they owe it to one another to succumb to their desires as well as help their spouse to explore their sexuality.

Mary Sue didn't want to dress; she wanted to lie unclad with her husband and feel reminiscent of their honeymoon, two weeks in a cabin, only having to have put on clothes once to restock wood for the crackling fire that kept their naked bodies warm as they got to know the entire bodies of one another. It wasn't lady like to speak of naked bodies, she never once heard her mother speak of love making or of the female anatomy so she was mildly insecure and unsure how to handle the subject matter, after the first few days fumbling through love making and trying to learn what each person liked. Mary Sue used her hands to guide her husband to her delicate areas of interest, Obadiah was clumsy in bed at first and felt the need to apologize often for many of the things that went awry between them, it was frustrating for them both as they struggled to learn the ins and outs of love making together, after a few attempts during the first day or two, they disrobed and agreed that neither would put on any clothes with the exception for an apron to cook in as grease splatters.

The two fumbled to explore each other's' bodies, wrought with nervous excitement the two slowly learned their way around. Obadiah had a strong chest and rounded shoulders from a life of hard work with his hands, Mary Sue felt her knees tremble and her stomach spasm at the sight of her new husband. Many summers spent working the hot South Carolina field without a shirt on had left Obadiah without tan lines and very lean in body, Mary Sue wanted to be everything she could ever offer to her husband.

Obadiah was left open mouthed and speechless when his beautiful and stunning wife had stepped into the light after removing her dress. The first night after the wedding was clumsy and in the dark, his hands roamed her body but without much exposure to the naked female form he had a hard time mentally mapping out her contours, his first view of her exposed, perky and supple breasts left him light headed and fighting the urge to pass out as the blood left his head. His eyes followed her sides from her shoulders, down her slender arms, down the outsides of her hips and down her tone, gorgeous legs and up the other side, the pair stared at each other's' naked bodies for what felt like eternity, their hands each shook as the slowly stepped towards each other for their first naked embrace as a married couple.

Mary Sue stared at the manhood of her husband and felt overwhelmed, she had never seen the specific part before in her life and only heard of a few references in hush tones as her aunts and mother had visited the topic over drinks occasionally, sans men. Mary Sue was scared at the idea that something bigger around than her fingers could wrap around was intended to be inside of her and she held her breath nervously as they began their lovers' dance of intimacy. The couple laid beside one another and slowly caressed the nervous bodies of one another and neither could stop smiling as they were overcome with the newlywed nervous excitement. Their love making had become much less one sided as each leaned what the other liked and what each could to to ensure the other continued to lust for one another.

31

Love making wasn't the foundation of a relationship but they were smart enough to know that it was the mortar of their marriage, the intimacy, the fiery lust, the sometimes physical exertion or anger release all came together as they used each other's bodies as their own. Their first year of marriage was as many others', a lot of learning, exploring, and sometimes struggling to work on perfecting communication between them, things had come a very long distance, both emotionally, and geographically but they have done it together, and together they can and will achieve everything they could have, everything they had ever dreamed of. They strove to work through any small obstacles that may have arisen, their first year of marriage came with the first obstacle, not having a home to move into of their own, they decided to spend a year of two with Norman, Obadiah's father, Norman had been a widower for some time and the house was only occupied by the two men, bringing Mary Sue into the house was a drastic change, at home Mary Sue had both of her parents and older sister Charlotte, to leave her family behind, even if only to move a few measly miles away, still created separation anxiety so they spent a fair amount of time back at the brides original home. Mary Sue became accustomed to the change and gradually improved at relying on her husband when insecurities flared up.

The two lovers sat and breathed in unison perched on the front wooden stoop, Obadiah glanced at the breasts of his wife, something about them always drew his attention, even when strapped into a tight dress which caused her cleavage to burst out or a shirt that kept them conservatively covered, Obadiah could glance at her chest and instantly mentally picture the chest of his bride. Mary Sue liked enticing her husband, she would occasionally brush her breasts against her husband's arms or rest a buttock against his hand as it hung by his side and he wasn't paying attention, in return Obadiah would randomly kiss the nape of his wife, kiss an earlobe or nuzzle his face against her chest, both would try to one up the other in a playful competition to keep their physical closeness full of passion and playfulness. Things continued to look up and up for the young couple, they stared out at the fields that encapsulated their new farm.

Obadiah brushed his fingertips along the outside of her right breast as they sat in the warming sun, both felt the warm love from one another and it was enlivening. The wind raised the sounds of rustling grasses around them, branches from the front trees made swaying motions like the lovers had just done, *"MMAAAAAMMMAAAAAA"* broke the silence, alerting the pair that they weren't alone in their personal quiet world they had withdrawn to, momentarily.

Mary Sue grasped the shoulder of her husband to prop herself up, she slowly buttoned up her top, slowly and in a teasing manner, she tucker her right breast back into her shirt, gently drawing some fingers around her nipple to watch the pupils dilate in her husband's eyes. Obadiah sat there on that cracked wooden porch, pants down around his ankles and thighs still sweaty from the backside of Mary Sue, both stared lovingly at one another and took stock at what greatness they had, Mary Sue smiled at the naked lower half of her husband, she finished buttoning her top and then lifted the side of her light flowery dress to expose her milky white, smooth thigh all the way up near her hip to leave an impression within the mind of her husband, planting the seed of lust for next time, small fun they volleyed back and forth to keep the romance alive. Mary Sue extended her hands to her slow to rise husband, he creaked along with the boards underneath him as he stood, saving him the bending, she leaned down to raise his britches up for him and she dragged her fingertips along his legs, she liked the feel of his right thigh hair and smooth sides as she helped him fasten his pants. The couple knew that any moment Elizabeth would come bursting through the front screen door to join them in surveying the scenery from the porch.

Obadiah ran both of his hands across the back of his loving wife; his arms were still heavy from the earlier days' venture as well as from leaning back upon them post coitus. Her hair glistened in the soothing sun, Mary Sue gazed up at her man, they locked eyes and those small back dots seemed to lead into infinity, when their eyes locked they could feel their worries disappear, their pulses become tranquil and their lips moisten for one another. There were so many requirements strewn out in their near future but knowing that they would boldly stand beside each other through thick and thin, in deep embrace they rested their chins on each other's' shoulders and rubbing each other's backs still longing for alone time. They knew it was only moments before the beckoning call came once again from Elizabeth, it had only been moments but they were already craving another round. Mary Sue often tried her best to squeeze her beefy man when they hugged, she loved to be playful and rarely could get his back to crack and when he returned the favor he lifted her off the ground with ease. Mary Sue felt enlivened with love as her feet often came off the ground, the corners of her mouth always lifted higher than her feet as a smile always overtook her, no matter her mood, Elizabeth even had the same visceral response, a great big smile when lifted from the ground by Obadiah.

Sure enough the spunky toddler came karate kicking through the door; she resembled a football player breaking a tackle. The parents felt relaxed from their second sexual expedition of the day already as well as time spent in the life giving sun, the toddler was recharged, rips roaring and energized to take on the rest of the day. Obadiah curled his baby girl into his arms and lift her quickly into the air to make her giggle with joy. Mary Sue welcomed her daughter to the afternoon then confirmed that Obadiah was going to watch the gal whilst she begin making fixings for lunch. With minimal ingredients Mary Sue filled the three bellies, they decided that the barn was the next task of the day, the sliding hinge of the door needed to be cleaned and creased, Mary Sue found some owl pellets on the floor towards the back, she used a stick to push around into the round feather covered lumps that were strewn on the floor, she showed young Elizabeth what mouse skulls and different bones looked like as she dissected the excrement from the night hunters. Owls were fantastic hunters and by looking within their waste, you could determine what types of varmint were about and how well they were eating. Up in the rafters towards the rear of the barn was a large bundle of bedding and the rafter holding it up was covered in dripping streaks of white droppings, evidence that there had been a few generations of owls all roosting in the same area.

Obadiah began to un tack some of the dry rotted boards and hang newer boards to hopefully further ward off rodents from making nests in the engine of his tractor or from eating the seat padding of his car. There was so much work that needed to be done, there were only a few short weeks to ensure that things around the house were ready in preparation for their first planting, both husband and wife were excited to invest in their future, there isn't any better way to put your faith in tomorrow than to plant crops, the hard work upfront is an investment, the tedious detail that goes in to making sure that the fields stay rotated each year, the hard work through the season and watching the weak, small, ambitious little plants break the surface of the ground and grow towards the sun as they mature and turn dark green, then age and dry out, ready for harvest.

Obadiah was new to wheat but farming was in his blood for generations, the pair planned a large garden for plenty to can or dry out to sustain them through the winter, Mary Sue loved fresh veggies and they planned to purchase a few chickens for the daily eggs. The farm was slowly coming together, little Elizabeth ran amok and her parents just watched over her with great big smiles and loving hugs, this was a family of sheer gratitude and blessings.

After the first few weeks at their new farm, Mary Sue wrote plenty of letters for the post to take back to her family, Obadiah wrote to his father and the couple continued to build on their dreams, Mary Sues' lower stomach slowly became convex as her second pregnancy slowly came along, the rosy color around her nipples gave way to a darker more tan appearance, as they had first noticed around the fifth month of pregnancy, things were still in a bit of a hurry around the farm. Obadiah spent all of the possible sunlit hours for almost eight days tilling and turning over the weed covered earth of their fields, the earth underneath was so rich and fertile that it only could mean prosperous crops and a wonderful harvest.

Obadiah was exhausted at the end of each day but his wife walked out lunch and dinner each day to make sure that her husband had adequate food energy to remain alert and perched on the metal seat of the tractor that puttered along dragging the rounded tines that churned up the earth and sliced through the weed root systems. Mary Sue spent her days teaching Elizabeth letters and numbers, they wrote them in the dirt over and over, singing hymns together and waving to Obadiah when his steal stead brought him close to the house before taking him back away again. Obadiah rode high upon the gas engine as his peered back over to his girls doodling in the dirt, he knew he was truly blessed and looked forward to his first harvest, one that should pad his bank account, afford them many years of bank payments, the financial security to finish fully furnishing their home and purchase more land, Obadiah was the kind of man that wanted to do it all, farm, family and do it all for everyone around him.

They went without their own home for almost two years in order to save every penny they could scrounge, they worked Normans farm, helped with Mary Sue's family farm and Obadiah also worked the cotton mill as often as possible, they had enough to buy their farm outright but decided it was a bit better to finance and keep most of their finances as liquid cash rather than limit themselves, they bought a used tractor and equipment and also a used car, all were in good condition so they needn't worry for a few years about replacing any of the machinery, a comfort the couple enjoyed.

The days grew longer, the temperature began to climb each day and soon April was almost over. The fiery passion of the couple had continued to rage on, Obadiah enjoyed the swelling of his wife's breasts, a subtle perk of pregnancy, even as she began to feel more uncomfortable in her skin, Obadiah did his best to reassure his swelling wife that he still loved her so, it was a rare event but she still had the occasional self-doubt. Being in the middle of her second pregnancy she was much less nervous about how to handle everything, the wheat seeds were ready to plant, Obadiah brought their trailer back from a grainer's, loaded with bags of seed ready to be locked below the surface of the ground. After the almost month long commitment to make the land ready for planting, the turning, the tilling, the chopping and finally the planting, the couple could finally leave, they could make trips to town and interact with more time and freedom than that of the previous month.

Many of the residents were all free from the bonds of planting time; many had the same process in preparing their lands for crop growth. Mary Sue had seen Doctor Martinez once by this point for a checkup, it was routine and things seemed on course for a late fall birth. Mary Sue wasn't looking forward to being big pregnant during the peak of the summer heat, her body was once again changing, growing, and she did her best to fight of the urges of momentary rage or anger, she held her own mental stability pretty well, it was just her appetite that was dialed up, as it should. Elizabeth took notice to the swelling in her mothers' belly and would ask about the baby inside, even just a *"baby"* would come from her tiny pink lips as she would rub her mommy's belly during story time in the evenings.

Obadiah often stood in the doorway as he watched his beautiful wife read bunny rabbit stories to their daughter, he just stood their glancing after a long day around the farm, he let her voice lull Elizabeth to sleep and also completely relax himself. At the ends of most evenings the couple would retire to their bed,

36

Obadiah would often massage his wife's body, he would kiss her growing tummy and also rub lotion on her to help soothe the expanding process. Each night as the couple laid in bed, they jostled profound knowledge among them, things like "we'll never be this young again, ever again" and then contemplate how their days were spent " this was one day of our lives, did we spend it appropriately?" these topics were some of the things they liked to keep in perspective, they both wanted to keep their closeness as well as take conscious steps to prevent ever taking one another for granted, something they both saw was a poison in many relationships.

The mornings each came with the sun rising earlier than the previous day, Obadiah cleared away the stubble that grew from his face before a hearty breakfast, there was minimal conversation over breakfast as Mary Sue focused on helping Elizabeth feed herself until Obadiah had eaten and could take over so she could eat. The couple made things work well in the household, today was another doctor's appointment in town with Dr. Martinez. The trip in was carefully planned out for the end of April, the farm needed some restocking of supplies as well as a long list of more items from the tack store and so on.

The last day of the month was already starting off warm, it was already becoming humid and the early sun was bright red, the old saying was "red in the morn, sailors be warn" Norman was akin to sayings like that to judge how the day might go along, and the red hue of the morning meant warm and humid, the later summer days that started out with the same ambient signs were often blistering hot. Looking out across the fields behind their home, Obadiah imagined how luscious the soon to be sprouting fields would look, he pictured walking through the planted rows of grain and the tips running through his fingers, the thought of those plant tips easing across the tips of his outstretched hands brought a soothing comfort to the already tranquil natured man, Obadiah stood near the back window peering out as he finished his morning cup of coffee.

The young girl needed extra hands this morning to get cleaned up, she had enjoyed her pancakes but thought that slapping her hand down into the small puddle of jelly might have caused it to splash said jelly straight into her mouth, most of it ended in her hair while her parents chuckled. Obadiah was sometimes taken back by the ingenuity of the toddler in the many ways that Elizabeth came up with to make messes of a monstrous nature. When the skies grew gray and the clouds above began to sprinkle, the three often played on the front stoop, watching the rain drops leave small pits in the dirt nearby. One day when the trio sat upon some chairs listening to the pitter patter of rain drops on the metal roof, young and wild Elizabeth ran in tight circles at the entertainment of her parents until she suddenly stopped, gave her parents a bright eyed glare and began to sidestep towards the porch steps. "*NOO*" Mary Sue tried to coax Elizabeth from her suddenly onset idea, Mary Sue lunged to snag her daughter by the arm before she leaped from the front step, with knees tucked tightly to her chest, Elizabeth was curled into a small ball, giggling loudly towards a puddle and headed for little girl greatness.

Mary Sue had almost caught her daughter, her finger tips had just barely graced the shirt of the belly laughing girl, as she flew through the air, Elizabeth looked back at her mom as Mary Sue slowed her descent towards the floor boards of the porch before the toddler plunged into ankle deep mud. Somehow this little girl had become a magician, she had used her tiny new powers to transform a two inch deep puddle into one that seemed to engulf the entire body of the girl, and also managed to spray the outstretched Mary Sue with mud splatter also. Obadiah had jerked forward as his wife had left her seat, he wasn't as prepared to snatch up the girl but Mary Sue dove for her as if she was about to fall from a cliff. Obadiah was now laughing heartily, his hands gripped tightly on his chair while his baby girl had begun to kick her bare feet in the mud water as Mary Sue spat out the muddy water that had accumulated in her mouth, Mary Sue had a slight inkling of upset about her as her direct order to Elizabeth had been ignored and disregarded as she flew off of the porch and into the puddle, but the three ended up in tears from the laughter so she was quickly over it.

The young Elizabeth was often mild mannered and into obeying her parents, the wee one was often glad to have stories read to her and tried to follow along with her finger, she also pointed to many pictures and pointed what they were. The girl showed great intelligence and Mary Sue was proud of the time she got to invest into her daughter and the well spent time showed through. The time was drawing near when the wheat was going to start to break free from the ground and sprout, Obadiah was always glad to see the large brown plot of dirt begin to give way for the small green speckles before the green completely took over and sprang from the ground. Farming was the greatest way to prove that you invest in tomorrow, invest in the near future a few weeks or months from now, owning a plot of land was the ultimate way to show that you were faithful in the world around you, Mary Sue shared in that pride as well and both parents passed it along to their daughter.

Obadiah slept every night with a clear conscience, he looked at the young precious daughter that often tugged his pant leg to convince him to hold her hand, every time he glanced at her, he saw his future, he saw her as his legacy, his way to immortality, through her she would tell stories about him to her children and her children's children. The young couple saw a grand future before them, they tried to contain their excitement when they discussed what the next few years, decades or even at the rest of their lives may contain, and the wonderment and amazement was endless.

It was getting near the end of April and in the morning they were planning to make it to their appointment with the dashing Dr. Martinez, Obadiah and Mary Sue knew that another mouth to feed would require extra work as well as even more time for the family also. Elizabeth didn't really understand what it meant to have a new baby enter the family, the couple knew that adding to the family was going to be wonderful. Mary Sue had written Charlotte and shared the news, Charlotte's return letter had just arrived, she was overcome with joy and a heavier desire to come and visit towards the end of the summer. Life seemed to start moving faster and faster, it almost seemed to just flow along and no matter how hard they struggled to come up with the speed or energy to make it through their day, it seemed that at the end of each day, there were more things left on their to-do list than time to do it. The couple kept their passion as stoked as possible, they would return to the front porch when Elizabeth was tucked in for a nap in their room, the barn or other exciting places around the farm when the option presented itself. Mary Sue and Obadiah were still very young at heart, even when the days' tasks had tried to overtake them as a couple.

As the night finally wound down, young Elizabeth ran in circles on the porch as the sun faded away into the horizon, the sky grew dark and the lights within the house became more and brighter. Obadiah and Mary Sue sat side by side and rocked in their chairs, creaking on the rickety boards, they gazed into each other's eyes and smiled wearily as Elizabeth slowly ran out of energy. Elizabeth climbed onto the lap of her strong poppa, Obadiah jerked to lift his darling baby girl and let out a hearty huff while doing it. Mary Sue kept her head rested against the headrest of the rocking chair while smiling at her husband and little girl. The porch light had reflected little speckles of light from the stubble of his cheeks.

Obadiah couldn't help but smirk, his exhaustion made it hard to fully smile but the corners of his mouth kept perched deep in his cheeks with true happiness at his life, he had worked so hard and god had seemed to add extra blessings to it. The temperature dropped with the sun, it grew dark and the brisk air became chilly and as they could begin to see their own breath, they decided to finally head in and put their heavily yawning girl to bed finally. Mary Sue lurched herself forward to get the necessary momentum to get her weary self out of her chair before helping to coax her also tired husband up and inside with her. The parents cradled their baby girl together and also kept their eyes trained towards the sinking sun as they shuffled their feet in.

It was getting late and little Elizabeth was safely secured in her bed, she was ever more peaceful as her breathing slowed and sleep overtook the beautiful child, her dark brown ringlets laid upon her forehead and Mary Sue brushed them gently to the left and graced her hand along the far side of her face. The light sigh that Elizabeth let out was a telltale sign that she was deeply asleep, her conscious was clear and her heart was at peace. The couple retired to their bed, their feet shuffled in smaller steps as they ran out of energy nearing their bed, Mary Sue dropped herself on the edge of her side to undress from a seated position, Obadiah stood, slightly slouched which gave his overalls an airy look to the chest of his overalls, he leaned over a bit and braced himself against his bed as he fumbled to undress too. As Mary Sue removed her clothes to put on a nightshirt, Obadiah tried not to stare but took notice and admired the body that was harboring and incubating his second child, her body was thin and yet, strong.

The tired and worn out man still lusted after his wife, she was all he ever wanted and needed in this life, Obadiah had begun to explore the world with Mary Sue, starting with their drive to the mid-west, together their adventure to be parents was one they shared and one that was an amazing dream come true. A small puff of dirt let out of the overalls as they dropped to the floor. Obadiah used his opposite feet to remove his socks as he backed down onto his bed, the springs sank under his weight, the middle had a divot from the weight from both of their bodies, Mary Sue let herself slowly lay back onto her side of the bed, the man reached his callused hand across the midline of their bed and grasped the hand of his supportive bride, she grasped his hand back with a loving embrace that often reassured him that he made all of the right choices in his life, all of the decisions that weighed heavily upon him when they needed to be made but were made with ease when he had to make them for his family.

Mary Sue rolled her head over to her right to glance at her leading man, she lifted her head a little to let her hair fall beneath her and out of her field of view, Obadiah smiled an exhausted smile at how cute she still was, he was overjoyed with the love he had for his wife beside him, with a large exhale, that was the end of their day, the couple relaxed and they fell deeply to sleep while still holding hands. The final houselights were off; some shadows appeared on some of the walls as the moon shone bright overhead.

42

May 1st came with the crow of a rooster, as the couple arose and stretched out their tired bodies, they greeted each other to another wonderful day with their routine morning kiss back and forth. Obadiah tried to swing his right leg over top of him to get his lower back to pop and relieve some of the light pressure that built up throughout the night. Mary Sue offered a light shove to his propped up leg and also to help him up and moving as he was a bit slower to rise. Mary Sue chuckled as he cracked and creaked his way onto his feet, she *"AWWWWW'D"* at his old man body and served up a harsh comment about it. "you OK gramps?" he returned a sarcastic *"hardy harr"* to express his displeasure at her remark but smiled it off ensure her that it didn't hurt his feelings and that all was alright between them and that it was all in good fun. They were often great friends and even on days when they may have been frustrated or in a sour mood that they occasionally had to vent to one another, they did so and were there in support of each other no matter what.

"MAAAAAMMMMAAAAA" came ringing out through the wall, the announcement came bright and early and the parents dressed promptly to attend to the young princess' needs. Obadiah was first out of the bedroom and won the race to the wailing girl, it was time for breakfast so Obadiah started the woodstove and put the coffee kettle on while Mary Sue caught up while tying her hair back for the day.

Today held a doctor's appointment for Mary Sue, there was also a long list of things to attend to once in town, there were a few stops planned, they needed to stock up on flour, kitchen foods and more seeds for a garden to plant to further sustain them through the coming summer.

Canned veggies and assorted foods were good and all but having been farm raised, hand plucked goods straight from the earth was the preferred method for food for meals.

The rooster that cockled the household awake at the break of dawn reminded Obadiah that he should pick up a few baby chickens to raise around the farm and once they mature, there would be ample fresh eggs daily as well as many birds for meals also. There seemed to be plenty of critters to hunt or trap to also feed the family, trapping rabbits was a fairly easy task when you spotted their running paths and a simple noose would snare them over and over again without having to spend money on ammunition. Obadiah had an over under rifle that Norman had given him when he was a boy, the rifle was trustworthy and pretty accurate, it was also the same rifle that he learned upon when he was growing up in Charleston. Elizabeth fed herself mushy handfuls of soggy biscuit into her mouth, she smiled at herself being a big girl and getting to do so, Obadiah sipped at his coffee, he tried to shake off his tired dreariness and go over his list of actions for the day.

Mary Sue sat herself beside the mush covered Elizabeth, the little girl offered up a smile through her faux goatee of jam and white squishy biscuit, Mary Sue ducked to the side to miss getting a smoochy morning kiss from Elizabeth but she gave her one on her forehead instead. The trio sat and enjoyed the morning meal together and mentally prepared for the hour trip to town and everything else that might come along. Obadiah mentioned to Mary Sue that he should grab an empty crate box from the barn so as to fill with chicks for the return drive home, he was certain that little Elizabeth would be more than thrilled to have a box of small, soft, yellow fluffy chicks to play with. After helping to wipe down some of the mess created by the mushing monster of the morning it was time to lace up the dirty work boots and get ready for the drive to town.

It took a short while to load up the depleted gas cans required to top off for the tractor as well as any other items that might need tending to while the girls got ready back in the house. The Dodge was still extremely dusty, the layer on the windshield needed to be swept off in order to be visible. The winds around the farm brought a lot of dirt with them, when the breezes picked up and reached a fast speed, it felt like being sanded by the coarse grit being carried by the breeze. The sun was rising, at a low angle the fields held a hue of green and also glistened from the morning dew. After closing the door and getting ready to head indoors to gather his ladies, Obadiah stood for a minute and took stock in the world around him, his family was growing right before his eyes, his farm was coming to fruition, and he was sitting tall at the helm of all of it.

44

It weighed on his heart having to leave his father behind, such was life he supposed but nonetheless, it was tough to stake out on his own and finally be the head of his own household, having to be the tall standing man that Norman had prepared him to be. With a light sniffle and a bowed head to move in the direction of his front door, Obadiah quickly put a stop to the brief emotion from getting to him. The dirt beneath his feet squished as he walked back into his home, the car held everything necessary for their day trip as he was also hoping his girls were ready to go. Three steps up the sun worn wooden steps, that creaked under his weight as he climbed, he could hear little Elizabeth running amok from outside, causing a bit of a hearty huff of a chuckle.

Elizabeth was wearing a light flowery patterned dress; her hair was combed back, even though both parents knew the combing wouldn't last the trip to town. Miss Elizabeth was giddy and excited to get in the car for their trip, it was still fairly early as the family set out, headed into the heart of Indian Gulch for an event filled day including a stop off to see the town doctor. Obadiah gave thought about maybe stopping off at the Ponsens' deli for lunch, maybe a cucumber sandwich sided with a sun tea or a few thin slices of one cured meat or another paired with a flat bread or baguette bun. Obadiah reached his dry cracked hand towards his wooden screen door, the screen was faded, dirty and had large holes in it from repetitive harsh closing causing tears near the handle.

Barely in the door long enough to kneel, the short little lady was already barreling towards him in a hurried pitter patter with wildly flailing arms, with an encroaching smile Obadiah knelt down to embrace his sweet little girl and promptly raised her into the air for a light toss to excite her. Elizabeth laughed and giggled as she flew up and into the air, Obadiah was reminded often that she was a little girl and should be handled with a more delicate set of hands but Obadiah wanted a tougher girl, he longed for a son to be rowdy with but he was adamant about raising his little girl how he wanted, and strong enough to handle life was how she was going to be raised. Obadiah often reflected how quickly life seemed to fly past, his baby girl was almost two, his marriage was already a few years in and sprouting their second child already. With a few more pumps into the air, Obadiah asked if his ladies were ready to go, Elizabeth was giggly and more than ready to follow her parents on any worldly adventure they may partake on,

Mary Sue was finishing rolling her stockings up in preparation for not only her appointment but also strolling through town.

Mary Sue was shining brightly in a light tan dress that was adorned with dark brown spots, she was stunning and while sitting with her ankles crossed in her chair, Obadiah was reassured that his wife was not only insanely gorgeous but also very classy. Obadiah sauntered over to his loving wife and with his baby girl propped up on his left shoulder with her arms outstretched pretending to fly, Obadiah offered out his hand to assist her to stand up, she was still small in her pregnancy and was more than capable of rising on her own but it was still a gentlemanly thing to do. With his wife on his arm, the man escorted his ladies out the door and onward towards the car. Elizabeth wriggled and squirmed as she was placed on the lap of her mommy; the young lady was giddy to be with her parents as her daddy set himself behind the steering wheel and turned the engine over with the twist of the ignition.

With a quick three point turn the family was off and headed to town, the surrounding fields showed more green than brown as they few past the fields that were stretched out alongside the dusty red dirt roads, the engine hummed as did Elizabeth as she tried her best to remain calm and seated per the repeated suggestions of her mother. Out of his peripheral view Obadiah could see his beautiful wife, sitting beside him with her hair wisping in the breeze that came from the cracked passenger window, her hair whipped and swirled around her head, adding to her true beauty as she used her right hand to crossover the front of her face and keep tucking her hair back behind her ears. Her lips were bright red, her cheeks a rosy blush color and her skin, exuding with a glow as she nurtured the child within, Mary Sue had large doe eyes, eyes that always brought a calming sense of security to her sturdy built husband. Both husband and wife were anxious to move halfway across the country, they discussed many of the what-ifs and unknowns of their uncertain future.

The fence posts flew past in a blur, the car often tugged from one wheel worn root to another in the road as they followed the tracks to the east. The sun was just above the brim of the windshield, it was high and reflected off of speckles of dirt that clung to the glass, the rooster tail that followed the car seemed to engulf and drape over the road they left behind. The grasses and ditch plants that lined the roadside were covered in the red grime that originated from the road, Elizabeth grew tired and restless, hardly much energy had been spent by her before loading into the car but the closed in space wore on her and she succumbed to the weariless motion of the hour long drive. The little girl was curled into a ball on the bench seat where they all sat, her head was still with the light jostles from the bumps in the road as she slept, and Mary Sue stroked the head of her sleeping daughter, brushing her hair aside and helping to ensure she remained asleep for the remainder of the trip.

The couple exchanged loving glances as well as reassuring smiles, Obadiah reached over to grasp the hand of his wife like they do as often as possible; Mary Sue held the right hand of her husband with her left and alternated between stroking her own hair out of her face and that of her daughter. The drive took the planned hour and by the time they reached the town limits it was warm enough out that both windows were mostly rolled down and the warming breeze soothed the vehicles' riders as they turned towards town at the final fork in the road.

After the left turn onto the main street, the laundry building was the first building on the left, the shop was small and inside the big windows you could see the Asian couple moving about inside, bags hanging and clothes strewn about just behind the counter. Obadiah slowed the vehicle down and parked in front of the second wooden building on the left, Martinez's medical practice. The appointment was loosely set around eleven, it was near that time according to his gold pocket watch. Obadiah stood firmly upon the brake pedal whilst shifting the car into park then turning the engine off, the engine sputtered before finally ceasing into silence.

Obadiah shifted his weight to ease the pressure up from the right buttocks to the left as the fleshy part of his body had tingled and was sore from the hour drive while leaning on it. With a grimacing face Obadiah looked towards Mary Sue, squinted his eyes and stuck his tongue out to express the discomfort, giving her cause to smile and let out a comical sigh at his playful nature. With a butt shuffle to the left, Obadiah jerked the handle to let himself out, it took a bit of a shoulder to pop the dirt laden door open and the noise coupled with the car shaking heave gave signal to Elizabeth that it was time to wake up.

Mary Sue shushed the startled little girl, patting her back to reassure her that all was well and that everything was OK,

Obadiah scurried around the front of the car to open the door for his ladies, and with a tug on the door, Obadiah popped open the passenger side and bent to lift his young daughter from the arms of her loving mother so they could begin their next new adventure. During the first appointment things were very formal and quick between Mrs. Withers and Dr. Martinez, it was a short meet and greet while Obadiah walked with his tiny daughter up and down the boardwalk of town while they waited. This time Obadiah asked if she wouldn't mind if the two waited in the waiting room of the clinic while she spoke with the doctor, of course she didn't mind at all, it would be easier to corral the toddler in a small room rather than up and down the sidewalks of town. Obadiah walked in front of his wife and held the door for her as a gentleman should, his darling baby girl toiled and played with anything within her reach, his hair, his shirt collar, her dress and shoes, she was curious about everything.

The main room was painted white, there was a small desk in which a lady dressed in white sat, the lady was the sharp doctors wife, not only was she a nurse but also performed a secondary role as receptionist while her husband performed his duties. The room was brightly lit, there were three padded chairs for sitting and a small table in the corner, the doctor served the citizens in town mostly and rarely were there appointments close enough to warrant waiting but there were times in which family members would wait for loved ones to finish with the doctor. There were a few wooden blocks on the table, the blocks had letters from the alphabet painted on them and Obadiah lead his daughter to the corner to play and learn with the letters while her mommy played the part of the patient in the next room. The young doctor came out promptly to greet the lady, Mary Sue extended out her right hand to shake the right hand of the doctor.

Martinez was a young successful practitioner; he wore small spectacles and kept his black hair short and neat. Dr. Martinez was the progeny of a successful Spaniard businessman and his wife, a Filipino descendant, Martinez held traits form both parents, a darker tan skinned from his mother and broad shoulders and good posture from his father, he was all of six feet, height which he didn't inherit from his mother's genes, his intellect was a combination of both smart parents, his ambition and yearning to travel came from both parents as they had traveled from other countries to New York where they raised and educated the bright lad and then prospered while he moved down and across the country before settling in to Indian Gulch to make a home. Joseph was very personable, his manner with patients was impeccable and his attention to his attitude was of note.

Dr. Martinez was quick to make the acquaintance of the little girl thrashing blocks into one another, he was really friendly and treated everyone equally, he wasn't some pompous arrogant snide doctor whom only saw people as patients and loathed them each, Hirsch was that way with the people of his own town in which he was trusted with their money, and yet he was still dictator to everyone. Martinez lead the way into his examination room and closed the door behind them. Obadiah kept his little girl occupied with building blocks while Mary Sue discussed the prenatal care for the embryo she grew within her womb, Mary Sue was excited to once again house the developing fetus, she was truly appreciative that she and Obadiah were able to conceive and add one more child into their lives and continue to expand on their dream of a large family and farm. With a long and lustrous future continuing to open up before the couple, they felt amazed each and every day when they woke up to greet yet another long day filled with potential. Martinez was efficient in his examination, he took the ladies' blood pressure and listened to her lungs for any crackling or other abnormalities that have become common among some of the town's residents.

The appointment went quickly, Dr. Martinez was aware that there were family members waiting for their matriarch, the doctor and his patient exchanged farewells and the well-spoken young doctor also shook hands with Mr. Withers as well as young Elizabeth whom by now, had surely marked her favorite "Q" block with her mucus laden saliva. The Withers were ready for their stroll through town and to further get to know more of their fellow townspeople. Mr. Withers held the door open for his wife while holding the hand of his daughter, with a squeezed hand extended towards the receptionist and her husband doctor, young Elizabeth gave her form of goodbye.

With a glance in both directions the family made their way across the street and to the butchers deli, by the midway point in the dirt road, Elizabeth was already leading the pack by pulling of her parents as she wasn't sure what was in store but she had great fun in the last building with the blocks so who knows what may lie in store for the family, especially because this new place had food inside, lunch was just inside the door that was getting closer and closer. Young Elizabeth dug her toes into the road to pull harder and hard to convince her parents to hurry while they played the role of resistance as they leaned back a bit to offset her oxen style pulling. Elizabeth stopped briefly at the large step up to the next boardwalk,

Elizabeth sized up the gap from her feet on the ground to the boardwalk which was about waist level, her parents counted from one and once they reached the highly anticipated "*THREE*" they cocked their elbows and the wee girl squatted down in order to jump super high when her parents tugged her from the ground and on up the boardwalk, "*WEEEEEE*" the little girl let out a fun induced squeal as she tucked her feet tightly towards her belly before extending them downward to thump onto the boardwalk with a *thump*. As the parents took a large step up onto the same level as their daughter and back to being pulled by the rambunctious toddler, Obadiah's' stomach began to howl like a lone wolf as they neared the Ponsens' deli/butcher shop.

A dust strewn car motored past the family and Elizabeth turned to watch it as it zoomed by, the dirt that was kicked up by the tires drifted up and onto the boardwalk as well as the couple standing upon it. Interstitial pneumonia was common with the dry air as well as with all of the dirt that was often inhaled from the winds, sputum heavily laden with brown streaks of dirt or mud was commonly found in the handkerchiefs of men whom blew their noses to clear a mud blockage from the sinus cavity. There was no screen door on the butchers shop, the amount of airborne dirt was too much to risk letting any into their deli, the door that creaked when you opened it was cracked and chipping white paint that began to peel up and off of the wood underneath.

The inside of the deli smelled of salt cured hams and sausages, there were many forms of meats hanging above the counter and the glass case was over packed with many animal parts, it was heavenly. Elizabeth was making motor noises reminiscent of the motor vehicle from a few moments ago, the little girl was dragging her hands against the case glass making streaks and squeaks, the couple looked up and browsed the menu that was written with white chalk on the black slate hung up on the wall over a shiny meat slicer. The specials included; "Thin sliced dried salami with tomatoes and dill." Jim's "shit on a shingle" sandwich which was dried roast beef, smothered in white country

50

gravy and between two slices of bread, a town favorite and named for a Jim Dailey whom came down from Detroit for some building of the towns' stores as a construction engineer and architect.

The sandwiches were all handmade by Kathleen; she had graying hair that was clipped back with pins on the sides. Kathleen had bright green eyes behind her tired looked eyelids. Kathleen's crow's feet where deep worn lines all angling to the corners of her eyes, the weather lines crinkled deeper when she smiled, her thin lips pulled tighter towards her gum line exposing her teeth as she spoke, her voice was a bit raspy from a diet heavy in salty meats and a lot of speaking in the dry air with her many patrons.

Murray worked in the back to keep up with his tasks to cut and slice to keep his meat case stocked and to also prepare the meats that hung from the ceiling. The family enjoyed their meal, and young Elizabeth ate well, made much less of a mess than usual all while being distracted by the lovely Kathleen and her fondness for the young girl. The couple were able to remove themselves from the moment of loud and chaotic noises that randomly spewed from the little girl, the couple stared into each other's eyes and at that moment, the rest of the world faded away, even if only for that moment. The couple smiled back and forth at each other, it only took a few minutes and sometimes that was all they could muster as their daughter was still at the young enough age to be a handful and require constant supervision. The drain of energy that was always looming within the parents did add strain to the already busy life as they still had to stockpile their pantries, their cupboards, and their farm.

The first day of May was a warm and sunny day, as the temperature climbed it was a sign that this day was leading to a long hot summer. With a tug to Mary Sues dress, Elizabeth blurted out an inaudible noise that shook her parents back to reality, lunch was at its' end and there were still more tasks that needed to be done, with a hearty heave upwards, both adults were once again back on their feet and heading towards the door. Mary Sue and Kathleen exchanged "goodbyes" and smiling waves as Obadiah once again held the door for his ladies as all three poured out into the streets.

Elizabeth disregarded the instructions from her mother to wave goodbye as they made their way back into the street, Elizabeth returned to holding the hands of her parents and while heading back to their motor vehicle, the little girl frantically spun

51

her head back and forth as she took a giant leap from the boardwalk platform back down onto the street. The parents struggled at times to keep the little girl wrangled and from running amok in the street, they quickly loaded back into their car and continued their drive east towards the gas station.

Obadiah needed to fill the fuel tank of his Dodge as well as the few metal gas cans to take back to the farm for the tractor as well as have spare gas on hand. With a twist of the keyed ignition the motor started back up again, with a full belly the parents began to feel docile but the little girl had recharged batteries and her energy spiked. Obadiah backed out from the slanted parking space, his car lurched in reverse and once again they were east bound, the gas station sat towards the most eastern end of the strip, on the north side across the road from the market. Johnson was inside one of the bays of the garage, laid out under a Mercury of some model as the family pulled in near the second gas pump, the alert bell rang.

Mr. Franks rolled himself over and pushed himself up to his feet to attend to his customer. Johnson was still tired looking as he straightened out his grungy overalls and brushed some dirt from the sleeves of his stained and tattered brown shirt. "What can I do for you Obe sir?" the tall thin man hollered out to the driver. Obadiah was impressed his name was remembered as he shifted the transmission into park and then killed the engine. Obadiah stepped out as he greeted the shop owner, "what's the prices running me?" he asked Johnson; "two bits" the man replied as he used his left forearm to smear more dirt on his own cheek in an attempt to wipe some off. "Fill 'er up fer me" Obadiah asked of the man as he located the scrub brush to clean off his own windshield, Franks made a motion to the washer bucket as Obadiah beat him to it to save him the hassle, Obadiah wasn't trying to do the task for the man in a manner to show disrespect, but rather in an assisting manner, one to which Franks nodded in gratitude.

The men spoke a bit briefly as Mary Sue wrestled with her baby girl in the front of their family car. There were a couple of thinly spoked wheels out front of the shop, the inside had a small standing cooler that was stocked with soda bottles and some display signage for "Pepsi-Cola", there were a few racks of magazines as well as packs of cigarettes hanging above the register. Having seen many farms of tobacco back in the Carolinas and how many of the old timers often smoked a pipe in the evening, it hadn't really stuck the few times when Obadiah tried to join Norman out on the veranda as the sun set after long work days.

"O'er there," Franks peered across the street and motioned for Obadiah to gaze at the hefty Pauline Curtiss as she took fast paced micro steps down the opposite boardwalk and into the market, "that bird has a loose beak my friend" the work worn man passed a warning to heed about the high nosed well to do woman. Curtiss was a proud woman whom was ignorant to her own affects when she gossiped about others; she floated from one listening ear to another. Curtiss would gather any form of ill-speak about anyone's business and would wallow in it as long as she didn't have to face her own short coming. Johnson spoke with a hunk of chaw packed in the side of his mouth; his tongue keeping the tobacco wad in place gave him a bit of a draw when he spoke as the left side of his face held stiff.

After the five dollar total exchanged hands for the gasoline, it was time for Obadiah to rally his girls, as well as the energy to lead his ladies into the supermarket, and also to do his best to tangle up the flailing limbs of the tight gripping girl that had very fast and curious hands while Mary Sue loaded up a basket with what she needed. With a pointer finger wave towards Johnson Franks as the family Dodge exited the station and crossed to an empty parking slot out in front of the food market. Obadiah hung his head for a moment, an almost silent prayer for strength and closed lips if he were to cross the path of the selfish heavy set woman that was sure to intrude into his family business as soon as her small beady eyes locked onto him of his wife.

Something about Miss Curtiss exuded discomfort, not only was she tied into her corset and seemed to bulge out of any loosely tied straps and it gave her an almost ingrained grimacing face, a scowl that everyone could see. The family climbed out from within the cab of the vehicle, brushed off some of their clothing and arm in arm, all stepped towards the glass doors of the market. The market was laid out in spacious design, black and white tiles alternated on the floor and the fresh vegetables were piled up on the shelves. A younger towns boy named Henry was stocking off on the right, beets it seemed from the entryway.

The store was a bit cooler inside than out, the coolers keeping food fresh all buzzed and hummed in an electric chorus. There were shelves upon shelves of foods, cans and jars all packed with foods from all over, fresh cuts of meat as well as bags of flower and assorted grains. With basket in hand Mary Sue dotted down the aisles, the basket filled rather quickly as she read from her list and stocked up on supplies to continue to keep her family fed. The couple sauntered briskly down each row, Obadiah struggled to keep his daughter from grasping each shiny item she could see, his hands had to work twice as fast as her and with better precision to deter her speed and reach. The Withers spoke between themselves and discussed the items for assorted meals and plans to cook throughout the summer; they also looked forward to planting a large garden from which they would be able to harvest their own goods for canning and storing.

Young Elizabeth loved last summer, holding Normans hand as he picked green beans, he would give her one to keep a wandering hand busy as he filled an old mail ouch with pounds of green beans to add with supper. Elizabeth was curious about every bug and crawly critter she happened to spot, with extreme dismay to her mother, Elizabeth ate a glow bug late in the previous summer, it was crawling on her hand and the glowing yellow light mesmerized the girl, and with fast curiosity the bug became a quick snack and the glowing ooze caused a really grim expression to overcome her face for the evening, coupled with a shriek and mild dry heaving sounds made from Mary Sue.

Obadiah was speaking softly to his daughter and reassuring her that she was being a good girl and behaving very well, "*OHH*", suddenly from around a blind corner rounded the rotund Mrs. Curtiss, Mary Sue gasped with the startle but the older unpleasant lady was stoic and almost prepared for such an encounter. "*And how are we doing today?*" the lady stood with firm posture over the couple that were coddling their daughter that was growing inpatient. Obadiah tried to avoid eye contact with the scowling Mrs. Curtiss as he replied "*well, ma'am, and yourself today?*" the woman gazed over the young family with the same look that a hawk has as it peers over a field looking for prey, Curtiss looked to figure out if there high end associated with their clothes, tried to size them up if they were in middle class clothing as a last resort or as their first choice for going out. Mary Sue tried to keep her eyes locked on her daughter and out of the notice of the ample Mrs. Curtiss, whom was blocking their exit of the aisle.

Elizabeth was growing inpatient and beginning to throw her head around from boredom and her parents were growing tired of trying to pass subtle hints to the older lady peppering them with questions. "*Bought the old Keenans' place did you? It was shamefully going to waste, they put a lot of work in that house and contributed largely into Indian Gulch and it would be just a disaster if the hard work from that family also went to waste*" the lady was fairly passive aggressive in her attempts to guilt Obadiah into making sure he picked up the dropped slack in helping to maintain his home as well as contribute towards events in town.

"*Ma'am it was nice to meet you and sadly the circumstances have come to a point in which we must part ways, it was nice making your acquaintance and in time I am sure opportunities to converse again will arise, good day ma'am*" with a shortened huff, Obadiah had to rush out the blunt and forced ending to the rude interrogation, Mrs. Curtis looked bewildered at the man's crude departure and began to walk down a separate aisle with a forceful walk, one which displayed her contempt for having been brushed off. Mary Sue snarled at her husband; "*sadly?*" she passed a sharply meant question to make fun of the fact that she knew he wouldn't be sad for a moment and found it quite funny. Obadiah did his best to always remain respectful and give anyone their moment to speak, but to be at the verbal rummaging from a complete stranger, whom also felt too self-righteous and entitled to dole out commands to strangers, took Obadiah to the end of his fuse really quickly.

Obadiah felt warm under his collar, he could feel the red in his ears as his blood began to boil and the sounds of buzzing in the store droned into a noise that seemed to further agitate the usually tranquil natured man. Obadiah could feel the rustling tone of his wife as she poked fun at how his demeanor changed along with his grammar when he addressed the leering Mrs. Curtiss, he normally doesn't speak in such an affluent way and he knew his wife would bust his case about it in a fun way. Mary Sue knew that her husband only changed the way he spoke to adapt to the company, he didn't like being judged and he knew that was all Curtiss had in store when she "accidentally" rounded the corner to end up face to face with the newer Indian Gulch residents.

Mary Sue held her shopping basket tightly with her left arm and tried her best to calm her husband by wrapping her free arm around his, they walked arm in arm while Obadiah held his baby girl in his open left arm, she was still restless and jostling a lot, giving Obadiah grief as he continued to try to keep her out of trouble and in his arms. Mary Sue squeezed tightly a few more times and still felt as deeply in love with him now as she did on their wedding day when they also walked arm in arm down the grass row between two groups of chairs with their loved ones staring at them from seated positions. Mary Sue was a gleaming bride when she and her husband strolled down the aisle, she loved feeling like she was on top of the world and a queen, with all of her subjects looking up on her from the seats, she and her king walked gracefully down waving at them and smiling brighter than a lighthouse beacon.

Each time Mary Sue held the arm of Obadiah, it took her right back to that place, that peaceful day that will always be her personal heaven; her wedding day. She knew she had chosen the right person to make hers as being with him was always soothing, comforting, and loving, by his side was her one true place in the world. Obadiah felt a calm take over him, his posture began to slouch a bit as his breathing calmed and his heart beat slowed, his body responded viscerally to the tender touch of his beautiful wife as she rubbed against his arm, her chest bumping into the outer side of his arm with intent to draw his attention.

Obadiah had a light perspiration upon his forehead from the intense feelings that he couldn't avoid when dealing with the less than desirable social self-appointed matriarch. Obadiah felt uneasy having surrendered some of his power to the lady by letting her parasitic festering near his family, even bother his homeostasis in the slightest, Obadiah was normally rigid in his ability to keep a level head and clear thought process to his world around him, he wasn't sure how a lady he had just finally met had any effect on him, it didn't make any sense and he gave his head a shake from left to right to realign his perception of his standing and gave his wife a loving hand squeeze to ease her worry that he was fine once again.

The couple continued to roam the aisles of their new hometown market, Obadiah scooped a large stainless steel scoop of raw almonds into a thin plastic bag to snack on, almonds were an amazing treat, he had even considered planting a tree or two on his farm but knew it would be at least ten years before he could begin to harvest the crunchy bounty of the investment. Mary Sue looked as darling as could be in her dress, the pleated end towards her ankles flowed back and forth as her hips gently swayed, the dress was conservative in regards to her form but Obadiah craved what was underneath as he recalled what the bare body of his sensual wife looked like. Obadiah kept a pleasant smirk on his lips as he relived so many of the cherished intimate moments with Mary Sue, they had partaken to many opportunities of silence and solitude on the farm when the energetic little girl was napping, sometimes the couple just laid together and napped as well, other times they enjoyed the romantic pleasantries that were benefits to being a husband and wife.

The Withers finished their successful shopping trip, they checked out with a young lad named Roger that was in need of a step stool to reach the height of the counter. Roger was a freckle cheeked and sandy blond haired boy, he appeared to be about eight and was familiar with his job, as if he had been at it long enough to be proficient. The Withers carried their groceries and proceeded to load up the back of their car, the last stop on this outing to town was to stop off to the tack and hardware store, it was time to purchase a few hatchlings to raise back home, the rooster that had called out the wakening alarm of the morning must have been a wandering rooster, one that maybe strayed from a neighboring farm, one that must have had steel spurs in order to avoid being picked off by one of the local coyotes somehow. After backing out from the market parking the family Dodge puttered back near the Doctors office, which was next to the hardware store.

The hardware store was fairly wide in comparison to the doctors building but it also engulfed a large plot of land out behind it which seconded as a lumber yard, green house, and open space for any number of critters for sale at any given time. Carvell often kept a hand full of livestock out back and also had contact information to other farmers that were often willing to sell piglets or other young animals to begin one's own farm if the desire presented itself. The hardware still smelled of iron and sawdust inside, Theodore was this time joined by his Indian wife Mary Catherine, she was from a long line of local Native Americans called the Kiowa, the tribe lived off of the plains buffalo for hundreds of years in harmony until they had been pushed, forced, and hunted onto reservations.

The Catholics that were forcing assimilation onto the still rather young country almost wiped out the long established culture that the Kiowa people had, once the Medicine Lodge Treaty was signed in the eighteen sixties, whites moved in and once again, began plaguing the secluded tribes of the reservation at the time to

57

adopt white practices and religions, once again by force. Mary Catherine was quieter by nature, she was in her middle teens when she married the stocky Theodore, he still takes pride in having tied himself into the lineage of the town's history, it gave him a sense of entitlement, he swears there is still a great love for his wife but her silence and withdrawn demeanor quietly shouted otherwise.

Mary Catherine hardly made eye contact, she often gazed towards the floor and nodded when given instructions, her obedience was more than a simple agreement between the betrothed, there was a gut feeling that abuse kept her in line much like what the government had done to her people. Carvell wore a light blue button up shirt, brown slacks with suspenders that part around his rotund belly, Carvell leaned hard on his left elbow as he kept his spit cup within reach of his right hand as he was positioned overtop a large laid out newspaper. With a piece of wad shoved between the teeth and lower lip of his mouth, he flicked tobacco pieces back and forth with his tongue while spitting bits into his cup. Mary Catherine was rather conservatively dressed, a white pressed shirt with ruffles that were tucked into a plaid dress of mostly green and black, with tiny stripes of yellow running here and there. Mary Catherine maintained her eye lock on the floor as she almost glided from point to point tidying things up.

Obadiah asked for half a dozen chicks to further propagate his farm, he wanted an assortment and Theodore gave a nod and a click with his mouth over to the next aisle where Mary Catherine was kneeling to clean the lower shelves, she stood straight up at attention and pivoted to turn towards her master/husband then towards the back of the store to retrieve the small poultry for the customer. Obadiah looked at some of the bone handle knives in a display rack near the register that the broad Theodore was propped near, he admired some of the intricate carvings on the small handles, scenes of deer or bear at different moments in the wild, he contemplated purchasing a new knife as the one he gotten years back had been worn down, the handle was smooth except a small crack, and the blade had been sharpened, then worn over and over again now and was only half the original width.

Having a fiscally conservative nature, Obadiah forwent buying a shiny new blade; he toyed with some ideas as to how a new blade might come in handy but maybe in the near future would such a purpose be warranted. Mary Catherine was petite in stature, she was maybe five foot two inches, even with the slight heal that was under her black leather boot, her hair was pulled back in a low ponytail and hung to her mid-back, her arms were cocked up near her side holding a small cardboard box with a few small triangles cut near the top. Mary Catherine carried a stern face, her displeasure with life hung heavy on her and it wasn't hidden from public eye.

Mary Catherine set the small box of chirping scratching baby chicks on the counter, the box gyrated and budged about from the small animals inside bumping into each other. Mary Catherine went right back to cleaning she shelves of paint cans and brushes after snapping to attention as her husband made requests. Theodore brushed some of the spit that remained stringing from his chin stubble off on the heavily stained cuff of his shirt as he continued to browse over the newspaper. Obadiah poked an outstretched finger at the small brown box, on occasion a small tuft of yellow feathers would fill a small cutout triangle then disappear back into the box again.

With a second mental scroll through a checklist of what was needed from Carvell and his store, Obadiah had concluded his business, after the financial transaction had been completed, Obadiah picked up the box and turned back to the awaiting ladies in the car, Elizabeth was standing on the passenger side of the seat, fingers firmly gripped on the half open window and bouncing up and down on the seat springs. The sun had peaked much earlier in the day and was now falling in the direction, leading the Withers to their home. With the front bumper headed west, the Dodge roared down the dirt roads, throwing plumes of dirt into the air leaving a long trail for miles before falling back onto the road or drifting outward to the ditch plants.

Elizabeth kept giving the box a small shake, the chirps and noises that came from the inside peaked her curiosity and she was adamant about finding out what was inside. The young girl kept poking her fingers into the small punched out holes, her delicate fingers fit almost all the way in, up past the big knuckle, *"MOMMAAA WHAAAHHHHHH"* the little girl dropped the box to the floor and grasped her forefinger, one of the baby chicks must have poked or nipped at the wriggling piece of flesh that was dangling near the top of their box. Mary Sue was quick to attend to her wailing daughter that was probably more scared than actually hurt at the fact that her tiny finger had gone from searching to feel something soft and cuddly to a spontaneous sharp pain when least expected.

Elizabeth had barely shed a tear, supporting the theory of more surprised or scared than hurt, Mary Sue coddled away anyways, it was her job as the mother and nurturer. Elizabeth had begun to take large gasping yawns, a solid sign that true tired was behind the howling cries she let out, the little girl curled up against her mother, there is always great comfort in being in the arms of your mother, whether you are two or twenty, Obadiah often wished his baby girl had gotten to know his own mother, he often missed her and that longing always shifted over to his missing Norman. It wasn't but a few gasping breaths to send the little miss into slumber. With hair stroking hand pats to sooth her daughter, Mary Sue sat quietly close to the right side of Obadiah as they finished their stretch home.

Mary Sue used her foot to upright the turned box that was discarded to the floor by the startled little girl. Mary Sue leaned back against her seat and angled a bit to fit into the corner between the seat and the door to prop herself up, Obadiah glanced at her to ensure all was well with the both of his girls, Mary Sue smiled causing a tired tear to fall from her left eye and stream down her cheek, followed by a deep lung filling yawn. The yawning was contagious, Obadiah fought as best he could but he too was overtaken with the urge to let out his own large exhale.

Obadiah tried his best to do so with his mouth closed to hide it, if he were to volley a yawn back to the other side of the car it would cause a match of yawns back and forth in the front seat and make for an even longer ride home. The driver turned his head to the left to peer out at the growing weeds whipping past, he kept an eye on the road ahead but also admired the long horizon stretching out as far as they could see. The final wide turn at the fork to take them down Saginaw Way and to lead them home came and passed. The couple fought but succumbed the urges to yawn more and more as they neared their home, young Elizabeth was nestled comfortably in the crook of her mother's torso, the young girl enjoyed the clear conscience that came with blissful youth, she was able to fall swiftly asleep with no knowledge or worries of bills or of the future, a privilege all enjoy but for different lengths of time as we age and become educated in the costs of the world, and the requirements needed to pay those costs.

The vehicle finally turned down the driveway, the drive was even longer when tired, the couple slowed to a stop near the home and then was shifted into park and the ignition finally turned off. The coupled stared longingly at one another, it had been an enjoyable day out and it was finally over, they were home and finally able to begin to wrap up their evening as well, it took a moment to take deep breaths, Obadiah felt tired begin to set in and if he didn't move quickly it would be off to sleep for him right there behind the wheel of his motor vehicle, the man lurched forward quickly to remove himself from the back of his seat, with a few quick shakes to bring the awakening needed blood to his head to continue on with the remainder of needed tasks for the day.

With a swift yank of the handle and shoulder to the door, Obadiah let himself out to stand and stretch beside the vehicle before heading around the front to let out his wife and sleeping daughter. Obadiah tried to pull the handle quietly to let his young daughter remain asleep, Mary Sue braced herself so she didn't follow the door as it swung away, Obadiah placed a supportive left arm to the back of his wife to help her swivel in the seat and move to her feet and stand while still carrying her sleeping child, Obadiah reached for the box of live critters still chirping a wriggling about inside, he scurried to open the front door so Mary Sue could lay her baby girl in her bed and shake out her arms that were also sleeping. Once he let his wife and daughter in through the doors, Obadiah headed towards the barn where he had already put together a wire mesh cage to contain the chickens and keep out any hungry coyotes.

With small brown shaking box in hand, Obadiah dragged his weary body over to the pen he had built for the chickens inside, nearing the barn Obadiah peered up and towards the back and there they were, a Sleeping family of owls, perched up on one of the back rafters in the shadows of the corner. The owls didn't budge, five small feathered lumps sat perched on a beam, they had neither worry nor need of concern as the man sauntered past the large opening and to the cage on the side. The winds gusted by, the light grit it carried speckled the man on his exposed skin, the grasses were growing and the fields were blooming green with the planted wheat.

Soon as the summer grew hotter, earlier in the day, and the sun dragged in setting later would ripen and dry the slender plants with their airy whiskers on top. Obadiah unlatched the top of the two part door and set the box open, releasing the small yellow chicks to figure out their new home, he stood tall and peered out over his fields, imagining running his outstretched and open hands as he walked the endless rows of honey colored life. Obadiah leaned against the chicken pen, his right arms propping him up against the wire as he just lost all track of time staring out into the distance, things were going so well, he thanked god and he never wanted anything to end. Elizabeth was doing great, growing bigger, stronger, and older every day, his wife Mary Sue was incubating their second child and they were still wildly in love and their passion for one another was still enthralling.

Mary Sue had tucked her sweet child into bed and pulled a light sheet over her to ensure comfort, then turned towards the window in the kitchen to keep an eye on her husband as he wandered about looking over things that might need repair as he carried the box of baby chicks to their pen.

Mary Sue swung her arms from front to back to stretch her muscles and get the blood flowing to get a second wind to get started to prepare dinner for her family. While staring out the window the weary wife watched her husband disappear around the far edge of the barn, after a few minutes of no return, Mary Sue kept a trained eye towards the barn waiting to see her overall clad husband return, there was no anxiety or concern but a small spark of curiosity poked at her, what might he have gotten into? Was there some small hint of adventure that called his attention, she wanted in. There was still very young adults within each of the pair, she put dinner on hold and discarded her apron onto the table and wandered out to investigate with her husband. The grass was soft beneath her feet, her slip on shoes were smooth on the bottoms and she could feel the contours of the dirt clumps in the grass under her toes, her ankles changed directions and the angles of her feet slightly to match the landscape as she walked towards the corner of the barn that she watched her husband travel around. Mary Sue slowed her pace as she neared the corner of the barn, Obadiah was standing tall leaning against the chicken pen, staring out into the evening.

Mary Sue leaned against the barn, she crossed her arms across the chest, leaning against her right side, Obadiah was shrouded in loose hanging overalls and his shirt underneath was slightly sweat stained, he slouched a bit as he stood, making him look tired from the rear view. His brown boots were layered with dirt, Mary Sue admired the strong hardworking man that she turned into a husband and father, she gazed upon him and she felt the corners of her mouth lift with a smile, her forehead lifted and her eyebrows raised with pure internal joy that consumed her every time she set eyes on him. Those brown boots were worn from work, the red tinted dirt had filled in the stitch holes near the sole, his left leg was straight while the right was crossed over it at the ankle and his toes were propping up, shaking a little.

Mary Sue wanted to reach for Obadiah, she wanted to stand by his side and embrace him as he held her tightly but she hesitated, she stood firm and gave him these quiet minutes as they were few and far between for the doting father and caretaker. Mary Sue stood and enjoyed the life giving air, she took in every smell of dirt, wheat, grass and smells of the barn that filled her lungs as she inhaled but remained silent as not to disturb her view; Obadiah in front of their fields. Both felt so unbelievably blessed and fit in to Indian Gulch like they had been specifically raised to move here, it all felt predestined. Obadiah took long slow breaths, he looked up and down the rows of wheat he had planted, the plants were just beginning to break the soil surface and the red tinted dirt was taking on a green tint as green took over.

Mary Sue stood idly by as her husband spent his alone time to himself, under the impression that Mary Sue was still back in the house resting. Mary Sue gave him his time, she was more than confident that her husband was OK and with a solid nudge against the barn edge she was resting against, she was straight upright and turning about to head back to resume her task of preparing their supper. As she gracefully walked back to the kitchen, Mary Sue gleaned with the knowledge that she couldn't have construed such a life, even in her sweetest of dreams wouldn't have been so perfect, with a pause for a moment Mary Sue rubbed her left hand around her belly and remembered, things were getting more perfect. Mary Sue was getting hungry, or maybe her baby was, either way supper time was well upon them all and even though she craved her husband, in a carnal manner, she knew their time for intimacy could wait, her hungry body would not.

The sky had grown bright orange and the eastern horizon a ruby red with purple clouds strewn here and there, the breeze was an amazingly sweet smell from the flowers of the nearby trees in near bloom preparation, with her eyes closed tightly, Mary Sue paused to imagine how things would be next year, two little whipper snappers to chase around, a much fuller farm teeming with life and their futures another year into fruition. The picture Mary Sue had envisioned when she was a little girl, a large family and a farm was coming true, her childhood hopes and dreams that she had worked to build with her husband Obadiah, was all happening and if she spent to long astonished by everything, then her eyes would well up and she would weep with the overjoyed feelings of true bliss.

Mary Sue popped her moist eyes back open, she was mid path between the house and the barn, she looked around to ensure that everything was as it was before she closed her eyes and she had lost track of time momentarily. The breeze was still uplifting, a strong gust had completely consumed her, it filled her dress, and gave her a chill, the breeze danced all over her body and gave her goose bumps that further fueled her desire for special time with Obadiah. Mary Sue felt herself tingle with passion, she yearned to be with his manly touch right now, this intense passion she held for her husband was a great feeling, and being able to have him at any given moment, anytime her femininity needed him, every chance they created to be together, was slightly strained with little Elizabeth around but getting creative was still a very exciting task for the couple.

Mary Sue let herself back in to her kitchen, with a few eggs and couple cups of flour, it was time to get biscuits started to join with the main course. Mary Sue kept an eye out towards the barn, she wondered how long he would lose while standing out by the barn. The wood stove burned hot and the stew was cooking along when Obadiah finally emerged from behind the barn. His head hung and his steps were slow but he was making a beeline right towards the house.

As Obadiah stood against the chicken pen, his eyes fixed on the horizon, an unbreakable stare in which he lost himself in, he was in a trance when the call of nature came in, he opened his eyes widely and looked around trying to get a fix on how long he had been standing statuesque, his right foot was numb and he could feel the crisscrossed pattern embedded into his right arm from the chicken mesh, the worn down feeling from the long day then had to shake off his numb hands in order to work the zipper of his trousers in order to relieve himself. A few steps past the chicken pen and any spot was just as good as any other to whiz, Obadiah could tell by the yellow tint of his of his urine that he should probably drink more water, especially as the days grew warmer and the summer came on.

After kicking a boot scoop of dirt over the small puddle he created, which was turning to mud and soaking in, he turned himself towards his home. Each of his dusty boots set a small puff of dirt into the air each time his foot stomped to the ground, his pant legs were worn on the fronts, faded from dark blue to the light jean color, Obadiah felt just as faded some days. Obadiah raised his eyes towards his home, he could see the silhouette of his wife in the kitchen window, a sense of happiness consumed him, he slowed in his already slow pace as he just looked into the window and watched the black outline of his wife toil away inside, he was so very lucky to have such an amazing wife by his side, she was inside creating a smell that wafted from the kitchen, then hitchhiked on the breeze and right to him.

As Obadiah stood and admired everything that he had helped to make happen, the odors drifting from the kitchen almost lifted him off his feet; it felt as if he were being carried up on his tippy toes to the kitchen. He felt powerless and didn't bother to fight as he was suddenly letting himself inside to make the presence of Mary Sue, he was bewildered that he didn't recall walking the last ten yards to his home but suddenly there he was, his lungs gasped, desired, needed to take large heaping breaths of her cooking, she made noodles to join with cubed beef, brown gravy and sided with baked potatoes, a favorite of her husbands. Obadiah removed his red dirt crusted boots, as he sat down and bent over to untie his boot, Mary Sue stepped closely to him, her knees were eye level and she pulled the front of her dress up to reveal them to Obadiah.

Obadiah hadn't even removed his boots when he decided that his wife was ever so much more important, he leaned forward to kiss each knee, she placed her hands on the back of his head and neck and began to rub as he continued to kiss upwards. Her thighs twitched and quivered as her excitement grew, her excitement began to affect her breathing; she had moments where she held her breath as her body filled with a fiery passion for him. Obadiah kissed the legs of his wife and continued to move upwards as he lifted her dress to better see more of her. His hands groped the back of her legs to brace her, her muscles tensed as she was pulled closer to him, her forehead began to perspire and her head lifted so her eyes could close, she continued to hold her breath longer and longer, she craved her husband immensely, Mary Sue grabbed the head of her husband out from under her dress, she absolutely had to have him, Obadiah spun his wife so she was leaned back against the kitchen table, her dress raised up and his overalls speeding to the floor.

Obadiah and Mary Sue embraced and made passionate love to each other, they kissed with a passion that held more heat than the wood stove nearby, they breathed heavy and sweated even heavier, they exchanged smiles between kisses, their bodies craved each other so carnally that they almost lost track of time, the sun set outside the window, the kitchen grew dim, Obadiah almost expected to see sparks with how hot things were between them, his hands roamed her backside as her left leg was propped up to his side, her dress straps fell down the sides, Obadiah took full advantage of the exposed body of his wife and ravished every inch of her with his lips or finger tips. The kitchen raised its' internal temperature, things were hot and steamy and even the open window couldn't keep it regulated. The couple was young and in their own world, when they were together in this way, the world faded away, things seemed to cease to exist, it was just the two of them, and the kitchen table this time.

As the time raced by and their young love continued on "*MOMMMAAAAAAA*" startled the intimate couple, suddenly the pair was sent scrambling to re-dress as they were alarmed by the waking toddler in the next room. Mary Sue leaped off the table with a whole body hurl, she looped her arms in the arm holes of her dress and tucked herself back in, her perspiration dampened skin made her dress stick to her in many places, Obadiah frantically pulled his clothes back on, he tried to keep from falling to the ground as he stood on one pant leg and ended up stumbling to the floor from the uncoordinated task of dressing in a hurry. Mary Sue began to chuckle, and was wobbly from already being out of breath from their love making session.

Obadiah continued to try to finish dressing as he joined his wife in laughing at his clumsiness. Both parents tried to dress in the dimly lit kitchen and in a frantic hurry to avoid getting caught by Elizabeth also. Obadiah simply rolled back and forth on the dirty ground, he felt dirt sticking to his skin as he pulled his pants back on, things were awkward as he wrestled the snaps on his overalls to make sure they didn't fall back down and expose him once he stood back up. Mary Sue was all but ready to go and get

66

young Elizabeth for their cooling dinner, first she straddled her husband as she hadn't quenched her thirst to taste his lips, that thirst for him and his body was never satisfied.

Many dinners had passed, the summer had grown hot and long, the couple had sweated through many passionate opportunities together as they could duck away from the awareness of Elizabeth, whom grew more and more ambulatory. The belly on Mary Sue continued to grow; the life being nursed within her body came closer and slower to arriving. The summer gave way to crops of golden wheat in which were nearing time to harvest. Obadiah had toned up over the summer.

Mary Sue had thinned in the face a bit with the heat but her legs and stomach grew together, she was uncomfortable with her size now and was often leery of his compliments towards her body, she knew he much enjoyed the swelling of her breasts but she felt like she had an oven within her as the baby grew more and more. It was becoming tiring to keep up with Elizabeth for Mary Sue, the constant up and down wore her out more and more as the days went by, Obadiah fought as best he could as each day passed to supplement the needed attention for his daughter as well as step up for his wife with massages for his wife.

Nights after their daughter had retired to bed and they lay in the nude to stave off the heat. The couple would often begin with light touching, Obadiah rubbing various parts of his wife, usually knowing that it would stoke her loins for him and he also knew he was privileged that his touch alone held the key to unlock her intimate desires. Rubbing her sore and tender calves would often lead to a giggle as he knew she was ticklish but he would also run his hands up her bare legs and body and she would quickly reach the point where it would drive her crazy and she absolutely had to have him.

So many nights had passed in which they spent in loving embrace, Mary Sue was nearing the birth of their second child and the fall harvest was closing in also. The family had canned and dried most of the bounty that their garden had provided. Elizabeth was growing taller each day and Mary Sue continued to educate the young girl in the alphabet, numbers and simple arithmetic. The family was surely at home, at peace in their decision to move west, and welcomed into Indian Gulch as fellow residents. There were a few trips in to see the town doctor, Martinez; he was already anticipating a phone call from the couple to alert him to make the hour drive out at any given time to assist with the delivery. The husband and wife had already stockpiled baby needs as well as grains and rice to supply them all through the winter.

Fall harvest came barreling down, the summer raced past and as the Withers came to know many of the townspeople more on the social level, many residents were also anticipating the harvest, once all of the grain reached its' ideal low level of moisture to ensure proper storage ability, everyone was planning to bring their crop into town where companies would buy it by the grain sack, load it up onto large wagons and then transport it all to the train station hours away. There were grainers with large storage silos all over towards the east still, the silos dotted the landscape on their drive west and many companies offered really good market prices for grain. Obadiah had begun to make preparations to harvest, his trusty tractor had new Havoline oil and a tune up to chug its' way up and down the wheat rows. When the harvest was finally over it was mid-September, the loving wife was ready to birth her second child, it was hot and sticky out as the summer had hit its doldrums, the air was stagnant, still and heavy, some days seemed to just sizzle from the roosters cackle.

With the grain piled up high on their wagon trailer, the Withers had planned to strike out to sell it all one warm Thursday morning in the third week of September. The couple was up with the sun as usual, it was hot out already, Obadiah gently woke his wife with some intimately placed touching and massaging, he kissed her neck and followed the nape down towards her chest. Mary Sue rubbed her hands over the still muscular husband of hers. With delicate kissing, they began their morning in the same loving manner they had so many mornings before, it was mildly uncomfortable with the heat but they still thoroughly enjoyed their time together, they lay in bed together, breathing heavily and glistening with sweat.

Obadiah traced many of his wife's contours with his fingertips; making circles around the darkened nipples of his wife had continued to send a shiver down her as she was still very sensitive with excitement towards her husband. With each light touch, each goose bump inducing shiver, blood rushed to the delicate areas of the pregnant Mrs. Withers and her smiles grew larger as her body contorted in a feeble attempts to control her own body, although moot. Obadiah kissed down the sides of his bride, her ribs tweaked away from his kisses as his facial hair tickled her, kisses down her hips lead to kisses on her thighs, he gently kissed down the outer sides of her legs, her thighs soft and glistening in the reflections of light protruding through the drapes hanging over the window. Her legs spread to welcome her husband again, her hands holding her chest trying to slow her breathing, fooling neither her nor her husband.

As Obadiah kissed his way back up towards his wife's' awaiting mouth, he noticed a spot of blood on the sheet below her, Obadiah paused for a second, disbelief kept him from processing what he was seeing just before panic kicked him in the already beating heart. "*Honey*" exclaimed Obadiah to alert his wife, their heat of passion was quickly extinguished and the sense of a coming baby set them into a fast pace to prepare for a very long day of getting many things done. Obadiah rang the operator and asked the lady on the other end to ring Dr. Martinez' office once the opening hour came. The trailer was already loaded to haul their harvest into town.

Obadiah was frantically rushing around to gather supplies for his family for the day in town as Mary Sue had roused Elizabeth and adorned the sweet child with a light colored dress. It was an hour into town, and coincidently also an hour before the doctor's office was due to be opened. The spotting was light but still enough of a concern, their home was a ways out from town and any number of things could happen between home and there. Obadiah was ringside for the birth of Elizabeth; he held his dear wife's hand through the entire time while a doctor and nurse worked diligently down below.

Obadiah loaded his daughter and a bag of clothing into the backseat, he assisted his wife to sit in the passenger seat, she was uncomfortable with her size but wasn't in any more anguish than she should be but her husband was still overcome with panic and concern. Mary Sue tucked her legs into the car, she tucked her dress under her leg so it didn't get caught in the door as her husband shut the door. In a hurry around the front of the car, to hurry into the driver's seat, as he rounded the driver's corner. Obadiah clipped his left leg on the front bumper of the car, knocking him to the ground. More embarrassed than hurt, the man stood up, his wife sitting high in her seat trying to peer over the edge of the hood to make sure that her husband wasn't injured.

With a small pain in his left thigh and a small frayed spot on his pant leg now, Obadiah brushed himself off after picking himself up, pulling up on the same bumper that snagged his leg thus knocking him to the ground. Obadiah knelt for a moment, feeling like an imbecile, he remembered his wife and the predicament they were in and he returned to the hustled mentality and got moving. With a pace slower than the one that left him on the ground, Obadiah shoved himself behind the wheel of the dusty Dodge then fired up the engine. With the ladies ready to go, Obadiah slowly started to head east towards town, the heavily loaded trailer hitched behind creaked and squeaked behind them, slowing their pace and making the driver antsy with impatience.

As the sun rose higher in front of them, they zipped past the ditch weeds and trees that lined the red dirt road as they raced into town. Nine o'clock came as they made the last leg towards the doctor's office; the dirt covered Dodge pulled past the laundry place run by the quiet Chinese couple and began to slow down near the front walk of the office. With a brake squealing noise that halted with the car, Obadiah rushed to the aid of Mary Sue to help her to her feet and out of the car, as a gentleman should.

Once Mary Sue was upright he then hurried to get his daughter out of the backseat and the family then headed into the office. Dr. Martinez was already opening the door for them as they got close, it was still early but he and his receptionist wife were already waiting inside for the urgency ridden couple. Elizabeth held tight to her daddy as she trailed the faster paced pair as they made quickly with the morning greetings.

Mary Sue was ushered into an examination room and the husband-daughter twosome was offered to follow in if they chose to. Obadiah lagged behind with his daughter to give his wife some time to be examined and asked the young doctor to inform him if he was needed for anything. The door closed behind Dr. Martinez and Mary Sue, with the click of the door handle, a final sense of calm his Obadiah and he was finally able to breathe easily with the comfort to know that his wife was in safe hands of a professional and she was going to be taken care of. Obadiah fought to keep his mind out of the adjacent room, he tried his best to dance with his baby girl, her hair was getting long and she was getting much taller, when she wrapped her arms around her father's legs they now reached around above his knees, it was incredible to see how she has grown and now over two years old, she was about to be a big sister.

Obadiah listened intently to hear a baby cry, or his wife scream, any sort of sign that things were doing well and that is beloved wife was alright, he was growing worried as time carried on. After a few minutes of tussling with Elizabeth, wrestling her to and fro among the chairs as he did his best to delude is thoughts; there was a turn of the handle, Obadiah snapped up and his head whipped towards the door for a much needed update. Mary Sue stepped from behind the door. Mary Sue moved ever so gracefully even with the added size of pregnancy, she walked swiftly and gallantly. Obadiah felt his face lift from concern to a befuddled confusion for a moment, he was overjoyed to see his wife and that she was OK but he was expecting to see the always classy dressed Dr. Martinez. His jaw fell open, pulled towards the floor by his bottom lip, his eyebrows moved in the opposite direction on his face. The brow of Mary Sue broke adding a sense of relief to the room, she joined her family on the far side of the light waiting room, *"everything is just fine, it was just light spotting and we are all set"* she reassured her concerned husband that she was in good shape and that the baby was very healthy and at no risk of any harm. The relieved husband leaned up from sitting on the floor to kiss the mother of his children; her stomach was firm and inhibited her from getting her kiss so Obadiah picked himself up by his overall straps to meet his wife's lips.

Obadiah often pictured their future, the kids grown and with kids of their own, maybe in the future they would move away from the farm and grow gray together, age and weather as the times pass on. Their town was still new to them but he could picture it growing with the times also, it only took a second to picture the couple, sitting perched on a pair of rocking chairs together, wrinkled and talking about their lives, all that they had done, accomplished and the wonderful family that they had created, all those moments, all the memories, they all began with their wedding, it saddened Obadiah's heart to think about the day when one of them had to deal with having to lose the other, she was such a huge part of his life and he enjoyed every minute he had been blessed to spend with her, he feels a heavy burden well up in his chest every time, dreading the thought of outliving his wife.

73

There will be a time when the ultimate challenge is laid out before one of them, loss, that moment when one of them ceases to continue to breathe, their heart stops and then the other persons heart has to find a way to keep beating, alone. The thought of that moment caused Obadiah's heart to slow a bit, to fill with worry that it made it hard to breathe sometimes. Mary Sue felt the same way, it was a hard subject to think about, she feared the day when her body no longer resembled what it had when her husband fell in love with her, she feared the day when her body dried up and became barren to having more children with Obadiah, the strong able bodied man she was overjoyed to call her husband.

The couple was all set for the day, they loaded up their little girl, with a few deep sighs of relief, the couple was all ready to head out and into town to sell a wagon load of wheat and maybe make some rounds among their friends. The weigh station was down past Franks' gas station, the weighing was going on for a few days so there was plenty of time to get to their business, the Withers climbed back into their dusted Dodge and headed further east, they passed the hardware store and then beyond the gas station and to the makeshift weighing arena that was set up by purchasers ready to cut checks to the farmers selling their crops. Obadiah took the left past the gas station, there were large trucks with even larger trailers hooked up and ready to pile on hundreds or thousands of bags of grain before heading to a final destination. Mary Sue took young Elizabeth off to a wayward side so the two were out of the way from the busy traffic; each bag of grain was weighed, tallied and then loaded onto the even larger truck trailer.

Mary Sue sat and played with Elizabeth in a patch of grass but she kept an eagle eye on Obadiah, his shoulders bulged as he heaved and unloaded his trailer, after several hundred grain bags were unloaded and exchanged hands, the task took several hours to finalize and there was a hefty check cut to Obadiah and as the day peaked, the family was able to head back into town and grab some sandwiches at the deli. There was a huge relief that their first harvest had gone very well for the new farmers and the weight of "what-if" had come and gone and now their relief was in the form of a blue tinted paper check in the pocket of his trousers.

Katherine Ponsen served the family their late lunch, young Elizabeth was much better settled after filling her belly, she was calm and much less punchy now that she had eaten. The man of the business was still cutting and hanging meats while the family ate, he had his phonograph on and the soft sounds of the new tunes made for soothing ambiance in which caused the young daughter to succumb to many yawns, she yawned more and more, getting to the point at which she was unable to fight the tears that came with exhaustion. Mary Sue and Obadiah swapped sly smiles and winks back and forth at the fact that their daughter was about to be ready for an afternoon nap, even if it's against her will.

With their tailored car right out front, Obadiah set his girl in the back and wife in the passenger side of the front, he ensured that they were safe and sound and he walked to the building next to the deli, the bank. As the thumping sounds seemed to echo a bit below his footsteps on the boardwalk, Obadiah thought about many things; his girls back in the car, having to grow older with each passing year and what may still lie in store for him. How will he accept the day when he has to realize he has more he'll leave behind than life left ahead of him, what about the moment when he can only remember what it was like to do things on his own? Will he be able to deal with the memories of being a strapping lad while having to face the old man in the mirror? So many things entered his mind as he thudded along, the bank wasn't all that far of a walk but his mind seemed to race for whatever reason, maybe the scare he had this morning set a bit of mortality in his mind.

Obadiah pushed open the door to enter the bank, the metal cage that separated the customer portion of the bank from the employees was a dark black thick iron bars, the two people sitting behind were Hirsch Morgenstern and a younger lady teller. Obadiah had dealt with Hirsch a few times to make bank note payments, the rest of the time it was to simply cash checks or get money orders to send money back east. Obadiah had a large check to cash, the stingy Hirsch tried to charge the farmer a small percentage to simply cash the check and hand over the money unless Obadiah was willing to leave a percent in an account for the banker to be able to use for further investments. Hirsch was a decent banker but still a stingy and tight fisted bitter man, his salt and pepper hair was short and his short stature coupled with his still growing Jew nose, gave him a rat like look that people talked about.

Hirsch convinced Obadiah that there simply wasn't enough cash to pay the check in full, that if he opened an account and left some of his money with the bank, that he would ensure a positive percentage that would show some appreciation to the new customer, Obadiah was certain he was scammed but there wasn't much that could be done. Things were booming in town as the pocket books of all the farmers were swelling, farmers were spending their hard earned money in the stores and shops; they were refilling their bank accounts as they sold off grains and end of the season crops then restocked supplies for the winter and beyond.

Hirsch extended his hours during this time to capitalize on the newly acquired wealth of the hardworking residents; he too looked to benefit from the hard work of others. Obadiah was unsettled about his business at the bank and with a little bartering on his side he had a checkbook to write checks based on his account to he could still sort of access his money, a smart move on his part. Obadiah nodded good day to the thicker blonde woman behind the tar black iron bars, she hardly looked up as she filed her nails and maintained her focus on some other order of business behind the cage.

Obadiah brushed off the rudeness and left it in the bank where he found it and made his way back to his family and Dodge car out front. It was as if a light switch flipped again and he was back to thinking about the future, he knew deep down that the next fifty or so years would rush by, much like the waters of a stream, gently flow from one point to another, not always leaving an impression or marks, but passing by nonetheless. It was incredible to think about his new baby girl already being two years of age, and his second child almost here also. The sun faded cracked boards settled under his feet, each step brought him closer to his family awaiting his return but Obadiah was in a hurry to get back to them. He still felt swindled by the banker, it left him irritated that he already knew he was going to be scammed and tried his best to deter it, then it happened anyways. Obadiah wasn't sure what the chief problem was. Was it his being schemed or his inability to do anything about it, even with the premonition that it was going to take place?

With a roll of cash in his pocket and two ladies waiting for his presence, Obadiah stepped more swiftly to take his place at the helm of his motor vehicle. The day grew warmer yet, he felt his work shirt wet and sticking to him, even in the shade. Obadiah removed his cap to wipe off his brow with his handkerchief before shoving it back into his pocket to where it belonged, all while keeping a brisk pace. The air was still, with no breeze the sun seemed to penetrate the skin of people and make their blood downright boil, Obadiah wanted to hurry and get a move on so the wind whipping past their open car windows would cool them off.

Obadiah was wanting to get his wife back to their home so she could relax near a fan and be more comfortable after the day she has had, it was his job to make sure she was taken care of to the best of his abilities, at all times. Obadiah always had a portion of his attention turned to Mary Sue, he also kept a parents' eye on his young daughter but his loving wife was always first and foremost. Obadiah walked closer and closer to his car, he didn't see his rambunctious little girl creating chaos in the back seat, he saw the back of his wife's head as she laid back in the front seat. As he neared the front door he admired the more busy town, a bit farther ahead there was a couple of colored fella walking towards him on the boardwalk, they weren't anyone he recognized but he offered a friendly head nod anyways. The trio of black guys was dressed in worn overalls; one had a dusty brown bowler hat while another was in a leather miner's hat. They were chattering among themselves and seemed to be headed back to the weighing station set up back past the gas station.

Looking across the street Obadiah looked over and noticed ole Carvell keeping a watchful gaze over the guests in town, his menacing stance wasn't very welcoming and his crossed arms overtop his portly belly didn't give him a look that he was trying to drum up much business, as Obadiah reached out his left hand to the door handle of his vehicle, he gave a half two finger salute through the air with his right hand towards the unpleasant looking man leaning inside his doorway. Upon pulling his stiff door open against the dirt filled hinges, Mary Sue popped her head up from the back of the seat to wearily smile at Obadiah and welcome him into the car. Elizabeth was laid out on the back seat, her hair was matted to her head from the sweat, her hair was soaked and her cheeks were blushed from the heat.

Mary Sue herself looked tired, it had been a long day and coupled with the exhausting temperature, she was ready for a relaxing afternoon spent in front of a fan to cool them all off. When Obadiah seated himself in his proper position, he leaned in to kiss his wife and she leaned in to meet him halfway. Mary Sue rocked back and forth to remove herself from the seat back, not only was her sweaty causing her to stick but her pregnant belly gave her hassle to sit up but kissing her husband was more important than anything else. With a brief loving embrace the couple resumed their seated positions and headed home.

Obadiah was glad he made the stop off at Franks' station right after offloading all of the harvested wheat to the buyers, with many full gas cans and tanks in tow, the were once again headed west to go home. The pregnant wife sat back and rested as Obadiah captained his vehicle and its' passengers back to their home. The afternoon was flying by along with the flowers and ditch weeds alongside the road that lead them home. The breeze that whipped past was cooling and relaxing, the outside air had changed its' smell, it progressed from potential to success, it was their first wheat planting and with a bundle of money in his pocket.

Obadiah was riding high on life and it felt great, all of the invested energy, the hard work, the sweat and back breaking labor that was put into the ground had sprung forth from the earth and made the family successful. Winter was still a ways out but there was so much to do, Obadiah wanted to continue to harvest goods from his garden, dry them or can them and stockpile more goods and supplies for the coming months. The engine sped along, much better without the weight of all of the canvas bags of wheat loaded on the trailer. The drive was long and past various farms along the way, as usual it took the better part of an hour and the husband and wife drove along holding hands. Obadiah was so relieved that his wife was OK and that they were still awaiting their second born child. The road was still bumpy, it hadn't really rained in a while and the roots in the road scooted the car from side to side as it drove back home, Obadiah did his best to keep the steering wheel straight and on course.

Elizabeth jostled in the back a bit but remained quiet and asleep, Mary Sue did her best to remain calm and relaxed as the bumps caused her head to shake a little here and there, after the subtle turn down Saginaw Way, they proceeded to make their way home, the passed the Basks farm on the left, it was large wheat farm also, owned and run by a man and his wife, their children long since grown and moved away. The last farm between their front bumper and home was their neighbor farm, the Lyzkas, another wheat farm with a few animals for slaughter, mostly chickens and some goats. Lyzka was a widow lady whom still struggles to run her farm but Mr. Basks helps to till her crops also.

There were only the three farms along the long Saginaw road, things were remote and quiet, and it left each home to their own tranquility and devices. The downside was little help nearby if things went awry but it also provided ample solitude, privacy that Obadiah and Mary Sue enjoyed frequently. Things were so blessed, the soils around them were fertile, their love blossomed and gave way to a lovely little girl, and another infant child to arrive any day, their home was cozy and should be warm through the winter, their farm was proving to be everything they had ever hoped it could be and they were making a living. Obadiah often wrote to Norman, Norman wrote more often as he missed his only child.

Mary Sue sent letters back east also, her sister Charlotte wrote and spoke about possibly coming to visit once the harvest was in and their parents were settled comfortably for the winter. Mary Sue suggested that Charlotte come to visit a month or so after the newest arrival to their family, not only would she be grateful to spend time with her older sister, she would also be grateful for an extra set of hands to help with the newborn for a month or so as the first few months are often the most trying for new parents. The two sisters reached an accord, Charlotte would be out by train in late October to stay until around Thanksgiving time before returning east.

As Obadiah turned down his driveway, he looked around at the once again bare earth, it had been cut and harvested and now only plant stubble remained. The golden honey colored fields that rolled with the breezes now had a dominantly brown tint, the earth shown through by the short cut plants, soon the leaves of the sparse trees would also turn and give way to the coming winter, fall had come and the transition into winter was already set in motion, the changing of the seasons steamrolled on and there wasn't anything anyone could do about it. As the motor vehicle slowed to its normal resting place just out from the front porch, nestling right back above the spot worn dead from having perched there most of the summer, the car coasted to a final stop, and they were home. Mary Sue spoke about sending Charlotte a telegram per Western Union once the baby was born so the news got to her family as soon as possible, Obadiah thought that it was a good idea and worth the nickel, the only exception would be the hour drives each way in order to get the news back to the east coast. Mary Sue was terribly spent, her energy was zapped from the heat

79

and toiling in the day, she needed help to her feet, it was the gentlemanly duty to hold the door for a lady anyways and Obadiah was there in a jiff.

Mary Sue pulled on her husband's shoulder as well as the back of the seat to finagle her body upright, she was less than thrilled at being this large pregnant and uncomfortable in the heat but she was still joyous to be nurturing a child within her, the baby turned and bumped around inside of her as it grew, she was still tickled when she could feel an odd bump protrude the tense surface of her belly, Obadiah would get to watch a lot of the baby jiving and moving when Mary Sue was in a bath, when she was submerged in warm water, the little critter tucked deep into her stomach would be energized, something about the bath encouraged the babies most active times. Mary Sue was about to take a step towards the house when an agonizing pain shot through her loins.

Mary Sue bent at the waist for a moment, the pain kept her from standing erect but bending didn't ease the pain anyways. Obadiah was stricken with concern, the expression on his face turned from strong and stoic to immediately concern for his wife, her knees began to buckle underneath her and the brawny man wrapped his second arm around her to keep her from collapsing. Elizabeth began to stew in the backseat from the commotion, Mary Sue struggled to take a deep breath, she had a small moment of clarity, this wasn't something wrong, and this was labor. "*It's time*" Mary Sue grunted to her supporting husband, Obadiah paused for a brief second, what was muttered to him through clenched teeth hadn't taken hold. "*OHHH*" Obadiah let out a half howl half screech as the information struck him about what Mary Sue had said.

Mary Sue grasped at the center of her pains, her right arm hung around the neck of her husband who was guiding her towards the steps, her left arm enclosed her stomach as her whole body seized and kept trying to force her to her knees. Three struggled steps from the car and they were halfway to the porch, the rickety steps were worn and faded with the sun but suddenly looked of promise, those steps proffered the hope that they were almost inside, inside the couch and other furniture gave the false hope of comfort, even if only a false sense of hope, it was better than being stuck outside fumbling to deliver a baby.

As Obadiah reached out for the small handrail to lead his wife's hand to the rail, a grunting painful cry let out, a large amount of fluid came rushing out from between the legs of Mary Sue, her water broke, this was a point of no return, this baby was joining them this day and Obadiah was going to have to figure out as much as he had to and quickly. Obadiah saw white for a moment, he wasn't sure if it was the looming prospect of having to deliver his child, or at the sight of all the liquid that had created a large mud puddle on the ground, or perhaps a combination of the two.

Mary Sue began to cry; she was not only frightened but riddled with pain as her entire body tried to evict the baby from her womb. Obadiah was struggling just as hard as his wife to get her up the few stairs, her fist clenched tightly more out of reaction to pain than to pull upon to rise her up the stairs, Obadiah was so focused on getting his wife indoors that he forgot about his little girl beginning to wake up in the backseat of his car. The puddle created when her water broke, trailed in spots from the puddle to a bloody mix streaming down her legs, her stockings were soaked and mud had clumped upon Obadiah's boots.

Obadiah felt as if his hand was being crushed in a vice as Mary Sue squeezed as a reaction to her entire body squeezing, her strength was immense, Obadiah felt his knees tremble a bit as her hand clenching came and went with the waves of labor contractions. Obadiah was guiding his wife through the door when she was overcome again and this time, was forced down onto one knee, Obadiah's heart sank seeing his wife in such dire pain. When Elizabeth was born he did as most men did and waited for a nurse to come and alert him that it was all over, only having witnessed a few horse births.

Obadiah was in a bind, he had to figure everything out on his own. It was a slow struggle to get Mary Sue to the comfort of the couch; her legs trembled as she dug deep for the strength to keep taking steps towards the couch. Obadiah tried to comfort his wife in this stressful time, he continued to coax her to the couch while speaking soothing sentences, all to no avail as her grunts and screams overtook the volume of his voice. Obadiah felt a fool, it snapped into his head that poor Elizabeth was still out in the car, there was so much that had to be done promptly that Obadiah was already becoming overwhelmed, shock and panic coupled with

81

fear and excitement, with all of the emotions flooding into his mind, his stomach was turning knots and he was feeling queasy.

Once Mary Sue was laid on the couch, and as comfortable as possible for the moment, Obadiah ran to ignite the woodstove, he had heard them talk about hot towels and such when at the hospital last time. Mary Sue was crying and grunting in pain, it all broke the silence in the house in between the banging of pots and pans as Obadiah hurried to fill as many as he could with water and get several placed onto the stove to begin to heat. The frantic chaos induced fumbling caused Obadiah to splash a large amount of water down the front of his bibs, the water soaked clean down to his socks; this only further aggravated the tense man.

With pots banging on the stove, a wife screaming in the next room, and soaking wet overalls, Obadiah was growing stressed and more panicked as the looming birth of his child was solely in his hands. With three large pots beginning to warm, Obadiah stepped back towards the main room in which Mary Sue was laid out on the couch, his boots growing soggy and wet as water ran down from his chest and stomach, down his legs and collected in his boots. Obadiah was already perspiring, his frantically hurried pace was only matched by his rapid heartbeat, he had so many tasks popping open in his mind, he wasn't sure what to expect, farm animals birthed on their own and with ease, they were mere animals, this is a human being, this is his second child and he was afraid to make a mistake.

"*Elizabeth!*" the memory of his baby daughter suddenly filled his mind, it had fallen to wayside and he had forgotten about her, much to his regret. Obadiah informed his ailing wife that he must rush back out to rescue their trapped baby girl, imprisoned in the Dodge, he felt so ashamed as he burst out of the door and rushed hurriedly to the frightened little girl. With a few large galloped strides, he neared the back door to release Elizabeth, she was standing on the seat, both hand slapping against the glass crying out for her parents. Elizabeth had red eyes from minutes of crying, her cheeks were red and stricken with tears, and her nose was bubbly with snot from screaming and crying so very hard. Calm set into the face of the little girl as her father came running to her rescue, she was so frightened having slightly woken to the howling of her mother's labor pains then woken up alone in the car and then was locked within. The poor young girl was

82

absolutely horrified, she was uncontrollably sobbing as her father released her from her motored prison.

Obadiah yanked the door open, the little girl was leaning on the window, pounding her open hands against it trying to call for any attention, from anyone that might hear the frightened child, Obadiah pulled the door open with his left hand and reached out for the upset toddler with his right, catching her as she flung to him. He couldn't have arrived any sooner, she was so glad to see him but she was still sobbing and crying. The little girl hugged him ever so tightly; she had instantly forgiven him for neglecting her and leaving her for much awful terror filled minutes.

As Elizabeth clung to the neck of her hero father, they hurried towards the howling screams shrieking from inside their home, Elizabeth was already overcome with a look of panic, she grew more worried as she neared her mother in agony as they sprinted up the steps, she and her father bounced in unison as they landed on the porch. The twosome burst in the front door and it was time to get back to work taking care the woman sprawled out and clenching tightly to the couch while labor completely controlled her body as if a marionette. The poor woman was on her knees, her arms around the arm of the couch, pulling it tightly to her chest as the agony and pain causes all of the muscles in her body to tighten, forcing out awful groans.

Elizabeth was still sobbing, coupled with yawning from wearing herself out crying, she held so tightly to her rescuer that he had a hard time breaking her hold on him, he pried her fingers apart in her grip on him to set her onto her bed so he could return to the side of his wife, Mary Sue's contractions were gaining strength and frequency, the task of birthing a child was as real as ever, not to mention right in his face. Elizabeth refused to stay where she was placed, Obadiah gave firm instructions to stay put as he set her in bed then tried to hurry to leave her behind and get to his wife. Elizabeth climbed out of bed as fast as she was put there, Obadiah had to hurry to shut the door between then, locking her now in her room rather than the car in which she was just freed from. Obadiah rushed to gather any and all towels and spare sheets he could find, he was certain he was in for a messy task, he was already introduced to the bloody mixture that spewed forth from his wife, he knew that the broken placenta proceeded the arrival of an infant, and he got the ground saturating signal that his second child was on its' way.

Obadiah panicked as his wife screamed aloud, he was growing concerned for her as his heart felt for her in pain. Obadiah rushed to gather all of the available towels and blankets, he couldn't figure out what else he might need, he was in such a flustered state that his head ran in circles and his feet seemed nailed to the center of the room and his eyes fixated on the grimacing face of his wife. Obadiah began to roll up his sleeves, his wife was still kneeling on the couch edge, writhing with uncontrollable contractions and leaning back towards her heels trying to alleviate the overwhelming pain, her arms hugging the sofa arm. The lights burned bright as the sun wore out, Mary Sue was in the throes of birthing.

Obadiah wasn't sure he could handle such an intimate role with his wife, he was also extremely racked with nerves as he was ill prepared to be a medic for his wife. As the bursts of groaning from the painful contractions grew into one, Obadiah was sure that he hadn't tripped on the porch and knocked himself on conscious, or perhaps even failed to wake up this morning, the reality of amniotic fluid and grunting from his loving wife were real, and really happening. The time was at hand, as was his wife's birth canal. The wailing howls of the once again entrapped Elizabeth could be heard through the door, the young girls' wails joined in chorus those of her mother, both of the cries burned in the ears of the over stressed Obadiah.

If there was a howling hound to add to all of the caterwauling, it would be enough to send Obadiah over his limit, his mental edge was nearing and he could feel his blood pressure filling his ears, making them hot and red. Obadiah fetched the first large pot of water and a pile of cloth and helped his wife to recline back onto the floor, she was breathing heavy and almost unable to speak, the grunts, groans, and crying wails were exhausting and she gasped large yawns to get enough air to continue pushing. Obadiah tended to as much as he possible could, he placed blankets under her and her back for comfort, he pushed on her legs to keep them elevated so she could push from deep within.

Mary Sue had been through this process once before but was still scared and duly worried, she was reassured with some comforting notion that her loving husband was by her side but she would have also felt much more reassured to have a doctor nearby. Obadiah had rung the operator as he was rummaging through the kitchen to begin to boil the water, the reformed Dr. Martinez was over an hour away and that was if the operator could even reach him first try. Obadiah felt his brow seep perspiration, it seemed to stream down his face and drip off of his nose as he tried to do his best to play catcher, but this wasn't baseball. Mary Sue continued to push. Obadiah was nervous to peek under her dress but he also knew it wasn't time to be shy. Mary Sue screamed out "*can you see it? Am I close?*"

Obadiah lifted the dress above her raised knees, he took a second to identify what he was seeing and with a succoring reply he was able to inform his wife she was doing great and that their young baby was nearing. The desperately nervous man could see the head of his second child get ever closer to joining them, closer to becoming real, the head was popping out and the fathers' mouth had begun to curl upwards. The eyebrows broke the plane of his wife, the baby's head was almost completely out, Obadiah was still bewildered at the amount of fluid that was leaking out with the newborn, the baby was almost passed its' shoulders and the husband was growing even more excited that things seemed to be doing well.

While cradling the head of the baby, Obadiah tried to ease the baby from its' mother, the baby was warm, wet, and pink, the flush colored baby had blue lips and wet matted hair. Once the baby had freed its' shoulders, the remainder of its' body slid the rest of the way out and that was that. Obadiah was immediately rushed with relief, it was a subduing feeling, suddenly his arms felt the weight of all if his concern lift, his body felt lighter and with his new son beginning to wriggle in his arm, he began to shed tears. Streams fled from his eyes as he looked at the baby boy that he and Mary Sue created, he could hardly keep from crying enough to speak audibly to Mary Sue. He did his best to clean up the mess spread out before him, it was in need of attention, Obadiah walked on his knees to hand deliver their child to its' mother.

Dr. Martinez, Joe, opened the door, there may have been a knock to announce his arrival but with everything that was going on, added with the crying of a freshly born baby, the knock went unanswered so the gracious doctor slowly let himself in and took stock of the room in which he entered. Martinez rushed to the aid of his patients on the floor, with a quick series of events; he was cutting the umbilical cord and cleaning the jaw waggling crying infant. The baby checked out healthy and next order of business was to inspect the mother, Mary Sue was growing tired, her

85

energy was fleeting and her yawns became closer together. The gentle doctor and Obadiah helped Mary Sue to her bed, a much more comfortable place for her to relax while Martinez checked the baby's airways, eye reflexes and skin color, everything on the child pointed to a healthy baby boy and Martinez was very congratulatory.

Mary Sue still wept from exhaustion, Obadiah was full of pride as he was tasked with helping to bring his child into this life and rose to the challenge. The baby was slowing in its' cries, the fatigued mother was struggling to even keep her arms up to cradle her new baby, she was pale and sweaty but still smiling at both the infant as well as her husband. Dr. Martinez gave both patients a seal of good health, his tan toned skin was also perspiring from the frantic chaos of the room and having to acclimate to the pace and bring order to the room. Martinez wore a gray derby with a black band over his shorter black hair, his glasses sat closely to his face that refused to slip towards the end of his nose as he worked. Martinez had put rubber gloves on before getting elbow deep in placenta and amniotic fluid; he used a pile of already dirty and soaked sheets to soak up more of the mess on the floor.

Doctor Martinez went above and beyond to help clean up, he explained to Obadiah "you *did a great job doing a large part of my job, so I'll even things up and save you some work for the night.*" Obadiah smirked at the quick thinking of the keen doc; he truly appreciated the help from the medical fellow and sincerely appreciated the thoughtful sentiment. The kind doctor spent time on his hands and knees over a pot of hot water scrubbing at the floor, Obadiah guided and helped his wife to sit up a bit better then ran to unleash his rather un-happy daughter from her dungeon. Elizabeth was asleep on her floor, Obadiah had to squeeze in the door to keep from injuring the passed out girl, his heart was so full of joy that he fought the feeling that it might burst, he smiled so big that his facial muscles ached and it felt like his ears were being pulled behind the back of his head. It was truly an amazing day; it was long and exhaustive but so wonderful and full of blessings. Elizabeth was hard to wake but easily scooped up and carried out to be with her mother and new brother. Obadiah laid the little girl near her mother on the bed and quickly made his way to the kitchen.

The man made a quick attempt to play host and hostess, he made several sandwiches as fast as he could and hoped that the feeble attempt was enough to thank the stand-up doctor for his heroic actions and kind hearted gesture by cleaning. Obadiah was fighting to stave off his own weary feelings, his head began to feel heavy as he laid out slices of bread and mounded up sliced deli meats on each one. Obadiah rushed between rooms as he took orders from wife and visitor as to what sides or additions each wanted on their meals. Doctor Martinez joined the man in the kitchen and began to spend a few minutes washing up as he continued to offer his assistance in any way that he could. Obadiah was amazed that the kind hearted doctor continued to help out, even after the medical side of his help had come and gone and then was no longer needed. Joseph finished washing himself up then helped to place the sandwiches on plates and carry everything out to the bedroom so all could sit together. Obadiah dragged an end table from the couch so they could all sit and take stock of how things transpired before all called it a night.

Elizabeth rubbed her eyes and yawned excessively as her father tried to wake her up so she could finally eat supper, it was late and all were mildly worn out from the day but with the new baby sleeping in the arms of his mother, no one wanted to part from the room. Dr. Martinez ate with the family and complimented the new mother on her strength to get through everything and how well Obadiah handled the stressful situation. Martinez had counted aloud and came to the realization that the Withers' baby was now the tenth one he had delivered; or almost, as he chuckled a bit. Elizabeth was overly curious about the small sack of pinkish skin wrapped in a towel, she kept trying to climb up on the legs of her mother to improve her view, each time she began to lean, she was reminded to sit and eat. Elizabeth was still yawning a bit, she had cried more today than maybe any other day of her young life before. The light in the main part of the house shone bright as the light from the sky faded to the dark of night and the hours carried on.

Dr. Martinez thanked the man of the house for his grace and welcoming, Obadiah tried to out-thank the educated and even more well-spoken young doctor from the northeast. Obadiah walked the doctor to the door as they made their goodbyes again and the father reached out to firmly shake the hand of the doctor whom made the hour drive to ensure the health of his patients, it was a much appreciated gesture and Obadiah couldn't thank him nearly enough for everything he had done. The doctor made his way to his car and then back down the driveway and headed east towards town.

Obadiah watched out the front window as the two bright taillights wound their way down the driveway, turned to town and slowly disappear into the darkness. Mr. Withers leaned against the window, his head began to throb as his adrenaline had subsided and now he was feeling empty, drained, and lethargic. The cold of the glass that supported his face felt wonderful, his eyes wore heavy and a violent shake was in order to feebly attempt a reawaken. With the now larger family just behind him, there was a lot to do, so very much more so, especially that Mary Sue was to be laid up for a few days and all of the chores were now on his shoulders. The little boy was swaddled in a towel and resting next to his mother, whom was struggling to remain awake as her head was nodding to a fro while trying to finish her sandwich and juice.

Mary Sue had a large bite of food balled up in the right side of her mouth, her medium brown hair was sweaty and matted up in a tumbleweed looking mess that mostly fell behind her, Obadiah had hardly ever seen her so tired before, one occasion of hauling and stacking fire wood for an entire day had gotten her close to such exhaustion but nothing can rival birthing a child. Elizabeth kept trying to peek at her new baby brother, she had so many confusing questions and her eyes were locked on the boy and she couldn't fathom where he came from.

The entire family was physically and emotionally drained, Obadiah dragged his feet to the bed to sit with everyone, he landed a kiss on the forehead of his wife, he was gleaming with how proud of her he was, he had to brace a wobbly arm on the bed to keep him from falling forward and landing on her. Young Elizabeth was now an older sister, she didn't know what lay in store for her and how much would change in her small world but she would gladly partake in anything she could, she was always happy to join in any adventure or help in any way. Falling backwards onto the bed, Obadiah tried to brace himself to slow the fall, even trying to fight gravity a little was moot, he still plopped down and the mattress was there to greet him.

As the air let out from behind his back he could feel his body relax, the air left his seat, and also his lungs, with a deep exhale, tired had suddenly presented itself to the proud poppa, his head rolled to the right to make eye contact with Mary Sue, whom was braced on her right arm which sat upon the pillows of the home.

The four tired bodies finished their quickly thrown together meals, Elizabeth pulled at her bread and kicked her feet up into the air and still played a little, even into the late hours. The light bulb that stuck out from the center of the main room buzzed, the light shown bright and unwavering, even as each family member yawned in chorus or struck out on their own to yawn as an individual. The day was late, the wheat had been sold, the new baby delivered, and all was as ready for the winter as it needed to be. It was time to retire, Obadiah escorted Elizabeth to bed and tucked her in once again, she seemed to resist as her earlier experience inside was less than pleasant, with a kiss to the forehead he left her to yawn again and shut the light off for her to sleep.

The newborn sat next to his mother, passed out from sheer exhaustion while his father was tucking in his older sister, he sat bundled tightly on the couch, sleeping from his own violent upheaval from his warm dark comfortable baby palace, through the birth canal and then dropped suddenly into a new, bright strange world full of sharp, no longer muffled sounds and sights that are many levels of scary. The baby sat unnamed for a few minutes, his parents had briefly volleyed a few names but none with any sincerity; Thomas, Mathew, Mark, Norman, Alexander, there were also girls names discussed but none of them mattered anymore.

Obadiah joined his wife on the bed, she was absolutely passed out cold and hard to wake, Obadiah moved his healthy baby boy to one side and did his best to ease his wife to the middle of the bed. Obadiah softly lay his wife down, he was still wrought with emotions towards the amazingly strong woman whom just gifted him his second child, a strapping young boy. Obadiah tucked his lady into bed and turned back to retrieve his newest family member, the nameless child squeaked and let out small chirps from the foot of the bed, Obadiah walked as if his feet were shrouded with cement, he sauntered over to fetch the small child and then make his way back to bed with great hope for some ever needed sleep.

The small boy was wide eyed and just staring out into the open, he was silent and content with his position and having been swaddled securely. The tired man gathered a second wind, looking down on his freshly born son, he was instilled with pride, a light heart, relief that everything turned out alright, he was so very grateful for so much and all he could do was well up and let a few tears of joy streak down his face.

Obadiah brought the bundled baby close to his heart, he wanted to hug the baby so firmly but was afraid to risk injury to the infant, and the baby had dark blue grayish eyes that just stared deeply at his dad. Obadiah suddenly couldn't feel his body, his aches and pains faded away, he was filled with such a relief that his worn out body no longer mattered. The two Withers' men made their way to their sleeping quarters, there was a bassinet in the corner for the arrival but the first night the baby boy would be nestled in the crook of Obadiah's elbow so he was close at hand for rocking for shushing to sleep. There was no way of knowing what time it was, Obadiah slid into bed, his body fit perfectly into his well-worn impression and his son wriggled a bit in his arm. Obadiah whispered to the baby *"son, my son, welcome to the world, you will be my heir, you will inherit all that I know and learn everything I can teach or have ever learned"* Obadiah let out a light sigh and murmured *"SON"* as he smiled to himself and fell asleep.

Sleep had fallen short as the newborn baby began to whimper and cry a little, it couldn't have been long past falling to sleep when Obadiah had realized that the screeching noise in his dream had come from reality and it had to take everything he had in order to pry his eyelids apart. Obadiah had managed one crusted eye open, his entire body felt depleted and tapped out, it took everything he had in him to reach over to try and arouse his wife and convince her to nurse. Mary Sue was stiff as a log, when she was shaken her entire body just rolled a bit, Obadiah shook a little harder trying to get her attention enough to help him out, he was getting desperate for sleep and the idea to attempt matters himself flashed in his head. Though extremely rude, Obadiah considered unbuttoning her top and hoping his baby would latch and feed, Obadiah was pretty certain that if he nuzzled his son to her and she didn't have warning, that he would end up with a hurt son and a fat lip for himself, neither were worth the risk!

Obadiah moved his hand from his the shoulder of his wife up to her face, he hoped that his soothing touch and maybe speaking her name might wake her up enough to help her husband out. Mary Sue lifted her head a bit at response to the request of both boys in her bed, she didn't have the energy to speak as much as just mutter something, she tried to half fumble her top off,

90

Obadiah helped as best he could to help facilitate but between the three tired hands he felt more of a hindrance than anything else. The infant nursed and all fell deep asleep, the Withers were all so extremely tired that even the breathing that each other found comfort in, became shallow and had no effect on the other, each parent fell so deeply to slumber that small noises and the usual branches rubbing against the front of the house didn't even register to either of them.

The morning came with a labored awakening, no one in the house was quick to rise, Obadiah had to spend a few minutes mustering the energy to raise himself, his head was heavy and throbbed with each heartbeat, his baby son was wide eyed and docile so Obadiah was thankful for the lack of crying and was giddy to greet his son to his first day on the outside. Mary Sue slept and hardly stirred as Obadiah rolled from the bed, he couldn't even force himself to sit up so he rolled to his left and landed with his right knee and arm on the floor, his head still resting on the bed.

Obadiah rolled his face back and forth against the bed, the awkward position in which he was seated seemed to ease his lower back, it may have just simply been the lack of ambition to arise for the day, still weary and worn from a late previous night. There was wood to chop and stock for the coming winter, there were eggs to harvest for the days breakfast for the family but first, there was a coffee pot to get brewing to try and start his day with a hearty liquid boost. Squatting on his hands and knees, Obadiah seemed to be pulled more by gravity this morning than any before that he can remember, he pushed his hands against his knees to do his best to stand erect and then lean towards the kitchen, hoping that shear momentum would take him there.

As he stumbled towards the kitchen, Obadiah felt like he was falling, just slowly and semi intentionally, he hadn't bothered to put a shirt on under his overalls; the day wasn't all that chilly at the start so why bother. He flipped on the coffee pot and dropped down onto a kitchen chair with a "thud" the chair let out a small squeak, as Obadiah bent slowly to reach for his boot to tie them on, he heard his new son begin to tussle in the next room, the combination of noises seemed to lead to another noise; "*MOMMAAAAA*" Obadiah didn't want to leave his young lady behind again, wearily he sauntered back over to open her door to find her sitting on the floor, her hair was rather disheveled but brushing it was often a misguided adventure that usually seemed to leave someone flustered.

Elizabeth picked herself up and ran with glee to her father, he did his best to brace himself against the excitement filled blow as she charged at him and hugged his legs, the worn down father reached and pat his daughter on her head and encouraged her to follow him, but quietly. Little Elizabeth did her best to tiptoe, she kept her arms tucked up by her chest and made a sneaky face but her steps were no more quiet than usual, it was still funny that she tried as her daddy lead her outside. The two stepped out into the fresh morning air, Obadiah was still slouching and the yawning failed at forcing him to stand tall for better inspiration.

Elizabeth carried the woven basket, there was a white and red clothe folded in the bottom to soften the wood for the morning eggs. There were plenty of eggs tucked under the few chickens in the coup, Elizabeth was startled every time a chicken would leap from its' perch and flap its' wings in a huff of panic while trying to flee. Elizabeth would clutch the basket tighter and close her eyes with all of her might trying not to get hit by a flying chicken as Obadiah scared them away one at a time to gather their bounty from each nesting roost. With nearly a dozen eggs trusted to the care of little Elizabeth, Obadiah encouraged her to walk gently and exercise extreme care with the eggs, the barefoot young'n had her left arm under the handle of the basket and with her right hand ending in her pointer finger, was trying to count the eggs inside.

The sun was breaking the horizon, beams of light made silhouettes of the trees and long drawn out shadows on the ground, the sun was a deep golden orange with red lining the horizon on both sides, the blue grew fierce around the lifting orb and the bugs nearby had begun to stir for their day as well. Obadiah was hungry, his body was requiring food to keep going, Elizabeth was most likely hungry as well but to distracted by her basket of eggs to pay any mind. Obadiah wanted to get breakfast cooked and serve his wife in bed as he was also tasked with taking care of the tough new momma, he had to get her to eat to continue to feed their son and it was his job as the man of the house to raise a strong family, and he was excited about it.

The two early risers entered their home, the coffee was the overbearing aroma in the kitchen, there wasn't a sound to be heard beside the random pop of the coffee pot on the hotplate. Elizabeth set her basket on the table and rushed to drag her small foot stool towards the stove, the little girl pulled with all of her might to position the light colored wood step stool just right, then climbed atop to be closer to working level with her pa. Obadiah stood firm and watched his growing daughter tug the stool, he knew she wanted to work right beside him and all he could do was smile, he didn't want to undermine her strength or confidence by stepping in so he let her struggle and enjoy the well-earned victory.

With cast iron skillet on a warming burner, the father daughter team began to prepare their morning meal, Elizabeth wore almost as many eggs as she made into the pan but she was adamant to do it just as well as her larger stove partner. Obadiah let her whisk the eggs while he sliced green peppers, grated some cheese and add a few dashes of spices for their pleasure. Obadiah toasted some thick slices of bread, poured some juice for his girls and sat his little helper in her chair to feed herself. With loaded plate and full glass in hand, Obadiah made his way to the side of his wife, the room was silent and he budged the door open with his left elbow to reveal the sleeping mother and child still where he left them. The smell of food alerted Mary Sue to the presence of her husband more than hushed carefully placed footsteps, the accidental clanging of pans in the kitchen hardly made her budge.

Mary Sue was so tired looking, her eyes were puffy and her cheeks drained of their color, Obadiah worried for her, she still looked absolutely washed out, the day after delivering Elizabeth she was ready to get back home and finish hanging laundry, this second time was different, she hardly had enough spirit in her to help nurse their son, she was half propped in a way to latch and feed. Obadiah placed her plate on the night table next to her, he reached in to give her a kiss on her cheek and lift her a bit to drink, he placed his lips to hers and took notice that the heat radiating from her forehead was more than normal, her lips were dry and she barely had any energy, his worry grew. Obadiah brought a glass of orange juice to her mouth and encouraged her to drink, she began to lean back after a short sip but the dutiful husband held the glass in place. Mary Sue kept drinking as she wasn't given much of a choice, the juice continued to flow into her mouth and she struggled as best as she could to keep swallowing until the last gulp or two near drowned her, causing her to spit some forward and shoot Obadiah a stern look.

Obadiah didn't much care for the sideways stare from his under the weathered wife, she seemed to have a fever and lacked the energy to do anything about it. The concerned husband hoped that the juice alone was enough vitamins and calories to give her some strength to eat, he told her he wanted to get back to Elizabeth before anything happened, he apologized for the near drowning and pleaded that she eat her eggs, the father excused himself to return to tending to Elizabeth, and his own breakfast. Obadiah sat next to his big helper, she was knocking eggs off of her plate with her fork but still reaching out and grabbing her eggs to eat. Obadiah spritzed a few streams from his trusty Tabasco bottle, the smell of the sauce caused him to flair his nostrils, also prompting young Elizabeth to pinch her nose shut because the odor was more offensive to her than that of his coffee.

Obadiah ate his meal alongside his darling daughter and then cleared their places, he encouraged her to play with her blocks while he again checked on her brother and mother. Obadiah drizzled honey on some toast, honey is an antibiotic and maybe the sugar in it would help his wife to feel better as well, he poured her a small amount of coffee, placed her toast on top of the cup and headed to her again. With the opening creaks of the door, Mary Sue looked up from her laying position to glance at her husband walking in, " *if you try and pour that down my throat too I'll bite you"* Mary Sue warned her husband that his antics to feed her won't be taken to lightly this round. Obadiah smirked at her snappy whit, he took it as a sign that she was feeling a little better, even if only for a minute or two. Obadiah held up his peace offering, he had hoped that the smell of food and other goodies would be enough to help perk her up.

Obadiah sat by Mary Sue's side again, this time she had enough gumption to sit up a little, with his help. Obadiah held up the honey soaked toast and encouraged her to nibble away, her facial expression after the first bite in response to the really sweet honey mixed with taste of juice still in her mouth gave her a reason to shiver a bit, with an encouraging smile from Obadiah, she continued to force down the toast. Mary Sue sipped at her coffee, it wasn't piping hot but warm enough to slow her gulping, which was to offset the overpowering sweetness of the honey that coated her mouth. Obadiah let his face relax after his wife had taken in some calories for energy, her color returned to her face a bit and she ceased perspiring, much to his delight. Obadiah was relentless in his pursuit of many things, this morning his attention was locked on his wife eating, and having to feed her so she could feed the wee lad was of the utmost importance. Obadiah reached for the plate of food and refused to heed to her hesitation.

Halfway through her mound of eggs, Elizabeth came bursting through the door with the mighty force of an adult; Obadiah almost fumbled the plate but saved it at the last moment from joining some juice on the clothing of his wife, causing Mary Sue to chuckle a bit at the close call. Elizabeth climbed onto the bed, she wanted to see her mother and brother, "*hi mommy, brother?*" the little girl crept close to the wiggling baby, "*MOMMY?*" Mary Sue took a labored breath and warned her little girl, "*mommies sick baby*" the little girl didn't quite understand, she looked at her mother, looked at her baby brother then back so her mother again: "*sick?*" she asked. "*No no, I sick, I sick sweetie*" the young girl seemed to grasp the concept for a moment, she turned to look at her baby brother "*Isaac, Isaac, Isaac*" the little girl chanted while tugging the most outward layer of her brothers' swaddling gently trying to wake him. Mary Sue smiled an ever so large smile at her daughter, looked back to her right and shrugged. Obadiah stuck out his bottom lip as if in agreement and so the baby boy was dubbed; Isaac. Mary Sue ate plenty and regained enough strength to bath and change for the day. The family had begun their day in the main room of their home, Obadiah decided to turn on the phonograph to maybe hear a radio broadcast or the upcoming weather perhaps.

There was some Morse code like beeping coming across, the beeping signaled an alert to news of some sort so he began listening intently to the words lightly covered but a fuzzy static that also came out of the speaker. "The stock market crash of yesterday had continued to have a shattering effect on finances today as prices still come tumbling down around the country, jobs are drying up and panic has caused several traders to take their lives in New York" the broadcast spilled out of the radio like a bursting damn. Mary Sue gasped at the news. Obadiah sat befuddled and tried to make heads or tails of what he had just heard, what could it mean? The adults let their heads spin for a moment; neither was certain what this news could possibly mean for them or their fellow Indian Gulchers.

Obadiah wasn't clear on how anything of such magnitude happened as he remained glued to the noisy box for the remainder of the afternoon; the news was intriguing and kept his attention. Mary Sue remained fairly idle and took to resting for the remainder of the day. Obadiah cleaned and hung the laundry, the winds were delicate in the afternoon, reassuring that the freshly washed sheets and towels weren't to be soiled. The rest of the fall came and the family remained hunkered down for the next two seasons and looked forward to the coming spring when they could leave their form of hibernation and bring life to their fields yet again. Obadiah ensured that the windmill was properly working with the generator so the strong winds of the mid-west helped to power their home, their well was well placed and the family was well prepared for however long the winter might become.

Spring of '30 was drawing to a close, over the course of the winter Isaac began to roll around and his parents took great pride in his growing. Elizabeth was much more versed in her alphabet and counting, Mary Sue worked with her to educate her when the young Isaac slept. Obadiah remained attentive to the chickens; he searched for bugs and ground corn to feed them as they helped to feed him and his family. News spread of the worsening hardships around the country through the radio, major companies were laid off thousands of workers, or closing up all together, the falling market shares were losing hundreds of thousands of people all of their savings and worse yet; many thousands of people were losing their homes from coast to coast.

The failing economy was of troubling note but little could be done from their small remote farm in Oklahoma so the Withers did what they could do; pray. The spring was mildly dry in comparison to what Obadiah had expected. April was closing in so it was nearing time to begin preparing the fields for planting their crops. Mary Sue was appreciative of all the hard work Obadiah had put into their farm, he chopped all of the wood that would help warm them all winter, he spent many days outside in the snow and cold blowing winds keeping up on his repairs to the barn or home, he kept the chickens fed and safe from any roaming coyotes brazen enough to get close to their farm, daring and dangerous from near starvation. Obadiah wandered out at times to hunt many of the rabbits for fresh meat for his family as well.

The spring was rife with promise again, the air smelled of the rich earth mixed in the wind, the family began their second year as independent farmers in the mid-west, things were still so very exciting, the farm was almost paid off to the bank, their equipment was still newer and stable enough to perform for another few years before the wear and tear caused the need of replacement. The Withers had planned a day to travel into town, Obadiah needed to purchase seed in which to plant for their crops, Mary Sue wanted a much larger garden this year as there was now a fourth mouth to feed. The days grew warm and longer, the ground had thawed and the grasses became green once again. The passion between the couple had rekindled not long after the arrival of little Isaac, the energy required to maintain a nursing infant was great and some days even greater than what the couple could muster.

The firewood supplies dwindled on the very cold days and when the blistering winds died down; Obadiah would shoulder his ax and make a day out of chopping and restocking. The winter didn't see them overtaken with snow as much as it kept them bunkered with howling prevailing winds. Oklahoma winds were a violent bunch, much more so than the family had known in South Carolina, the vast open plains gave force to the gusts and the long stretches of land made for ample straight-aways for the winds to gather speed and when they whipped the house, windows rattled and siding boards rustled together. The couple was glad to see the sun break more and more frequently as the worst of January had blown over, February wasn't very friendly either but March brought warmer weather and brighter days, coupled with great relief.

One welcoming Monday morning the ambitious Mr. Withers had made arrangements for the family to all make the trip into town yet again, they wanted to see what has developed over the course of this financial depression as well as see what may have come about as the slumbering town awakes from the winters' binds. The piker Morgenstern still held some of the money the farmer was obligated to leave under his care, he had hoped to use those funds to help finance the purchase of several hundred pounds of grain for planting, the wagon was loaded up with many large fuel cans, his loving family and a winter grown excitement to once again sow then reap a mighty harvest. Obadiah's hands were callused from a long winter full of wood chopping, his shoulders were still brawny, he had hadn't regained his normal winter weight, his cheekbones seemed to protrude a bit more than they had in the past, Mary Sue was also slightly more petite than usual from a long winter of breastfeeding the infant Isaac.

Mary Sue spent a great deal of calories breastfeeding as well as keeping herself warm and healthy over the winter, it was most noticeable in her spring dresses that hung more loosely off her collarbones and arms. Mary Sue looked worn from the winter, her skin was still much lighter from the reduced amount of sunlight, she had been spending more and more time outdoors as the weather permit.

Three weeks ago Mary Sue left her children to the care of her husband and disappeared around the far side of the barn, the parents took turns giving each other plenty of breaks with the children. Mary Sue chose to duck away for a stretch of fresh air while the sun was warm and the breeze was subtle. Mary Sue looked over her shoulder and spun her head around to ensure she was alone. Mary Sue began to unbutton her shirt nervously, her winter induced lethargy had begun to drag down her mood, her entire body craved sunlight, her mind needed it to lift the haze that had set on her mind. Mary Sue was semi hidden behind the chicken pen, it was wide open fields as far as she could see and even though the trees swayed ever so gently, there wasn't a body around, besides her.

Mary Sue was a little self-conscious stripping down to bare skin to lay out in the sun, her skin rose with small goose bumps as more and more of it became exposed to the world beyond clothing. Mary Sue laid down on top of her clothing to keep dirt out of some of her more intimate areas, the sun was warm on her skin, with her eyes closed she still saw the red from her eyelids. The sun kissed every inch of her body, she laid out and let the sun fade away the stresses from raising two young children, the worries of the unknown and the residual effects of cabin fever.

The sun warmed her whole body, she could feel parts of her begin to perspire as her hands stroked smoothly up her legs and her skin felt ever so soft to her touch, she preferred the touch of her husband, she began to think about the many sensual times she and he had shared as husband and wife, she felt her skin go flush with passion as she squeezed her eyes closed and craved being touched. Mary Sue felt blood rush to her breasts, they felt engorged and her heart began to race. She cracked a cautious left eye to double check that she was alone, there was no one nearby and some of the taller bushes helped to conceal her nude sun tan session. The titillating private time stoked her passion, her heart kept beating faster and faster, she suspired to be touched, pined for her husband, absolutely needed her husband's body right now. The urge became overwhelming, Mary Sue found her left hand moving up her stomach towards her chest while her right hand ventured down below her belly button, her skin was warm to her touch, and her own touch gave her shivers.

Mary Sue clenched her eyes tight, her bottom lip was pinched between her teeth, as her fingers traced areas of her body, her breathing was almost uncontrollable, the thought of being outdoors and completely exposed made everything that made her a woman, throb with blood. This moment was confidential, the subject of a woman enjoying such things other than to please the ego of her mate was taboo, a woman was meant for the pleasure of a man and that is how all of society viewed women, Mary Sue felt like a rebel, a dangerous and wild girl and would die of embarrassment if anyone knew. Mary Sue felt herself holding her breath, she tried to fight it but she didn't care, her small hairs on her body stood up in places from the slight breeze that roamed her body, she felt her skin tighten and constrict in places as she enjoyed her private time outside.

The sun was warm, it kissed at the exposed body of the weary mother as she spent a quiet two hours without her family, she loved them dearly but sometimes the strains of anything can eventually overwhelm anyone. Obadiah helped Elizabeth clean up her toys and air out the house while his wife disappeared, he didn't suspect anything was amiss whilst she was out, he knew that she tanned sans clothing because the sun gave her a golden hue and faded away the tired look that she got during the first few months of being primary caretaker to Isaac almost full time. During her time outdoors, sprawled out on top of her dress, exposed to the quiet serenity of the world around her, she was too distracted to realize that the left arm had been covered by the sleeve of her dress dislodged itself from beneath her and stuck to her sweating arm, shading it from the sun and leaving a much lighter triangle on her left arm, right in the crook of the elbow.

The area on her arm that lacked the darker tan from the sun, was a comical point and Obadiah pointed it out later that evening, the whiter triangle among her pink arm was hilarious, she smiled and shied away as she just kept trying to convince him that she simply fell asleep in the sun. Mary Sue could still feel her skin flush as she would gaze out the window and reminisce about her little adventure, she was still insecure about her dillydallying but she was also slightly liberated, she always craved Obadiah in the carnal sense but also, she felt she had unlocked a whole new door for herself.

Obadiah traced the three week old strange tan on his wife's' arm as she rode silently beside him as they headed into town, she leaned on her right hand and her fingers rubbed against her lower lip, the sun was shining and offering promise to another warm and luscious day, Mary Sue enjoyed the wind whipping by, Elizabeth sat in the back and played with a few of the blocks she decided to bring to help keep Isaac distracted enough to refrain from wailing in the back seat. The Withers were loaded up and headed east to Indian Gulch, Mary Sue was intrigued to check out any new dresses that might be in season, make rounds to meet and greet the folks and just spend a day socializing, out and away from the remote farm of theirs. Obadiah was bent on loading up fuel and grain, not as much on the gossiping as Mary Sue but not opposed to the change for the day anyways.

The family bumped and jostled along in their old hay burner, Isaac seemed soothed by the hum of the engine and to gentle rocking in the back seat. Mary Sue rested back against the seat, comforted that her family was strong, healthy and growing, her love and lust for her husband grew stronger each day, his broad shoulders were already toning from springs hard work, his arms were browning from the sun and his eyes had already returned to their worn in squinting to keep the sun out of his eyes.

The red dirt kicked up as they drove towards town, the orange and yellow flowers dotted the roadsides and speckled the view. Mary Sue was still feeling rather randy, Obadiah's' chiseled arms flexed as he gripped the steering wheel, navigating the ruts in the road, his jaw was clenched and his hands gripped firmly. Mary Sue kept glancing at her husband out of the left corner of her eye, she alternated between biting at her lower lip or at her finger that was near her mouth. Obadiah noticed that Mary Sue was nibbling a bit, he threw her a sly smile, a form of nonverbal communication they shared to prevent Elizabeth from catching on.

Obadiah was already in the mood for married time with his wife, the problem at hand was that they were heading towards town, and a long day from being able to get intimate. The husband and wife held hands and squeezed back and forth in a flirtatious manner, the two young children in the back seat were keeping themselves busy and giving their parents time to reenact their younger years when they would neck at every opportunity and they wanted to ravish each other's' bodies. It was a lot less frequent that they were able to hide away for a swell bit of whoopee, they were still so very stuck on each other and when they were able to capture intimate time together, they fought their best to be together when they could.

The car drive dragged on, the rear ends of the front passengers lost feeling, they grew restless as they turned from Saginaw Way onto Flint rd then down to Main Street, there were a few more cars than usual, the warm weather and bright sun encouraged people to wander town and roam about. Mary Sue and Obadiah passed glances back and forth at seeing new faces and the hordes of bodies strewn about, their children in the struggle buggy of the car were growing antsy to get out, Isaac was merely fussy but Elizabeth was all but hurling her blocks into the front seat like a hired gun for attention. Elizabeth was often mildly behaved in the car but her patience wore thin after the thirty minute mark, she was still balled up about why they were in the car for so long but she willingly went along with her parents no matter what, she absolutely loved to venture the land with her father, holding his hand and kicking her small feet at the dirt clumps or taller weeds.

Obadiah would leave his daughter standing by once in a bit to chase and catch a small critter, one such critter was a small snake, he snatched it up by the tail and repositioned his hands to grasp the wriggling critter near the head. Elizabeth was pensive at first about the snake, her young curiosity overtook her and her apprehension dissipated as she followed suit of her father as he handled the snake. Elizabeth petted the snake, her hands went with and against the course scales of the animal, she investigated by rubbing her finger on the animal, curious to why it felt so much different than her own skin, it was cool, yellow and black while her skin was light pink and warm, she liked the way the small snake felt and wanted to show her mommy, Obadiah quickly put the nix on the thought of Elizabeth taking the snake to her mommy because not only might she hurt the snake, if he brought a snake into the house, Mary Sue would surely hurt him!

Mary Sue was more than ready to leave the car and stretch her legs, they had made the trip two months before when the weather was still dicey, they made an appointment with the spiffy dressing Dr. Martinez, he inspected the infant and congratulated the family on the health of Isaac. Mary Sue wanted to head to the Ponsens' to gossip and chitchat, she wasn't usually into others' beeswax but she was itching to get herself the mental relief by divulging into the business of town, catching up on the goings on of things and able to get away from her day to day back at the farm. The deli made for a central hub for which people could mill around and beat their gums. The town seemed to be crawling with all sorts of people, it was as if there was a convention that culled people from all over the country.

Obadiah pulled down the side street next to Martinez' office, there was room for the car and trailer attached as well as room to turn around to head further into town when their social tasks were over and they were ready to load up seed and refill the fuel cans before returning to their home. Obadiah pulled over onto a long patch of grass that lined the side of the building, after shutting down the motor, the Withers began to remove themselves from their worn impressions of the cars seats. Obadiah tried to reach for the sky to stretch, his lower back was numb from the trip, his feet lost sense of feeling for a moment causing a stutter step like stumble before catching himself on the front fender of his Dodge, Mary Sue was much more cautious to rise, she swiveled to the right as she opened her door, she straightened her legs and shook her feet for a moment to encourage blood circulation, she smirked at her husband fumbling about for a moment, mixed with Elizabeth's growing inpatient that she hadn't been released from the back seat entrapment yet.

Elizabeth was violently shaking at the door handle as Obadiah reached to let her out, she was happy to get out and get to the ground to run about, she stayed close to her parents but the commotion of town drew her attention. Little Isaac was stirring in his carrier basket also, he wasn't far from needing to be fed, the cars trip wore on the family as a whole but it was over with and their new day in town had begun. The sounds of folks were muffled from their parking place but as she headed out from between the laundry building and the doctor's office and walked out towards the center of town.

There were cars lined up and down the streets, people were scurrying all about and the Withers made a beeline towards the deli to chat and catch up. Obadiah carried young Elizabeth and her head turned over and over to pinpoint the voices around her as well as people walking on the wooden planks of the boardwalk. The couple held the hands of each other as they walked through the street, Mary Sue was giddy to get a wiggle on with Mrs. Ponsen, her pace was much faster than Obadiah's and by the midway point of the road, she was a stride ahead of him and pulling him to keep up. Obadiah tried to "*whoaaa girl*" to settle her excitement but she was quick to ignore him and keep trudging along. The family stepped up onto the boardwalk in front of the deli and without hesitation, right on in.

103

Kathleen was in a green dress with black plaid striping, her hair had become a little more gray near her temples and was once again slicked back to a tight ponytail type of bun, *"welcome all"* she kindly greeted as Mary Sue pulled the screen door open, Murray was behind the counter straightening his meat counter, offering a nod to the new patrons. The deli was fairly busy, three of the four tables were occupied with townsfolk sipping coffee and creating a dull roar. One table was the solo and uppity Pauline Curtiss, she was hunched over a teacup, leering out over the rest of the patrons, judging without saying a word, she snickered and sneered as people moved about, and when addressed, she forced out a crooked smile that showed her snarled yellow teeth. Mrs. Curtiss was in a crimson red dress; the material seemed almost satin smooth and was affixed with lace.

The next closer table sat perched the dolled up Leslie Martinez and her spiffy doctor husband Joseph, the two were on a break from their practice and enjoying a bit of time out. Leslie had her blonde hair pulled to a loose ponytail, she had several strands of her hair hanging out and off to her right side, framing the side of her face, her green eyes gazed lovingly at her husband and then randomly around the room. Leslie and Joseph sat close to one another, they chatted about things out the window, cars going by and sparsely interacting with other diners.

The third table had a few cackling ladies, it was also the origin of most of the caterwauling, it seated three women that had been seen around town, Mary Sue sat at the fourth table and began to make acquaintances, she had sat down with baby Isaac and let all of the ladies *"oooh"* and *"awed"* over the waiting to be fed infant. Obadiah said good morning to the owners and shook hands with the doctor and asked how he was this fine morning, Joseph smiled back with a gracious nod and rolled his eyes hinting to listen to the gawking table of hens conversing. Obadiah sat himself next to his bride and lifted young Elizabeth to sit in her own chair between them, Elizabeth let her lower lip slide out, she was displeased having to sit again, Mary Sue requested two cups of coffee and a small chocolate milk for the pouting little lady, it helped to lift her mood at the thought of the treat.

Obadiah listened intently at the table with the three ladies sitting and chatting, the topic finally clicked as to what Joseph was snarling about. Sally Vreml, a late forties woman with a medium build, was a housewife, she had short curly blonde hair that had white streaking in it, she was engaged in conversation with two other ladies. The other ladies were; Katherine Mohs, an early forties lady with jet black hair that was long, brushed straight down between her shoulder blades, her makeup was a bit bright for her washed out complexion and wore a dark brown short sleeve dress that further washed out her face. The third lady was an early fifties woman named Donna Wells, whom was on the heavy side but averaged in size for most ladies of that age.

The women all adorned gaudy jewelry, the appeared to be in the same coffee group, Mrs. Curtiss often met with them but grudgingly alone but close enough to be associated with the group. The topic of the table was about aches and pains, which had what snap crackle or pop as they arose for the day. Mrs. Wells spoke about lumbago and bad knees, probably arthritis. Sally spoke about last summer when she had a rash and was so certain that it was probably shingles and was almost fatal but how a "certain doctor" refused to pass along sound medical advice in a deli so she wouldn't have to pay for a medical checkup. Dr. Martinez was doing his best to remain under the radar as each lady continued to attempt to solicit free medical advice from the next table. Sally extended her left arm and hushed everyone to listen, she was trying to get popular opinion about whether it was cartilage going bad or rheumatoid arthritis setting in, Dr. Martinez just tried to stare down into his coffee cup to avoid eye contact as he huffed off their feeble attempts to get him to crack.

Joseph was the darkest skinned man in the room, his Spanish and Filipino genetics gave him olive based skin, and his fair skinned blonde haired wife snuggled firmly onto his right arm and chuckled every time he exhaled heartily with exasperation. The medical couple fought to keep their attention to themselves, Joseph was a caretaker and it was in his nature to want to help, three summers ago the coffee club lured him into some advice, simply for a splinter as to if it was infected, at the time it was mildly red as it sat and festered in the left thumb of Donna, she whimpered about her thumb for the entire coffee hour until finally Joseph gave in, he took a quick peek and told her to put a little sodium bicarbonate paste on it for a bit and remove the splinter. Donna put the mix on it then bandaged it and three days later it was finally infected, much to her dismay, then the second guessing and doubting came.

Donna still complained about that residual pain she still felt in her thumb, each time, Joseph suggested that anyone of the ladies make an appointment if they really felt they needed medical advice rather than aches and pains from aging, Donna looked down at her thumb and winced whilst flexing it in a weak attempt to get her way. Joseph tried to explain to Donna that her lack of cleaning it after three days of leaving it dirty wrapped in a bandage is what lead to the infection, not the bicarbonate mix that he suggested. The other ladies at the table volleyed sides; they often sided with Donna and her quasi leadership of the group but also flocked towards the chance of free medical advice.

Katherine was discussing her fancy dame of a cousin Shanae coming up from New Orleans, she was a dancer-entertainer in a swanky jazz club, they often sold bootleg liquor in a speakeasy she danced in, and she made the trip to Oklahoma to visit her cousin because things had slowed down a bit at her club. Shanae was tall for a lady, she was slender and in tone shape from dancing six to seven nights a week, she made great money and lived a stars life down in the French Quarter, Katherine wasn't jealous of the lose style life but of all the fancy dresses and feathered boas that Shanae kept in her wardrobe. Shanae was considered a bearcat by her cousin, she was flashy by trade, she wore low cut dresses with a bustier that gave her ample cleavage and attracted even more attention. Katherine loved her cousin and only saw her infrequently, especially as they aged, Katherine was almost twice the age of her youngest cousin and having a place to stay when she and her husband traveled was a glorious perk.

Katherine spoke with her lady friends about the wardrobe her cousin brought with her, dresses that were the latest in French fashion, she had a bright red silk dress that had black lace overtop, the dress was ever so elegant but Shanae wore it without anything to conceal her bosom, Shanae wore small black leather boots with tall heels which added to her height, and made her legs even more slender. The other girls joined Katherine in fanning themselves at the thought of considering wearing such revealing attire, mixed with jealousy that they couldn't squeeze into such a dress.

Katherine continued to describe some of the flapper hats Shanae wore, some were just big enough for her to tuck her long blonde hair under, others were big wobbly tweed hats with peacock feathers hanging out, such outfits would be rather frowned upon in the Bible Belt but thankfully the reaches of such fundamental

106

lunacies were restricted to some of the farther east states. The ladies at the table were of Bluenose morals, they each held themselves in high regards to lord over the other ladies nearest them but in their own home, deeply they were all the same and wished they had the ability to free themselves and flaunt what they had when they were younger. Shanae was aware of her ability to attract men, her chassis was firm from dancing and it had made her a luscious living down in Louisiana, she had a new car, a breezer as they were labeled, had closets full of glad rags and was living like a big egg.

Shanae was one of the most well-known dames from the Quarter, she had light blonde hair, bright blue eyes and a few light freckles, she seemed to be what most bell bottoms wanted to see when in port and they called all day and late into the night , which made her a huge hit, very hotsy-totsy. Katherine went to visit her cousin a few years back before her fame had taken off, Shanae could still hardly walk down Bourbon or Canal streets without causing a crowd, and this was before her name was known or lusted after by eighty percent of the men in town. Shanae began her lifestyle as a chorus hoofer, a dancer that did so in the background behind a headline dancer, it hardly took much time before Shanae had proven her talents and earned her own spotlight, leaving all the other "Janes" behind in that first juice joint.

Shanae had learned her way through the larger city, she had been dancing since she was fourteen, she was nervous to take the stage and as she blossomed over the next two years so did her fame. Mary Sue shot Obadiah a quizzical look, her eyebrows raised as high as they could possibly go, she wasn't sure what to make of the topic a table over, she glanced at Kathleen as Kathleen brought a fresh cup of coffee for Mary Sue as she nursed the sleepy Isaac in her cradling arms. Obadiah was not interested in much more of the squabbling but he wasn't going to leave his wife to tend to both kids as he made his way through town, Elizabeth was licking off her chocolate mustache and beginning to grow antsy again, Obadiah had had all of the bird heckling he could take, he sat up straight and was starting to lean in to speak to his loving wife; "*I am taking*" when suddenly she cut him off " *had enough?*" he smiled grandly and replied with: "*now you're on the trolley love.*"

Obadiah stood tall, squeezed his leg muscles to push blood through his body and reached out for his little girl, Elizabeth jumped from her chair at the first instance to leave her seated position, he didn't want to be a pill so Obadiah greeted all of the other deli guests a good day and turned towards the door, Elizabeth in tow. Obadiah left Mary Sue behind, he kissed her on her cheek before fleeing, he didn't even turn back to leave her with a cheerful glance, he was out and in a big way. Elizabeth had no idea where she was going but she sure wanted to lead the way, she pushed open the wooden screen door to let herself out into the world, the air was dusty and there were still lots of people milling around. The cackling of the table full of ladies became dull as the father and daughter pair further distanced themselves from the deli, little girl in tow, Obadiah made his way next door to the bank.

Obadiah wanted to confirm his account balance with Hirsch and the bank, the "stingy Jew" was spot on when he referred to himself in the harsh derogatory term, he was a scowling angry man and had nothing but contempt for everyone around him. Obadiah didn't necessarily feel like standing before the shorter, growling demon that hid behind the iron bars that kept him safe from being pummeled when he spoke unkindly to people. Hirsch hasn't really done any physical work, he isn't really built for much, and maybe his ill view of those around him is out of a jealousy because of his meek physical attributes, even compared to the ladies. Elizabeth tugged and hurried her father along, she still had no idea where she was going or why she was going there but she still leaned forward with all of her might, she dug in her toes and held tightly to the much larger hand of her father.

Elizabeth trudged right past the door of the bank, she had momentum to keep heading east and was set on maintaining that direction. Obadiah reared his little girl back and used her energy to fling her into his arms, he positioned her into his left elbow crook and pushed the door to the bank open with his free right hand. The lady behind the cage jerked herself upright as the pair entered the bank, the lady seemed in a huff and short tempered at being disturbed from whatever the heck she was doing, *"How are you folks today?"* the lady teller greeted the father daughter combo.

Obadiah responded and told the lady his intentions and asked what the balance was on what Hirsch owed. The lady looked up in the record book what money was owed back and reported to the man that he had a fair sum in his account, under the care of the tight fisted banker. The teller was steel guarded against letting go of the farmers money, the teller came up with the balance and shot right in with how the bank was low on disposable cash as everyone was spending their money to make ends meet as the economy was slipping out of financial stability in addition to all the farmers were purchasing all of their seed for the upcoming planting season. Obadiah clenched his jaw as he was already tired of being undermined around by the short bastard hiding behind a mildly attractive teller.

Hirsch had been turning away many of the people he owed money, he was skilled at ducking people, the man came from a long line of stingy bankers, of course he embraced all of the stereotypes of being a money grubbing Jew and what-not, and he used to barter anyone possible out of any funds he could. Obadiah could feel his blood pressure raise as his young daughter wriggled and fought to be free of her bonds and get to run circles in the bank lobby. The teller lady continued to play games and despite the feminine exterior, Obadiah wanted to raise his voice to match his blood pressure. Obadiah realized he was getting nowhere so rather than spin a yarn and end up storming out sans money again, Obadiah asked if he could take a cashiers' check with him to put towards his grain purchase.

The teller excused herself before printing his check, to clear the notion with the cowardly Hirsch whom was probably urinating in his pants at the idea of releasing any funds. The cahier cut a check for almost thirty dollars and handed the pink perforated paper over to Obadiah and his little girl, she was reluctant is typing out the whole check and the faint sound of Hirsch groveling in the background seemed to match the pace of the typewriter.

With cashier's check in one hand, and Elizabeth in another, the Withers' two turned back into town, Obadiah felt uneasy knowing that the check he intended to hand over to the man at the end of town in exchange for a few dozen bags of wheat, was going to bounce like a heavy girl running. Obadiah had listened to the phonograph radio and heard about how things were becoming tight financially coast to coast and he wanted to get enough seed to plant this season and put even more of a hearty wad of cash into his pockets to better provide for his family, Obadiah felt a bit guilty that whomever he handed the check to, would then have to take on the burden of trying to pry their money from Hirsch's' small cold hands.

Obadiah held the hand of his young daughter, she was whirling her head around here and there, there were so many people wandering about, the morning grew late and as the time wound on, more people filled into the streets. Some redheaded lady waddled by, a large feather bounced with her stride as she crossed the street, it was comical that the bouncing large white feather caught the attention of Elizabeth, she reached her left hand out wanting to grab it, Obadiah smirked thinking about his daughter grabbing that feather and watching the lady panic. There were groups of people standing about gossiping, there were many people sitting on the boardwalk just letting the day pass on. Elizabeth waved to many of the strangers lining the streets just beating their gums, few spat hefty streams of chaw spit out into the dirt, some of the men loitering around seemed to have nowhere to go and were alright with it.

Mary Sue sat in the cafe awaiting for the return of her family, she sat along with Sally Vreml as she twirled her short curly hair with her fingers, the lady's hair had speckles of gray forming at the roots and her eyes continued to squint, forming deep creases in the outer corners. Mary Sue carried on different conversations with the ladies at the adjacent table, Katherine Mohs boasted about some liquid libation her cousin Shanae brought up from New Orleans, a cocktail mix called Steckler, it was rum mixed with lemonade and a splash of Maraschino cherry juice. Shanae had vacationed in the Florida Keys, she danced one night for a dance parlor that sold bootleg rum, the joint was always hopping and couples danced and drank long into the night. Shanae loaded her car up with the hooch and brought plenty back to her home.

With prohibition being stringent, she took extra care on the drive back, the Steckler was such a fantastic drink that she had to share it with her own dance hall. With New Orleans being a port city, there were plenty of boats that made midnight deliveries up and down the waterways to different cities. Steckler was a drink with a large popularity in Florida because the bartender, an I.Steckler, he was well liked in popularity and extremely versed at his job, he ran a booze joint that everyone knew about and it made the Keys a premier vacation place with the tropical setting and drinks to match. The Steckler on ice was the preferred method for consumption; it remained cool and helped to fend off the hot Florida summer sun.

Shanae brought a few cases of Mason jars full of the Florida rum up for her cousin, whom was bragging about having an illegal stock of rum. Katherine mentioned that she should have all of the ladies over for a mediocre night of playing music and maybe even letting their men play poker. Vreml and Wells sat and nodded their heads in agreement to the notion of an impromptu drinking and poker session, the ladies tried on several occasions to host such as session but often flaked out on such plans. Katherine felt now that she held several cases of liquor under her care that maybe she held the power to sway their plans to actually meeting up for the gathering. Mary Sue rebutted with how well the Steckler sounded, she knew that Obadiah was more of a Bourbon man, prohibition had gripped the nation for quite some time and many men opposed having to deal with dry states, the idea of no alcohol was enough to encourage rallies and marches on the crooked congress. G-men were often making headlines by busting stills and dumping barrels upon barrels of moonshine and bath tub made whiskey.

The southern states were the mainstay of liquor production, the humid summers and cool winters aged bourbon in oak charred barrels to such perfection that only a few states could claim top names, Kentucky and Tennessee were the origin of some of the best liquor in the history of inebriated man. Mary Sue and Obadiah had a few rare nights when the couple would sit beside Norman on the porch and pass around a bottle of whiskey, the southern drink sure brought comfort to some nights, despite a bit of a heavy head the following morning.

Mary Sue cradled her still small baby boy Isaac, the ladies cooed and awed over the bundled boy, he only fussed a little and Mary Sue knew that Obadiah and Elizabeth would be back soon after their stroll through the walkways of town. Donna Wells spoke about her husband, a trucker by trade, he still drove around the country shipping goods from one place to another, his deliveries had reduced in number but he was still getting some driving jobs. One job Mr. Wells received was to haul bundles of marijuana out of Virginia to a facility, apparently the government hired certain farmers to grow the crop for hemp rope and goods, Wells commented that her husband always took pity on the hemp farmers as they always seemed dim witted and not very bright, probably as a result of exposure to the crop. Something in the hemp seemed to dumb down the people who handled it.

Wells couldn't make out any reason as to why the hill people were hardly smarter than a potato but if the government hired these people for a mediocre task, than up the line it employed her husband to drive the crop a few times and he then sent money back to her in Oklahoma. Mr. Wells had written Katherine on few occasions to tell stories of how the country was struggling, jobs were drying up, and companies were losing millions by the day.

The ladies continued to exchange ideas and fears about how things had come along over the winter, last September they said the stock market fell, major companies lost stability and began to crash, there was rumor that people had heaved themselves off of buildings to take their lives as their future had been ruined and with having lost thousands of other peoples' dollars, many stock brokers had fled to avoid responsibility. The gals each jockeyed to share their input, observations they have made from their small seats in their own town. There had been an influx of new faces in town, the additional people really hadn't added to any revenue, some people have come from other places in the country to stay with relatives, and others had simply floated into town in search of work.

There was a large trailer full of grain bags at the end of town near the gas station, the same place that was buying the wheat during the previous fall. Obadiah had calculated that he would roughly need twenty bags of seed to plant his property, hopeful that this season would be another reassuring harvest that would keep them afloat as farmers. Obadiah wandered back to the cafe to rejoin his wife and son. Elizabeth enjoyed wandering about, she looked all over at the people, men in overalls and boots, ladies in light dresses, ladies in full dresses that were adorned also with hats and nice shoes, some men were dressed very well.

Nearing the door to the cafe, Obadiah and Elizabeth came across a Negro man; "Willie Bennett's the name, vacuums are the game" a dark skinned man with a fast paced speak spat out his sales pitch to the man. Obadiah reached for the door handle but was stopped by the man with a side cocked bowler hat, as Obadiah reached for the handle the man reached and grabbed Obadiah's hand, startling him. Willie spoke really fast and loud at Obadiah, "don't let the color of skin dissuade you from a great bargain" Obadiah was taken aback by the accusation as well as extremely

112

insulted by such a notion, he had no need for a vacuum and yet, there was the blunt accusation from some stranger.

Obadiah responded with" sir it's not your color but rather your aggression," while trying to escape the sales noise spewing out of the mouth of a man in sharp dress clothes and vest. Willie was relentless, he barraged the man and daughter about some new shiny confounded vacuum that was all the rage in New York, allegedly, Obadiah continued to apologize and decline while trying to excuse himself from the conversation. Willie half followed Obadiah and Elizabeth into the cafe before Katherine Ponsen rushed toward him to shoo him back out yet again, he had been chasing potential customers up and down streets trying to make a sale, it was a pathetic job and everyone looked down upon sales people.

Willie was a short pudgy man, his palms a light pink while the rest of his skin was dark in tone, his eyes had a tint of yellow where the whites should be, he had a sly smile and a bit of a lazy eye, the kind of lazy eye that makes you skeptical and warns you not to trust them. Obadiah felt relieved that the harassing man was off his back, he was slightly hesitant that he would also have to risk walking back across the attention of the salesman again on their way out; he let out a heavy sigh. Donna had mentioned that her husband Arthur ran into all sorts of salesmen on his drives, from vacuums to house siding and even new types of plastic storage containers that they "guarantee will extend the life of your food by two weeks."

Obadiah brushed his sleeves off as if he had just narrowly escaped a near death tragedy, he knew it was just a sales guy but it was a very awkward situation all together. Elizabeth shed her father's hand upon entering the Ponsens' cafe and hightailed it to her mother. Elizabeth had enjoyed her time with her father but she longed to be perched back on the chair next to her mother and baby brother. Mary Sue was more than ready to depart from the cafe, her backside was numb and it was time to wrap up the chatter. The Withers paid their tab and it was time to head out and make their seed purchase then get back to their farm. The young family made their way back to their parked car over by the doctor's office, on their way over all the mingling bodies strewn about had frozen, not a person moved and the husband and wife had no idea why. Mary Sue looked up to notice the tall elegant

113

woman gliding down the boardwalk; her demeanor demanded all of the attention without having to say anything.

The woman was tall, blonde, and well primped and put together, Obadiah fought his best to keep from staring but the moment he caught a glance of the dame, he couldn't even blink, Mary Sue assumed from the earlier stories that the woman gracefully walking the boardwalk was Shanae, cousin to Katherine Mohs. The lady strolling along was elegant, full of poise and her posture made her appear tall and slender while hoisting her bosom into the air and leading her to her destination.

Shanae was dressed in a dark green satin dress with black lace adorning most of it, her short blonde hair was done up and tucked into a small hat, her dress flowed behind her, each step she took caused the lower edge of her dress to bounce and flow in a rather majestic way that attracted the attention of both men and woman within view. Shanae was used to the attention, she didn't even swivel an eyeball to see everyone frozen among the streets in awe of her elegance. It took a moment but Mary Sue caught on and threw her elbow into her husband, the elbow to the ribs caused Obadiah to come back to his senses and change his line of sight. Mary Sue smirked that she caught her husband glancing at another woman but wasn't insecure in the least, Shanae was of gorgeous beauty and the admiration was simply that, not the lustful drooling of intense sexual desire, like how he behaved towards her.

Mary Sue had an amazing life with her husband, there was no need for jealousy or insecurity, the pair had a strong marriage and having birthed two of his children, Mary Sue had a small gaff to poke fun of her husband about. Shanae peered out of the corners of her eyes at the men gawking, she liked the attention, back home when she danced she wore a shorter dress without a bustle underneath, men hooted and hollered and then threw her money all night long for her company. Katherine Mohs was covetous that her cousin Shanae lived such a lavish lifestyle, the latest trends in clothing as well as her own motor vehicle. Shanae reveled in the attention, everywhere she went, she could pick any man any night and simply neck with any of them, she very seldom brought men home and into her bed but she didn't feel any remorse or moral conflict when doing so. Shanae had a life that many could only dream of, footloose and fancy free in many aspects and despite being so quickly judged, she hardly ever offered any real reason to be judged, she just exuded beauty and elegance in her stride as she glided to and fro.

Obadiah stuttered and murmured for a minute as he tried to avoid admitting being caught by his wife while gazing at another woman. Obadiah felt a bit guilty about having been caught up in eyeing another girl, Mary Sue laughed it off and didn't give it a second thought and redirected the focus on the rest of the tasks at hand for the day. The family made their way back to the car, they had to fill the gas tanks with fuel as well as the trailer with seed for planting back at the farm. Obadiah turned left down Main Street and headed to Johnson's gas station. With an ease to the left, they drove passed many men sitting out front waiting for various patrons and headed towards a large truck attached to a long trailer loaded down with burlap bags full of wheat. Obadiah loaded the trailer, secured his purchase and thanked the truck driver for the supplies.

Obadiah pulled into the gas station and headed to greet Johnson, it had been a while since they last spoke and this stop was towards the end of their list of tasks for the day. Johnson shook hands with Obadiah, the men exchanged pleasantries and before Obadiah could offer his response to how he had been, Mr. Franks cut in with having met the extravagant blonde beauty Shanae, she had come in for a top off, Johnson was befuddled as he recalled how her long nimble hands shook his, her touch was soft, her fingernails polished a bright sensual red to match her lipstick, her cheeks lightly dotted with light brown freckles accenting her light blue eyes, she made Johnson feel alive again. Obadiah tried to silence the conversation as he still felt that he was in hot water over the earlier staring issue. Johnson chuckled at Obadiah and his tiptoeing over the subject matter.

Johnson and Obadiah filled the glass measuring reservoir atop the gas pump, when the appropriate amount of gas is measured out up in the glass container, gravity then released the fuel down the hose and into the car and fuel tanks. Obadiah roused Johnson for being a bit of a spry old goat for having eyed the young blonde vixen, Johnson had no need to apologize for being a virile man still full of life, Obadiah didn't blame him, men were men and when an attractive dame came into view, men were allowed to just take a glance. People were simply people, everyone takes notice of one another, it doesn't always mean there was a sexual or romantic component to everything and a passing look is usually just to simply take notice.

Obadiah let the events go, he loaded up his crew and then made a last stop to the market for groceries and supplies. The Withers were all loaded up and headed west back to their farm, baby Isaac was whiny and tussling in the back next to his sister who was also tiring and rubbing her tired eyes, drained from her day of exploring the world with her poppa. Mary Sue was glad to get the opportunity to chat and make nice with the ladies from the upper crust of town, not for the gossip but to enjoy talking with other adult gals, a pleasant break from the daily make believe tea time with her Elizabeth. Mary Sue was second guessing her interactions with the superficial and most judgmental lady in the cafe... Mrs. Pauline Curtiss, she was quiet today and simply stared over her coffee cup at the other patrons sitting near her at the Ponsens, the lady was hard to read and was suspect in nature.

The long and barren road that laid outstretched through the windshield of their old and dirt worn Dodge seemed endless, it was mute and devoid of much activity. Obadiah and Mary Sue held hands and fought to keep their wits as their two young children increased their volume in the backseat, the bellowing screeches from the backseat ranged from that of a cat in heat to the wail of a fire truck siren mixed with something that resembled a goose choking on a bullfrog. The husband and wife alternated squeezing each other's hands as their blood pressure increased and their patience ran thin. The speed of the car with the addition of the trailer loaded down with ready to plant wheat hauled and buzzed on down the road, leaving a rooster tail of air born dirt kicked up a long ways behind them.

The couple arrived to their farm before sundown, Mary Sue unloaded the car of the children and goods while Obadiah hauled the grain bags into the main room of their house also, Obadiah was partially tempted to take them to the barn but knew that the rodents would make quick work of the burlap and pour the grain all over the barn. There was a lot of work ahead of the man and woman, they had struggled to remain passionate but at the end of each day they found themselves in deeper need of sleep than of intimacy. Obadiah still lusted for his wife, there were many opportunities that he wanted to ravish her, anytime they thought they had a few quiet minutes while both kids were asleep or quiet, they took turns napping to keep up on the struggle to stay awake and keep the children overseen.

The two young children were spent; young Isaac hadn't nursed in over an hour but was asleep from over thirty minutes of fussing and fighting off sleeping until finally succumbing to it. Elizabeth had cried herself to sleep just as they reached their driveway after unloading over thirty bags of grain, as well as almost a dozen colorful fabric bags of flour from the market and several cases of jars of food for the upcoming months. Obadiah was swooping his arms in large circles as his shoulders were engorged with blood from the second workout of the day, Mary Sue was more than ready to plop herself down on the couch and all but pass out from the day as well, with both kids put away in their beds, the couple found themselves at the rare intersection of rarer events, it was as if a solar and lunar eclipse happened in the same day, that was how rare this event was.

Obadiah dragged himself over to be beside his wife, Mary Sue laid back on the couch and laid her left arm across her forehead to hide her tired eyes from the light overhead. Obadiah eyed his wife, her breasts still swollen, her dress was raised to just above her knees and it was most enticing to Obadiah, whom was nearing her knees and gazing upon his bride. Obadiah knocked Mary Sues' right knee with his left in a playful manner, she peeked from under her forearm to meet eyes with Obadiah, it had been a long while since she had received his encouraging smirk and was met with a tightlipped puckered smile from Mary Sue as she had longed for the touch of her husband also, they weren't sure they contained the energy for a romp but they desired to have playful husband and wife time.

Obadiah knelt down to one knee, he began to kiss on the exposed leg of his wife while she ran her fingers through his hair, they longed for one another and even though they had several months behind them since Isaac had joined them but with the length of the months somehow weirdly was made up of short days made up of long hours. Each day seemed to exhaust the couple, leaving them to struggle for adequate sleep at any given moment. Obadiah slid up the bottom of his wife's dress to expose more of her, she was accepting and motioning in approval for her husband, he took her body language clues as a go ahead for further advancements in their passion. Mary Sue spent the first few months after birthing Isaac feeling unattractive; fat, disheveled, as if she was trapped in a body that wasn't hers, Obadiah spent those same months confused and confounded at the whole mentality of the female post pregnancy thought process, he didn't try to understand it, just support his wife.

Mary Sue felt unattractive, which caused her to forgo undressing in front of or for the visual pleasure of Obadiah. Mary Sue often commented on being unattractive and accused her husband of not finding her young and fit anymore, which often spun out of control to him "not loving her anymore." Obadiah often rebutted with "how can I find you attractive when you layer up and hide away?" which he lamented that her hiding her body hadn't caused him to fade in his lust but he still longed for her. The conundrum was uncanny, she felt unattractive so she made herself unattractive to Obadiah when the whole time he just simply wanted to have access to his wife, she made herself into a self-fulfilling unattractive prophecy and it often left Obadiah frustrated and with needs for his wife.

The couple finally had their time, it had been several months in the making and it all finally culminated at the end of a very long day. As Obadiah kissed the thighs of his wife, she pulled on his face to come up to meet hers for lust filled kisses, the scruffy face of her husband had hardly fazed Mary Sue, she was in such a need for her husband, it was almost overwhelming for her and she simply wanted to explode at the mere finger touches of her husband, he touched her delicately and yet, it was such an intense feeling for her that her whole body writhed and her lower back arched so she could be closer to her husband's hovering body. Obadiah kissed along Mary Sue's jaw line, he aggressively nuzzled against her cheek causing her to smile, her eyes closed tightly and her breathing became erratic.

Obadiah was more turned on when his wife was at the mercy of her primal urges, she was thrusting in cadence with Obadiah. The couple finally had their chance to relive their younger more energetic years, ones they had before children required so much of their time and energy. Obadiah was days from having to sow his seeds, the fields needed plowing, the tractor needed maintenance and the spring was easing into summer and there was a lot to do, but absolutely none of it mattered. The pair had let the world around them blur into their breathing, there was no world outside, no town, no struggling country and no worries for the future, all they had was each other and that always made everything alright.

Mary Sue always had her breath taken away in the strong arms of her husband, they exchanged kissed back and forth as they made love for the first time in months. Obadiah felt his fiery passion race, his desire for his wife had all but erupted as they lay together on the couch, Mary Sue took control of things, she took a straddled position atop of Obadiah so she could run her hands over the large tan shoulders of her muscular husband, she ran her fingers through his hair as she rolled his head back to bite kiss on his neck, she grasped her hands around his neck as she rode up and down on his lap, their bare thighs sticking with sweat, their bodies became moist in the evening air. Mary Sue let her unbuttoned dress fall off of her shoulders, exposing her chest for her husband to suck upon, Obadiah grasped her legs, thighs, waist and sides.

The couple had deeply missed one another, their tired and weary bodies struggled to function, at the expense of rhythm and grace, the couple laughed off clumsy bumps and uncoordinated fumbling as they fought for control in their animalistic snorting and grunting. As Mary Sue gained momentum in her straddling, both in speed and intensity, Obadiah took command to work harder, their intensity increased and the couch seemed to rock with their bodies, Obadiah wrapped his arms around his wife and hoisted her up, in a swift graceful motion he lifted her while keeping her close to him and they worked as one body. Mary Sue wrapped her legs around her sturdy standing husband as they crossed the living room, Obadiah set his wife down on the bags of seed, her bare bottom flexed as it touched the course burlap and the rustling of the seed inside the bags was hushed by their heavy panting.

Obadiah kept the slender tan legs of his wife raised up by his shoulders as they enjoyed each other's bodies, Obadiah smiled at the triangle on her left arm that had gone without the sun when she was sunbathing before, her queer tan line was comical and a point in which Obadiah could tease his wife. Obadiah kissed every inch of his wife, She was so overwhelmed with intense pleasure that all she could do was grab his muscles and hold on to the strong arms of her mate and completely submit to the man, her nails digging into the back of his shoulders, holding him close. The couple heaved and writhed in the late hours, their heavy breathing was synchronized, and their bodies entwined with one another were their only focus of their evening.

Obadiah kissed all over her chest, her neck and her face, and his hands roamed her exposed body from her ankles tucked near his armpits to her knees that were above his shoulders and her arms draped around his neck, their foreheads were rested against one another and they both gazed down upon their conjoined bodies, their bodies were pressed so tightly together that there was really no telling where one ended and the other began.

Obadiah had been long without the loving tenderness of his wife, he missed her touch, her body, the delicate curves and fleshy parts of her bare body, he craved her in every sense of the word and his thirst couldn't be quenched, even after having been married for several years, their lust for one another was often like a spark that quickly lost control and became a blazing wild fire. The burlap bags of seed settled under the motion from the couple, a few of the bags moved creating a small impression where the backside of Mary Sue was settled while receiving her husband.

Late into the night the couple slowed their pace, their carnal activities had finished draining them of their energy, their thrusting and heaving slowed to a standstill, Obadiah stood pressed against his wife, their chests were pressed firmly against each other, and they kissed and volleyed back and forth to suck on each other's' lips causing each other to smile. "Shhhhh" there was a sudden noise, Obadiah popped his eyes open, his eyebrows clenched as his mind raced to place where the sound came from when suddenly the pyramid of bags began to slide, taking the couple with it. The bags piled in the corner slid to the left, the top bags raced towards the door, Mary Sue flung her right arm out in failed attempt to brace her, Obadiah hurried to try and grab his wife and steady himself before they both ended up in the fray.

Bags slid all over the floor, the flailing body parts made feeble attempts to keep from ending up underneath seed bags, one bag trapped Obadiah's right leg, causing him to stumble backwards and lose his footing. Obadiah began to clumsily fall backwards while trying to retain his supportive hold on his wife to keep her from falling to the floor also. Mary Sue rode on a few wayward bags of seed in the direction of the door while Obadiah stumbled back towards the couch, Mary Sue was rolled back onto her shoulders as gravity held the upper hand, Obadiah fell backwards and thudded to the floor, landing on his bare backside and then falling to his left arm. Mary Sue did her best to flatten out, her hands frantically searched for something sturdy to grab onto to ease her descent to the floor.

Obadiah finally stopped falling and locked his eyes onto Mary Sue, whom ended and an almost upside down angle and fighting to lift her head to keep her hair from being further pulled. The exhausted stupor had caused Mary Sue to begin to chuckle, the laughter took hold and Mary Sue found great humor in the situation, they had finally managed the time and opportunity to make passionate love and as they finished, their intensity had brought down part of the house. Mary Sue looked to be a major disaster, her dress was hiked up and pulled down to end up looking like a sash, her hair flowed behind her and her naked body glistened in the dark.

Obadiah used his shaky hands to free his legs from the weight of the seed bags, his legs shook from their hoisted position upon the mounds of seed, his tired body was trembling as he had spent all of his energy pleasing his wife. Mary Sue was still laughing about the situation, their efforts to finally enjoy each other's' company sexually had ended in a comical situation and Mary Sue was out of control with laughter and it had become contagious to her husband.

The couple laid sprawled out in contorted positions among the bags of seed, Obadiah's muscles twitched. Mary Sue just watched the leg muscles twitch on her husband as she wiped tears away from her eyes from laughing so hard, the couple acknowledged that they must have been a sight to see, he being trapped by bags of seed and unable to muster enough strength to become free. Mary Sue was all sorts of misconstrued, her clothing was discombobulated and her body contorted among the bags, her feet much higher from the ground than her head, causing her to become light headed with the laughter. The couple whimpered a bit post laughter, they tussled to get close enough to hold hands, the cooler night air was a relief to their hot humid bodies, they gazed on each other, the couple managed to wearily haul themselves to bed yet again.

The following summer brought less rain than the previous year, the crop yield had suffered in comparison to the previous year, or even expectations. Obadiah had put in all of the hard work and yet the return on the investment suffered, the reduced amount of rain stunted the crops. The children continued to grow, Mary Sue did her best to educate her children as well as fix healthy meals and be the wife her husband needed, the summer drudged on and turned to fall, the fall fell cold and another abrasively bitter winter kept them enclosed inside.

Much of the blistery cold was much like the previous winter, days of chopping wood managing food stores passed on slowly but the spring had broken and the snow melted away for another year. Things were still engulfed in love and support for each member of the family, their farm required the usual maintenance and chores, all the while, leaving ample time to be a hands-on parent for their children, the Withers still felt blessed and most fortunate to have their lives, and in Indian Gulch.

1931 was another year for the Withers, there was seed in the ground and their third planting was on its' way. Obadiah had tilled and turned the soil again, last year's harvest was much less than they had expected, it had been a long winter, the cold was bitter and wretched, the winds whipped and had a bitter bite when it hit the exposed skin, the family hunkered down indoors to stay warm and close together. As the spring passed on and summer began to set in, Isaac was running by now and getting into all sorts of mischief, Elizabeth was much taller than her brother and she was wearing her long hair in a braided ponytail most of the time.

The winter winds seemed to carry on through the spring and there had been some higher winds into the planting season and Obadiah was puzzled as to why it was unseasonably dry. It was early May when the first large storm left the Withers in a situation that warranted worry and panic. Two weeks after planting, Obadiah had spent three days tilling and then three more planting, the second Tuesday started out with jam and biscuits for the Withers, Mary Sue scurried through the kitchen while Obadiah fed the children and nursed his coffee, the sky was mockingly gray, the two weeks since the seed had been promised to the land was without rain, Obadiah took advice from the surrounding farmers as well as the phonograph radio on when to plant, the forecasts also continued to promise rain, an empty promise that left him feeling let down each time.

The skies grew gray; the clouds in the distance looked bleak and black as breakfast passed. Obadiah took a second cup of coffee out to the porch and wanted to stare out in the distance and continue to hope for rain. The storm looked like it was going to wallop the area, Obadiah pondered thoroughly about the effects of a torrential downpour on the dry soil, if the land took on to much rain, the seed that was planted might float up and un-plant itself, a waste of the seed if that were the case. Obadiah watched the dark black clouds rumble in the distance and the lightning flashes within the clouds, with a quick sweep around the perimeter of the property, Obadiah wanted to check to make sure that everything was as secure as it needed to be if the rain or winds had gotten forceful.

Mary Sue joined her husband on the porch, the smell of rain was absent, she leaned upon the shoulder of her husband and wrapped her arm around his back in a loving embrace, while the children played and hollered just inside behind them. The lack of humidity was off putting, it was a strange, usually Obadiah had aches in his well worked hands when the barometric pressure fell, reassuring that a looming storm meant rain, this storm was bleak, it was ominous in the distance and the winds began to pick up. Mary Sue had a tinge of worry on her face as she looked out into to distance at the rumbling storm, she held her husband tightly and had a strange sense about the storm, the children played away without a care in the world but their parents lurked around on the porch with an off sense as they stared to the west.

It was growing dark and the sky was becoming overtaken by swirls of dark black off shoots from the storm, the thunder rolled in and the walls of the house began to creak under the pressure of the wind as its' intensity ushered the couple into their home, they nervously hunkered down for safety until the storm passed. The winds howled from the west, the windows taking the brunt of the storm were rattling under the weight, Mary Sue wandered over to place a towel on the window to lessen the rattle. *"OBEEEEEEE"* Mary Sue beckoned from the far room, the tin room was making noise under the storm and her holler was a higher pitch sound among the roaring of the storm. Pressure inside the house grew ferocious, Obadiah wondered what in the blazes his lovely wife was frantic about, and she was un-shakable in the face of snakes or spiders so those country risks weren't the matter.

Obadiah turned the corner in hurry to see Mary Sue standing near the window, it was still in one piece so the shattering of glass wasn't of concern, it was much scarier. The black skies weren't pelting the entire house with rain, it wasn't a life threatening tornado or anything else that had ever been witnessed or even spoken of by anyone in Indian Gulch, the gates of hell had opened up on the prairie and, a fierce thunderous cloud of dirt was blowing through the plains and trying to swallow the Withers and their home. The eerie noise that growled within was similar to two rusted sheets of steel grinding with bits of sand, the coarse metal on metal screeching echoed in the house as the tin roof was getting sand blasted with the wind and airborne pebbles clinking against the glass as the storm encapsulated the farm.

The storm raged on, the family hunkered down and the children cried. The howling and growling from the storm scared both of the children, Elizabeth was more brazen about the natural goings on but Isaac was overtaken with fear, even as his mother held him closely. Obadiah did his best not to pace with nervous energy, at best he sat on the couch and bounced his knee while trying to converse with his wife and daughter, he did his best to be a stoic pillar in the homestead but he also worried about the biblical hell that was whirling around the home. The reverberating noises of the tin roof made for a baying in which you would expect from the hounds from hell to unleash before reclaiming a soul that may have eluded Hades. The small hairs on the back of Obadiah's neck stood up, his skin had become overtaken with goose bumps and it had made Mary Sue quasi nervous also, Mary Sue knew her husband to be firm in the face of all adversity. The family huddled around the couch in the main room, Obadiah held his young daughter while his wife sat beside him on the couch cradling their young son.

The pressure in the house caused by the air penetrating cracks in the home on the strong side caused ears to begin to pop and create discomfort; the young Elizabeth covered her ears and clenched her eyes tightly hoping for relief soon. Mary Sue thought about maybe eating, the chewing motion often relieved ear pressure when traveling high up in the mountains, Mary Sue made a motion to rise up to start fixing sandwiches for her family, just as the howling moaned through the house, the boards rattled and tin roof vibrated to a tune that a cello would make when you slowly drag a bow across the strings. Isaac was growing scared, he began to shake and tears formed in his eyes, Mary Sue held her young son tightly and caressed his hair in an attempt to sooth him while Obadiah held the hand of Elizabeth.

The dark skies enveloped the home, the windows rattles in one vibrato while the roof another, and the outer boards another still, all the commotion in conjunction with the commotion of the sand shearing at the home almost muted the cries of the children and continued to unravel the nerves of their parents. The overbearing noise was so much to handle that the tension threatened to cause nosebleeds.

Mary Sue scooted closer to Obadiah, fearing that the family may not survive the storm, the couple held hands and embraced their young children, there was still so much to do in life, Mary Sue began to weep at the encroaching idea that doomsday was upon them. The gates of hell were opening to swallow the world, their farm was nearing the cusp of Hades, the underworld had risen up and was surrounding their home. The couple both worried about their families back home, was Norman going to die alone back in Carolina? It had been a while since Obadiah had seen his father and just as long for the girls, Obadiah felt remorseful that his father had not met his grandson, Isaac deserved to get to know Norman, as Norman was a handy and useful man as well as a kind and loving male influence.

The storm raged on, it carried more fury than an invading Roman army, the home swelled and settled as the weight of dirt piled up against the western wall, Obadiah didn't think about the weight of tons of dirt bashing their home, the sand blew in cracks of the walls, the window sills caught piles of dirt on any jutting surface. The soot blew into the rooms, the roof had begun to take on a low hum, the sand filling in any open space essentially dampening the vibrations. The quiet became eerie, ominous and began to slow the heart beats of Obadiah and Mary Sue, their pulses slowed and began to thud in their ears, they began to perspire. Isaac cried alongside with Elizabeth whom merely wept. Mary Sue gripped her husband's hand and awaited the final moments of judgment following the wrath.

The phonograph only contained static as Obadiah tried to wishfully tune in some form of distraction to pass the time, Obadiah turned and twisted the worn gray knobs hoping to hear a news report, or any form of human voice reassuring them that the world was not ending. The Withers had hunkered down through many storms through their years, South Carolinas humidity and ocean proximity gave way too many storms and the occasional hurricane, which often pelted and soaked the state causing ample crop damage. The couple did their best to entertain the children, wood blocks clacked as they tried to stack and organize based on color or letters, Isaac refused to partake in the play time, the dark skies still shunned away the sun, it was as if the dark of night had descended on Oklahoma and the grips of the darkest fury of the universe had overtaken the world.

There were no distinguishable sounds outside of the abrasive dirt spraying the home, the ruckus made it hard to make out what each family member was saying when trying to converse, it made the day long and dreary. Mary Sue was frightened but grew acclimated to the setting as lunch time slowly passed, with stomachs rumbling and the family forcibly locked inside for potentially forever. Mary Sue gathered her bravery and headed to the kitchen, a few lit candles sat within storm lanterns to assist the family in getting around in their home, Mary Sue was too worried to start a fire to cook but instead slapped together sandwiches and drinks for all involved and they gathered around the kitchen table to eat maybe one last meal.

Layers of roast beef atop slices of bread were adorned with a dollop of white gravy, "Jim's shit on a shingle" had been served, the lunch idea that originated at the Ponsen cafe. The chickens outside were out of sight and sound, Obadiah had wondered if they had simply been taken off with the storm, there was no viewing past the dark clouds that blotted out the sun, it was darker than a cloudy night in the midst of winter, at least in the depth of a dark night it would often reveal stars or brighten some of the smallest lights that shimmered out in the distance. This magnitude of darkness amplified the light from a flickering candle to the level of a military search light, the candles shone bright as the sun in stark contrast to the absolute depravity of light outside, the emotion was heavily strewn on the faces of Obadiah and Mary Sue, the drying skin deepened the wrinkles near the outer edges of their eyes, Obadiah was sun worn and it gave him the appearance of being much older than he was, Mary Sue had her long brunette hair pulled back to a ponytail to keep it out of her face, she too looked worn and tired.

Elizabeth ate well, she managed to chomp down her whole sandwich and finish her juice, the full stomach began to soothe her, it had been a tense time trying to wait out the storm, Elizabeth was on edge, she didn't know what to make of the dark day, night had charged across the plains like a herd of buffalo, wild and damaging, it had taken over the farm as far as Obadiah could tell but he couldn't exclude the possibility that the world may have been swallowed by Hells vortex.

The family sat at the table together, the looming storm rumbled on and on, the sounds and noises just roared against the house, everything shook and rattled; the sounds of boards creaked and hummed, glass tinged and rattled and the hell hound howling of the wind grew closer to taking the lives of the family to atonement. The wrath had continued to thunder on, the house shook as it seemed that the four horsemen of the apocalypse grew ever closer. Obadiah was eternally troubled, he had an overwhelming dread growing within him, his chest burned with concern and panic as his home shook and boards bowed around his family, the present danger was upon them, Obadiah fought his best to swallow his fear, he wanted to grow old, watch his children have children, watch those children grow up and older as he and his wife aged together towards the grave.

Obadiah tried to stave off the desire to stare out the window, the long distant stare was hard to fight, Mary Sue had to keep snapping her fingers to re-orient her husband, his worry fed her worry, she didn't have to hear anything to read his lips, eyes and eyebrows and all were heavy with worry. The kitchen flickered on with a few candles inside of storm lanterns, the sounds of sand and dirt running along the floor in some of the side rooms concerned Mary Sue, she wanted to excuse herself from the table and go to investigate the bedroom but she also hesitated to leave her family. The family sat at the table and watched the dark outside of the windows, there were swirls and mounds of airborne dirt flowing from off of the roof, preceded by a blood curdling screech as it slid down and off the tin roof.

The roof vibrated and created a pitch like a cat in heat, a moaning that can't be sanitized from the mind and it covered the body with goose bumps, Mary Sue held Obadiah's hand, the sweaty palms and sturdy embrace didn't relieve any fear but it was a slight comfort to one another, they also revisited their vows. Mary Sue and Obadiah promised to be there for each other at the end of days, both were filled with dread that it seemed that the end of days were upon them. The family decided to head back to the living room, it was ironic that they may spend their final hours of living in the aptly named room, the family was going to stand strong, and together, even as the weather beat their house in on top of them.

Obadiah had no idea what was going on, but was certain it was hell on earth as sand and silt snuck in through any crack in windows or doors. Even the smell of the room became earthy, Mary Sue wanted to sweep but found it to be moot as dirt wafted across the floor from the bedrooms, Mary Sue was certain that silt and dirt had been pouring in around the windows and then dusting the rooms as well. The hours toiled on, each minute drummed on, the house taking a severe beating from the winds heavy with dirt and debris, the occasional harder thwack or thud hit the house as heavy bits of this or that had taken flight and found a mark to hit somewhere on the home.

Isaac had found solace in the barraging of the house, the small boy had the comforting cradle of his mother and with a clear conscious, the boy had tuckered himself right out. The home was still rumbling from the storm, there was no knowledge of how long this would last, no lessening of the assault on the land but the humming and buzzing that filled the home had made it hard to converse so the family sat in silence as they just kind of fidgeted with Isaac's wooden blocks and lounged around on the floor while the small boy slept on the couch behind them. Elizabeth sat snuggled between her parents on the floor, Mary Sue tussled with her hands while Obadiah brushed her hair with his fingers as he attempted to comfort her and his wife.

The candles slowly burned down, they flickered as they neared the base of the storm lanterns and made shadows dance on the walls. There was no clear way of deciphering between night and day with as dark as it was, the sun had been snuffed out and it seemed to be the end of the world and there was very little left to do but sit huddled together and wait for the house to collapse in, smothering them all to death. Obadiah was panicked, his heart weighed heavy that his young children may not ever know the love of a marriage like he had, he was more than lucky to have Mary Sue and always felt the same in kind from Mary Sue. The house was stagnant, the air hung heavy around the family bunkered down within their living room, Mary Sue could smell the faint hint of her own breath in the air, the windows were closed to keep out a majority of the dirt and wind but there was still sand seeping in the cracks and any opening, further sealing them from fresh air.

The storm howled on into the late afternoon according to Obadiah's pocket watch, Isaac jostled a bit after a while had passed. Mary Sue held and Obadiah had played with Elizabeth and all had hoped to wait out the storm, they were growing inpatient and by now it was carrying on and still showed no signs of stopping. The family had read books, talked about the biblical proportions of the storm and how Indian Gulch may have been

129

consumed by the worst storm anyone may have ever heard of. The storm raged on, it was like a hurricane but it spat sand, dirt and debris, there didn't seem to be any limit to the power and intensity of the storm as it bore down on the home with the Withers holed up within, the family grew weary, hours without sunlight left the family restless, Isaac had stirred and awaken but simply stared from his curled up position on the couch while his family sat on the floor and let their hind ends go numb. Mary Sue noticed that her young son had risen and wasn't startled as badly with the roar of the storm bludgeoning away at the home, he gazed about aimlessly but remained silent, Isaac just watched the limited goings on in the room as his family sat near him and just read aloud to Elizabeth.

The lights grew dim as some of the candles burned down, it was later afternoon now and there wasn't much to do. Mary Sue wanted to open some of the bedroom doors and take stock of how much dirt had entered into the rooms through cracks in walls or windows but opening doors may give the dirt full access to the living room and cross breezes inside would make an even larger mess. The adults had grown semi comfortable while the storm fiercely beat against the outer walls of the home, Mary Sue paced nervously awaiting the end result of the storm no matter what it might be.

Obadiah stood near the front window and watched sand and grit blow past while drawing circles in some of the sand that blew in the window edge and settled on the window sill, it was tempting to open the window to change out some stagnant and stale air but the wind howled on and on and changing the air flow rates in the home would have only further filled their home with the soil that had been uprooted and sent into the air. Dinner came and went by candle light, there was no end in sight and the family only hoped that the morning would bring refuge or relief and that things would be back to normal. Obadiah just stood vigilant near the window and pondered as to when the storm might wear out and finally subside. Mary Sue finally gathered the courage to head into their bedroom to gather bedding to simply camp out in the living room.

Opening her bedroom door was silent in comparison to the growls of the outside, the tin roof still let out moans eerily as the winds still whipped just as strongly as it had when the gust's gathered strength and speed from the plains while barreling down on the farm. Mary Sue felt the energy from the room behind the door, her hands trembled at what she might find, almost concerned that maybe the room had no longer been there. She felt a bit childish but she also thought that maybe entering the room with just a lantern that maybe she wouldn't come back, maybe become trapped in a pile of dirt and never return.

Mary Sue froze solid as her feet entered the bedroom, she gazed deeply into the darkness, looking for anything that she might recognize, maybe the bed she had shared with her husband or any sign that her belongings hadn't been swallowed by some of the sand storm residue. There was a glint, a tiny shimmer off to her right as lead the lantern before her into the room, her vanity mirror magnified the light into the room and all seemed as it was, except her reflection gave her a small startle. She viewed near the window to see sand piling from the floor to the base of the window sill, she was disheartened that there was a mess but so much more relieved that it wasn't such the mess that she had worried herself with, she grabbed a few blankets from her bed to pad the living room floor with for the whole family to lay down on for the night.

The morning came; the light cackle of a rooster brought with it the morning light, Obadiah and Mary Sue stretched and took stock of their aches from the floor. Obadiah dragged himself to his feet and headed straight for the window to ensure that the morning had actually arrived; he gazed about through the dusty glass and kicked at the mound of dirt on the floor beneath the window. Mary Sue smiled at the gleaning sunlight filling the room, the hope had been restored in her heart and even the air inside seemed anew. Mary Sue wanted to get to cleaning the house, the storm had left the inside a mess and Obadiah wanted to head out and check on the property, he was terrified that all of the seed he planted weeks earlier had been torn from the ground and blown around the countryside. Obadiah took a step back, sick with the realization that he might be out all of the fresh seeds he planted and all may have gone to waste, the time, the money, the hope that had all gone into the ground around his field had now been ripped out and blown away. Mary Sue had been focused on the interior and what had to be done until she also realized the costs of the storm and the risk it had inflicted on the farm. Mary Sue quickly whipped together a breakfast for Obadiah so he could head out and begin assessing damages, the amount that needed to be done was suddenly endless.

Obadiah pocketed his thermos filled with water and headed out while Mary Sue and Elizabeth began to clean the inside, with broom and dust pan in hands, she headed to the first room to begin hauling out buckets worth of sand from each one of them while Obadiah began to shovel away piles of dirt and what have you on the outside. Obadiah shouldered a spade shovel and made his way out, the front porch had drifted dirt strewn from right to left and on the farthest edge, it was more than ankle deep. Obadiah looked out over the farm, everything was a disaster, there were mounds of dirt piled of against the west sides of everything, trees, the barn, the house, even the posts that marked the end of the driveway, few grasses poked up from the sea of dirt that now covered everything, it was reddish brown forever in every direction, and it was all filled with desperation. The dirt that once held so much hope and potential had been depleted, there was no longer anything that the ground could offer, it had spat out all of the seeds Obadiah planted, his future had become bleak, there was no longer potential in the land around and he could only stand still and fight to keep his breath, he felt strain in his chest from anxiety as the sun rose higher.

Obadiah spent a majority of the morning digging out his home, the west side was mounded up to the windows with the dry sandy mixed silt, shoveling the mixture away continued to plume up dust into the air when shovel fulls were heaved out of the way, the silt filled his nose and grit filled in around his teeth as he worked. As the day warmed up and sun grew higher, Obadiah slowly made progress in digging out around the farm, the chickens had climbed into their roost to avoid being sandblasted or buried under the flying gravel, the digging was tedious. Obadiah worked his callused hands on the shovel for most of the morning and once a majority of the work was through, he headed in for lunch with the family. It was after lunch when Obadiah had the notion to head to the next farm over, the Basks, an older couple that may have needed the help digging out.

Obadiah was worn from the work but he also wanted to be as neighborly as possible, this storm had caused such a disaster that it was hard to tell what could have been salvaged. Obadiah shouldered up his spade shovel and a bottle of water again and headed down the driveway and down the road. Mary Sue stayed behind with the children; there was still plenty to do at the house so she passed on tagging along as Obadiah began the long walk.

Obadiah kept his eyes locked on his destination, there were a few dead birds along the road as he made his way over, it was disturbing that the birds weren't keen enough to avoid the storm. The road was soft and dusty as he walked, the sand in his boots wore at his heels and even with as dry as the air was, his backside was sweaty and beginning to rub itself raw as it was filled with dirt, the discomfort had elongated his walk ever more. Birds were chirping along the sides of the route, the sky was blue and almost clear of clouds, a strong opposite to the day before. Finally reaching the Basks' farm, things were calm and still as Obadiah turned down the driveway. Nearing the house, Obadiah was already tired from a day's worth of digging and now almost an hour's walks down the road to reach his neighbors.

Obadiah grew curious about the homestead, neither person were out and there hadn't been any clearing of the storms' residue, there hadn't been any motion or hint of anyone that had entered or left the home, no signs of anyone. There were closed curtains in the home, and outside there were a few goats near the barn that sought shelter from the previous days' storm making a racket as they pawed at the dirt foraging for any grass hidden underneath. The goats all shared a color similar to the dirt that had overtaken the countryside, their hair had been dusted and dirtied and even when shaking off piles of dirt, their kicking and pawing kicked up more that seemed to recover them once again with more dirt. The air was so dry, the hearty cover of dirt that blanketed everything as far as could be seen seemed to absorb every speck of moisture from everything, his mouth parched and eyelids sticking to his eyeballs as Obadiah neared the front porch to check on his neighbors.

Obadiah climbed up the few steps to knock on the front door to arouse the Basks, his boots had an equal percentage of sand as that of the landscape. With a hearty knock on the door to alert his neighbors to his arrival, things were still silent, no movement from within, no noise or rustling and the only sounds from around were from the goats clambering around in their pen. After a minute of scanning the perimeter looking for any signs that they were even home, and not having any luck or progress, Obadiah reached for the door knob and turned it to let himself in, there was still no response as he alerted his entry to the home, the air was stale and warm, it didn't give any indication to having been aired out in some time and it held some weird musk in the air. The living room had a slight dusting of sand as everything did today; trekking through the home yelling for Anita Basks, there was no response from her or her husband Rupert.

The kitchen was sans dishes or signs of use, a quick eye search of the home lacked any tracks that anyone had walked through the dusting of dirt that had blown in, things were oddly in place but out of sorts, the couple had hardly any family near and with the whole previous day having been a dirt blowing storm that tried to bury the countryside, there didn't seem to be any reason to have left the home.

Walking to the first room Obadiah had a strange pit in his stomach as he reached forward to knock before he let himself him, his stomach twisted and let out a howl that broke the silence, it caused for a split second pause from the startle. The door opened with a creek, there were feet resting on the end of the bed, as the door opened further it continued to reveal more of the elder Anita Basks. Anita was laid out, her shoes were nice, she was in stockings with a darker colored floral pattern dress with a sweater over her shoulders. As Obadiah pushed the rest of the door open and called out her name, it took a moment to affix his eyes on her face, in the dim light it was almost hard to make out the woman's neck, in the shadow of her chin, as Obadiah neared the body, he took notice of a hole under her chin.

Obadiah took a moment and his eyes trained on the body. Obadiah stood bedside and felt really nervous, he waited for her to prop up and respond as he called out her name, his hands shook as he reached to shake the lady, hoping to wake her. Obadiah could feel his forehead begin to leak, he was filled with dread and worry as his heart pounded with anxiety. The lady rested in a pool of blood that poured from the hole in her neck, the blood had no shimmer, no glint to prove that it was still wet, long dried and her body had lost its' warmth, breath, life.

Obadiah left the room where Anita Basks had taken her last breath, he was nervous to think that maybe she took her life while fearing the worst in the storm, or maybe Rupert had done this, he exited the room before further investigation as he was nervous to sit near the body and feeling ill. The rest of the home was empty, no sign of Rupert or that anyone had been through the other rooms. Obadiah stepped outside to plot an appropriate place to bury the lady of the house, the tree directly out back seemed like a good eternal resting place for the lady and he headed in that direction. A few steps past the midway mark and the sand and silt grew deeper; it had really blown past the barn and left deep drifts that overtook the amount of ground behind the home.

Obadiah shuffled his feet through the finely grained dirt that had piled across the ground. "*THUDDDD*" the already worn man had tripped on something buried in the dirt, causing him to land hard in the dirt, his shouldered shovel landing ahead of him. Obadiah lay for a brief moment, face down in the dirt, fighting to muster enough strength to continue on with the remainder of this tiresome day. Pulling his arms underneath his fallen body, Obadiah pushed himself to his feet while spitting out his mouthful of dirt before he panned the area behind him to see what had tripped him up.

A hand protruded from the earth, it shared the same color as the ground around him, it was hard to distinguish at first but then the shape of a half gripped hand stood out from the ground underneath it. Obadiah had already had enough dead surprises for the day; he took to a knee and wiped his forearm across his face to clear away dirt and sweat. Obadiah nervously brushed away dirt from around the hand to reveal the attached arm, this was as strange of thing as he had ever crossed, there was a body buried under mounds of dirt and the farther he dug to continue to uncover the rest of Rupert Basks. Rupert was outstretched, angled towards the home and only four yards from the back door, he looked close before succumbing to the power of the storm. Rolling the body of Rupert Basks over revealed a grimacing face, his eyes were open and full of sand, his mouth also full of dirt, it appeared that Rupert had gotten caught up and turned around in the storm while trying to return to the safety of the house.

Obadiah now had two bodies to bury, there was a lot to suddenly handle, his generous favor to his neighbors had turned into funerals and burials, the days' tasks had increased exponentially. The discovery of bodies had shaken Obadiah to his core, the pair had boggled the chivalrous Obadiah, if Rupert had been overtaken by the storm, then it must have left Anita alone to endure the breadth of the storm, curious as to what happened to her husband and then break down to the point where she felt no other option but to take her own life, an absolutely horrid notion.

Obadiah picked himself up by the straps of his overalls and continued to head towards the large oak tree behind the house,

Obadiah was heavily burdened by the days' set of events as he picked up his shovel again. Obadiah began to dig; the hard work was a much needed break to clear his mind, chopping wood was often the preferred method to work out any mental troubles. Norman always told his son that chopping wood often lead to clarity and helped to resolve internal conflict, " the tree doesn't always fall on the first chop" and each swing of an ax was a step towards progress" meaning that with hard work, anything could be accomplished. Sometimes when you look ahead and the things that needed to be done mounted and piled up, taking things one swing at a time, you'll eventually be able to look at a winters worth of firewood and realize the progress that you can make by taking things a little at a time. Obadiah shoveled one scoop of dry dirt at a time, each scoop that was heaved to the side let a plume into the air and it seemed to be an everlasting fight against the dirt.

The sun rose high and had begun to break towards the west; Obadiah kept the sun on his back as he dug and dug. Rupert had been dragged and placed into the ground, his eyes didn't close and the dirt filled eyes stared up at Obadiah as he reburied the man that had life in him the day before. It was time to head back into the home and prepares Anita for her burial, it still unsettled Obadiah to have to face this situation, it was an uneasy burden to stomach. The grimacing face, full of anguish, that Rupert had, sat poorly with Obadiah as he headed into the home, the hole had been dug and Obadiah had to now wrap up Anita and carry her to her grave now.

Reentering the bedroom where the body of Anita laid, it was still an anxiety ridden situation, Obadiah looked for a minute, her hair was gray and white, done up as if she was headed to church, her clothes were pressed and looking keen, her face was peaceful, like she simply fell asleep, knowing she'd never wake up again. Obadiah decided to pull the side of the comforter from under her to roll it over her, he walked to the far side of the bed to wrap that side overtop of her when that's when he kicked a hard chunk of metal that was on the floor. The light was growing dim from the window; it was hard enough to see so Obadiah simply looked for any shape of what he kicked in order to place the sound with what he kicked.

Obadiah tapped his foot a few times in an arch to find what he kicked, sure enough a "clunk" informed him that he kicked and then found a pistol, "*thee*" pistol that Anita used to take her own

136

life, assumingly when her husband never returned from the fury that engulfed the home. Obadiah shoved the pistol in his back pocket and hoisted the cold clammy body wrapped in a blanket and carefully fumbled out to the second grave that he dug for the other discovered body. Obadiah fought his best to make his way to the dug hole, it was hard to keep his footing and on few occasions he almost fell as the loose dirt under his feet slid and gave way. The sun began to sink into the horizon as he finished re-scooping dirt into the hole that Anita was now at the bottom of.

Obadiah had the hour trek back to his home to ensure that his family was safe and sound, it had been a long day and his body had been more than depleted of energy. Obadiah headed towards the barn to throw a bale of hay in the internal stall for the live goats, they had probably gone all day without being fed and he'd have to figure out what to do about them come the morning anyways. Obadiah headed back down the driveway, it was growing darker and darker as he walked the shovel that started off on his shoulders now dragged behind him. Obadiah's' hands were swollen and thick, they hurt and it took all of his strength to even grip the shovel while the pistol in his back pocket hit his behind with every other step.

The day had been long, exhausting and more than the physical depletion, the mental strain had left Obadiah trying to shake off the faces that he had seen, the expressions, Rupert's anguish and pain, probably from suffocating in the dirt storm, Anita's peaceful and tranquil look even after having to make the choice to take her own life, he tried to imagine what they had gone through in their final moments in life, all the while trying to clear his mind of it all. Obadiah found the evening strange, other than his boot steps hitting the softened dirt of the road, there weren't any other sounds, the air was as still as the Basks', there weren't any noises or sounds, no coyotes in the distance, no bugs chirping or birds settling into trees for the night, it was as if most forms of life had been extinguished. The sky was clear as the stars shone bright against the blackened sky, the moon was only a quarter sliver but it still illuminated and offered enough light to highlight and outline tufts of grass along the sides of the road that hadn't been covered over by the windblown sands.

The outlines of a few trees could be barely made out against the distance, the silhouettes stood tall and proud, having weathered the worst winds of the last hundred years and even when the winds blew sand, dirt or tornadoes, they still stood. After the day like he had, Obadiah felt like one of the trees, not as strong or sturdy as an oak per say, but a tree nonetheless, after the storms he had withstood, the punches life had thrown and as wind worn as he felt, he could at least say that he was still standing, his family was safe and together, it may have been the most basic of requests that he could have made through anything but it was the most important request that would always be made, that they were all safe.

After the sun began to dip into the far and beyond, Mary Sue had begun to grow worried about her husband, the children ran and played in the house, she did her best to clean out the piles of sand and beat the dirt from blankets and such in each room. Elizabeth helped to keep an eye on her baby brother as they both ran about around the home while their father was away and their mother cleaned. As the afternoon wore on, Mary Sue was doing her best to ensure that her focus was on cleaning, she didn't want to worry her children and also wanted to keep herself distracted. Mary Sue trusted that everything was well with her husband, his absence hung heavy in her heart but she had an equal amount of comfort knowing that he was an able bodied and sharp minded man, she was most fortunate to call him her husband. Elizabeth and Isaac played in and around the barn, the sand drifts had piled up near the opening, trapping in both the tractor and the Dodge parked in the opening. Isaac liked to squat down and "hoot" at the owls perched towards the back, they made noises when aroused and those sounds entertained the young boy, not to mention the large eyed birds that could look almost directly behind them.

Mary Sue kept a weathered eye towards the driveway for her husband's return, and another eye towards the barn where her young children played as she shook the dirt out of blankets and towels from within the home. Lunch sandwiches had come and gone and now dinner had passed before the sun set and her worry began to swell in her throat. Mary Sue worried that there might be another looming storm headed their way sometime and wanted her loving husband home to ensure his safety, she tried to pass the time with the children and then also kept a few lights burning bright in wait for his return. With the children tucked in tightly to their beds finally, the lone time without her husband passed slowly, the clocked ticked on as she watched the sun capsize into the horizon, the darkness and shadows grew from behind trees and buildings, the darkness spread and became the majority. Mary Sue tried to fight off the coming night, she worried that once the dead of night took hold, that it somehow signified that she would be forever alone; she feared that her husband might not ever return and that rearing their children might have become her sole responsibility. Mary Sue fought to keep her wits, her panic organized, and ambush in the background. She felt its' presence in the undertones of her mind as she kept her eyes trained on the driveway, praying at any moment he would materialize from the darkness, to her relief

Mary Sue replayed the pending apocalypse, she recalled the long hours she spent with her family, long hours that she mostly comforted her children and sat dutifully with her husband in the living room awaiting any potential fate that may have been set in motion for the Withers. Mary Sue reflected to her childhood, her time with her sisters, Gertie and Charlotte as they often tore down to their undergarments as young girls and frolicked in the nearby creek. The girls often spent warm summer days splashing each other, of course Mary Sue being the youngest often ended up almost over her young head in water as her bigger sisters would always create monster tidal waves of splashes to almost drown the much younger sister. Mary Sue had plenty of adventures with her sisters, even after Gertrude's untimely passing, she and Charlotte would go out into the nearby woods and pretend to be Laura Ingalls Wilder, living on the frontier plains and living by wood stove. Mary Sue missed her parents and Charlotte, she needed to write them more, the distance between them hastened the intimate relationship between sisters. Mary Sue couldn't stop her mind from racing to every corner she mentally had, she thought about the romantic drive from South Carolina, the intimate stops along the road between husband and wife.

Mary Sue longed for the intimate touches of her husband, the prospect of losing him made her long for him ever so much more. Mary Sue recalled many of the moments she shared with her husband, she went back to when he took her on the porch, outdoors and exposed to the serenity of nature. Mary Sue found it most erotic and titillating that as they made love, Obadiah displayed his sensual wife to the world outside, she knew she was the center of his attention; she enjoyed his roaming hands and soft touches. Obadiah had work worn hands, hardened with the labor of life but still had the most gentle and delicate touches reserved for his wife and children. Mary Sue replayed so very many of the trysts that she and Obadiah shared, those engaging moments that took hold of the loving couple and made the world disappear when they were together. Thinking about having to navigate the future without Obadiah saddened her already heavy heart, the prospect of having to try and figure out what to do, how to handle the farm or leave the farm and return home with her children and restart from a lost position, was all so very overwhelming.

Mary Sue donned a position on the front porch; she sat quietly on the steps and peered out in to the distance, awaiting the return of her strong and sturdy husband. The slight breeze filled her light dress causing goose bumps on her arms as she sat in the dark alone, she strained to hear anything that resembled the boot steps of Obadiah returning home. The darkness was unsettling, the silence gave Mary Sue more of a chill than the breeze, and the life lacking sounds outside made her own heartbeat the loudest sounds in her ears.

There was very little rustling, minimal movements or noises, there was no motion or movement anywhere, the loneliness was deadening and it began to fill Mary Sue. The doting wife sat idly on the front porch, the top step warmed with her backside resting on it, Mary Sue huddled by herself and fought to remain optimistic that Obadiah was just moments away from returning home. As Mary Sue listened to hear, her heartbeat away time, the thumps were maddening and with each one growing harder, fueled with anxiety, she grew more worried. The dark blanketed everything as far as Mary Sue could see, The dim lights buzzing away inside let out enough of a glow that it obscured her ability to see the stars dotting the nights' sky, the moon was visible in the distance and she just gazed out wondering if life existed elsewhere in the grand universe.

Mary Sue fought to retain hope, staring out into the darkness she replayed each sensual touch from her husband when they made passionate fiery love on the same steps, she smiled at the warmth that filled her and it helped to fight off the gloom that was filling her mind. Mary Sue shook back to reality as the night air was beginning to nip at her bare skin, she stood and began to brush off her dress from the dirt she sat upon, she turned to head towards the awaiting home when she heard a voice, it sent shivers over her entire body. Obadiah made the final stretch down his driveway, he saw the shadow of his wife perched on the stoop waiting for him, and he mustered his last remaining strength as he carried the shovel and dragged his weary tired feet towards his wife.

Obadiah smiled, the lack of energy he had left him merely smirking and he was too tired to realize that the smile remained because his brain lacked the energy to stop, he felt like his eyes were crossing as he closed in on his home. Obadiah neared the edge of the shadows when Mary Sue began to stand, he felt his smile turn to a pout as she turned and began to walk away from him so he blurted out "*hey.*" Mary Sue was already on edge after sitting in the dark after the vile storm, hearing the voice grumble from the darkness sent her airborne with a wild windmill flailing of her arms in defense of herself to the unknown behind her. The spastic reaction of his wife left Obadiah wide eyed and with a bit of a small spike of adrenaline in response to the unexpected Kung-Fu motions of Mary Sue.

Obadiah didn't realize that she couldn't even make out her husband in the dark, her spacey tired mentality from the long day had clouded her attention to much, and she didn't even realize her husband was walking towards her as she headed into her house to break things down before bed when Obadiah let out his warning. When Mary Sue finally returned to her feet after her deep startle, she was so relieved that he returned to her that she began to weep, her eyes glazed over and began to leak tears down each cheek.

Obadiah didn't understand why his wife reacted the way she did, he was glad to see her after his day, he really had time to take stock of everything he had and he remained grateful for his farm and the safety of his family. The worn and weary man trudged up the three steps to be on even standings with his wife, they locked eyes and it was suddenly clear to each of them that they were both in need of one another. Mary Sue set eyes on her husband and could tell between his absence and exasperated look, that his day had brought him much more grief and sorrow than had been planned for. Obadiah reached for and embraced his wife, simply holding her brought a tinge of relief to the well-worn farmer, he had simply been drained and there was nothing left in him, as she held her husband she could feel him sink into her embrace, after a moment she was holding him up more than his own two legs and she truly began to worry.

Mary Sue coaxed her husband inside and to the couch for him to unburden himself to her. She held her husband closely and shared that she had missed him dearly, he told her about his journey to the Basks, the long walk and the dusty earth pelting his body with each gust of breeze while on his way. Mary Sue consoled her husband but failed to understand what was so laboring about the day, Obadiah continued to tell her about entering the home and what he had discovered, Mary Sue gasped and tried to hide her expression about the grisly discovery, she found it simply awful that the sweet Anita had gotten to such a point of desperation that she had to resort to such a violent and sad ending of her life. Obadiah continued to tell Mary Sue about what else had happened, his fumbling discovery of Rupert Basks and the struggle he must have endured before his demise in the storm. Mary Sue continued to feel terrible for her husband, she had no idea when he set out that he was in for such a daunting day, and Obadiah had no idea what he was in for either.

Obadiah finished explaining his days' events to Mary Sue, she filled him in on what she had done with her day in the absence of her husband and felt that Obadiah had had just an awful day. There was still much to do come morning light so the couple retired to bed for the evening, both halves of the tired couple were glad to finally get to sleep in their bed instead of on the living room floor, Obadiah ached and had pains in every nook and cranny of his body and Mary Sue could tell by his winces that he needed some massaging and womanly touching on her behalf. Mary Sue helped to escort her husband into their room and get him ready for the nights slumber, Obadiah still fought his best to remain standing but he leaned heavily on the shoulders of his wife, the day of digging and hearty work mixed with the heat and arid air simply exhausted every ounce of energy the husband had within him, she laid him down into bed and before she could untie his first boot, he was already asleep and snoring.

Mary Sue carried each boot back outside to dump the footwear of its' sandy contents, the man remained passed out as Mary Sue continued to unclothe her husband and get him tucked in for the remainder of the night. Mary Sue was almost as tired herself, the fresh air and physical labor was some of the best exercise anyone can get and it depletes you of your energy with enough hard work to make an ideal sleep recipe. Mary Sue laid herself next to her husband and admired his exposed torso, his muscular chest twitched as he lay asleep, his shoulders and neck muscles remained swollen and engorged with blood from the extensive labor, the woman found herself once again revisiting some of the tender moments she had shared with her husband.

Mary Sue traced her fingers along the meaty chest of the sleeping Obadiah, he hardly even responded his slumber was set in and there was no disturbing him, Mary Sue made an attempt to test his resilience to arousal, Mary Sue let her hands wander the landscape of Obadiah, his skin glistened with tiny beads of sweat in the warm night, the exposed body of Obadiah made her body become hot with passion. Mary Sue craved her husband, the man lay there without any worldly hint that anything was going on around him, all the while his wife had caressed his body, Mary Sue let her left hand roam his body and her right hand hers. As Mary Sue began to perspire, the hairs right at her hairline above her forehead began to stick together, the nape of her neck felt cool with sweat in the night air and she could feel her chest begin to swell with passion, her nipples hardened.

Mary Sue desired Obadiah, she needed her husband, his soft lip kisses, gentle hands that enveloped her body in areas when her grasped her and she carnally needed him at the very moment. Obadiah lay there breathing shallowly, he did not stir and there was no flinch or response to any of the stimuli from the room around him, he was oblivious to anything and everything about him as Mary Sue delved further into her desires, she had continued to hope that her husband would awake at any moment and just take her, or catch her, which further excited hear. Mary Sue felt her nipples become hard and filled with blood, they had a slight pain to them as they were so engorged with excitement and sensitive to her touch, to explore herself within such proximity to her husband was adventurous, she craved his body and wished that he would wake up and take over, take over her entire body.

Mary Sue continue to breathe heavier and heavier, her chest heaved up and down as she continued to explore herself, Obadiah still remained motionless, there was no change in his breathing, it remained slow and shallow as hers increased with each breath. Mary Sue held her breath as her excitement peeked, she was overcome with excitement. The night toiled away, as did Mary Sue, after the embers of her loins had been brought to full flame and then burned out, the lonely wife was now without much to focus on, she thought further about how the week had come along, the storm and its fury and how it raged in from the west, the darkening skies and how the Basks had succumbed to the desolate situation, Rupert having fallen in the storm and must have suffocated with lungs full of silt and dirt, and what a horrible way to have passed on. Anita, realizing how dire the situation was for herself and didn't want to risk facing the world alone, she must have needed her husband by her side and when he hadn't returned, she took her own destiny into her own hands, what a scary situation to come to, it truly filled Mary Sue with deep appreciation for what she had. Mary Sue finally let her mind go blank, she fought to stave off any more thoughts and finally fell into a deep sleep.

The morning came and with another day of new light, the weary couple dragged themselves out of bed and shuffled their feet to attend to the waking children and another days chores. Obadiah wanted to head back over to the Basks' house and figure out what to do with the damn goats, there must have been about a dozen of them and he was in no shape to make the hour walk or even drive each day to tend to the woolly critters, if by chance the road became passable. Obadiah explained his plan of action to his wife, he also loaded up Elizabeth to take with him, he figured she would love the adventure as well as possibly lend a hand. The mother was really hesitant to let her young daughter go with her father, two people had passed away just the other day and it probably wasn't an ideal place for the young girl to be.

Obadiah reassured the worried woman that all was safe and that the bodies had been buried deeply, his arms and shoulders were still worn sore and slow to move from the previous days' work. Elizabeth had no idea what was going on but she was very enthusiastic to get to join her poppa for the day, leaving behind her brother and her role of watching over him. Mary Sue was filled with dread over the ordeal, she also had no desire to deal with goats for that matter but with the economy suffering and now with a blow to the state such as the storm, things were only sure to get worse so Mary Sue trusted her daughter with her husband, he was her father after all.

Obadiah tried to plan his course of action, he wasn't sure how everything was going to move along, he stewed over a cup of coffee, his body still twitched from exhaustion and he did his best to roll his head around to stretch out his neck. Obadiah laced up his dirty brown boots and made sure Elizabeth had a hat on her head to help keep the sun off of her face as they headed out. After

144

a stop to the barn for a few hand tools, the father daughter duo headed down the road towards the Basks farm again.

The girl kicked at some of the pebbles she came across, the sand drifts still closed off most of the road, the uneven terrain made travel a bit of a challenge, Elizabeth climbed the mounds and jumped from the top of each one to the road underneath, after the twentieth or so mound her enthusiasm began to wane and the journey became long and tedious. Mary Sue stared down the road and watched her husband and daughter head off and on their way, it was nice to have the home to just her and little Isaac, she enjoyed having a full house but ensuring that both children were plenty entertained, was tiring. Mary Sue finished washing the dishes and prepared to launder the linens before she pulled her focus back to her son as he kicked around his wooden blocks passing the time.

Elizabeth climbed each mound of sand, taking such large strides began to burn in her legs as she kept a hurried pace keeping up with her father, the walk seemed to take days, weeks, even hours, she felt it might be night soon they had been walking so long. Elizabeth was enthralled to get the invite, she wasn't sure where to go or what they were doing, or even her role in the day but none of it mattered, she was going to have a good time.

Obadiah tried to recall what he had seen at the farm, he felt a bit guilty about going to rummage through the property but he only planned to gather the goats along with some wire fencing and haul everything back to their home. The farm was still solemn, it was spooky to walk towards the house, the faces of the deceased flashed in the mind of the father, he was comforted that he wasn't alone this time and didn't have to discover any more bodies suddenly, he was better prepared to handle anything that might come along this trip. The goats were still filthy, a few of them sounded to be making a rough cough type of hack, presumably from inhaling lungful of dirt while trying to feed. Elizabeth changed her course direction and ran to climb on the fence that enclosed the goats, she began to click and snap trying to get the attention of any one of the critters inside. Obadiah shouted that she stay put for a few minutes and then he headed inside to look for and salvageable goods, he still had the pistol from the day before so he would at least need more bullets, not to mention there might be other items that could come in handy.

Obadiah let himself in, the house was even more spooky knowing that Anita had taken her life just inside the bedroom, it was that knowledge that made him even more uncomfortable as he entered the room looking for anything of value, he opened the curtain a bit to let in more light to see better. The curtains blew plenty of dust around when he whisked them aside, there was a box of ammo on the top of the vanity, Obadiah began to rummage through the drawers looking to find any cash or other items also, the country was hard up for work and the complete loss of all planted crops would be devastating when the end of the harvest season comes along and there aren't any crops to actually harvest. Sure enough in the bottom drawer there was a cigar box, the white box had red writing all over it, the cigars would have made for a decent treat at the end of a summer night, the box had eighteen cigars in it, and a clipped bundle of cash amounting to over one-hundred and sixty three dollars, money that would sure serve a huge help when things get even tighter in the coming days.

Obadiah scavenged several items from the home, he found a canvas apple bag to sling over his shoulder and fill with stuff that he needed to take back home with him. A box of cigars, a half box of ammo for the .38 pistol he recovered from the floor of the bedroom, there were other odds and ends that Obadiah found useful, he made sure to take everything he could and headed back out to check on his daughter. Obadiah left the home, pulling the door shut behind him again, the landscape was all different shades of the reddened dirt strewn across the entire property, just like the rest of the country, it was depressing that the dark dirt fields had been blown to the east coast rather than nurture planted seed inside the ground preparing it for growth. It was disheartening that all the work he had put into the land for his farm had become piss in a river. Obadiah turned towards the barn to begin roping goats and removing pen wire to take home with him and catch up with Elizabeth.

Elizabeth was standing against the goat pen, next to her stood a tall negro, rubbing her left shoulder, panic set in, he could feel his own pupils dilate. Obadiah dropped his bag of acquired goods and began running with the heft of a bull towards his daughter and dark skinned stranger, Obadiah was bewildered, there shouldn't have been anyone around and it was just yesterday when he buried the residents and living out in the countryside things were really remote and secluded. *"Get your hands off my daughter"*

146

Obadiah shouted as he rushed to defend his young girl, the man in jeans and a button up shirt jumped to the side, the man threw up his hands and began stuttering something in gibberish. Obadiah spun his daughter away from the fence and put himself between her and the strange man. The man started rambling about how pretty the girl was, how lonely he had been, and how he watched the farmer bury the homeowners the day before and assumed that the little girl had just wandered over and was there for the man to do what he wanted to with her. Obadiah's blood boiled, his rage sent him flying wildly towards the man, as Obadiah left the ground he reached for the pistol that was in his back pocket earlier, his anger flared wilder and wilder as the man continued on talking, the man didn't recant what his intentions were, he began trying to bargain for time to spend with the young girl, whom began to panic and cry that her father was physically attacking a stranger, the commotion was unsettling.

Obadiah landed atop the stranger as they fell to the ground together, there was no pistol, there was suddenly no sure upper hand in this squabble, the negro offered his hat, money, anything, to escape the death grip Obadiah had upon his throat but to still try to bargain time with the little girl, Elizabeth was near the house, crying uncontrollably, as her father turned from anger to a raging fury that changed his slew of swear words into a spit strewn babble of inaudible words as he continued to squeeze the strange man's throat. Elizabeth cried from being upset, Obadiah stared into the eyes of the sick stranger as his legs clamped down against his ribs and pinning his left arm, Obadiah's left hand was vicing down on the esophagus, his right arm pinning the man's free arm, and his eyes, growing more and more bloodshot as the life drained from the stranger. A white flash of enraged fury turned to wrath, the man stopped struggling and as Obadiah's fingers began to touch, he realized he had crushed the windpipe in his vexation. There was now a lifeless black man at the end of his grip, his eyes bloodshot, the world flooded back in to view as the clouded corners of his eyes cleared away to reality. Obadiah had struggled to loosen his grip on the man, he fought but the hand was closed and now cramped shut and refused to open on command.

The crying of Elizabeth brought her father back to his senses, there was now a murdered man that he was straddled on top of, he was absolutely stunned, he couldn't believe what happened, he was ashamed and suddenly things were out of control. Obadiah began to panic, he was freaked out wondering what to do, he had just killed a man with his bare hands, there were laws, rules, punishment for murder, he would be locked up and his wife and children would never see him again. Dread was the only thing on Obadiah's mind, his daughter was shaken, she had just witnessed the most tragic situation that she may have seen in her entire life, he had so many things that were assaulting his conscious, there were many things that should have taken a priority, he was supposed to be doing things but for the life of him he was entangled in the present, consumed. The goats were stirred from the commotion, there was a dark gray one, who's fur was full of dirt and dust and had red tints and tones to it, the gray goat was climbed up on the fence and riled up causing the other goats to panic as well. The "baa'hing" of the goats broke the controlling stare that Obadiah had on the now deceased man within the hold of Obadiah.

It took the goat to bring the awareness back to Obadiah, his daughters' crying made him jump to his feet to get a better angle on the situation, he side straddled to his daughter while keeping a watchful eye on the body now lying near the fence of the goat pen. The man just laid still, his blue jeans were dirty and worn this, his boots were more worn than Obadiah's, his originally light blue shirt was stained from sweat and filthy from rolling in the dirt with Obadiah now, his body lay motionless and now without life. Obadiah comforted his baby girl as she continued to cry as her upset state of mind was so strong, she didn't understand what had happened, her blubbering cries seemed to fade into the noise echoing from the penned up creatures. Not a single thought had any form of organization within the mind of Obadiah, he rifled through his options, he knew that he was alone at the farm, there was a dead body sprawled out on the ground a few feet away, his daughter had been the witness to an event that may trouble her for the rest of her life if she remembers it. Obadiah tried to stroke the hair of his little girl, she trembled with uncertainty of what took place, Obadiah was shaking, his arms ached and his right arm remained clenched and his forearm felt seized.

Obadiah began to think better on his feet after a few minutes of close reassuring embrace with his daughter, he asked her to head into the barn and look for a pair of pliers and some rope while he headed in right behind to find a shovel to get back to more digging, for the second day in a row. As Obadiah dug a deep hole at the far end of the barn, away from the innocent eyes of Elizabeth while she tried to find enough rope to tie up the goats in the pen. Obadiah shoveled in a hurry, he was pinched for time and couldn't waste a single moment to dig as deep as he did for the Basks.

Obadiah panicked, he was overtaken with what had happened, how could he have done such a thing? He was a god fearing family man whom settled peacefully into Indian Gulch and now, everything had changed. Obadiah dug in a hurried manner, he scooped away at the red sand to be able to place the dead body of the stranger in it, Obadiah dragged the body behind the barn to get it out of eyesight from his little girl, and she was young yet and needn't be exposed to such things in life. Obadiah was still stricken with grief, guilt, and rage, his arms still throbbed with blood and his grip on the wood handle felt like he would snap it at any moment.

Obadiah covered the body over, after checking the man's' pockets for any form of identification, the man's wallet was empty with the exception of a baseball card of Babe Ruth and a faded and crinkled driver's license, the man's name was Mickey Williams, a man whom was a sicko, he made disgusting advances towards a his six year old daughter and rightfully so, Obadiah killed the man. Everything happened in such a rush, Obadiah was at the whim of a white flash of rage, his adrenaline had caused him to blank and when he came to, he had taken another man's life and it was all too late to retract what he had done, there was a daughter in the barn gathering things to herd goats back home with, he was burying a strange man that he had only met for a moment and then had taken his life, there was a heavy pit in his stomach as he continued to dig, these two days had compounded all of his stresses and worries for his family, and himself, the country was sinking into a financial depression and things continued to look every so much more bleak.

Obadiah's mind ran faster than it had ever run before, his adrenaline was causing his heart to pound, his mind ached and he fought off a lightheaded feeling as he dug hurriedly. Obadiah threw the first scoop of dirt over the mentally twisted Mickey, that a deviant, his absence from the world would not be missed. Mickey was a man that deserved to be buried in a shallow hole, there wouldn't be any solemn words of goodbye, no psalms to mourn his passing, just a squinted look of agony burned into the memory of Obadiah, the man that attempted to have sexual relations with the temporary undertakers' daughter, just looked asleep, his face was without pain, anguish, or even life itself.

Obadiah was a changed man, in just a few days, any prospects that the farm held, had simply blown away, any life bringing seeds that were gladly planted, had been ripped away and had been swept to the heavens. Yesterday Obadiah had buried his elderly neighbors, the old man had died in a gruesome sandstorm, his last moments must have been spent choking and gasping on the fine silts that filled in his lungs, his eyes, his nose and mouth. Obadiah felt haunted at the eerie sights of now three dead people that he has had to bury in under two days' time, he finished covering over the deceased negro, his gray sweat stained hat lay over his face and hands crossed over his body, Obadiah scooped and heaved shovel after shovel full of dirt onto the body before his daughter had caught on to what was going on.

Obadiah felt sick, his body was spent, his emotions had run amok and he had no idea how to handle any of it anymore. He missed his father, the senior Mr. Withers held so many answers to everything and he just wanted to run to the safe side of his father, like he had done when he was Elizabeth's age. Obadiah snapped back to attention from staring off into the sand now covering the dead stranger, he came back to awareness and shook in his overalls, patted down his legs trying to brush off some of the sand and dirt from his labor, and began to motion to join his daughter.

Mary Sue sat at home and kept Isaac occupied, she sorted the remaining seeds she had, seeds that she hadn't planted in the garden that blew away. Mary Sue plotted and schemed how she was going to plant in order to prevent the seeds from being blown away again if such a storm were to brew in the fires of hell and unleash on Oklahoma again. There were a few flour sacks that Mary Sue had retained, the sacks were a simple fabric but if she cut the bags out to large squares and stitched them together, than she could sprout the seeds inside the home until the plants had study enough roots to hold to the fabric and stave off being blown to kingdom come.

Mary Sue worked on her idea, she gathered as much of the life giving soil from under the silt and sand that had covered everything, she played with Isaac and together they molded dirt with water into small cups, tucked in to paper cups to hold everything together, her idea to start seedlings inside near a southern facing window should help to give the garden plants a healthy start to the coming year. Isaac was bobbing and wobbling he took his uncoordinated steps around the home, he was slowly becoming more verbal, he could easily point and grunt and was getting much better at identifying the objects of his attention and desires. Mary Sue continued to sweep off the steps and dust out the barn, the car had taken a heavy layer of dust, it had eclipsed the windshield. Mary Sue couldn't help but flash to the neighbors, her mind wandered to the story her husband had told her about how the Basks were found, their final moments had been spent apart, there was no last loving embrace before their lives expired, no last kiss, no hand holding as the eternal darkness took over.

Mary Sue began to weep, her eyes became misty and she became stricken with emotion, she was ever so loving and in need of her husband for the rest of her life and the thought of losing him, was just too much for her to bare. Mary Sue had to take a knee, her emotions were overwhelming, she had no idea what had come of her, the way things had continued to spiral downward towards Hades and her poor young children may never know the kind of love that she was blessed to have. Mary Sue wiped her eyes when Isaac waddled to her, he noticed his distraught mother was in need of his loving touch, a hug was the only thing he had in this world to offer but it was just what his mother needed.

Mary Sue used stakes to hold down the large area of clothe that she intended to use for her garden, she placed tall sticks to map the corners of the garden, if the sands blew in again the garden would have slight shelter from the home to protect it, it was crucial that the garden prosper, there was slimming stockpiles of food, and according to the radio, things all around the country were becoming more and more bleak. Mary Sue fought her best to keep from worrying about the future, she held her husband and his abilities of being a husband in great faith but she also could see past his weather hardened facial expressions and could see that he had worry in his heart also. They didn't want to face the looming truth, they both knew that things looked less and less promising but if they never spoke of the topic, if they pushed down the sad truth deep inside them then maybe, their ignorance could keep them from having to face the frightening reality.

Mary Sue stored seeds from all the winter and spring vegetables, she had a large hoard and half were already put into the ground, then up heaved and blown away. Mary Sue longed for her husband and truly missed him, she was considering taking her son and heading to join Obadiah at the Basks farm, she knew that he was working and didn't want to be a burden and frankly, she wasn't convinced that she would be enough help, especially while she had ample work to do at their own farm.

Obadiah and Elizabeth worked together, they roped all of the goats together, they began tied off to a barn post while Obadiah and his cohort unwound the wire fencing and rolled the pen wire up, after placing the wire on a wagon, the pair then loaded up as many more items as could be salvaged, cans of gas and fuel, tools, especially hay and goat feed that could be scavenged as the hours waned by. Elizabeth was growing weary as she had struggled her best to keep up with what her fathered asked of her, she sought out rope, she helped to yolk the goats together, the goats were lined up in pairs to a cut boards of timber and attached to the wagon, Obadiah was unsure about how this would transpire, he was about to dogsled goats and use the stubborn creatures to move them and all of their supplies to their new location.

There were a few goats that hadn't survived the storm, the four bodies lay in the dirt, half covered in dirt or some form of natural burial, Obadiah just figured he would leave the critters in the pen as they were, they had been in the sun too long and there was no salvaging any of the now rotting meat. Elizabeth tried to wake the dead goats as the rest were roped and tied up, she didn't understand why they wouldn't wake up and kept shaking them with no avail. Obadiah worked feverishly, he constructed makeshift harnesses for the goats to secure to to help pull the wagon now loaded with supplies. Obadiah used several types of twine or rope to ensure that all of the goats that were alive, all eleven of them, were ready for the journey to their new destination. The road was still choppy with sand ruts and Obadiah knew that it would be havoc on the ability to haul the wagon back to his farm, he was full of self-doubt about how well, or not at all, this venture would go.

With a wagon loaded with pilfered goods and supplies, his young daughter adorned front and center on the same wagon, Obadiah was as ready as he could ever be to begin fighting the road to get the salvaged wagon to its' new place near his barn. The goats all tried to head in every direction but the one they were pulled in, Obadiah held and pulled the lead rope, the stubborn bastard animals fought everything they could before finally just beginning to mosey. As the goats followed suit, Obadiah was finally making some progress in heading towards his home where he could finally unwind and try to forget the day's events. The meandering animals tugged at the wagon as Obadiah continued to tug them in the right direction, Elizabeth whipped at the reigns to keep the goats moving. Obadiah also used some extra rope to also whip some of the lazy and worn out animals, it was one of the longest afternoons he had ever experienced and as the long minutes slowed to what seemed like a halt, he struggled on and on to lug all of the gear and supplies to his farm, Obadiah was spent, and the days' work and completely tapped out the father, but it wasn't anywhere near over

The day after the goats arrived, they spent the night tied on long ropes to the barn and left to wander after being watered appropriately. The goats survived the night, the couple had spent the better part of the day establishing the goat pen in conjunction with trying to ensure that they would be taken care of, the animals offered meat now, game in the area had become scarce, birds were no longer plentiful, the rabbits had thinned out and who knows how many more had now become buried in their holes, food sources were growing and more thin and the Withers began to realize it. A few days after the goats were re-homed, the Withers decided it was due time for a trip into town, Isaac was outgrowing a lot of his clothing and Elizabeth was also.

Mary Sue had a long list of goods and food requirements; she had a list of what she wanted but also knew that the funds to purchase the groceries were very limited. Obadiah was worried about running very thin on money, things sounded more and more desperate around the country, the radio spouted news briefs that declared thousands of companies closing down and laying off millions of employees, things had continued to grow frantic for millions. Most of the afternoons were spent nibbling suppers that decreased in portions more and more, Mary Sue became ever so talented at making the most of meals with very little, food supplies waned and ran thin, but her family remained fed and her children remained healthy. Obadiah noticed the downward slope of the food supply, he never said a word as he was the man of the house and the supplier, when birds or rabbits became scarce, and they both knew that feeding the kids came first.

After a watered down cup of coffee, the morning was much like many others, Mary Sues seeds hadn't sprouted yet, there was hope in her heart about it, she found it harder and harder to struggle to retain faith about anything, the country had continued to fall into despair, the radio broad-casted how terrible the stock markets had become, how millions of jobs and billions of dollars had blown away, just like the hopes and seeds of the fields had. Obadiah hadn't had the heart to tell his wife what he had done at the farm; he couldn't bring himself to change how his wife looked at him.

Mary Sue held her strong and tender husband in such high regards that Obadiah felt trapped, he felt her expectations and the added stress of that truly bore down on Obadiah and he feared failing in the eyes of his wife or children. Obadiah felt burdened by the expectations to be the ideal husband, he felt like he couldn't fail, while failing, his farm had become desolate, his crops had taken to the air and will now no longer provide a crop for harvest or for sale.

Mary Sue kept strong hold of her husband's eyes and heart, she was growing further worried about how they would continue to provide for their children, or even themselves. Mary Sue struggled to remain composed when Obadiah was around, she sometimes hid away in the kitchen and wept as she prepared a meal, the clanging of pots and pans masked her sorrows when she felt she was at her weakest. Mary Sue watched the levels of flour or rice dwindle, her anxiety also increased as she thinned out recipes for meals. Mary Sue was filled with dread at the thought of letting Obadiah feel like a failed husband, she needed him to remain by her side.

The couple hid their fears from each other, they were both afraid of being truly open with their deepest fears to one another, they didn't want to shame the other person, they struggled to keep a smile on their face and remain committed to one another. The children were none the wiser when their parents stressed and worried about the adult concerns. They remained fed and entertained, unaware that there may not be a next meal any day.

Both parents felt blessed to have one another, their children and the farm; all had held firm to this point but the dam could break any day and when the bottom falls out, there is no telling how things might turn out. Obadiah had the cash he pilfered from the Basks home, the bundle of cash would help to stockpile food and cooking supplies and hope that they could make it through this year, there was no telling if it was even possible, neither adult in the home could foretell if there was hope worth hoping for, but for the sake of their legacy, the children, they had no choice but to hold out and keep wading through each day. The family gathered what they needed to in order to venture past the end of their road, it had been over a week since the storm had completely wiped the country clean of planted seeds and there was no telling if the roads were passable. Obadiah loaded his shovel just in case they might risk ending up stuck, the empty gas cans were trunked, there was a lot to try to figure out but they did their best and got on their way to town.

The kids had become accustomed to spending most of their time at the farm so the trip into town was a bit of an exciting change for the day. The family loaded up and headed down east to head towards Indian Gulch, Obadiah guided the motor vehicle carefully over many of the windblown ruts in the road, it jerked and pulled from one side to the other. Passing the Basks farm filled Mary Sue with grief and her lower lip quivered at the thought of the elderly couple having been buried in the backyard near the large oak, Obadiah eyed the slight bump in the ground near the roadside ditch, where he buried that bastard scumbag named Mickey.

Obadiah felt uneasy as the Dodge putted past, he sat tall and struggled to keep his eyes on the road in front of him instead of on the body behind him, he began to sweat and felt a spearing guilt in his gut, his temples pulsed and he could feel his face become flush. The couple sat tall in the front seat of the car, Mary Sue scoured the horizon looking for signs that maybe it was only their area that had been almost wiped from the land; it was heart breaking to look out from behind the windows and see such an infertile desert. Mary Sue pictured the family as if they were traversing a desert, maybe such a grand desert as she had read about in stories, both fiction and non. Obadiah tried to listen to the motor of the car to make sure the intake wasn't clogging with sand and silt, anything to keep his mind off of his brutality that had taken a life.

The young children in the back jumped and bounced along with the contours of the road, they found comedy in watching the heads of their parents sway back and forth in front of them as the whole vehicle swayed and navigated the rough roads. Nearing town things had not fared any better, the sights were covered with reddish sand and dirt, the piles were still packed up against trees and mounds drifted as far as the eye could see.

As the family neared town, the roads became better navigable, it was a comfort that many of the town's people had survived and that there had been enough traffic to help clear the roadways. The large windows of the laundry store had such a thick cover of dust on them it almost obscured the closed sign taped to it. The family pulled up to the Ponsens deli, they figured they would stop in for a lunch break and some informal news on the goings on in town over the last several months, and especially since the wicked storm. There were people loitering over most of the boardwalks, it was intriguing to whom most of the people were, there were so many people in different levels of dress, some kids lacked shoes and appeared dirty enough to support the suspicion of not having bathed in weeks, it was a poor sight to see and it also made for the upsetting confirmation, that the country was surely sinking into poverty.

The normally chipper Katherine was sitting at one of her tables, Murray leaning on the counter, the couple hardly stirred as the Withers entered in, Katherine looked unusually tired, she was often spry and glad to welcome any that entered, Murray looked ready for a nap when the family came in, he had a relaxed ease to his position at the counter when he recognized those who came forth. The family was also weather beaten from the storm, the sand in every corner of their lives and seeing the despair spreading from the outer corners of the country was seeping into the friendly Indian Gulch. Murray was usually slicing any sort of meat for patrons, at this time he was merely hunched over his counter, reading a newspaper that seems to have been well worn from excessive use.

There were no other patrons, the window sills were dusty, it seemed that the deli might have been closed since the storm, it was dark in the store, the dust draped windows blocked out some of the light, letting in streaks of light and displaying misshapen shadows all over the floor. Katherine offered a weary smile towards the children, she was impressed to see how Isaac had grown since last fall, Elizabeth remembered Katherine as the lady that offered hard candy in the past and was glad to see her. Obadiah asked what was available, Murray snickered back that things were tight, other than opening around breakfast time for coffee, and closing just after lunch time, it was all they could do to remain open for business at all.

Obadiah was bewildered that things had gotten so thin, Katherine pulled up a stool near their and began to let them in on all of the latest goings on around town and how many of the citizens had simply moved on to find work or better land to farm. Katherine flailed a snapping hand to her husband for sandwiches for the customers before returning to storytelling. First it was Hirsch, the short statured and even shorter tempered bank owner next door, when the rumors hit that things were tanking in the financial markets, he grew even tighter with returning money, at first he continued to take peoples house payments, without forwarding them on to the respected banks, he greedily stockpiled funds and continued to Jew citizens out of their finances.

After a few months and several of the town's residents lost their homes to foreclosures because of the deviant practices of the crook Morgenstern, he then simply boarded up his bank and fled, taking thousands and thousands of dollars from the resident, leaving them to suffer the evil natured after effects of what the scamming half midget Hirsch had done. The Withers had gasped at the devious actions of the scoundrel, they had never heard of such betrayal, Katherine proceeded to speak.

Katherine Mohs and her husband had just left town a few hours previous, they had held out and last year's harvest had given them the confidence to purchase new farm equipment for this season. Last years was dry, it had shown them that even with a dry year they could afford to expand their parcel to farm so three weeks before the storm, they had spent all of their liquid cash on seeds, and all of their credit on equipment, they had extended themselves beyond what they could afford, they forewent paying house notes for a month or two but because the lack of forgiveness from banks, they had to leave their home pronto. Katherine Ponsen was saddened by Mrs. Mohs leaving, they were friends and Ponsen's just simply shrugged to accept it. The Mohs had taken to loading up everything they could transport and headed to Louisiana to take up residence with Shanae, her fancy dame cousin whom was still faring the depression financially well with her stardom and talents with the men. Shanae had continued dancing; the speakeasies were still hopping, especially with the shipping ports of the Mississippi right at her front stoop.

Donna Wells was struggling, her husband had left her for a much younger woman in New Mexico he had met while trucking. The burden of sending her money had finally pushed him to see how the country was struggling and that he was completely supporting her to sit around and have coffee time with her friends while he bargained and bartered for any job he could get, sans intimate time. Mr. Wells, Michael, had crossed a strikingly young Latin beauty, and had walked away from his entire past to wed her in under a month's time knowing her.

Michael expressed his remorse in his letter, he had come to the realization that he had been doing all of the work for them as a couple, her aging was at her behest, while his was at a much faster pace because of the work "they" required of him to continue to support her. He had simply realized that while he spent long lonely days on the road, with minimal comfort as a reward, she lived luxuriously at his expense, he had grown lonely while married and it wasn't right, he had realized how selfish and portly his wife had become, as many truckers do as well, fat on the earnings of their men. Mary Sue raised her eyebrows at the shock of what she was hearing, people that seemed to have had solid marriages, ones much longer than the Withers, were shaken and had now crumbled.

Murray apologized for the meager accommodation, their deli was often minimally stocked lately as they couldn't afford to waste much and their business barely kept itself open as it were, he warned the Withers that there was no credit and as Obadiah reached for a few dollars to pay for the sandwiches up front, the front door hit the small bell. As the lady of the business was about to begin telling stories of drifters and hobos that had wafted into and then out of town, a young girl was trying to enter the deli, she was maybe young teens, her hair hadn't been washed in months, her clothes were rags and she was without shoes.

The meek girl still held the handle with her right hand, her head hardly above her forearm and she tried to avoid eye contact as the man of the business piped up, "*HEY, NO MONEY NO FOOD, this isn't a soup kitchen*" Murray threw a stern voice towards the little girl, whom stopped dead in her tracks, the look on her face was just dreadful, it appeared she hadn't seen a good washing in weeks, she may have blown in like a tumble weed she was so thin. The girl dropped her head as she turned around and headed back to the blowing dirt, from which she came.

The booming warning startled Issac and his lower lip slipped forward from under his upper lip and it began to quiver as his upset look turned to Mary Sue. The ambient atmosphere was uneasy, the immediate silence left the Withers to settle in their chairs, the following was unknown and Murray stared at the door for a few more moments before returning to his worn paper.

Katherine turned her attention back the her guests, she shook her head for a moment and apologized to the withers, "*it happens all the time, sometimes dozens of people a day, all wandering in and either asking for a handout, grafting anything out of the already struggling business owners or just simply trying to steal anything small enough make off with."* With the nearest railways less than fifty miles away, people rode the train cars across the nation looking for work, east coast natives sought cotton or wheat harvesting in the mid-west, mid-west residents uprooted and headed west in hopes of fruit harvesting to bring in money to feed families.

Obadiah and Mary Sue found themselves propped on their elbows without a word as Katherine continued on. *"First it was the bank, Hirsch reduced his hours very rapidly and within a few months, he had simply boarded up and fled,"* Katherine spoke about how the greedy little Jew, made good on his self-prophecy and left town, leaving many of the towns folk without the money he owed them, he swindled many people whom shortly after the financial hardships choked Indian Gulch, stormed the bank and went near lynch mob for the short statured sour faced man.

Katherine spoke about one of the heartbreaking groups of drifters that had pulled a scam on them, a family of Armenians had wandered in, there was a family of five, the three kids were tan, dirty and smelled; "a*s most Armenians did*" the father ordered three sandwiches of bread with butter on them, all cut into quarters, as Murray prepared the food behind the counter, the three daughters pillaged everything they could, maliciously. The swindling family of gypsy scum had pilfered jars, salt and pepper shakers, silverware, cups, two of the chubby little beasts had climbed under the counter so when Murray turned around to hand the food over, they were still swiping everything within reach.

The mother fumbled in her handbag when Katherine was ringing up the sale at the register, just long enough for one of the girls to take the last lamb quarter and a loaf of bread and as they began backtracking, Katherine caught on to what was going on. With a startled yelp to Murray, the father gave the orders to scurry, the mother of the gypsies shoved the register at Katherine, with extreme disregard to her well-being, the father also caused ruckus as he threw the bread and butter sandwiches into the face of Murray and then flipped over the nearest table to prevent the Ponsen's from following them out the door. When that encounter was over, it reassured that every Armenian was a scandalous, untrustworthy, smelling bunch of grossly obese and unintelligent people, these just showed that they also lacked any form of sympathy or compassion and robbed from a couple that was already giving them some help, showing just how ruthless and inhumane they were, like rabid animals.

Indian Gulch had slowly bled citizens as finances dried up, and the previous years' harvest wasn't of note, Murray kept a vigilant eye on his store and strangers that passed by the front door got a stern look to warn them not to enter and waste anyone's time. Murray kept a stern posture as he continued to flip pages, Katherine continued on, there would often be gaggles of people simply moseying down the road and into town, it was hard to figure out where so many of them had straggled from, their origin was unknown and their destination was just as mysterious. Some of the wanderers would stop in for a few slices of bread, Murray would charge them two cents each or three for a nickel, it wasn't much but often times the strangers would take some wrapped in butchers paper and simply breeze back out, probably to fill the bread with who knows what from along their journey. Katherine and Murray had struggled to keep their deli open for the fellow citizens, even when there was no money, the still tried their best keep the coffee warm for the morning residents, even as they waned. As the coffee club disbanded and it often left Katherine and Murray to take up seats and just simply watch the time pass by.

The well to do doctor Joseph Martinez had taken to his good nature, he had simply given up on billing when his office had become packed with the homeless travelers, all seeking treatment for any number of ailments from their travels or the weather. Joseph had seen a grand number of people with blisters, sores, dehydration or malnutrition problems, all whom wandered in, sought treatment and continued on. Joseph did his best to treat those who needed him the most and remained humble in the knowledge that he was able to help so many.

Joseph and his wife had forgone many of the privileges that a doctors' family should enjoy, they saw this time as a type of missionary to help, as if they had traveled to a third world to help the poor or hungry for humanitarian efforts and not to profit from the misfortune of others like so many other doctors. There were a few hard pressed business owners in Indian Gulch that didn't want to walk away from their lives, they fought to build a lasting future and like the Ponsen's, the Martinez's weren't going to pack up and blow out of town, they were certain that this town was where they were meant to reside, and reside they were going to. Katherine

162

spoke about how most mornings Joseph and Leslie would come in for coffee, it was often just them but it was at least consistent, a slight glint at normalcy when everything else was going chaotic in the country during this depression.

The uptight and snobby Mrs. Curtiss was struggling to keep up precedents; she still strutted around in silk fashions but her morning coffee meetings had reduced to once a week at best. Katherine had gotten to know the pretentious old bird, she had lost a husband whom was an oiler, he passed when they were in their thirties, his wealth had amassed and she used it to lord over those in town that couldn't afford what she could. Pauline wasn't always the most sociable, she kept a strong arm to any form of bond or friendship but after a few years of sipping Katherine's coffee, she made some headway getting to know the old bird. Pauline had traveled with her husband, he invested in oil wells in Texas and the proximity to his investments made Oklahoma somewhat ideal. She mostly enjoyed the luxuries of New York and California, she was aging and growing lonelier as her closest companions in town were leaving, like the Mohs.

Pauline had slowly bled her accounts, the crook Hirsch had really put her in a bind as she only had the money stashed in her home and no longer could access her larger bank accounts. She was hard up not able to get new clothing or drive out to shop fashions or things for her home, she once again had to budget and live off of mediocre means, not something she had ever imagined having to do again. Pauline often growled her contempt at the way the country was being run, her life had changed from her lavish styles and tastes and she was displeased.

Katherine expressed that Pauline was still a judgmental and unrelenting harpy but now being in her graces and serving her coffee, Katherine had taken favor from the lady. Johnson Franks, the man whom ran and owned the gas station at the end of town, he had had a tough time dealing as well, he fought to remain open to sell gas and assorted items. Johnson had given up his small home and took to living out of the gas station; it was hard to keep the lights on in two places. Johnson often found hoards of people trying to steal his gasoline when he was out of sight; he remained armed with a revolver as if it was once again the old west.

The thin old Franks was hyper vigilant about his store, most of the tobacco he stocked he chewed, fuel was his biggest commodity but keeping his tanks full was hard to do as it was overhead money simply sitting in tanks underground. Johnson sold many Marlboros and Lucky Strike cigarettes and not much else, the few remaining businesses were fighting to remain open while hundreds of people poured in looking for handouts and freebies. Katherine had a worn look in her eyes as she peered out the main window, random people sauntered passed and so many of them looked depleted of life and will.

Joseph had walked in the door, he was still dressed well but not as dapper as he had the previous two years, his dress shirt wasn't as neatly pressed, his gray suit pants had dirt on the legs and the lowest parts of pant-legs were starting to unravel and wearing thin. Joseph also looked tired, he struggled to smile as his nature was of caring and helpful but the past several months had been especially tough on him. With admirable posture and classy manners, the reverent doctor greeted each member of the deli by name, he was certainly glad to see the Withers; it was a very nice surprise and impromptu visit. Joseph asked Murray for a few salami sandwiches then made his way to the table in which the Withers were perched, his gate was slowed and his once black wingtips scuffled a bit on the floor, they had dirt in the crevices and eyelets of the leather.

Joseph extended his arms to Isaac and looked into his eyes, as Isaac sat on the hip of the doctor, he looked unsure about the tan, man with thin eyebrows and glasses perched on his nose. Isaac was unsure about the man but he had a soothing voice as he gave the toddler a once over to double check his health as a favor to the parents and to ensure the boys well-being. Joseph handed the wee lad back to his parents and congratulated them on his health, since the dirt storm, there had been a major increase of dirt induced pneumonia, silicosis and travelers arrived hacking and coughing from the fine airborne silt that kicked up on their travels and into the airways.

Joseph ate for a few moments and shared stories he had heard from travelers, many had taken to riding the rails and after certain periods of time, people would dismount the iron horses and search for work or food. There was a young man whom showed up at his clinic the other day, what a heart breaking story. A young boy named Carl Niks, was nine years old, and showed up with a broken arm. Carl showed up alone, he had run away because he was worried his parents couldn't afford to keep him and he didn't want to be a burden any longer. Carl had been pushed from a train as an older boy wanted his can of soup and place in the train car, the boy said he held tightly to the side rail to keep from falling under the train when the older boy kicked him in the side so hard he could no longer hold on, and let go.

The boy suffered a large deep purple bruise on his left ribcage and a broken left elbow; the doctor offered the boy a sandwich and water and wished he could do more. The boy only showed up because there was a post near the tracks that he came across, the sign had a few marks on it, Carl said he couldn't read but he remembered a few of the symbols and one of them meant there was bread available in the town and he headed that way. Carl traveled for two days, just simply falling asleep near a tree at night, even listening to a wolf howl one night, he expressed that he was scared but that he would be tough enough to find work to help out his folks.

Joseph continued on; "*I asked the boy if he was scared of the wolf, of almost dying falling from the train,*" Carl responded that each morning he woke up and could only think about eating, each day was spent in search of food or work and each night brought the attempt to sleep, death wasn't scary, it meant not having to be hungry anymore. Carl had a morbid outlook but Joseph was unfazed, the sense that hunger was to overwhelming to be taken lightly and even many adults would cast aside the moral rights in the face of starvation. Mary Sue fought to keep her mouth closed, she held Isaac tightly as she couldn't help but to imagine Isaac fleeing home much like that little boy.

It was a frightening reality that things in the country were getting so glum, any sense of future or hope set with the sun each day and for some, it didn't rise again. The radio had spoken about Hooverville's, Katherine and Joseph exchanged light conversation about having heard about the makeshift cardboard hobo style homes of blanket tents that now housed thousands on the coasts where the hope of work was the gospel of urban myth. Katherine had heard from a wanderer that Washington had accumulated a large gathering of homeless people, all demanding rights and work for their families, the police in Washington had fought to keep people in the Hooverville's from getting out of hand with rallies and protests, many people got arrested but many who were arrested were at least given a meal, so many people protested over and over again.

Obadiah sat perched over his cooling coffee and listened, as people moseyed along the boardwalk or just simply sat along the walkway, each held a story and the need to survive, it was saddening that so many people had been uprooted and displaced, left to the wind to blow over this great country. The storm had blown dirt all over, news reports had commented that dark skies and dirty clouds had left dirt from the mid-west strewn all over the east coast, there were reports of both Virginia and Florida getting silt blown in. The storms held a ferocious power that hadn't simply localized in the Oklahoma area but barreled in from the mountains and charged the plains like a military assault. It was just so overwhelming to contemplate how bad thing were quickly getting, harvests were drying up, people were migrating and desperately leaving behind their homes, anything in an attempt to survive another day. Obadiah felt a lump in his throat, his mind flashed back to Mickey, the stout Negro that he fought with and killed with his bare hands.

Obadiah had felt bad already for what had happened and now he felt even worse, the displaced man may have traveled from wherever and whatever his final destination may have been, will no never be. Obadiah recalled that Mickey had made sexual advances towards Elizabeth, even as the father confronted the stranger, the stranger tried to barter for time to spend with the little girl, it was appalling that the stranger only had one thing on his mind, he must have been akin to the older boy that kicked young Carl from the train, just purely an animal and the world was probably better off without him. It was shameful that as people age, many men don't outgrow the most basic sexual urges, they attempt to lay with anything they can find, their intelligence doesn't overtake their Neanderthal portion of the brain, the one that causes hard-on's and not much else.

Obadiah and Mary Sue flashed back over some of the faces that they had passed on their way through town, men, woman, children, elderly, many people that had just stopped off in Indian Gulch and each with dwindling assets. Mickey had a baseball card and the clothes on his back when he died, Obadiah had no idea if the man left behind a family, and probably parents but maybe a wife and kids, maybe he set out to search for work and maybe with the promise that he would send money back to support them. Obadiah felt sincerely sick and he could feel himself grow pale with each thought. Joseph took notice and ensured that the man was feeling well, Obadiah skirted the question and just mentioned that he was well and fought to focus on the cup of coffee in front of him. It was hard not to imagine everything that had taken place in the few days since the storm, burying the Basks, Rupert and his face full of sand and probably having died with lungs full of dirt and the struggle he must have endured. Obadiah's mind kept darting back to shoveling over Mickey, the still body lying in a shallow grave kept the lump present in his throat.

Joseph stood and bowed his head to the Withers, before parting back to his clinic with lunch for himself and his wife, before exiting the door, he waved a two finger salute to Murray and a smile back to the table where Katherine was entertaining the Withers. Katherine spoke of a few more instances that reassured that things really were that hard in the area, the Asian launderers had closed up shop some time ago and moved along, as so many others had. The news that broad-casted over the phonograph told tales of the government failing over and over again to bring relief to the people of the land.

The dry regions of the country had already had stressed food supplies, cattle herds began to dry out, in the southwest, the uprooting and destruction of crops with the wind storms was certain to further crimp the economy. With simple sandwiches and a new perspective of how things were carrying on, the Withers began to gather themselves and make another trip to the grocery store. Katherine stood out of courtesy when Obadiah and Mary Sue stood to head their way out the door, Murray hardly shifted his weight when he glanced at the parting family, he snickered a bit in time with a half attempted wink and that was the extent of the quiet man.

Obadiah and Mary Sue escorted their children back to their filthy Dodge, the streets still kicked up dirt as they shuffled along, and Elizabeth stomped into the dirt with each step to leave behind her footprint. The family headed to the grocery store at the end of the street, across from Johnsons' gas station, there were people sitting along the boardwalk lining the streets, Obadiah felt uneasy about trying to park as people hardly bothered to move out of the way for the vehicle to be able to park right in front. Obadiah parked at the edge of the row, he grumbled a touch about having to walk such a distance through the beggars while towing purchased goods. Mary Sue wanted to load up on flour especially, the chickens would still put out eggs to make biscuits with and now with goats at the farm, there was the better availability of meat.

Obadiah wanted to purchase plenty of salt to cure meat with on his own back at the farm, he figured that once he slaughtered a goat he could cure it and ensure that the meat would last a very long time if necessary. On the way in to the store there were two young girls standing out front, they weren't much older than Elizabeth, they were wearing worn out shoes, all that seemed left was a bit of the leather for the soul and their toes sticking out, there may have been socks under the dirt but you really couldn't tell as their feet were so filthy.

Elizabeth walked over to the two girls and introduced herself, the girls told her that their names were Elsie and Frances Holmes, their father was a police officer from Detroit but they were moving to their mothers' sister in Arizona, means wore thin by Oklahoma, their gas tank and food resources had run dry, their mother told them to beg for any sort of edible stuffs while she bartered for fuel across the street, the girls looked absolutely pathetic, their hair hadn't been washed in who knows how long and it was in different forms of matted, it looked like a rats nest. Their dresses were tattered on the bottoms and ripping to ribbons, their legs were bruised, dirty and it was apparent they had been sleeping in the car or on the ground for weeks; their eyes sunken in and the dark circles underneath gave them an almost dead look to them.

The girls sat against the wall of the grocery store and waited for anyone to walk past, asking for change or morsels to snack on, and any few calories that may fend off the hunger pains of starvation. Mary Sue gasped at the sight of the two girls, her heart just sank and Obadiah immediately sensed that she wanted ever so desperately to help in any way. The family walked into the grocery store, many of the shelves were empty or thinly stocked, the resources were diminishing and the man standing near the entry door kept a watchful eye as the family walked in.

Obadiah nodded to greet the man standing guard, the man welcomed them, he was a medium built man, his hair had grayed and was covering with silver, he stood with poor posture as he continued to survey the aisles, the man told the Withers to enjoy their shopping experience and encouraged them to ask if there were any questions or if they needed any assistance. Obadiah and Mary Sue placed Isaac into a shopping cart basket so they could mosey up and down and load up whatever they could find from their list of needs and part ways with the stores. Obadiah and Mary Sue tried to fill up on curing salts, sugars, canned goods and finally to the flour, Mary Sue found the sacks of flour and wasn't sure what she was seeing, the sacks were usually brown and plain, these were flowery in pattern and she found herself suspicious of what had changed or why. Flour had a decent shelf life so they loaded up almost a dozen large bags, the bags had flowers on them and Mary Sue found them cute as could be.

The Withers headed to the register, the lady was filing her nails to pass the time, there was no sign of the younger stock boy from previous visits, it was just the middle aged register lady and the man nearest the door, it was strange that things were so empty but it was a sign of the times. Mary Sue exchanged pleasantries with the lady, she was looking over the top of her eyeglasses, the lady wore a peach colored top under a maroon smock, and the lady was pleasant but let out a big huff as she rang up each item in the basket. Mary Sue tried to make small talk with the lady, her curiosity was boundless about things from this end of town. The lady explained that the man at the door was her husband, the owner, he had to remain vigilant as he was often looted of things from passersby. The woman spoke of multiple situations in which adults would send their children into the store to pillage while they pretended to browse, there were so many times that the man would do inventory and find hundreds of dollars' worth of goods missing at the end of each month, with each loss of money, there was less that could be ordered for replacement, less that could be paid out to employees, less to even keep employees, the husband and wife now ran the store themselves just simply to keep the doors open.

The lady at the counter finally got to answering Mary Sues' final inquisition, the flour sacks, each sack was patterned differently; some with flowers, some with swirls, each had different main colors and some faded colors with shapes on them. The flour companies had learned a year or so ago that when things became desperate for families, the company had learned that many people were purchasing the flour to feed themselves, then fixing the fabric into clothing for young children, the flour sacks that were originally brown, had taken on color and patterns for the sake of making the clothing much more fun, exponentially easing the transition into almost poverty for millions of children.

The gesture the flour company took upon themselves to help their countrymen ease the burden of hardships, was almost to kind to bare, Mary Sue began to get teary eyed at the thought that giant business tycoons somewhere, actually thought of the little people that made the majority of the population, the compassion had touched her heart and she struggled her best to maintain her composure. The Withers began to head to their motor vehicle, Mary Sue grabbed one of the jars of canned peaches and handed it to the girls for a lunch, she didn't have much in the means of things she could offer but she felt relieved being able to do something, not just pray to clear her conscience, but actually do something.

The Withers headed across the street to top off the fuel tanks, it took a few moments to cross as people just meandered around and failed to politely get out of the street for traveling cars. The fuel depot was almost empty, there was Mercury sitting nearest the forward pump so Obadiah parked at the rear pump and made his way out of the vehicle and headed into the station office to check in on Johnson Franks and pay for gasoline before he pumped. There was no sign of the driver of the Mercury, it may have just been abandoned, left to sit in the parking lot, the top of the Mercury had a roughly packed luggage rack, there were suitcases crudely tied and the black paint had been dirtied and rusted near the fender wells, there were mounds of dirt along the back bumper and near the taillights, juts a filthy car and it was hard to tell if it had sat through the dirt storm or had traveled from a great distance.

Obadiah pulled on the door to enter the gas station, the owner Johnson was out of view, no sign of the man in sight and it was concerning, especially as vigilant as all of the other shop owners had to have been over their facilities. Obadiah heard a heavy breathing coming from the back room and immediately, his heart raced, there was a worry that the man may have been injured or suffered a heart attack, it struck the patron and his pace took him to the back room to assist the shop owner.

Obadiah peered into the back stock room of the gas station; as soon as he cleared the door he promptly realized the error of his ways. Johnson was standing tall against the side counter, on the counter sat a nude woman with her arms around his neck and her legs around his waist. Johnson's pants were around his ankles on the ground and his buttocks flexed and relaxed as he humped away at the lady and didn't break concentration on what he was doing. The woman had a dirty face, her hair was short, dirty blonde and

170

her face wasn't one of pleasure as she winced, she looked as if just focusing on keeping eyes closed as her breasts were small, looked deflated and bounced unevenly as Johnson shook the counter top while he worked.

Obadiah didn't mean to look long and with a two second glance, the images gave more than enough time to gather a full view of the man and woman in the buff. The woman had bruised legs, her feet were crusted with dirt and left dirty streaks on the lower back of Johnson, her legs locked ankles behind him and she pushed his head towards her sternum as she arched her lower back and heaved her chest towards the hard heaving man. Johnson grunted and huffed as he worked hard at the lady, she was thinner than he was and between the two bodies, there wasn't a rib bone that couldn't be counted, his frail legs showed his flexing muscles above his knee as he worked and her hip bones still jut out even being semi seated.

Johnson strained as he climaxed, Obadiah spun around to back into the main portion of the gas station to avoid the awkwardness, he gave them a minute to finish their hanky-panky and then headed back to knock near the back room after a short minute to get the help of the man whom was short of breath now. Obadiah cleared his throat to announce his arrival, Johnson was bending over to retrieve his pants from the floor, Obadiah saw a bit more of the old man than he had anticipated and quickly averted his eyes from the wrinkled pale posterior of Johnson. The woman stood firmly, she didn't shy away when the strange man gazed at her nude body, she brushed a bit of dirt off from her leg near her pubis, the woman spoke before Johnson had finished picking up his overalls. The woman looked right at Obadiah when she spoke; she had a dress on the counter behind her and didn't bother to reach for it to cover herself, "*would you like a turn? I need the money for my family, we're heading to Arizona and we, I really need the money.*"

Obadiah was amazed, the shock made his eyes open but his vision had blanked and gone white as he felt his blood drain from his face for a moment. The woman took two more steps towards the man that had just entered the back store room, the man that had just climbed off of her was buttoning his filthy shirt and fumbling his shaky hands to button the clasps of his overalls, and his eyes hung low and refused to make eye contact with Obadiah. The woman used her right hand to caress her breast to attempt to entice the stranger, her left hand rubbed her flat stomach and poked at her bellybutton, she was trying to slowly walk towards Obadiah, she greeted herself; "I'm Cadence, what's your name?'

Obadiah was frozen for a moment; his vision was blank for a moment until suddenly he realized he was staring at the body of a naked strange woman, now only two steps from him. Panic struck, his hands trembled and Obadiah instantly began sweating profusely as he realized this woman was almost on him, Johnson walked past the man and newly met woman on his way to the front of the gas station, he didn't say a word. The woman took a wide stance, she waited for Obadiah to reach forward to touch her, she stood tall to raise her head to look upward, hoping to feel his touch and hoping that it would go quickly and be over in a moment. Obadiah began to back up, his nerves made him fumble and his feet hardly worked, he attempted to speak to excuse himself but as his temples pulsed and pounded, he tried to reach behind him with his right hand for the door handle to guide him out backwards, almost tripping.

The woman stood with her head pointed upwards, her arms were straight down by her sides as she waited for the strange man to take her, to use her, to pay her some gas money in exchange for time with her flesh. The woman sniffled, her sense of self had been demolished, she was willing to once again trade time with her body to ensure that she got herself to Arizona, Obadiah looked past her dirty body, above her small chest that inflated causing her breasts to rise, her neck was full of veins and tendons poking out through her thin skin, he looked at her face.

Obadiah could see tears begin to stream from her eyes, they were subtle but still left trails through the dirt on her face as they made their way towards her ears, and she stood there waiting whatever might happen. Obadiah finally found enough of a gasp of air to make his vocal chords work; "no ma'am, I am married and even if I wasn't, this ain't right" Obadiah spoke to the woman, the break in the silence gave her a bit of a shake as she whipped her head around to look at him. The woman tucker her hair behind her ears and a small bit from the front refused to stay put, her green eyes held a lot of pain and sadness as they locked on the man passing up exclusive intimate time with her, she desperately needed the gas money.

The woman caught Obadiah before he had completely escaped from the room, "*why not? You'd be doing me a favor and getting one in return, I don't like to beg and if I can do something for work or money, I'd do it, whatever it might be"* Obadiah tried to avert his eyes as the woman dropped her dress to the ground and began to step into it, *"you can look, I don't mind, its more personal to look at a girl when she talks to you"* the woman told Obadiah as she slowly pulled her dress up over her hips. The woman wiggled side to side to get her dirty yellow dress with black swoops on it over each thigh and hip, as the woman wriggled her belly button stretched on her flat stomach that sat just above her raised hip bones.

The woman pulled the dress up as Obadiah responded as respectfully as possible; *"it's not that you aren't attractive miss, it's that I'm married and you just climbed out from under a man not three minutes ago"* the woman paused as the dress was getting hung up around her rib cage, her thin shoulder wedged into the dress one at a time. The ladies green eyes watched Obadiah as she slowly slipped further into the dress, she watched for any sign that he might take her up on her offer to mate with her, she hoped he would flinch or reach out as she slowly used her left hand to grope her right breast enticingly tucking it back into her dress. Obadiah felt like the first time he saw his wife naked, his pulse coursed through his body with might while his hands shook, his knees shook even more.

Obadiah felt guilty, he was torn between his lustful male desires to eye the body of the nude woman, his urges as a male forced him to keep an eye on her for a moment but after several seconds of pause, his character still forced him to look away. The lady asked Obadiah to look at her as she dressed and Obadiah was now conflicted, to respect the woman he felt he should keep eye contact as she spoke but above all, he respected his wife so he peered up and to the left as to give false security that he was looking, while he looked at the corner of the room instead. The woman made one last attempt to sell herself, now with her opposite hand she handled her other breast and as she held it she asked one last time if he was certain, Obadiah escaped through the door before having to answer verbally, his exit was enough.

Obadiah glanced quickly to meet Johnsons' look at the register, Obadiah handed money to the man with the bristly facial hair covering his mouth, his eyebrows arched down around the corners just above his eye sockets, the man began to stammer out words to his customer, " I uh uh uh um um mmmmm" and then he gave up and just let out a long sigh. Obadiah assured the man that it wasn't his place to judge and "*I tried to get out as soon as I could.*" Johnson explained that she was desperate to get herself and daughters to Arizona and didn't have no money, Obadiah gave Johnson his money for fuel and they headed out towards the vehicles. Walking between the building and gas pump, Obadiah apologized for the interruption and appreciated the assistance from the worn and weary man, whom half hobbled from having tired legs.

Johnson pumped gas up into the clear cylinder that topped the pump, you had to measure up what you needed and then let gravity feed it down the hose and into to tanks. Obadiah took turns looking between Johnson and the door of the gas station, waiting for the lady to exit right behind them, she never did. As the gas emptied into the tanks, Johnson caught Obadiah's' searching eyes and offered up an answer, "*she hasn't earned a full tank yet, she wanted another go around but wanted to see if she could get a dollar or two from you.*" Obadiah could only respond with a wide eyed look and quickly tried to wipe his forehead with his arm to attempt to hide his unraveled nerves.

The trunk was loaded with the full gas cans and the back seat held most of the flour from the grocery store. There wasn't much money left from the pillaged Basks home but they had enough to supply themselves for a decent while if necessary. Obadiah shook the man's hand in thanks and let him return to the scantily clad woman residing in the back store room of his shop. Mary Sue had hardly noticed his delayed return as she was playing with the children in the back along with setting some of the groceries so they won't slide or shift while driving home.

Obadiah tried to control his breathing after the strange encounter, he smiled at Mary Sue and started up the engine then proceeded to make his way back through town, Mary Sue didn't seem the wiser to anything but her husband didn't want to wait but a moment to tell her everything, his guilt tore up his stomach. Obadiah fought off his nerves, the corners of his eyes felt clouded as he drove and he wanted out from under his guilt immediately. Obadiah spent the whole drive back home navigating the ruts in the road, the bumps risked breaking jars or spilling flour in the back and Mary Sue made her best attempts to keep things orderly. Obadiah's' conscience wore heavy, the last few days had been an upset to all that he knew, things weren't as simple and serene as they were, the exposure to how things were in town was a small sample of the large scale of just how the country was, Obadiah surely didn't want to think about the woman that just stood in her birthday suit in front of him in the shop, her body was worn and tired but her form was still ideal and very attractive, but in conjunction with his mind thinking about her breasts and thick pubic hair, the vision of Johnsons naked and wrinkled bottom flashed across his mind, unevenly strewn with tan lines at his waist.

The Withers had arrived, the road towards their home was without travelers, it was comforting that all was tranquil and unperturbed, they pulled in to the driveway near the front porch and the rambunctious children were weary from the car travel and more than ready to stretch their legs. The children exited in a hurry, Elizabeth helping Isaac to slide down the seat and jump cautiously from the side of the car and into a puff of dirt as he landed and off they ran. Mary Sue felt something had been burdening her husband but also knew that with the food supplies waning, the stresses increasing and above all, the hard tasks of having discovered and then bury the neighbors, she knew her husband had hardships but she knew deep down that he was strong enough to handle everything that life could throw at him and that they would be each other's' sides through it. After hauling all of the flour bags indoors and piling them in the kitchen, Obadiah sat down while Mary Sue began to prepare things for the family supper. Obadiah wasn't all that hungry yet but he knew that Mary Sue knew what she was doing and a good meal took better than an hour, sometimes two.

Obadiah set the kettle for a cup of coffee, Mary Sue found a cup this late in the afternoon odd so she opened the conversational door by asking if all was well. "Honey I need to tell you some things," Obadiah lead with a heavy opener, Mary Sue wasn't always the easiest to confide in and her often quick reactions made him feel guilty opening up to her sometimes and her excessive worry made it harder to tell her things. Obadiah took a deep breath and lead with the lesser of his burdens.

"So you won't guess what I walked in on at Johnsons" he remarked, Mary Sue didn't divert from her tasks as she began preparing to make some thin noodles for the family supper. Mary Sue didn't budge as her husband told her about walking in and hearing the grunting, assuming that maybe Johnson had had a heart attack, Mary Sue turned an eye on Obadiah in anticipation for him to continue, she had seen Johnson come out so a heart attack wasn't the surprise. "You know them girls whose mother told them to beg at the grocery store?" Mary Sue raised her eyebrows as the change in topic had confused her for a moment, before she figured out what her husband had stumbled on, he quickly followed up with "sex, the ole' bloke had that girl pinned up on a counter in the back., Mary Sue cracked a wild smile at the inkling that there was coitus, she had been without the touch of her husband for some time and was feeling her needs for intimacy herself. It wasn't polite to talk about the lives of others but to think of old Franks heaving and hoeing back and forth made for a funny mental picture in her mind.

Mary Sue asked a multitude of descriptive questions about what was discovered, Obe described the position of the lovers, her embrace and his thrusting into her, Mary Sue felt her blood heat at the steamy details that her husband explained to her, Obadiah felt guilty and expressed his remorse at having lingered at his glance upon her, she ensured him that he absolutely hadn't touched her nor encouraged her to participate in anything, Obadiah unburdened his guilt to his wife and she smirked a bit at his worry. "What takes place in that head of yours?" Obadiah prodded his wife for information trying to understand, she found it humorous that he was such a good man to her and yet, he still doubted himself, she had no reason to feel betrayed and in such a fact, she was partially tempted to thank the woman for giving her husband some mental fodder to titillate himself with next time he was with his wife, it was a win for the couple from her perspective, she was unsure if she liked her husband imagining another woman while they shared their bed but Mary Sue saw the accident as a bit of a gift for her husband and with the vision of the other naked woman fresh in his mind, maybe it would make their passion that much more wild next chance they got.

Obadiah continued to speak, he spoke about how troubled he was about when he went to retrieve the goats from the Basks farm, Mary Sue didn't understand why wrangling a bunch of smelly and stubborn goats would have troubled her adoring husband so much. Obadiah worked so hard to fend for his family and sometimes Mary Sue wondered if she was doing enough to take care of him. Obadiah lead into going into the house to search for money or goods that no longer benefited the late couple, he felt a tinge of guilt for stealing but his family was alive and he was responsible for keeping them that way. Mary Sue found herself growing uncomfortable as Obadiah told her about the dark skinned man standing beside their daughter when he exited the home and went to join her, and his panic as he stepped onto the porch on his way to the pen and watched the man, whom was much larger than the little lass, put his hand on her shoulder and rub her back. Obadiah explained that he saw red, his pulse didn't even race, his veins just ran hot as he charged at the negro to defend Elizabeth. Mary Sue sat across from her husband and encouraged him to keep talking.

Obadiah told his wife that as he neared the man, the man tried to bargain with him for some time with Elizabeth, much like the woman tried to barter with Obadiah in the store room of the gas station. Mary Sue clenched her eyebrows as she stared at Obadiah awaiting the resolve of the situation, Obadiah continued to hang his head as he spoke, his voice quivered and cracked. Mary Sue took the nonverbal cues that things didn't simply end with a stern warning. Obadiah explained that the men began to brawl, the squabble broke out and as the men fell, the other man continued to express sexual interest in the daughter which caused Obadiah to fight violently with little reserve. Obadiah explained that by the time he heard his daughter crying, the man lay limp on the ground, the man sat at the end of his clenched fist, lifeless. As Obadiah detailed his hand grasping the throat of the man and having ceased its ability to pass air through it and into his lungs to keep him alive, Mary Sue realized that her husband had killed a man.

Mary Sue tried not to be startled and suddenly she looked at her husband in a strange new way, he suddenly wasn't just the kind caring man that she knew, he changed from the man she fell in love with and adored for years, she birthed two of his children and suddenly, he found himself in a life or death situation and although he came out on top, he was now a murderer. Mary Sue was overcome with emotion, Obadiah was upset and as he finally admitted to what he had done, he felt a slight relief to his guilt but was also ashamed to finally admit what had happened. It suddenly became real. Obadiah had planned to take his secret to his grave, he didn't want to morph from what his wife saw him as, to the last thing she ever thought he could become.

Mary Sue held the hands of her husband, she didn't know what to make of it and she was terrified of what the future might hold for them. Obadiah just focused on the table in front of him, his hands shook and it felt like forever as he sat perched over an empty coffee cup. Obadiah was terribly concerned about what his wife now saw her husband as, he suddenly realized that he was holding his hands, the laughter of his children appeared in his ears and he realized that Mary Sue wasn't crying, she looked concerned but she was shushing him in a soothing way, trying to reassure the concerned man that she was to remain by his side as she vowed, for better or worse.

Obadiah felt an overwhelming sense of relief lighten his heart. A smile broke over the man and despite his reserve in telling his wife, she took it surprisingly well. The following conversation was even stranger, he explained why he felt he couldn't tell her and that her expectations of him often made it a tough struggle to simply talk about things. Mary Sue did her best to reserve her emotions and not feel offended by the comment and promised to do her best to be more receptive to him and his needs emotionally. The couple discovered a wonderful new found sense of maturity in their relationship, Mary Sue had no idea if Obadiah would be able to shake the notion that he took a strangers life, but she did her best to repeat that he did it to save and protect their daughter as a good father is supposed to.

Obadiah took the advice and different perspective of his wife, he had a hard time blocking out the lifeless face of Mickey but for her sake he would certainly try and continue to carry on, for the sake of his family. Obadiah was relieved about the stance of his wife, he was fortunate to have his two children and their farm which still held some potential to one day proffer fertile crops, also, his renewed visions breathed some life back into some of his dreams and it gave him a new outlook. Mary Sue finished on with her supper preparation and Obadiah headed out to watch his children play in the yard.

Obadiah gazed out and took stock of what lay out before him, the dry fields were barren, infertile and without seed. It would be a long year and unable to produce any form of crop or profit but maybe next spring might bring rain in the New Year. There was still plenty of hope in the dirt filled glass jars that perched on the windowsill, Mary Sue had a stroke of genius to start her garden plants indoors and once they were hearty enough to thrive in the less than ideal environment, they would be planted and hopefully take strong enough hold to bare food and provide for the family. Things still wavered as spring gave way to a hot and dry summer;

there had been weak storms that blew dust and dirt but never rain. The garden struggled but as Mary Sue and Obadiah kept watchful eye and plenty of water from the well, the plants survived.

Times continued to grow bleak as the days wore on, the trips to town grew farther apart as 1932 ticked by, the severity of storms were of mixed variety, there were two more large storms that buried a large part of the country in reddish silt and fine dirt that blew in from every crack in walls or spots near windows that weren't as sealed as they should have been. Mary Sue attempted to hang cloth near open parts of the window to act as a filter for the dirt so they could have some fresh air as storms whipped and thundered across the vast open plains before they further barreled east. Newscasts continued to echo from the phonograph, more and more people had taken to riding the railways, hitching onto the moving beasts to travel to potential areas of work or the promise of work, more and more businesses faltered and failed.

American citizens were waking up each day to find themselves out of work, their savings gone and their local banks going Morgenstern and fleeing with whatever funds they could steal from their customers. The Withers avoided the Basks farm as best they could, Elizabeth never brought up the fight that she watched her daddy in, Obadiah was the one who bore most of the guilt and he fought, struggled, and usually pushed down the strain that came from the knowledge and memories that came from taking the life of the stranger that attempted to make inappropriate advances towards Elizabeth, Obadiah knew that he didn't take the law into his own hands, just maybe justice.

The year brought more turmoil than benefit, Isaac had grown and become much more independent in his mischief, he liked to tussle with the goats, he liked to entice them to come near with grasses or weeds to eat and when they were near, he would yank on their horns, thus giving them cause to shake their heads and get worked up and jump around or butt heads with other goats, leading Isaac to laugh in such a giddy way that you could hear the hysterical belly laughing back at the home.

Isaac was growing further into a comical character, he had no awareness of the hard times, Elizabeth took notice of some of the makeshift patching to her dresses or that as she grew, and most of her dresses were tailored to fit rather than simply replaced. Mary Sue kept tedious care when cooking, she felt the pressures mount as the year went along, the availability to hunt rabbits of birds became nil for Obadiah, it was difficult to put fresh meat on the table all that often and anytime Obadiah slaughtered one of the goats, the blood would be drained to the garden so the nutrients would further fertilize the ground. The goat quarters were salted and cured in the late fall, the heavy salt was packed onto the meat then it was wrapped in cloth, the thickness of the salt along with the cooling temperatures kept off the potential bacteria that would be cause for the meat to rot and spoil, the salt penetrated the meat and in turn preserved it well enough to shave off hunks during the winter so the children had plenty to eat. The winter turned cold. The snow was enough to blow and drift but not enough pile up against everything everywhere and makes life difficult; it certainly didn't replenish the drought ridden land of the needed hydration.

1932 had ushered in more storms, the blowing wind and pelting dirt, each storm brought more struggle, despair and even death. The radio broadcast always sounded off each evening with "maybe it might rain, tomorrow" it was disheartening and robbed each tomorrow of hope for rain. Obadiah passed on the planting crops, the dry winter preceded a dry spring, with the dirt becoming more and more arid, depleting the ground of its' potential to sustain plant life, trees struggled to come back to life after the winter stagnation. The heartiest of prairie grasses didn't seem to find the life to fully come back, the grasses that lined the ditches filled with sand, the grasses filtered dirt from the air and left dirt piles at the bases to kill off new growth underneath. The sand and fine dirt choked off plant growth, there were blowing winds that carried dirt as far north as Maryland according to weather reports, one such winter storm had taken dirt form the plains, mixed it with moisture from the gulf and blanketed the eastern seaboard with a red mud rather than the white snow that it should have been.

One Wednesday in early March, the family was hungry and the meat was running thin so Obadiah packed a burlap satchel, his rifle and adequate clothing to go hunting, he kissed his wife and planned to head out for a day of hunting, he planned to walk down the road and try kicking up game along some of the field edges where some weeds were still holding root. The walk took almost two hours of kicking at weed pockets, points where the plants had bent over crating a hiding place underneath for rabbits or squirrels, each step was slow as Obadiah had to sweep his foot at each place hoping to spook up any form of dinner, the game numbers were as thin as the rain, the lack of fresh vegetation made it just as hard for the wild animals to survive as the people of the country.

Each time a kick to an air pocket in grasses that came up empty, seemed to take more hope from Obadiah, he had watched his wife grow thin, he fought to barely nibble at his meals to ensure that his family had enough; the children needed plenty of food to grow. The family was eating a form of wheat three times a day, the dried or canned vegetables were rationed, the meagerly stocked cans of various fruits, diced pears or peaches from the south-east that had been purchased from the grocery store, were doled out sparingly as desert with dinner, Mary Sue often stared puzzled at her pantry as she mentally figured how to prepare a meal that wasn't much better than flour and water, heated and served. The morning biscuits that the woman of the home made, often had grated remains of the previous night's fruit desserts, the bits of fruit made the hard biscuits easier to palate, despite being bland, the flour cakes mixed with an egg and diced fruit bits still eased the hunger pains after a night of fasting.

There had been talk of coming elections, there were often broadcasts about political parties, each fighting or squabbling about whom would better serve the struggling country, which would be able to turn the economic ruins of the country back to a positive for their country. The Governor Kerry was boasting about how he would provide enough jobs to all so that each family could once again afford bacon and beans rather than the flour gruel that had taken the top staple of every diet, it was a far stretch to believe. The other candidate was Franklin Roosevelt, whom had his own ideals, but politics are for the poor. Obadiah watched the skies as the clouds passed overhead, each was thin and sans enough moisture to bring rain to the region but kept a suppressing gray haze to the world.

Obadiah felt parched and despite a small canteen of water, he wanted to be sparing with every bit of sustenance that was served to him, it was his sole responsibility to ensure that his family came first, his children needed ample supplies to grow and he didn't want to take any more than bare minimum to keep himself strong enough to continue to provide for his family. Obadiah came upon the creek that parted some far fields. During the storms the sand had changed the geography of the creek, it was shallow with a few deep spots, it hardly brought out enough wildlife to sit nearby and hunt but it was a severe backup if things were tough, there was often field mice along the deep banks and with a few mice, the meat could help add some calories to a pot with boiling water and some thickening flour and some other grain or fillers, Mary Sue wasn't fond of mice but a few of them caught in a water pan trap would still add a type of meat to the family meal.

Obadiah decided to search along the creek banks, maybe a mink or river rat might make the menu, a turtle or couple of frogs would make due as well, the hunger of his family bore down on him as a man, the need for fresh meat rather than always falling back on the stored salted goat meat, the berry plants of the previous year's hadn't produced, the drying skies had withered the grounds and when you looked around, awaiting the luscious green of the spring to arise, it was undermining to realize that they may never come. Obadiah stared at the barely trickling water of the stream as he slowly walked the banks, the desperation to find life was growing infinite, it had been hours since he left his family with the hope that he'd bring back supper, his stomach howled and gurgled, his body had felt different from a year ago, as he watched his wife grow thin, he too felt his body lose weight as well, he could tell as his body grew tired much more easily each day, that he grew weak because he had forgone necessary nutrients day in and day out to maintain his ability to work day in and day out. There were some weeds that had tough stems, the branching seemed to twist and stick out from piles of dirt, they seemed to resist the dry environment or maybe tap into the mere trickle of the stream at the bottom of the bank.

Plucking a small twig from the plant, Obadiah pondered the edibility of the plant and wondered if was even palatable, the plant was hard to the bite, the taste was akin to the dirt and his already dry mouth made it a tougher plant to try and swallow. Obadiah stood near the dull green plant and looked up and down the creek trying to find any type of life, even small critters were edible and could salvage some sense as a provider for the man of the family. Mary Sue knew the urgency for Obadiah to bring food to the table, as the stresses of times opened up any potential for food and hungry bellies seldom complained about what was on the plate as long as it wasn't bare.

One of the strange dinners that had become common was goat tongue, the tough and chewy muscle was much more possible when sliced thinly and cooked slowly with a tomato type of stock, it was still an uncertain meal but it was edible nonetheless and very little was wasted. Obadiah stared into the creek, the deeper pockets ran still, almost stagnant as the blowing sands changed the course of the water and made the travel of fish or even minnows damn near impossible. Obadiah once had a meal that was a few handfuls of minnows, with a few slices of celery and a few peppers with country gravy, the minnows softened and as small as they were, you didn't have to worry about anything but eating them, their bones and skulls were soft enough to just eat.

Obadiah watched a mouse climb out from under a leaf near the water's edge, it was a small gray thing and jumped a few times, probably in search of seeds or nuts, like Obadiah, it probably was just looking to scavenge one more meal before the next sunset. The mouse interested Obadiah, he stood still as his back teeth grinded on the course plant he picked a twig from, he locked his eyes on the small furry creature, just staring and losing himself in the business of the creature, it didn't have a farm to maintain but it too probably had a family to provide for, like himself. The mouse was sporadic; it would jump once or twice, zig uphill than zag back down. It was intriguing to watch; suddenly the mouse pounced up and then ended up in the water.

The divots in the water were dark underneath; the shallow winds of the water just connected the puddles while sandy mounds kept separating them from joining back into a working stream. Obadiah thought about digging out some of the creek, it would only store water, not attract much life. The mouse swam in the water for a moment; the ripples grew in size as the small critter paddled along towards the bank. The man partaking in solitude just watched the small struggle mouse, part of him held his breath in anticipation of when the mouse would relieve itself from the water trap it was caught in.

As the mouse neared the edge of the water, suddenly a fish appeared out of the dark shadow below, swallowing the small mouse and then returning back under the water. Obadiah blinked a few times to ensure what he saw, had he really just witnessed a fish large enough to swallow a mouse? A fish like that could feed his family, maybe twice. Obadiah fumbled, he felt urgency fill him to get to the water and capture that meal, he bumbled a bit as removed his boots, he rolled up his pant legs and eased himself down the creek bank. The water felt cold, it was shallow, the sand

185

beneath his feet sank and gave way, his feet sinking into the bottom as he stepped towards the dark hole he watched the mouse disappear into. Obadiah bent down to try and reach into the hole, there was no telling how deep it ran as he couldn't see or feel the bottom immediately, it was an impressive depth, it seemed like the fish had kept the hole dug to remain able to sink to the bottom.

Obadiah slid almost waist deep into the sink hole, he felt around with his bare feet, it was unnerving at the thought that any moment a fish might bite down onto his foot, he squatted down to feel around with his arms as well, he neared the far side edge of the hole, sure that any minute he would feel the slimy skin of the fish and have supper ready for his family. Obadiah waded through the water, the edge of the bank under the fallen grass wasn't solid, the bank had an indentation to it, he nervously reached into the deep, dark hole, the temperature of the hole was cold, Obadiah began to second guess himself as he knew muskrats, beavers and turtles often resided in the same types of holes and he was not in a rush to lose a finger or hand to the ferocious bite of some wild animal. "SPLASH" the silence was startled by a hunk of dirt falling into the water from the grass ledge above the hole, the startling commotion gave the extremely nervous man cause to have to urinate and jump, he retracted his outstretched arm and breathed heavily, this time with a bit of a chuckle at how childishly scared he was and then being frightened from a simple splash, he felt like a fool. A moment of calming passed, Obadiah chuckled off the brief moment of concern and got back to the focused task at hand, he was mostly submerged in the water and duly impressed at the size and depth of the hole and cavern, it seemed to engulf most of his body as he waded in.

Obadiah reached through the water, his fingers touching the muddy sides as he felt around the walls. The water rushed around the palm of his hand, the water became murkier with the mud he had kicked up with each step. He began to second guess what he may have seen as the moments passed with no luck, there didn't seem to be a fish, no mouse eating prize that could have been a feast for his family, maybe he had conjured it, maybe the mouse never existed, maybe as Obadiah munched the straw like roughage from the branch, maybe there was some substance that caused a delusion, maybe he's not even in the water, maybe he was in the final stages of starvation and maybe he fell ill or was in limbo between life and death and all was imagined.

Suddenly he felt something, his hand graced something coarse and then slimy in the water, he hardly had a second to grasp something when it clamped down on his hand, the jerk on his arm felt like he was being pulled by a tractor. The pulling was immense; the struggle had caught Obadiah off guard. Obadiah had stumbled forward a bit, face first into the creek bank and he scrambled back to his feet for a sure footing to gain the upper hand. The coarse mouth of the beast grated at the back of his weathered hand, the force on his fingers made it hard to remain clenched for a hold.

The beast thrashed, water swelled backwards into the cave, gathered power and then rushed forward, the waves and splashing continued to wash over Obadiah until he found a solid portion of dirt at the bottom of the hole he was standing in. Once he gathered firm ground beneath him, he gained the power to pull back as forcefully as possible on the wild beast he held tightly onto, the fish fought for its' life and it was yanking at the hand and arm of Obadiah, it also had the upper hand until Obadiah, a forceful enemy that washed in the wake found his balance.

Once Obadiah found his footing and also his inner strength to fight for a meal for his entire family, he yanked the monster fish from the water and up to his chest, taking some of the fight from the catfish as it didn't have any water with it to empower its' thrusts. Obadiah was drenched, his hair matted down on his forehead and murky water soaking his clothes. The fish must have been thirty pounds; it had a head almost as large as Obadiah's torso and a dark blue green skin. Obadiah felt alive, he had barely glided through the last year, even in deep passion with his wife, there was still a dull tingling deep within him, and a fleeting sense of life, the life had been thrust back into the heart of Obadiah in the life or death fight with this strong fish that was tiring but engaging.

Arched backwards to keep the fish from the water, the successful fisherman tripped and struggled to climb back out of the waterhole and up the creek bank back to his gun and clothes. Obadiah still fought against the wiggles of the fish, he had the notion to remove a bootlace and string it through the lower lip of the fish and tie the other two boots together while heaving it all over his shoulder to begin his trek back to his home. It was a fair journey back to the family; Obadiah didn't want the fish to spoil while on his way so he left it alive and picked up his pace to get back. Barefoot and shouldering a monster catfish, the man of the family stood tall, he felt a renewed sense of duty that he could provide for his family, he felt his manhood swell with excitement and he looked ever so forward to the feast that awaited the evening. The dirt roads wore on his feet as he walked, he could feel his heels rub against the sand and the sound from his feet rubbing against the sand was strange, between the sounds under his feet and the puckering struggle of the fish under its' own weight on the shoulder of Obadiah. As the walk wore on, Obadiah fought off exhaustion as he neared his home, he wore tired but excitement continued to carry him home.

The fish expired while in route, the fish seemed to grow heavier over the trek along with the dead weight of the beast rubbed his shoulder raw as it bumped with the shirt against his skin. Obadiah walked up the driveway, boots slung around his neck, rifle over one shoulder and monster fish over another, the thirty pound fish shouldn't have been such a struggle but Obadiah knew that he had grown weak over the past winter and spring as the food resources dwindled and the needs of his children far outweighed his own. Obadiah climbed up the three steps to the front door and into the house where his family was gathered. Mary Sue looked up anticipating her husband's return with a few rabbits or some form of critter, the hunting luck lately had gone the way of the economy and lost its' presences. As her husband entered the living room, Obadiah walked in with a gargantuan meal strewn over his shoulder, her amaze caused her to leap to her feet, the large mouth of the creature had given alarm to Elizabeth and absolutely frightened Isaac, the poor little guy had begun crying when he took a good look to the beast atop of his father's shoulder, it appeared as if it were attacking.

Mary Sue offered a hand to her husband to unload his affects as they both wandered in towards the kitchen. As Obadiah unloaded the mega meal onto the table, Mary Sue began to unload utensils from a drawer so they could begin to butcher the creature. As Obadiah cut, yanked, tugged and ripped the leathery skin from the fish, Isaac still whimpered in the other room, Elizabeth stood near the corner of the entryway near the kitchen and ducked and peered at the large head of the monster as her father cursed and struggled to pry its' flesh from its' body. Mary Sue scurried about in the kitchen as she hurried to begin cooking and preparing the cutlets and fillets, she wanted to brush some of the meat with cooking oil and freeze it so as to preserve it for future meals.

Obadiah pried the pink flesh from the body of the fish, it was tough and hard to pull but with each cut hunk of flesh, there was another handful of meat to go into a pot of water and spice, each handful of fish meat was the size of a meal and the excitement of the kitchen attendants continued to smile and become more lively at the prospect of a filling meal, and then some. Obadiah told the story of how he wrestled the fish from the hole, his accidental discovery and overtaking of the beast that now lay out on their table, slowly withering down to a giant head and skeleton frame. Obadiah put the fish guts into a small bucket and placed them into the freezer, he thought that maybe he could chop it up, rinse it out and maybe mix it with flour if they got hard up for meals again; he also planned to smoke some of the meat to preserve it as well.

After the largest meal the family had in over a year, the couple sat around and let their bellies gurgle while their bodies returned some of energy that was rather depleted; they decided to rest upon some chairs on the front porch to watch the sun sink into the horizon. The children grew sluggish as the evening advanced, the day was the first great success they had in such long time, Obadiah felt as a renewed man should and his loving, adoring wife had a new way to look at him. Obadiah reclined back and took stock of the emaciated world around him while his wife ushered their children off to bed for a night of slumber with full stomachs finally.

The silence of the late afternoon was less than ideal, still devoid of the ample sounds of birds chirping and carrying on, the world was still strained for life and the hope for a return to normalcy was fading like the days' sun. As the evening set, the one positive that had been noticed was that the sand that covered everything had killed off many sorts of bugs; there wasn't the buzzing of biting insects whiles sitting out as the air cooled and the bright oranges and reds twisted into dark purples and wisps of black clouds against the background.

Mary Sue returned to her husband, she had on her face the look of desire, Obadiah missed that look, he knew what it held in store and his body had craved hers as hers craved his. Mary Sue stood next to her husband on the porch and dropped her light dress; it slid down her frail body and crumpled on the ground next to the chair. Her breasts had lost considerable size, last time he noticed she explained that it was from the birth of two children and not from lack of sustenance, Obadiah was suspicious out of concern that his wife had been neglecting herself for the sake of their children, much like he had been.

Mary Sue ran her left hand on thinning head of her husband, she looked weary and tired as she smiled down on him, he lifted his right hand to rub along the outer contours of her left leg, and her legs were thin and made a large gap between her thighs while her skin hung a bit. It had been a harsh two years and both parents felt as if they were wearing thin, the sake of their children depended on their ability to feed and support the young but their own survival was an important matter to ensure longevity of the children as well. Her pelvis jut out from under her skin, her hip bone and her ribs were much more prevalent now than even a few months ago.

Mary Sue tried not to dwell on the thinning hair of her husband, his cheek bones were sharper, his eyes sat deeper in his face and his lips thinned when she kissed them. Mary Sue turned to sit on the lap of Obadiah, her rear was thin and bony on his thighs, she unbuttoned his shirt and unsnapped his overalls as they continued to kiss and get back to their romantic youth that still sparked deep within them, underneath the rigors of parenthood. The couple passionately passed along most of the evening, their intimate time was a rare treat, and they were both fed well and had the energy to express their love for one another finally. With children requiring most of their energy to keep entertained or having to hunt and search the entire day long for food, the couple often found themselves without the time for themselves, let alone each other. It was an extremely pleasant change for the couple, the chance to spend intimate time together was long overdue and it helped to bring closeness back to the couple that was put on hold over and over again.

Obadiah had his confidence renewed, he had come through and provided a great meal for his family, it was a long time coming and it brought more faith back to the couple that together, they could persevere through and continue to thrive. Next few days the passion that the couple shared had continued to blaze on, the porch, the barn, the kitchen, any time the couple had a few moments alone, they found themselves entangled and expressing their lust for one another together, it was as if they were newlyweds once again, fueled on the back of the catch and great meal. Mary Sue was able to feed her family for over two weeks from that fish, she was able find a variety of different meal options as time passed on. Last week of May brought another disastrous storm, the winds howled, the skies grew so dark by mid-day that the chickens went to roost and the goats headed into the barn to wait it out.

The storm lasted three whole days, it was three days of being locked indoors, fending off dirt and sand blowing in the cracks under the doors and near the windows. The three days were full of child games and crackly radio broadcasts bringing in updates of the storm and the suffering citizens. The news reported that the numbers of bodies discovered among the sand was climbing, the estimates were reaching the thousands, people caught in the storms, like Rupert Basks, just fell during the blowing winds and suffocated from inhaling dirt and sand, others were passing away from pneumonias and illnesses from the storms, not to mention the starvation.

There were tough Russian weeds, the kind that Obadiah had bitten a piece off of near the creek bank that held firmly in the ground during the dry and windy conditions, people were taking to mashing up the fibrous plants with water and slow boiling them to make it palatable, it was a cheap meal that those whom were the most desperate to eat, were. Skirmishes were breaking out in many areas, people were flocking to Florida and California to work fruit harvests and farmers were turning desperate seekers away. Many people were climbing aboard trains to travel away from where there was no longer food or work, the numbers of dead bodies found in proximity to trains had climbed, many people simply fell from the trains and died or starved to death and were shoved from the trains. Obadiah remembered the story of the little boy that was kicked from the train by the larger boy, it sounded like more and more people were getting desperate, the masses were getting ruthless in their ways of attacking one or another. There were stories of city folks being evicted from their homes, citizens were robbing one another and armed muggings had peaked in New York and other cities of high criminal concentrations.

The stories from the news casts were ever so grim, the strain had now strewn coast to coast, the cotton and tobacco harvests of the southeast had also taken a major hit from the dry weather, the west coast had reduced fruit harvests, the economy was faltering and even on one wobbly leg already, the weather kept kicking at what may have been a saving grace farm harvests. The year ticked along, there was no hope for the future anymore, each time the weather was broad-casted, it was always concluded with the hope for rain in the future, only hope, no promise, no guarantee. The nights' conversations between husband and wife were rife with concern, each day was a struggle to feed the young and each news report brought more information but never any hope or sense of relief.

Every few days Obadiah visited the creek, further upstream and further downstream to continue to bring back food, anything that he could muster. Frogs, turtles, muskrats or other varmint, on a few occasions Obadiah waited out with his rifle into the evening to wait for nocturnal animals to near the water, the smell of rotting fish guts had brought out a few raccoon's over a few different days, the meat was greasy and tough but it was still sustenance. The Withers were making due, their bodies were still growing weary and thin and their energy levels depleted earlier and earlier each day as they continued to run low on food, calories, energy.

Obadiah often wandered past the home of the Basks, he felt queasy thinking about Mickey buried near the back of the barn, it was strange that it still hung on his conscience, he hardly thought about the couple that he had to bury near the tree in the backyard, the home had become dilapidated, as the storms blew on, the roof had taken on hundreds of pounds of dirt and sand and parts of it had begun to collapse. The whole west side of the home was a large pile of dirt, a slope all of the way up to the roof. Boards on the barn had blown in and then filled with dirt also. As the winds blew, the sand mounted and slowly swallowed the home. It still haunted Obadiah about having to fight Mickey, the hand to hand struggle for his life wore heavy on him, especially when alone hunting or searching the area for items of use.

As a child Obadiah spent time wondering when that moment would strike when he would know he was a man, it was a strange thought process to have but it was a question most young boys would often ponder. He often wondered if he would simply wake up and look in the mirror to a man staring back, or look for a moment and think back to when he was a mere boy. Life was fading, the country was growing further into what the news had described was a "Great Depression" and things were not looking like anything might change.

192

The following summer brought on more struggle, Obadiah had to continue to venture further and further out in order to scavenge, pillage, collect or hunt, the creek had since dried up and as sands blew in, it erased the creek from existence. One fall day Mary Sue gave Elizabeth her newest dress for her birthday, the girl was growing before their eyes and the couple could barely keep their children fed, let alone clothed. Mary Sue made a new dress for Elizabeth using the empty flour sacks, she searched for sacks that were of similar in pattern and made a dress that sent Elizabeth into an enlightened frenzy, she couldn't even wait to wear it and in her crazed dancing and spinning in the living room that fall evening, she shed her current dress and was diving into her new one from the bottom. The couple laughed at her antics but in larger emotions, they felt most blessed that they could bestow such a gift to her and her joy from it, brought tears to the eyes of her mother.

The struggle of the family continued to wear down on the parents, knowing that their children were slowly starving to death, having to go without so many niceties that the parents hoped to provide when they moved all of the way out here, they have gone without. Each night used to bring a beautiful warming sunset, those sunsets now were mere reminders that life sets on everything, the sun remains on orbit without worry or concern of the planet around it, or the struggles going on the third planet away. Sunsets became empty, now just a reminder that each day moves at a slow pace and like life, once it ends, there is no going back.

Obadiah and Mary Sue fought off the overwhelming concerns about how they were going to feed their children, and themselves. There was no hope anymore, no sound of any rumors of relief that might swoop in and save the country, or its' countrymen. Sands continued to blow across the land, each radio broad cast each day spoke of more and more people just abandoning their homes or cars in trying to cross the country in search and hope of work. Thousands were migrating every day, the coasts still had crops growing, tobacco and cotton in the southeast, corn and legumes on the northeast, fruits and vegetables on the west, but the drought has brought hardships to all and even those with crops to harvest, were being flooded with out of work people or families that came from nothing and only had one last hope remaining.

The remoteness of the Withers' farm offered them separation and seclusion from the wandering hoards of people seeking work, it was also inhibiting in the proximity to searching and hunting down food sources or being able to collectively find food with the help of others. With neighbors, city people can work together or garden in groups to keep themselves fed, the remoteness of the country offered up things that the city would not, the animals, rabbits, gophers, and now catfish.

There was hardly a month's supply of food stored in the pantry as the days fell shorter. Obadiah had to haul wood from further and further away to stockpile for the coming winter. Using the tractor and wagon to travel an hour away through the fields to the far edge of the tree row for firewood, Obadiah could feel his body give away faster as he swung his ax that seemed to grow heavy with each swing, he sometimes clumsily missed his mark and risked injury in many ways with the ax. Obadiah fought each tree, each chop that sent splinters in all directions, each log that was sawed off was the only way the man of the house could try to fight off his own cold, as well as keep his family warm during the coming winter.

Obadiah could feel himself struggle as he had to argue with his own weak body, he moved slower, found himself taking more breaks and with wagons full of wood, he would putter through the fields to head back to his home. Many days were spent with ax in hand and saw in tow, Obadiah left behind his family to go and gather firewood. Sometimes Elizabeth would join in, the father would encourage her to wear his heavy coat to keep her warm while she searched around for sticks and picked up the wedges of wood that went airborne as he chopped. Obadiah remembered chopping wood with Norman back in the Carolinas, the life lessons bestowed on the son seemed to have fled from his mind in lieu of the way life was fleeting now.

"Each swing of your ax may not seem like much progress, like each day of life, one at a time gets progress made" Norman once told Obadiah, there was a large need for wood and although tedious work, the first few chops into a tree seemed to be the first few steps towards climbing a mountain, but after enough time spent, you can look back and see that you've come a long way. As Elizabeth gathered sticks and helped her father load up any available wood onto the wood wagon, she still seemed bright eyed and grateful to spend hardworking time with her daddy. Some mornings would be much more brisk than others as Obadiah awoke and then headed out to search for good for his family; he had to balance his time between gathering enough firewood for the long cold months for warmth but also for enough food to fuel the wood chopping. In the months since the summer had gone, the Basks home had fallen in on itself, the western wall had finally succumbed to the weight of the sand and rest of the structure that was leaning on it. Obadiah hardly crossed the mailbox as he felt guilty about having cleaned out the home of useful items for his own family, and buried three bodies on the property, one that he himself had taken. The Basks fields were just as barren as everything else around them, Obadiah had planned to acquire the open land and farm it as his own if the ability to farm ever returned to the land.

With a seventy foot tree finally finished being cut and hauled to his own farm, Obadiah decided it was time to head to town again, he was running out of money and it was almost depleted entirely. He wanted to load up enough canned goods to leave his family enough hope to feed off of while he heads out to the country for a while and forage for more, from somewhere, anywhere. Obadiah explained his intentions to Mary Sue; she was hesitant to let him go and worried that as people grew more desperate, that they might become more dangerous. A stupid person is a dangerous one, a desperate person becomes a stupid one and when the pains of hunger are what you wake to or fall asleep to, there is hardly anything else you can focus on during your day, except the pains of your children maybe. Obadiah needed to head out and search for something that might fill the bellies of his children. There was one last goat in the pen, the grasses were gone and there was almost nothing left for it to eat and it needed to be slaughtered before it just starved to death and went to waste.

It was growing dark as the father and daughter wood gathering duo neared the home, the lights were dim and the smell of the wood fire wafted through the air. Elizabeth began asking questions and it broke the evening noise of the tractor pulling the wagon; "*Pa, why are you always gone, How's come we don't eat lots, when will I get to go to school?*" the young girl had a right to question the way things were, she had seen her parents grow much older than rightfully should have in the few hard years that had burdened the country. Elizabeth stood tough alongside her father, the young girl was blessed with the ignorance about the world around her, she knew that she wanted new dresses and more to eat, luckily the little girl had no wants for much more but as children age their needs grow, their requirements increase and one day, they become independent adults.

Obadiah was frightened at the prospect that his children would continue to grow in the world that had nothing to offer, a weak government that couldn't feed its' people and the despair forcing people to become increasingly animalistic in order to survive. Once back at home Elizabeth headed in to join her brother in waiting for their mom to have dinner ready, she was famished and her little stomach had rumbled half the afternoon away as she helped to load the wagon with wood with her father. Obadiah unloaded his cache and dragged his fatigued body into the home, he could feel the bones in his knees grind and rub against the thinning clothes that hung from his body, his body had exerted every last ounce of energy and he needed to sit for breaks frequently as he unloaded his wood wagon near the house.

Mary Sue moved around in the kitchen, a few slices of meat, shredded into a pot of water along with a cup of flour to thicken and a few spices to change the flavor was another meal, it hardly had a smell but it was sustenance nonetheless. Obadiah planned to slaughter the final goat in the morning; he also wanted to leave his rifle in the reach of his wife to protect her and their children in his absence just in case a wanderer or some nomadic hobo stumbled upon the farm. Mary Sue had been taught to shoot by her father and though she wasn't of the hunting mindset, she still felt comfortable enough with a gun to defend her home.

Obadiah helped to put his children to bed and joined his wife in theirs for the nights' sleep, Mary Sue sighed heavily, their children ate well but both parents had meager feedings and knew things couldn't stay on this path for much longer, they both exchanged worries, they cuddled to remain warm under their thinnest sheets, the children had the warmer everything. Obadiah kissed his tender wife for the last time of the evening, they both struggled to sleep and as the hard days passed on, the ability to sleep soundly was often interrupted by hunger pains or the worry about tomorrow, they had each other but there were still minds full of fear to truly find that peaceful mind to sleep.

A night without decent sleep woke the weary Obadiah from his bed, his mind raced about how desperate things were getting and how he was backed into such a corner that feeding his children was the only thing he could hope for now. Before the sun rose, before any other members of his family awoke to meet the cold air, Obadiah was stoking the wood burning stove in the kitchen, he couldn't feed his children well but keeping them warm was still within his abilities. The noise woke his wife, wrapped in a sheet she sauntered out to ensure that everything was OK with her husband, she could often read the worry lines in his forehead and the concern on his face, there was little that he could hide from her.

The pacing of her husband gave her reason to be nervous, he poked and stirred the hot coals and blew into the firebox until flame finally broke out, throwing a few split pieces of wood atop the embers satisfied his desire to heat the home, Mary Sue whispered to prevent waking the children. Mary Sue poked at her husband, she peppered him with questions about what was on his mind, she wanted him to unload his mind, his worries, and his burdens to her. Obadiah knew what his wife was getting at, he knew what she wanted to hear but he also knew that she still held him in high regards and he had her expectations to live up to, besides, it was his role to be the strong one of the couple.

Obadiah struggled enough to feed his offspring, he failed enough at being the husband and father that his family needed, and he failed even worse at life right now. Obadiah kissed the tired forehead of his wife and did his best to sound reassuring, his could only whisper but he still wanted his whisper to be convincing, his wife already worried enough. Obadiah headed out to do his part for his family, the lone goat was knelt down near the inner corner of the pen, it was asleep and even when he neared the shaggy creature, it didn't even budge. Obadiah clenched his ax and knew he wanted to deliver one strong blow to the base of its' skull, maybe an inch or two down its' neck, delivering a swift death. Obadiah leaned against the top wire of the fence, unsure of how to feel for the moment, he almost felt jealous that this animal would receive a much more just death at the end of one hearty blow instead of slowly wasting away. The farmer decided that as the light broke the eastern sky, that he had wasted enough time contemplating his role, the air was crisp and Obadiah let his nose run long enough before gathering up enough strength to hoist his ax high into the air before delivering the deadly blow that was due for the goat.

Blood poured out onto the ground, the warm crimson liquid met the cold ground and caused a plume of steam in the early morning, the body didn't jerk or twitch, it just stopped breathing and fell limp. The deed was done and now it was time to drag the carcass near the garden to begin the butchering. The creature was heavy, maybe eighty pounds now, the creature had lost weight and size over the last few months as food sources became more scarce. Obadiah had taken the goat on a rope to walk down the grass and weed grown field edges as far as he could so the goat could keep eating, he knew that by spending the time and making the effort to feed the animal, that in the end, the animal would feed his family, the goat droppings were also mixed into the garden to further propagate growth in the coming year from the fertilizer.

The gash in the neck of the goat let blood out, a trail followed him as he dragged the meal by its' legs. There was table near the garden that Obadiah butchered previous animals on, the blood dripped into the garden, the innards were also buried in the garden along with other scraps and food wastes, the compost helped to keep the ground fertile once spring came again. The family garden brought food during the past summer, planting them along the window sill in glass jars gave them a much better chance to root before going into the ground and risking being blown away by the winds. Mary Sue laid out a long sheet that covered the garden, the garden plants were placed in small holes in the sheet, it helped to keep the soil where it belonged and kept it from blowing away as well.

Mary Sue stepped out the rear door to help her husband, she brought the necessary pans to put the meat into once it's removed from the animal. The skin was tough, hair was hard to pull out as the winter coat was course and thick, the body continued to steam as more of the warm blood let out from the cuts before dripping to the dirt below, leaving small divots on the ground with each drop. Mary Sue rolled up her sleeves and helped to cut the hide away from the carcass and helped to prepare the pelt like the previous goats skins before. Layering the windows with skins helped to insulate from the cold. The Withers worked away a good portion of the morning, together they cut and stripped away as much of the usable animal that could be salvaged, the meager animal didn't offer as much to eat as the previous slaughtered animals, as they were of larger size.

Mary Sue carried in the pots of meat and began rolling most of it in the curing salt to preserve it, more of it went into cloth sacks and hung from hooks just outside of the window so the cold air would freeze it and it was still hung high enough to avoid being taken away if out of eyesight, by any sort of predator. Obadiah tried to shuck off the drying blood on his achy hands, the cold made his hands burn, they were hard to open but also hard to hold closed enough to continue working the knife to flay meat away from the bone. The husband and wife worked diligently to get their bloody chore done, the blood soaked the ground and the steam stank, it reeked of iron and dirt, it was thick and the steam cut through the dry cold air with an aroma that can't be duplicated.

Obadiah finished his task and put the remainder of the carcass in a bucket in the barn, he planned to use the bones for stock or to add with some pot of boiling water for gravy. Obadiah headed indoors to thank his wife for her help and to take a look on the food supply that had been partially restocked. The weary man was thankful for the life of the goat, it would get his family on through the New Year and then no one knew from there. Mary Sue minced some of the meat and added it to a boiling pot of flour and water, she wanted her husband to have a few meat biscuits in his stomach before the rest of his day ran long or late.

Obadiah was nervous about heading out, there was no telling what he might run into nor what may happen, it was a different world now and anything that may have been familiar once, was no longer anymore. Obadiah readied himself early and counted some of the last remaining funds they had, he hoped his thirty six dollars would be enough to get him to town, a few dozen bags of flour and maybe some spices to make the bland type of slop palatable. The sun was warming through the windows; the light beams brightened the room, reflecting off of shiny objects in the east facing kitchen to make shimmering projections on the walls.

There was too much uncertainty in life anymore, prayers had gone long unanswered and there were thousands that died from starvation while waiting for a sign. Radio reports spoke of hundreds that were found dead on a regular basis, people that had gotten caught up in one storm or another or just had their life extinguished. People from coast to coast had taken to prayer, tithing, and waiting for their savior, all to came up empty, many perished while they waited. Obadiah gave up praying, he gave up putting hope and stock into an invisible entity when there was a visible problem with logical solutions, food, his family was starving to death and empty prayers weren't filling stomachs. Obadiah had taken a back seat to his destiny, he sat back and just prayed for things and two years later, he was in worse shape, his family had become desolate and time was fleeting for them.

The time spent praying had not resulted in anything but wasted energy, it was self-defeating to think about how much time could have been spent foraging or gathering and things may not seem so bleak by this point. Mary Sue often hid her fear and emotions from her husband, she knew he was already heavily burdened and she didn't want to pile on so sometimes she just wept when she found herself alone. Mary Sue feared her husband leaving, there had suddenly become a small knot deep in her gut, and she couldn't place the origin of the worry so she just chalked it up to the concern about her husband's plans to leave and doing so alone.

The pilgrimage of thousands in search of work or means to survive was new to the country, the gold rush of the eighteen hundreds was the last large scale movement of people. People were fleeing homes and in the past few years had even taken to simply living out of cardboard boxes, tents made of sheets or just under bridges, anything that would protect groups of people from the elements. Radio reports spoke of President Roosevelt, there was finally motion to begin reversing the distress that plagued the country, the Hooverville's that had dotted the country like acne on a preteen had amassed larger percentages of the population than people that resided in their own homes. The daily news spoke of riots and protests, Hooverville residents marched on government buildings, instances of clashes with police were becoming more common and even with arrests happening almost every day, there was no real sign that anything was going to change anytime soon.

Obadiah headed out, he climbed into the Dodge after kissing and hugging his family goodbye and headed down the driveway and turned left. Mary Sue returned to her children, they were counting on her and the weight of it was pretty heavy, she struggled with the knot that surged from the deepest depths of her innards and it now assaulted her stomach and throat. Mary Sue found herself unable to breathe, she wheezed as she gasped to inflate her lungs, panic made her sweat, her children had been playing with wood letters and hadn't bothered to notice their mother becoming overtaken with dread and worry. Mary Sue stumbled to the kitchen to take a seat away from the sight of her babies, she didn't want to cause them any alarm as she leaned back, sitting tall to get a better inspiration. Mary Sue tried to slow her breathing, she already wanted her husband back, his absence was already felt and as she replayed his departure in her mind, her struggle to breathe worsened, she realized she was panicking and was struck had a notion that he may not return.

Their marriage had its ups and downs as all did, the strain of the past few years had really put pressure on the couple, their attempts to spend time intimately together had reduced, there just wasn't the desire when their most important tasks were eating and tending to the children and each adult spent their own energy for the sake of the young, and hardly left any for one another. Mary Sue poured herself some water from the cooling kettle, the coffee had run out long ago so the parents took to just sipping at hot water in the mornings.

Sipping the water was soothing; the sounds of the children giggling and playing in the other room had brought relief to the nerves of Mary Sue as she chanted to herself that her husband would return to her before the end of the day, and hopefully with some supplies, food, and news. Mary Sue stood from her chair, brushed her hands straight down the front of her thinning overalls to straighten her appearance, she needed to remain strong for the sake of her children, she tightened up the bun she kept her hair in before stepping into the room to join them. Mary Sue glanced out the front window, it was as if the storm had just happened, dirt strewn as far as she could see, the landscape was brown, brown dirt, brown skies, brown trees, everything was brown, just different shades.

Obadiah slowed as he neared the Basks farm, he was a good distance from his home and even as his hands shook, he brought his car to a halt just in the driveway from the road, his left hand clenched the steering wheel like it had done to the man's throat. Obadiah was unsure about what he was doing but he knew what he was after. Obadiah walked towards the house, or where the remnants of the house lay buried under years of dirt that had now piled on top, almost erasing any history of the property. Obadiah retraced his steps between the front steps, and the skeleton of the barn, he shuffled his feet to kick up dirt, row after row, and step after step, Obadiah traced a grid pattern in search of his first item of need. On his seventh or eighth pass, there was the thud in the dirt that he needed to hear, a break in fate that finally favored him.

The pistol that Anita used to take her life was still where it landed when it fell from his pocket as he charged the man whom was making advances on Elizabeth. Obadiah picked up the firearm, it needed to be cleaned but the lack of rain since it fell hardly left it with any rust, with cocking the weapon and moving it around, freed it from the dirt the filled the barrel. Obadiah clenched the gun; he held it firmly as he turned back to his awaiting car. The half box of bullets he recovered last time he was actually in the house was in the car, he left his rifle and only means of his wife protecting his family with her but now wielding this handgun, Obadiah felt more confident that one way or another he could return with supplies for his family.

Mary Sue ran a large basin with water to heat over the stove, with a little bit of soap on a cloth, and the basin filling with warming water; it was time for everyone to bathe. Starting with Isaac first, the warm water was nearest the wood stove warmest part of the home, the kitchen would help keep the chill off of the wet and exposed body. Isaac fought vehemently, he did not want to be bathed, and he didn't realize his body odor was appalling but didn't want to be wet no matter how much his mother pleaded. Elizabeth was given the task to pick up and sweep the home as Mary Sue carried on with her chore. Elizabeth struggled with the broom that was much taller than she was as she performed her duty, she dragged the awkward utensil as she could hear her younger brother yelp and wail against their mothers' orders to remain still.

The fight was hardly worth it, the pestilent little boy had given his mother more than a handful while she attempted to help him wash all of his body, he really gave her grief when it came to cleaning behind his ears and when she was finally done, he had gone through all of his crying and fit throwing expertise. Elizabeth shuddered knowing that she was next; she finished her chores while her mom warmed the basin with pots of water from atop the stove. Bathing day was mildly unpleasant in the winter, the pipes to the wash room often froze near the exterior of the home so bathing reverted backwards one hundred years for the Withers to a large washtub in the kitchen.

Isaac shot out of the kitchen as if he'd been running from a deadly predator, he was red in the face and his hair was still damp from the washing as he pouted on the couch. Elizabeth stepped up for her turn, Mary Sue handed over the washing cloth to the older child, and she was entrusted to wash accordingly and was given her privacy to do so. Mary Sue joined Isaac on their sofa, he was more than uncooperative after the struggle and his eyebrows clung tightly together, almost closing off his eyes as his arms crossed his body and his bottom lip hung lowly in pout. Mary Sue nudged her son in order to shake off his coarse exterior, he tried to shield his eyes and not join in her playful antics. Elizabeth finished her bath time, the fire was warm and felt nice on her skin, the children's clothing was re-worn most of the time, for cleanliness they had sleeping gowns they wore and their clothes were laundered weekly or as required.

Elizabeth slid her dress back on and ran her shoddy brush through her hair as she headed towards her family on the couch and joined them for the radio show. Mary Sue was surrounded by her much more pleasant smelling children, the soap had cleansed them from layers of dirt and they were in much better spirits. The unhappy Isaac missed his father already, as did Mary Sue. Isaac had fallen asleep shortly after the beginning of the radio show as he warmed and dried. The Withers ladies kept their seats on the sofa and listened along to the radio show as they waited for the return of the Mr. Withers.

Obadiah fiddled with the reclaimed gun as he drove one hand on the wheel as he navigated the rough streets that lead him towards Indian Gulch. He had run over and over his list in his head, the measly funds in his pocket were meant for flour and things to make hard tack, he had a box of ammo and a firearm that may or may not work. The morning loomed on, there was no telling how things would progress but something had to come out at the end, Obadiah fretted about so many things as the dodge twitched and jerked left and right across the path. The road was hardened from the cold, the feeling of the hard bumps on the springs vibrated up and through the driver, making his bones ache even worse. Blood still stained the knuckle creases on his hands as he gripped the steering wheel and fought to stay on course as he followed the winding roads to town, he stared at his callused hands, the goats blood stained in blotchy patches on his hand, the thick portions of his hands were hard to wash.

The sounds of the tires rubbed along the roads, his temples ached and throbbed, Obadiah took stock of how much different his body felt as the stresses and strains wore him thin, he noticed his knees had grown knobby over the last year, his bones sat closer to the surface of his skin, looking in the rear view mirror, Obadiah looked over his own face, his cheekbones protruded further, his chin has since thinned, and even after a meal and a night's sleep, he still looked tired.

Obadiah sat uncomfortably on the seat, the long drive and thin body made for an assault on his back, the front seat was rough and each bump in the road was amplified and beat against his torso. The sun beams poked through holes in the clouds, looking out over the flat countryside, the highlighted areas that dotted the land made for an impressive sight against the dark portions in the morning. Obadiah rubbed his forehead to pass the time, his bones ached, his thinning muscles tightened with each move and he was quick to tire.

As Obadiah neared Indian Gulch there were a few small camps along the roadside, the makeshift tents had menial goods such as plates or chairs sitting near the opening flap. It was cold out, some of the tents were erected side to side, the neighborly fashion made for mediocre security or comfort, as well as to make use of the close proximity to fend off the bitter snaps of the cold. The residents of the small tent camps didn't seem aroused, the tents sat still, unstirred, it was as if they had been abandoned, except you could see feet near the openings.

There was a unsettled feeling in his stomach as he eyed the tents while he passed, he felt terrible that the people sleeping in makeshift tents were probably starving and freezing, there was a dog tied to a stake in the ground laying near the opening of a gray tent, some gray and brown mongrel. There was clutter and litter near some of the tents, papers and wrappers that indicated that there were people inside that were at least there the day before. Obadiah worried that the sound of the engine might awake some of the people within the tents and sent them out begging, it made Obadiah nervous.

Obadiah made the last left off of Flint road and into the main street, the road was bare, few signs of life had remained, the laundry station had been long closed and the layers of cobwebs almost blocked out any light from penetrating in though the large front window. The crisp air was without many smells, the echoes of the engine reverberated between the buildings, there was hardly anyone stirring within the windows of the buildings, the deli was closed, the tack and hardware store was dark and looked as if Theodore Carvell and his wife Mary Catherine hadn't been in the store in some time. Obadiah hadn't crossed Carvell in quite a while, the stalwart and guttural hardware man. It had been a few years and he hadn't heard much about him, his wife had ample family in the area but he had three children to provide for and the money from the town's people may not have gone to home fixtures but rather for food and menial supplies. The only store along the boardwalk that seemed to have any activity was the grocery mart at the far end, it was a sense of relief to see it still open as the rest of the town had faltered and closed. Obadiah pulled in and shifted into park before turning the engine off, he eyed the building, the silence was welcomed for the moment, there wasn't any sign of people awaiting to rush the man that might be able to purchase a few goods from within.

Obadiah made his winding way through the aisles to load up on flour, few measly spices such as chicory root, and a few bags of potatoes. Potatoes were still cheap as their harvest wasn't as affected badly as many others in the country, Obadiah loaded up everything he had acquired and filled his backseat with all of his goods. Obadiah kept half of the money he brought so he had some saved for a future trip if necessary or perhaps for seed to plant come spring if the rains return. The grocery store was all but bare, the shelves had basic essentials and fewer and fewer goods were replenished after they were purchased, times were the most dire they had ever been and there was no longer any hope.

The lone man in the store was slow to converse at the register, the slow falling businesses failed one by one, the good Doctor Martinez was one of the last to go, there just wasn't anything meant for survival for the intelligent man and wife, he stayed long past necessary to perform his duties as the care taker in town. The larger percentage of people that came down with black pneumonia, a coughing and hacking as a result from inhaled sand and silt from the environment, passed away. Joseph Martinez helped to bury many of the discovered bodies after storms as people passed away from the elements over the years. The doctor gave and gave himself, long past his own sense of self was worn thin, Joseph took his medical training seriously and took the lead when it came to the delicate handlings of bodies of deceased people to show them the utmost respect.

The man behind the counter continued to ring up supplies as he described the out flux of residents, the man's wife was home this early morning but she randomly received postcards from some of the more upstanding Indian Gulch members that had left. Johnson Franks had finally given up also, he lived out of his gas station for the previous several months until there was no longer anyway to hold on and he took to the road to Florida for a late year fruit harvest, like many others. Obadiah felt dizzy for a moment at the notion that so many had fled after hope had run out. The winter had not offered much more than mere flakes, the cold was moving in but there was no sign that it was going to bring any moisture for the relief of the desert like ground. So many residents had gone, taken to the breeze just like the fertile topsoil had when it blew away.

Obadiah felt the bleakness of things truly sink in his stomach, the profound sadness had swelled in the quaint town, and then fleeted out and hardly left a skeleton, empty buildings dotted the main road in town, the once booming promises of wheat had dried up with the soil. Obadiah had doubted himself more than ever now, was his choice to move out here really god's will? He left his father's home with wife and child and headed west, head full of doubts but heart full of hope only to be let down and abandoned. Obadiah continued to second guess everything he had ever done, should he have gotten more dry beans? Was he being a caring enough husband? Was the death of his family going to be on his hands? What if everyone dies because a storm buries them in their home or if they just desiccate with everything else around them. The gentleman at the counter was still talking and it brought Obadiah back to awareness, he was staring at the flour bag with a bright pattern and had drifted off as the man spoke, with a few blinks he realized that the man was asking him if he was alright.

Obadiah shrugged off the long stare and apologized to the store owner for the rudeness. The two men finished their business and Obadiah parted to load up his remaining supplies, his body was depleted, there was hardly enough energy left to load the bags of beans, rice, potatoes and few other goods that had long shelf lives. Mary Sue had tended dearly to her garden, it wasn't the most successful but with her diligence she still made it prosperous enough to bring them fresh peppers and tomatoes through the summer and fall, as well as can a fair amount of the goods for the long winter.

Many of the homegrown vegetables had come up short, the lack of rich topsoil left sandy dirt that didn't provide much nutrients to the growing plants so Obadiah decided that as he slaughtered animals, the blood and unusable organs would be churned into the garden dirt under the cloth that was weighted down to keep from blowing away. The left over plants after harvest were fed to the remaining goats, any inedible plants and weeds were brought for them to keep them fed enough to later provide food for the Withers, it was an unending task of keeping animals, and family fed, Obadiah felt like he was wasting away trying to do everything for everyone else and at the end of each day, he felt as if there was less and less of him remaining.

The day had continued on, the supplies had been loaded in the backseat but the relief that purchased supplies should have brought was empty, there was only a pause in the knowledge that it wouldn't be long before the bellies of his family were once again empty, and as each day drew on, the man of the family continued to tap and run dry each last frantic option he could muster, he wondered how many last options there were before the well ran dry and his family finally perished. Obadiah drove past the edge of town, things had begun to stir a bit, there were a few measly dressed people sitting around the opening of the tents that sat behind the city limits, the older man looked as if he had been mining, he was filthy and his clothes were as well, the woman perched near him on a bucket was huddled under a blanket and had her face down, assumedly to keep warm.

The sight of the disheveled couple was hard to see, Obadiah had an urge to stop and offer them some help, even a few potatoes to eat but his family had to come first, his guilt had already caused indigestion and internal conflict over having murdered a man to protect young Elizabeth, Obadiah passed by without even tapping the brakes. The clouds patched across the sky, there were still open holes in the gray overhead letting light beams show chunks of the distance, the enlightened areas in the view gave little hope in his heart but he pulled over to the side of the road to sulk, hesitant to return home so quickly. The car slowed to a halt, Obadiah felt the weight of his overalls on his collarbones, his chest was tight and taking a deep breath was a labored task as he dropped his head to focus on his chest rising and falling in the idle vehicle. The air was still, cool and smelled of dirt when Obadiah stepped out onto the road, there was no need for him there, there was no driven need from him to stop, nor a reason to have stopped, not returning promptly to his family, but something in him made him stop anyways.

Obadiah ran his hands along the warm hood, leaving streaks in the dirt but absorbing some of the radiating heat. The air was still, the absence of noise other than the ticking of the engine as it cooled, was calming, the tranquility seemed to lighten the weight on his chest as he sat himself on the edge of the road that overlooked a small gully, in the distance was a low depression in the land, the lines that traced the fields were mere darker field edges, the shadows from the taller weeds or grasses faded away into the fields themselves, there was no sign that the land had held life in the previous year, there were hardly any trees in the distance, nothing to act as a wind screen. Man had used mechanical tractors to rape the land of its' native buffalo grass and trees to make room for more wheat and money, man brought this on themselves, Obadiah was hit with the realization that the chaos man had been suffering, was self-inflicted and that the great migration to the west for money, or the greed of, was ill fated.

Obadiah sat long past when his backside had grown numb, thawed the ground beneath and formed to his buttocks. The ground was covered with hard grass and pebbles but the serenity was soothing, breathing in the crisp air helped to relieve much of the constriction on his chest with each breath, the stream escaping his mouth with each deep exhale dissipated into the air and left the tip of his nose moist as it began to run. Obadiah still couldn't figure why he was perched roadside near the coulee, just letting his eyes wander while his brain fought to find silence. Obadiah reflected on his upbringing, Norman was more than adequate in his role as a father and Obadiah was really missing his father, dads always came up with the right answers and strength to remain steadfast day in a day out, Obadiah struggled to emulate his fathers' example but his will was growing weak.

Obadiah thought about wading in the creek down the road back near his father's farm, the cool water flowing past him as he searched for crawdads and polliwogs to put in a bucket. Norman taught him to be able to cook and make a meal out of many things that could easily be found in many places, a large craw-fish broil would be an amazing feast right now, a large table draped with newspapers and family gathered around laughing and chawing on as they ate into the evening, Obadiah was missing his family back home, it was only Norman really but he missed the Kelsonovichs too.

Obadiah ran his fingers up his temples and through his hair as he sat with his elbows on his knees, he could feel his hair line had receded over the past few years, hair wasn't the only thing he felt he had lost, Obadiah felt hollow, his guilt was burdensome and it seemed to eat away at his insides, his internal conflict gave him headaches and cost him sleep. He killed Mickey to protect his daughter, man's life ceased at his hard working hands, hands that were to bring food and life to his family's name and carry on his lineage. Obadiah was blessed to have Mary Sue, she was slow to judge and easy to love, she stood firmly in her womanly duties by her husband, she made her husband stand tall by her side but he also felt burdened some days at the pressure that having a family placed on him and he fought the urge to resent them for it.

Things were always taught to be black and white back home, in the shadows of the churches people ruled with the gospel and each pastor clearly defined the laws of man, each was tasked with carrying out the word of god, disbelieving false prophets and so on, but it was a time of gray, people were starving by the millions and even churches and food lines were turning their people away when they could no longer pay. Mickey may have just been trying to scavenge to support a family back wherever he came from, he may have just been delirious or maybe in his own rage, maybe he got it all wrong.

Obadiah rocked back and forth as he sat rubbing his temples, there was enough food for his family to last till spring, as long as he didn't stay to eat with them. What if he left, what if he just didn't stay after dropping off the food, would his family be better off? what if he just wandered off in search of food or money like so many other traveling gypsy like countrymen, maybe she would understand if he ventured out, and maybe while on the road he might just not look back, maybe head to New Mexico. Obadiah surveyed the horizon, the break where the clouds of the sky melted into the landscape, it was serene as far as he could see, if it hadn't been devoid of life or prospect, it might have been peaceful. The lack of life or life giving soil out in the view was a shame, so much land that could pump out thousands of bags of wheat and make thousands for thousands of farmers, and yet, it had all dried up.

Obadiah finally picked himself up, brushed off his backside before stretching and leaning back on the car to delay getting back in. Obadiah had turmoil in his heart, he really didn't have any answers, things were so strained and there was no sure way to know that he was doing the right thing anymore. Prayers had long gone unanswered, people were losing everything that they had, the bible said not to store grain for it might rot and go bad but to have faith that the "lord would provide," except he hasn't.

Obadiah looked around closer to the edge of the coulee near him, he noticed something shiny, there was something in the dirt, the mounds of grass and dirt that lined the hilled portions of land had left drifted sands to change everything, creeks and streams filled and disappeared, much like the creek he caught catfish in back near his home. There wasn't a stream or crick anywhere in sight as Obadiah peered out over the distance. Obadiah climbed down the shallow ravine, it was a wide gap to stride but with a few dusty steps, he was stepping up to the other side in search of what had been glinting in the sun. Obadiah dug his toes into the incline for better footing; he reached out for a small metal ring that barely sat out from under a dirt dusting.

Obadiah reached forward, his fingers grasped a small ring and broke it free from under the blown earth, the ring came from under a heap of dirt, it was attached to a green canvass tarp. The tarp was layered in sand, the sand gathered on top and rolled on itself as Obadiah continued to tug away at it revealing a face, or the remains of a face. Obadiah was startled so bad he tripped backwards into the shallow ditch, if he hadn't let go of the tarp its' hidden contents may have come down after him. Obadiah slid down the the slope landing on the back of his shoulders and his boots throwing dust and sand all over him. It took a minute for the startled man to gather his bearings and wits, not in his life would Obadiah have expected to find a decomposed skeleton like that and it was downright frightful.

Obadiah panted for a moment and took a mental check of his physical capabilities and checked to make sure he hadn't soiled himself or become entangled with his discovery. Obadiah rolled back a little more to upright himself, dirt was sliding down the side of the ditch as he tried to climb back up and take stock of what he had found. The skeleton was outstretched, laid out, it looked a lot like Rupert Basks, open mouth and with a look of agony. The skull barely had any skin to it, the eye cavities were filled with dust and the clothing, had become exposed as Obadiah pulled back the tarp. Obadiah recognized the robes, this man was a priest, there were torn and tattered black threads adorning the man, a rosary around his neck that had rusted and faded with the sands, and what appeared to be a bible or the remains of one wedged under his arm and body.

Under the tarp was also a few sticks, probably to hold the tent upright as it appeared to be a makeshift housing for the man as he walked to a near town before perishing. Obadiah didn't see any signs of food, the man probably died hungry or suffocated from the blowing winds and sands during abrasive storms that blew dirt and sand over him. Obadiah felt queasy, his stomach wanted to dry heave but the minimal food he had eaten lately was already processed so it was fruitless spasms of his stomach muscles before a few deep breaths helped him to calm his nerves Obadiah pulled the canvass back over the man, a few kicks of dirt to weigh it back down and Obadiah was on his back across the ditch.

As Obadiah hiked back uphill towards his vehicle, his day had taken an off course turn and he had to once again swallow down his memories, the faces of the Basks, and the Mickey guy all flashed through Obadiah's mind again, leaving him dizzy and unsure of how to progress, he felt truly lost in the world. Obadiah sat in the front seat of his car and folded his hands to begin to pray. With eyes clenched tight and head bowed, Obadiah began the normal routine chant that happened with all prayer until the rotted skull of the priest twenty feet away just entered his mind, the man died probably praying, spent his life praying and serving the lord and still died in pain and agony anyways.

What might become of the Withers if a man who gave his life for servitude of god ended up without a peaceful and merciful end? Is there a god and if so, why no mercy for one such servant or follower? If god is all knowing than why would he allow such punishments, if all loving than why wouldn't at least the children be saved? Obadiah began to truly feel abandoned and gave up his bowed head, affixed his eyes back towards his route home and turned over his ignition. Sadness sank in to Obadiah , his heart dropped in his chest as he searched his mind for answers, he came up blank each time he tried to start from the beginning on how things had gotten to this point, his family should be well fed and warm, not barely keeping a stoked stove and nibbling beans one at a time and counting them until they run out.

Obadiah felt tasked with the urgency to provide, he tugged at the fabric wedged into his buttocks as he sat behind the wheel of his vehicle and slowly made his way back to his family, with no urgency. The backseat was loaded with food stuffs and supplies for his family, but he still felt they would be better off without him there, his portions would be better served to his children to help them along and better ensure their survival until the summer when maybe a garden would produce a bounty and if there was a god, that the rains would return and once again, make the land fertile and produce a harvest. The bible tells stories of god flooding the world because he was displeased with how man used their freewill in a manner that he didn't wish, is this drought and more punishment being doled out by a vengeful god? Is god even a god of love or has the devil been the one recruiting souls in the name of Jesus and god just remained idly by? If god were all powerful he wouldn't need to recruit so feverishly.

Obadiah felt his temples throb harder, his heart caused them to pulse with anger, he was mad at god, he was mad that he spent his life praying to an invisible deity that would forsake his whole family and let them starve to death, even innocent children that hadn't known anything but the love of their parents and the aches of malnutrition and starvation. Obadiah clenched the steering wheel in hatred, it was originally the love of God that helped the man just ease through life on his faith, it was an early baptism and the early teachings in the faith, no child is raised with neutrality and given the right to choose a faith when they are old enough to make an informed decision, would religion still exist if it wasn't ingrained since birth or would people realize the stark indignation placed on gods own children.

If man was created in God's image, and they have flaws and sin, then is god even just or without sin, or even exist? Obadiah was lost, he just had a lump in his throat that almost gained control over his breathing, it was anger and dreads coupled with panic and concern about what the future held for his family. The road was still long and drawn out as the absent father made his way back to his children, there was so much doubt and uncertainty and he had no idea what might happen but he wanted to be there for his family, even if he wasn't doing them any good.

Mary Sue was practicing letters and numbers with her young children, Elizabeth read aloud to Isaac and he followed along with his finger to mimic what she was doing. Mary Sue had a handful of navy beans in a jar and that was the extent of the legumes she had to cook with the meat, she sliced the beans thinly to join a cut up piece of goat to simmer in a pot with two cups of dwindling flour to thicken up the broth, meals required mincing small pieces of vegetables in order to make them last longer and go around better, each time Mary Sue cooked, she wanted to weep at the lack of cooking supplies, she was truly missing her childhood when she had so few worries and her sisters were her best friends.

Mary Sue had felt herself slowly diminish, her legs had shrunk in the thighs, the tendons in her feet stuck out on top, she noticed as she walked around the home, her hands ached often from the chill and her cheekbones seemed to stand out and her lower eyelids seemed to always appear dark and baggy, she felt herself wasting away, as much as she noticed the same of her husband. Mary Sue often fretted that she was failing at her duties as a mother or wife, the children were always fed first, she and her husband often shared a portion that was smaller than one of the servings the children received at each meal.

Mary Sue could often feel her husband losing weight each night they lay down together, his muscles had lost size and his skin began to hang on his frame. Mary Sue tossed and turned most nights as she mentally scavenged her cooking supplies for any better means of food, she had started to eye some of the Russian weeds that lined some of the fields, she thought about maybe cutting up the coarse plant to boil until soft and edible, maybe that would make for a meal filler for the family and offer enough calories to fill the whole family back up.

The stresses the married couple suffered independently was similar to that of each other, they both wore the strain of providing for all of the other members of their family and it was even more of an important task to care for their children, to ensure a safe and healthy future and maybe even see them have children of their own if the lands ever turn around. Mary Sue wished she could do more for her family, she could shoot and hunt but there was no game to hunt, no more squirrels in the area, nor rabbit, their food sources had blown away and not returned, the food chain was missing many links in the middle and the Withers may have been sitting on top, but there was nothing underneath. Each day that passed, the children only continued to voice hunger pains while their mother fought off grimaces of her own hunger pains to remain stoic for them, her husband also. Her menstruation had sporadically ceased, her body could no longer support the events that might enable to become pregnant, and she kept that to herself.

Mary Sue felt her own concerns, she worried about not being able to feed her family also, she thought back to her mother Margarete always pushed the point that a good wife always supports her husband and never gives him reason to doubt himself that was her role as his wife. Mary Sue felt comfortable in her position in the home until the routines skewed, the change of things was significant, she took on any task she could think of when the opportunity presented itself, such as helping to skin and

214

butcher the goats, clean rabbits and chickens and still keep the house tidy and her husband satisfied in the bedroom.

The role of farmer's wife was always changing, she often had to come up with new and educating ways to teacher her children things they needed to learn and carry on with their childhoods and if there was a school that hopefully it might be open in the area come next fall for Elizabeth. Mary Sue worried about the effects of the solitude way out here for Isaac, Elizabeth spent a part of her early life with her folks back in Carolina. Norman was affectionate and really good with the young girl, the Kelsonovich's loved having Mary Sue and Elizabeth around when Obadiah was working all of the extra shifts at the cotton mill and farming the fields with Norman.

Mary Sue found herself at times, alone and contemplating the future, so many things had progressed over time when it came to her, how she had spent her childhood playing in the cotton fields at home, creek swimming with her sisters and holidays spent with extended family. Now it's the four of them, the stress on Obadiah was sometimes visual, he had to be the hardest working member of the family, the bread winner and when the fields were planted, he had to be the best father possible, she knew that his children noticed the long days and his absence and also knew if wore on him. It was a struggle balancing being a parent, you become invisible and when you give so much of yourself each and every day, sometimes you don't have anything left for yourself. It's hard when you strive every day for everyone else, and hardly get noticed, fail to exist other than when kids or husband wonder where the meal is. It was terrible feeling invisible, nonexistent and having to turn around and do it all over again each day.

Her children loved her, there was no doubt to their endless love, they often hugged and snuggled with her as they gathered around the phonograph radio in the afternoons, resting their heads on her lap as they stayed warm under a blankets on the couch. Mary Sue rubbed the heads of her babies, their hair wasn't washed all that often so it felt thick but it was still clean enough to be soft.

Isaac sucked his thumb when he grew tired, a habit with unknown origin and seemed to sooth the young boy when hunger pains or the cold overcame him and he needed the comfort. Mary Sue tried to religiously sweep up and keep a tidy house, the dirt that blew all over and kicked up at every slight breeze made keeping things clean an ever encumbering task. Elizabeth was a tough little girl, she witnessed her mother and father butcher many goats and just watched, she helped to pluck geese, ducks and chickens when it was time to kill one in order to eat, she knew that as part of the family, she had chores and roles to take upon herself to contribute, most of the time it was to keep track of her younger brother while her parents took care of whatever business they had to. Isaac laid on the lap of Elizabeth, her head rested on the arm of the couch they were resting on while Mary Sue moseyed about cleaning up and sorting things in the kitchen.

The dull clings and clangs of pots and pans didn't rouse the weary children, the constant hunger and chill of the winter often left the children hungry and without much energy, they usually ran to the kitchen for the warmth when their mother heated up the stove but the sibling warmth and comfort of remaining stationary took precedence most of the time. The children grew docile, as each day grew dim, so did the energy of the family members, it was growing hard to find the energy each day to run, jump and play as children do. It was hardly past the sunset each night as the children tucked in for the evening, the shorter days left the home cooler and cooler, the children began sleeping each night together on the couch, Obadiah and Mary Sue bundled their children and themselves up as best they could each night before bed.

Obadiah and Mary Sue alternated nights of remaining vigilant over the woodstove and woke up every so often to feed the fire and stave off the brutal cold of the nasty winter weather. Obadiah spent most of year chopping wood, the stack of firewood that lined the home and barn often lasted longer than the winter itself, even if the food didn't. Mary Sue sat in the kitchen, the stove had been stoked and a splice of wood added to the belly of the black stove, she could feel the warmth of the stove radiate through the layers of clothing and warm her skin, she bit at her fingernails as she tried to figure out how to feed the family.

The pot let out small plops of sound as it cooked the thinly shaved goat meat and beans in the light brown liquid that was thickened with flour yet again, a few small pieces of carrot added color to the brown stew like meal and it even smelled as bland as it looked, Mary Sue wanted to cry, there was nothing left to offer her children, hardly a place to live, it was hardly habitable and warm, it was edging closer to being a prison, a place for the family to remain until their last days brought in the crows to pick at the last of their flesh, the outlook had no promise, there was no telling

216

how long before the last ounce of whatever luck was keeping them alive failed and luck peters out and then their lives are over.

Mary Sue sat at the table with her elbows propped up and her eyes buried in the palms of her hands, too afraid to waste the energy to cry. The temperature in the kitchen rose slowly, it brought some relief but it was only for cooking purposes, the meager midday meal was almost ready for the children to eat, the smell was hardly pleasing but the children were hungry and it brought them to their feet. The radio show crackled on and the children listened intently. Mary Sue dished each child a bowl of the stew and herself a partial portion once again. Mary Sue wondered about what had become of her husband, her nerves were still frayed from her strange feelings that plagued after he left the home, she tried her best to keep an eye out the window and wait for his return but there was an unsettling feeling that he might not. She called to her children for their meal and as they entered the kitchen, she fought back more tears, she fought to remain strong for her children, and tears wouldn't change a thing so there was no point in bothering.

Mary Sue sat with her offspring; they sat around the table and spoke about how the stew tasted, how the fire was warm and about what type of weather they might expect over the rest of the winter, might there even be snow finally? Isaac had never seen snow, a few flakes last year but not snow, brutally cold, piling high, encapsulating white powder that entombs homes and the people that lived within, snow. Mary Sue closed her eyes and thought for a moment about when she was younger, she saw a picture show in a theater, a large screen that displayed images, orchestra music played in the background as a man with a stubby mustache danced and pranked around to an audience and everyone laughed. Mary Sue felt guilty that she hadn't been able to offer the same treats to her children, they had never experienced a picture show, nor live orchestra, no experience of a live play or much personal interaction. Mary Sue began to bargain that if her husband didn't arrive home, than she was bound to find a way back to be with her parents, back to her home, back to a place that was familiar and comfortable.

Mary Sue felt her heart thump in her chest, the notion that her husband would run off on his family wasn't a reality until hearing the story that it has happened, no one believes such atrocities could happen to them until someone wakes up and realizes that it has already happened. The midday meal was over and the children were carrying their half full bellies back to their radio show from their perch on the couch, Mary Sue waited for them to be out of the room and almost out of sound when she needed to take a few deep breathes of fear, her blood ran, causing her hands to tremble.

Mary Sue felt just awful that she doubted her husband; she never wanted to be anything but the wife that stood attentively by his side. She wiped away the moisture from her eyes so tears didn't leave her eyelids and stream down her cheeks before she joined her children on the couch for more afternoon radio program entertainment. Isaac was laid out and sucking his thumb while cuddled under a blanket with his big sister, he knew so little of this world and it was so heartbreaking that there was no telling how long he would have, each day that passed lacked any prospect of hope and it wore heavy on the dreary mother.

The tone of the house was melancholy and stagnant, there was a dire need for a change, it was time to dress warmly and get outdoors for some fresh air and stretching the bodies so she instructed the children to dress warmly for an afternoon outside while their father was absent. Isaac was slow to rise as he was full and comfortably warm but rose to his feet and searched around for his warm clothing while Elizabeth gave their mother a sour look of objection and stalled on her wanting to even bother moving. Mary Sue gave another set of firm directions to hop up off her backside and get her rear moving and join them outside around the barn.

Elizabeth dragged her feet in disapproval as she fallowed along, Isaac lead the way, he knew exactly where the barn was and how to get there, he was glad to lead the way, and with a half skip. Seeing her bright son hop along made her smile a bit, he had no awareness that things were so lean, no worry that there might not be food come the next day, he enjoyed the day for what it was, the adolescent perception was admirable, he still looked at the world with fresh eyes, when the news reported Hooverville's, cardboard box cities that sprung up when people moved to clusters when there were no homes for them, Isaac didn't realize the struggle people faced, he was blissfully ignorant to many hardships and strife that people went through, Mary Sue felt she carried his portion of world stresses.

Isaac reached the corner of the barn first and turned his head back to await his mother and sister, Elizabeth still stomped her feet bringing up the rear. Mary Sue had no plans while they were outdoors but she needed the air and the time outside to take in nature, even though it was nature that tried to take everything the family had, whether it was ripping all of the planted crop seed from the ground and dispersing it across the entire eastern seaboard or trying to bury the family alive inside their home, that was nature, it wasn't unfair, it wasn't fair, it was just nature. Mary Sue once thought of how unfair life was when she was younger, right after her sister passed away, she was torn having lost her older sister and great friend, her father was struggling with the loss and was desperate to try and comfort his remaining daughters so the only solace he could muster was *"life is only fair by being unfair to all, life lacks the ability to be just, it merely continues on and in the end, we all lose."* The words of sage wisdom had been skewed but it made sense, the words had been lost to her for some time but their resonance had come to the scared mother on this day.

Elizabeth kicked at some of the dirt, there were clumps of frozen sand that rolled towards the heels of Mary Sue as they walked in line towards the barn, Mary Sue tried to peer out the corner of her eyes towards the driveway with a profound sadness that her husband may not return, she was struggling not to panic struggling to retain the slightest spark of hope for herself, her marriage, her family. Mary Sue felt terrible about her doubt in her husband but there was an ill feeling that was binding up her guts, twisting and straining at her insides making it difficult to stand up completely straight and fight the urge to make a grimacing face, giving her children reason to worry.

The pebbles rolling at the backs of her worn and filthy shoes was an irritating distraction, infuriating the urge to snap at the drudging little girl but she was just being a kid, you can't bark or lament the child for just being a child. Mary Sue was sometimes in need of just a friend, she wanted to be able to confide in someone, it wasn't Elizabeth's place to listen to her mother's confessions, it wasn't fair of Mary Sue to put the weight of herself onto the mind of her daughter. It was lonely at the farm, no sister or parents to have adult conversations with; she wished she could sit back with a southern cocktail on a warm summer's eve like some of her days back home.

Isaac ran to the old chicken coop, it was sans birds for some time now, most of the birds didn't survive some of the storms, as the needs of the family came, the chickens went, it was desperate to slaughter the last few birds but they had stopped laying eggs so there was no reason to continue to feeding them if they weren't going to feed the family back. There were no signs of owls in the barn, they hadn't been seen in a long time now, the dust in the barns had piled up in the edges, the mood in the barn had followed the family from the home and it was still somber but the air wasn't still or stagnant.

Each family member could see their breath, Mary Sue shivered within moments of stepping outside but she tried to ignore the biting chills. Mary Sue asked both of the children to help haul wood from around the barn back to the pile at the house, Isaac struggled to carry one piece of firewood at a time, Elizabeth carried two and Mary Sue carried large armloads. The stacks of wood around the barn had dried during the summer and fall; it needed to be enough to restock the woodpile that sat near the side door of the house for easy reach to add to the woodstove to heat the home for another month or two. Mary Sue could feel her body warm as she burned off lots of her energy hauling wood, it was nice to not shiver but it was also extremely taxing on her body.

The gray skies hardly stirred any emotion, the dull colors of the sky and the monotone browns of the surroundings made for depressing moods, the only ambient sound was that of the breeze, no sounds of birds in the air or on the ground, no sound of Obadiah returning from the distance or any other sign of life beyond the children working and breathing heavily nearby. "Hard work always made a better person, the worse you feel about yourself the harder you should work" Mary Sue always thought, as a girl when she was the last of the sisters to develop breasts or be noticed by boys at school, she would toil away harder in the kitchen, she would bake, cook, or even join her father hunting. Mary Sue learned to shoot and hunt with her father, there was a therapeutic release to shooting guns, the adrenaline rush, the cold metal of a rifle and the concentration to hit your target, and the small win when you could put dinner on the table for your family. Mary Sue needed a win right now, she needed to be able to go out and hunt and be able to feel good that she helped to make a grand gesture in helping her husband to provide for the family. There were no signs of groundhogs, woodchucks, ground squirrels, rabbits, grouse or any other form of edible game, hope was long gone too.

When Gertie passed away, everyone offered condolences, a condescending "I'm sorry for your loss" was always murmured but it only masked the gratitude that they had that it didn't happen to them. People often spoke about things happening for a "reason," things being a hidden "blessing" usually people are in deep denial and try to persuade themselves that things aren't all that bad when in reality there is no hope, no faith, and no reason to believe in the uncertainty. Uncertainty can cause an intelligent person to become complete fools, the uncertainty of what happens after death leads many people to waste their once certain life, praying, tithing, and sacrificing what they have for what they heard from someone else.

Mary Sue found herself having a real struggle after Gertie died, it was a long cold winter and Gertie fell sick early on but it was a slow sickness and it took a while for death to take her. Gertie was young in her life when she took sick but had a sense of awareness that this life was all there was, she listened to the gospels and found no reasoning with any of it, there was no sense in any of the stories, no comfort in the delusions that someone else had conjured up and fed to congregations for baskets of money each Sunday, no different than play performers on Broadway.

Mary Sue felt confliction, she was raised on the word of the lord, but her brain and need to make sense of things gave her great grief over the matter. Gertie gave her youngest sister a key to many things regarding the internal struggle between hope and wisdom; "*the only real hell is a burdened conscience, heaven is each day with a positive outlook*" those words echoed in the ears of her sister for a long time. Mary Sue let the empty ramblings be just a puppet show, she spent her time wandering outside and then once she became a woman, she sought out true love and the blessings that would make this time on earth count, not be held a slave by a set of rules that were thousands of years expired.

Mary Sue shook back from her blank staring at the wood pile, she wasn't sure how long she had missed, her nose was running and when she breathed the cold stung higher up in her nose, her finger tips were also cold. Isaac was throwing small pieces of kindling at the larger wood pile, he was tired of being obedient and it was almost playful at this point, Elizabeth was trying to scold him for not working as diligently as she was, or that he should be. The nitpicking tattling of the two children was comical, Mary Sue sometimes found the nagging unbearable, especially when her own stresses were more than she could handle and she just wanted to explode, this time, she realized that they were just children, unknowing, innocent little children, and sometimes tussling is what they did, the change in her perception of her young children helped her to smile, the smile made her realize that her skin was tight, it felt dry and bunched as the corners of her mouth raised slightly and her eyes watered.

Isaac had green slobbery snot hanging from his nose and following the contours of his upper lip, his little nose was pink and his cheeks were red and showing that he had spent enough time out in the cold for now. Elizabeth was still doling out instructions to her younger brother when Mary Sue piped up that they return back in by the heat, Isaac had no hesitation and threw one last stick at the woodpile and raced his sister inside, presumably to the comfy portion on the couch, Elizabeth dropped her two chunks of split wood at the base of the wood stack and followed her brothers' speed in doors.

Mary Sue looked around, she was alone again and took a seat on a thinly wired chair near the table that the goat was butchered on, it was stained with the blood of many animals, covered with cut marks, and dried blood that by now had frozen. Elizabeth let the door slam behind her, she seemed irritated at having to be her brother's caretaker, a role that she often did well but was also resented sometimes. Mary Sue did her best to give the young girl her own time to play, either with dolls or her own letters or to practice writing without her younger brother. Mary Sue would often take the boy into the kitchen, he liked to help cook, usually stirring batter or breaking eggs, he usually made a rather large mess but kneading dough gave him a clean productive chance to get dirty, and it gave his sister her own time as well.

Mary Sue thought about how different things would be if she never moved out here with her husband, they would be nestled in the middle of their community, much closer to help and friends, even as things turned sour around the country. Mary Sue felt awful about how things were getting tight back in Indian Gulch, their new friends were suffering much like the rest of the country and each news program that spouted about many thousands of people had taken up root from their homes and communities and ventured to new and strange parts of the country in search of the most token of necessities.

The notion of leaving again deeply bothered the already distraught mother, she was confident in moving across the mountains with her husband, but now, she had two young children and no vehicle to help get them all back to her parents homestead where she may get some help. Everything was quiet, there was a faint noise inside the house, assumedly from the radio that was making sounds and keeping the children entertained indoors, as well as distracted from the hard reality just outside of their living room. Mary Sue tried her best to keep focus on the happiness of her family, she wondered if there were any happy people left anymore, any happy families anywhere, she thought about how much Obadiah had changed in the recent years, his head hung low and his burdens wore heavily on him, especially the things that happened to him at the Basks farm, she desperately wished she could do something, anything to help him.

Obadiah puttied back down Flint road, the drive would have been over by now if he hadn't stopped, or driven faster than at an idle speed, if he would have mashed the gas pedal down at all, he would shorten his trip by an exponential amount of time. With flour and potatoes as well as several others supplies for many, many meals for his family, there was some relief, but for how long? The ups and downs exhausted his nerves, there was such a need for some form of relief, any form, in anyway. The dusty window sparkled in the mediocre sun beams as he drove through some of the few sunlit spots along the road, the view was a mix of emotions, the open span was almost inspiring, except it had been devoid of life for too long, the arid land no longer smelled fertile, no lush vegetation to harvest and support or promote life in the area any more.

The drastic change in things over the two years of being in Oklahoma manifested in so many ways, the parched earth just blew away most plants, the few weeds that were strong enough to survive in the area, were Russian thistle, it was greenish black and just an abrasive looking plant, often times the plant would merely stop some of the blowing sands enough to cause it to pile up near its' base, but it wouldn't root enough to secure the ground beneath it much, the larger plants in the stronger winds would turn to tumbleweeds and roam the vast openness. The worsening of the lands were exacerbated by the dry winders, not enough snow to hard pack the sand or soil in place, or replenish the diminishing water table when the snow melted come spring.

The driveway came into view for Obadiah, he hadn't had nearly long enough to decipher his feelings about things but he was looking forward to getting back with his family, or maybe just out from the car, he wasn't sure how long he would be able to stay, but he wanted to ensure that they had a future, even if that meant that he didn't. The load of supplies in the back seat may not promise longevity, but it was enough to secure seeing spring time. Obadiah felt his heart lighten seeing his wife, she was still seated at the table awaiting his return, he found himself surprisingly elated to be home. Obadiah was grateful to get home, he hedged on telling his wife about yet another body, she was already shying away from her husband enough, he didn't want to sabotage her hope or spirits any more than they already were.

Thousands of people were already starving to death, all while still praying and waiting for salvation, only to pass on like so many others, with prayers gone unanswered. Obadiah wanted so much for his family when he moved them to the farm, he truly envisioned a splendid life, to be able to provide, to grow bountiful harvests to sell and help feed more in the country. Now there is no money, no seed, no hope or even the prospect of hope any more, there is just abeyance, and it all sat upon the heavy head of a lone and desolate Obadiah, as his family slowly wasted away in their remote domicile. As Obadiah neared the driveway, he was filled with hope to see his wife turn to watch him turn in the driveway; he sincerely hoped she would show joy as he arrived, her head didn't even turn in his direction.

Mary Sue heard the car in the distance, turning her eyes towards the road she was curious as to whom it was, it should have been her husband and it certainly looked like their car, she still held the pit in her stomach as she fought to remain still. She was uncontrollably hopeful that he was returning, and with good news and fortune from his travel but the fact that her stomach was still knotted, she still felt things were off, that maybe he wouldn't stay. The humming from the distant vehicle drew closer, tears began to run more than her nose when she positively recognized her husband's vehicle as it neared the home. Mary Sue could only hang her head, there were so many worries, even with her husband by her side still, there weren't enough signs of hope to lessen any of the problems.

Her arms hung heavy, her legs felt like cement and refused to budge after sitting in the cold so long, her pulse beat and her head swayed lightly along with each heartbeat and it clouded her mind from much, normally Mary Sue could hear an approaching vehicle from over half a mile out, this vehicle was only a few dozen yards out before the rumbling had registered with the limpid woman, plopped on a cold metal seat, it was the cold biting at her, she was beyond shivering, just simply beginning to give in to the cold and slumber it brought on. As the vehicle turned up the driveway, Mary Sue tried to pry her cold hands from underneath her armpits but the lack of feeling just caused the painful parenthesis and all she could do was re-cross her arms tighter around her chest and struggle to keep her eyelids open.

Obadiah neared the home, the ground was mostly white with frost, the setting sun thawed portions of the ground that the sunbeams touched, but the shadowed portions of the ground, still held the frost in place, Obadiah didn't feel the sense of relief in his heart when he laid eyes on his wife, he hadn't been elated to be in her presence in so long he couldn't recall the last time they embraced one another in the passion they had when they first met. Obadiah felt a darkened sense about things; he tried to stave off the notion that his family was becoming a burden to him, or him to them.

The day grew cold, as did the distance between Mary Sue and Obadiah, both parts of the couple sensed the distress in the marriage, and it began to manifest into cold days apart. Obadiah spent many days out in search for firewood to keep his family warm, Mary Sue delved into the education of her children, their enrichment was her primary goal around the house, both feared resenting the other. Obadiah put the vehicle in park and turned the engine off, Mary Sue didn't budge, she remained huddled on the chair and kept her head down, it was odd that she hadn't moved to come and see what her husband been able to scavenge or bring home, there was no motion to move. Obadiah felt a sense of fear kick him in his stomach, his wife wasn't moving, she must have heard the car pull in, even if she was asleep, she should have awaken when he pulled in closely but she remained still.

Dread hit Obadiah as he stepped out of his vehicle, Mary Sue still didn't budge, her head didn't even swivel in his direction as he took hurried steps in her direction, his pace picked up, each step closer to his wife made his adrenaline surge, his veins ran hot on the cold winter afternoon, concern for his wife filled his senses, his eyes began to water, either from the cold or the overwhelming dread of what he might find as he neared his wife. Obadiah had come across enough death since his move out to Oklahoma, he had been pressed to face death on his own, and very personally when he crossed the demise of Rupert and Anita, he also has still had to accept what he had done with his own bare hands to the negro that was making advances towards Elizabeth, or seemed to be back at the Basks farm as well.

It was a hard label to wear, "**MURDERER**" the life he took had no legal ramifications but the black spot on his conscience still flared up and ate away at him more often than it should have, it was out of necessity. Obadiah neared his wife, his steps slowed at the realization that his wife, the mother of their two children and the woman that stood beside him through each step since their marriage, might not simply be resting. It wasn't the cold but Obadiah had a seizing chill strike from his spine and ravishes his body making it hard to move during a momentary lapse of self-control.

Feeling tingled back into his fingertips, his mouth dry and parched and his chapped lips cracked and ached as he tried to silently mouth her name while reaching out towards her, his hands shook, the color left his hands and they were pale with spots of blue dotting the backs of his hands. With two quivering fingers extended from his hands, Obadiah reached for the slumped forward wife, her shoulder was almost within reach when she lurched upright. The gasping breath and action of sitting tall startled Obadiah so fiercely that it upended him, made him trip over himself in his disturbed panic. Obadiah landed harshly on his rear and rolled on his back and right side, causing a spike in adrenaline that almost caused his surprise to result in voiding in his wool trousers.

With heart beating like the hooves of a race horse coming down the stretch, Obadiah curled his legs towards his body and laid his head back onto the cold hard ground for a moment, breathing heavily in the disbelief in what had just happened, again, but in great appreciation that she seemed alright at the present moment. Obadiah laid on the ground and watched his breath steam into the cold air as his lungs expelled large volumes of steam filled breath out into the air as he lightly chuckled in exasperation.

Mary Sue had merely drifted off as her body grew cold, she wanted a few moments of solitude and as her hands grew cold, she tucked her hands into her armpits, with her body growing cold, the chill taking over and arms folded across her, she felt comfort while seated out in the fresh air, the sound of her approaching husband gave her great comfort and relief, to see the family car as the chariot that delivered the patriarch of the family back to them. Mary Sue hunched forward, her torso leaned forward onto her arms and arms onto lap, her cradled arms warmed slightly and the little bit of warmth made her drowsy, her eyelids hung heavier and heavier as her husband neared.

The relief of seeing the return of her beloved husband brought on her exhaustion she felt able to finally rest with the reassurance that he was back, and the happiness that he brought food. Her life and those of her two children depended upon him for existence, his hunting and gathering was what kept them warm every day, and fed, even if merely. each night. It was a balanced subject; either all of life or everything in it is a miracle, or nothing, to have spent your life having faith in the unproven only to find proof in each day that there was nothing to have faith in caused internal conflict for Mary Sue.

Mary Sue half fell and found herself draped on the chair she was seated on, her drowsiness had won the battle over her consciousness, only for a moment, ending with the startled arousal back to an awake state and a bit of panic, resulting in the lurching upward and finding herself startled as Obadiah had reached out towards her, startling him, startling her, and both finding themselves astray after a split second of mutual surprise. Mary Sue spun her head around to get a fix on what happened, where she was at and tried to process how she had gotten to the distraught mess of her right leg still on her chair while the rest of her was on the ground, much like her husband. Obadiah rolled himself to his right and brought himself to a seated position, winding his right arm front to back to work out the knot from landing on his back. He was glad to see his wife was well, the ground was cold, hard, and the pebbled frozen sand was leaving divots in his backside.

Mary Sue locked her eyes on her husband, he was sitting on the ground, in awe of how they both landed each other on the ground and bewildered at what was going on. Mary Sue kicked at the chair that ejected her to the earth as it was hindering her ability to gracefully get herself to her feet, she negated the ladylike ability to stand up straight so she kicked the chair, tried to coerce her legs underneath her and used her cold numb hands to push herself upwards, as she stood up and brushed dirty frost from her clothes and turned back to her husband. "*Hey*" Obadiah was almost toe to toe with the spun woman and once again, she was startled.

The couple met foreheads; they volleyed smiles and sniffles as they shared a laugh at the clumsiness from the thick clothing, as well as how unstable everything was after the fright. The couple was together again, breathing heavily, Obadiah didn't want to admit he thought not coming back would be a great benefit to his family; Mary Sue didn't want to offend her husband by admitting she doubted his character and doubted he would return. They were happy to be back together, it had only been a matter of hours and it wasn't worth the upsetting of the other by adding the honesty of the internal conflict and opinion of each other, to each other.

Mary Sue felt guilty that she had felt so troubled about her life partner; she began to tear up and cry at the return of her husband, she was lucky to have him back. Obadiah had missed his wife, he still felt alone and abandoned on earth but he had her, they had been through so very much together and after only being a few years into their marriage, they had many long hard decades together ahead of them, especially without any changes to the dire situation they were in. Mary Sue was grateful to wrap her cold achy arms around her husband and sob lightly with her face buried deeply in the crook of his neck, her tears began to soak the collar of his shirt, and her nose began to run.

Obadiah persuaded his weak wife indoors, he added a few logs to the stove in the kitchen and encouraged his children to engorge their mother in warmth and love while he unloaded the car and took on the task of cooking a larger meal, a sort of feast for the family. Obadiah padded the meal with breads and beans, foods that would help to insulate the bones of his family, he didn't want to go all out but the remaining food left over from after the meal, was saved until after the children went to bed, and he then insisted his wife join him in a pre-bed meal to help restore some much needed weight back to their bodies, and give them a miniature date for the two tired parents. The return of energy with each bite during dinner was worthy of smiles, the added food above a bare minimal meal just before bed made the couple almost giddy, they were alone together and nibbling on cooked beans and thick hard-tack crackers, the food was spiced a bit and as it dwindled down, Obadiah pulled out one last surprise for his wife, Chicory!

Mary Sue saw the canister of root, it was often added to coffee and made it rather bitter, was an amazing gesture, the chicory was much cheaper than coffee and not many Yankees had a taste for it, Obadiah splurged on the treat for them and planned to stew a bit in the morning and give them a whole new day and new way to start it in the morning. The chicory by itself can be bitter and strong in flavor but with as bitter cold as the nights have become, a small bit of ground root in hot water would enliven their spirits enough to carry them on through the most brisk portions of the winter and hopefully keep them mentally afloat and enduring until more food can be sowed in the warming year.

The winter was another one that lacked the snow to restore any faith or hydration that the coming year would support a crop, as the ground became drier, even the water table was at risk for depletion and if that happened, the Withers were done for. The days slowly grew longer, the sun hesitated more and more to set, it hung in the sky longer each day, the longer days brought hope of the coming spring then summer, it also brought further worry about crops and whether a garden could be sustained enough to support the struggling family or not. Obadiah and Mary Sue spent their days enriching their children with writing activities and mathematic, it was a priority that even if things don't improve in the area, than the family could look into going back home and the children going to school well prepared.

The ground softened, the crumbling earth broke easier underneath the footsteps of Obadiah as he walked his fields in search of resilient seeds, signs of small game to hunt, or even areas that retained enough soil underneath the blowing sands that it could be transported to the garden plot and help to further grow garden sustenance. The sand and silt mixture that was left after the winds blew the mid-west topsoil all over the east coast, couldn't support plant growth, other than the Russian thistle that grew in patches around the landscape, without decaying plant matter to produce more rich topsoil, there couldn't be a continuance of plant growth, it was a vicious cycle of soil starvation, Obadiah had begun to spill the goats blood in the garden with each slaughter, and the buried entrails rotted and decomposed, returning needed nutrients to the soil in the garden.

Obadiah and Mary Sue discarded any decomposable items in the garden and buried it, including their waste, the smell was wretched as the spring thawed out the earth but with consistent mixing and churning, the earth continued to grow black and retain the promise that the ground would grow food for the family to continue to feed from. Obadiah was ever watchful over the patch of ground, it remained under a blanketed tarp to keep its' contents from blowing away like so much already had, the ground churned easily and each time, it grew in size. The plant remnants of the last garden were fed to the few remaining goats before they were slaughtered, which had to happen before they wasted away and starved to death.

The farmer swept up the goat droppings to fertilize the garden as well, it was a scavenge sometimes to gather enough to find plant matter or animal feces to mix into the garden dirt to assist the plant growth come spring. The few snowflakes that fell, were measly and desiccated in size, not enough to accumulate or replenish some of the parched ground when it melted. The winter skies remained gray, some days it grew dark and teased the notion of flurries or storms, and with each passing day, the defeating let down hit harder and harder. The warming spring air that blew in from the northwest didn't bring any glint of moist hope; it was just a little warmer in temperature each day.

One much cooler day in early March Obadiah had decided to stake out on a trek, it was about fifty miles to the north to the train tracks, he was curious to know what he might find up there, even if only news of something nearby, work perhaps. Norman once told him that nearly all apple trees that crossed this country had originated with Ole Johnny Appleseed, and with each tree sprouting more apples and people tossing cores and more seeds about, than more trees shot up. As a boy, Obadiah used to pretend he himself was Appleseed, he would save all of his apple seeds and scatter them about during all of his travels and adventures, either through the mountains or toss one every spring into the raging spring rivers and imagine that they would take root in any one of the downriver tributaries and a mighty tree would grow, all thanks to his efforts.

Obadiah thought about some of the seeds he spat out of his window as he drove across the mountains with his family on their way to Oklahoma, there was always a small part of his inner child that went back to his Appleseed times, when things were easier. Obadiah had spoken to his wife about his curiosity to head out; he packed a few handfuls of beans to chew on along the way, and a few small potato sandwiches to load his pockets for meals while he was out. Mary Sue was nervous again, his presence had been needed around the farm, even with very little difference, he was still the man of the home and needed by his family. Obadiah figured it would take two days to walk and two to get back, it would be a long journey but he might find the prospect of work, or maybe even surveying the landscape might reveal a pond or stream that hadn't been choked by the sands.

Mary Sue still worried about the return of her husband, would he jump on the trains and take up a new life somewhere else? The notion of Obadiah leaving was more than her stomach could handle, she was nauseas and she could no longer hold in her emotions about things. The night before Obadiah had scheduled to begin walking north at first light, she approached her husband and expressed her concerns, she began to weep, she held her husband close and expressed how much she needed him in her life Obadiah had no idea how strongly she felt against his travel, or why, and further encouraged his wife to tell him everything that was on her mind.

Mary Sue finally gave up trying to keep in all of her thoughts, she finally unleashed her emotions and her doubt in his return last time he went to town, and especially how she felt the same torment and despair again. Obadiah felt his heart sink as he heard his wife express her doubt in him, he understood why and also knew that there was nothing he could do to change her feelings, except reassure her that he would always come back to her, just like he always did. Obadiah withheld his urge to tell her about his pause to soul search on his way back, he knew that it would only fuel her insecurity while he was away if he ever admitted to thinking about not having come back.

Mary Sue held her husband tightly, his scruffy face didn't deter her from kissing on his neck, he was warm, and his arms were visibly smaller than they were in the past but she craved his touch. Obadiah caught on to what Mary Sue was hinting at, it had been long since they shared their bed in such a loving way together, he began to caress the neck and jaw line of his wife, the couple had spent many days working with their children and not nearly enough time on themselves, this was their time. Mary Sue ran her hands on the shoulders and legs of Obadiah, her fingertips tickled his legs a bit as she progressed in her antics to get him to join her.

The couple caressed each other's smaller torsos, smaller frames, and bodies that had reduced in muscle tone due to the slow starvation of the times. Mary Sue removed her top as Obadiah undressed himself and helped to undress her also, they hadn't had such close time in a while and both felt a bit clumsy, Mary Sue accidentally grazed the cheek of her husband with a forearm as she positioned herself to straddle her husband, their bodies grew warm as their blood pumped, their touches excited each other and passion began to grow. Obadiah groped and caressed the breasts of his wife, licking and nuzzling her, she eased up and down upon him, her legs beside his. Mary Sue ran her fingers through his hair, taking her back to when they were young, curious and aroused. The enflamed love making found its groove, the writhing was in rhythm of one another, Obadiah grasped his wife along her ribcage and coerced her up and down, her body quivered and jerked sporadically as they progressed and further aroused each other.

Mary Sue knew tricks to enflame her husband's loins, letting her hands roam his body and cradling his manliness as she took him into her, it excited him enough to grasp her tightly around her waist, his grip further turned her on, heaving her chest into his face as she arched her back, their hip bones ground into each other. Mary Sue continued to fondle her husband, his thrusting increased in both intensity and pace, she needed him, she only felt complete when she was with him, she needed him inside of her, to feel him, to taste him. As intensity grew, Obadiah had to change how they were positioned, he needed better leverage to ensure that his wife's' desires were met and fulfilled. The couple rolled together, lying flat on the bed, Mary Sue dug her nails into the shoulders of her husband as he thrust into her, her back arched with his arm underneath her, her legs wrapped around him.

Mary Sue needed more of him, she continued to arch her chest at her husband, her nipples were filled with arousal and overly sensitive, each time they touched the bare chest of her husband, it continued to drive her wild with excitement. Mary Sue felt herself become her most basic sexual being, she let go of the stress and worry of being a mother, she had even let go of the strains of being a wife, this was about her and what she wanted, her pleasure and meeting the needs of her body.

Obadiah was fortunate to have such a wife that still craved him and his touches carnally, the most basic of animals still have their urges to mate and copulate. The angle still wasn't right for the lust filled husband, he rolled his wife over and climbed back on to her, her cold buttocks was a relief to the warm stomach of him as they continued their intimacy long into the night. Mary Sue grabbed the left hand of her husband, lead it down past her tightened stomach and between her thighs. Obadiah pushed against the backside of his wife, groped at her chest with his right hand and kissed at the back of his shaking wife, nibbling and suckling at the bare skin of her back, neck, earlobes and cheeks as she coaxed his left hand down below, guiding him.

Obadiah dug his toes into the mattress for a better foothold, her thighs clenched against his as she arched her back and signaled for him to keep kissing on her, her pleasure mounted and with body straightening spasms, her muscles twitched uncontrollably, the whole world and all of its' troubles ceased to exist, random colors filled her mind. Mary Sue had her husband, she had his undivided attention and it was all being focused on her deepest sensual needs. His touches made her womanhood tremble, she desired every touch from her man, his muscular frame was much smaller than it had ever been but his stamina held true. The touches to her body left Mary Sue with goose bumps, each caress, grope, and finger touch made her body shiver and quiver.

Obadiah grasped at the small rear end of his wife, her body twisted and thrashed as he fondled at his wife, her body was moist and warm. The couple had lost sense of themselves, both just only thought about their own pleasure and how to make the most of it for themselves. Her body squirmed with his touches; his hands worked her body over as his body lay atop of her. The slight puffs of cool breeze was a moderate relief as the bodies parted randomly during the amorous activities of the married couple, the moist skin cooled when exposed to the air in the room, the skin to skin grew damp and warm. Obadiah increased his thrusting, Mary Sue thrashed and grabbed at the bed sheets, biting at the pillow to fight to keep herself silenced, the bed growing in disarray, the sheets in shambles, the jerking of Mary Sue inched Obadiah closer to climax, feeling the trembling body of his wife shake violently underneath his surges, her lower legs rolled below his, his stuttered thrusts at her caused her whole body to jerk and thrash in the pinnacle and culmination of their passion.

Obadiah had felt a surge of energy rush through him and into his wife and she began to breathe so heavily it made her moan in a sporadic banshee like manner. The bodies of the couple were beyond exhausted, each person had given every last ounce of their strength to the other, and the height of their lust had filled them while they enjoyed each other. The bed sheet was soaked with sweat, the couple remained locked in their embrace, any move from one or the other caused an overwhelming sensation through the whole body of the other person, they worked in unison to wriggle to a dry side of the bed to retire for the evening.

With arms embraced around the naked body of his wife, Obadiah ran his fingers along the outsides of Mary Sues' breasts, her small buds still poked out and the goose bumps around them brushed against his fingers as he caressed her supple body. The couple finally let go, they gave up fighting sleep and the overwhelming desire for each other had transitioned into slumber as they drifted off to sleep, holding each other closely. The reassurance of their own worth to the other cast aside many inner demons for each other, Obadiah found his place in the household, cuddled up right beside his wife.

It was early when the family arose, the breakfast was fairly hearty for once, the parents didn't skimp on the meal to ensure the children had plenty to eat. Obadiah heaped a second scoop of home fries on his plate, he intended to head out and needed all of the calories he could take in before he ventured out to the train tracks to the north. Obadiah packed a few sandwiches loaded with cooked beans or potatoes smashed between pieces of bread, he also loaded up his thermos with piping hot chicory, his satchel a canvas bag hung on the chair while he donned a thick flannel shirt and laced up his boots.

The children ate and goofed around a little as Mary Sue tried to convince Obadiah to stay, with her big doe eyes, she gave longing looks and endearing smiles in hopes that he would change his mind and stay with his family, her attempts failed. Obadiah wrapped a few measly sandwiches in paper and in addition to his thermos, he packed a few matches and rolled up a small tarp from the barn for some form of makeshift shelter if in fact things took a turn for the worse, after years of hunting in the harsh South Carolina winters, there are always things you need to take in case of a binding snow that buries a hunting camp or even snows in a blind and you have to hunker down and last a day or two on your own in a snow drift. Obadiah thought about his childhood, heading out into the woods with Norman, the two of them with minimal food accommodations for a camping trip and off they would walk.

Obadiah gave Elizabeth and Isaac tight hugs as he knew he would miss them, each also received a pat on the head, Mary Sue held her husband tightly, her arms locked around him and she couldn't seem to squeeze tight enough, she feared him leaving again but she wasn't as reluctant as before, their night of embrace had rekindled her sense of security in her marriage but she still didn't want her husband to part ways from his family, her slender arms wrapped around his bony ribcage. The weather was gloomy, the skies gray and the whipping wind rattled against the outer walls.

Obadiah put on a wool cap to help fend off the breeze as he wandered about; he knew that his wife would worry so he made sure she saw him bundle up warmly as he readied himself before staking out. Obadiah kissed his loving wife on her forehead, it fortunately met the same height of his lips as they both stood flat footed and toe to toe, she turned her head sideways and rested her face against the chest of her husband, the embrace seemed to last just shy of long enough. Obadiah gave each member of his family one last kiss goodbye and stepped out the side door. With a double check of the woodpile to ensure that his family would be warm for the few days in his absence, he knew they had ample food to last them through to spring but there had to be more out there than the small retreat of his home, maybe just the news of something better.

Past the barns and out towards the north field, the wind whipped across the vast openness and gave Obadiah reason to tuck his chin down into the neck of his jacket and lean forward as he trudged through the cold sand that topped the once green field. The leather on his worn boots felt cold against his feet, the flat souls bent and slipped atop the sand and it seemed like an endless journey strewn out ahead of him, the fields were dark gray in color and offered very little to change the view, except for the occasional Russian thistle that littered the view. The sun hung low over the right shoulder of the wandering man, the home he left behind grew smaller and smaller with each step. After kicking pebbles to pass the time, Obadiah stopped to look around the midday, it was a long haul and there was still plenty of time and distance to travel, it was probably going to take all of two days with a steady pace just to get out there, then have to turn back again if he didn't find any sort of hope or information.

Obadiah hoped with everything he had in him that he would find some bit of fortune at his destination, even if it meant just the hope of work in the coming days. When civilization headed west in search of gold, many prospectors simply loaded up what they had on the notion of hope, no promise or guarantee, just mislead hope, the same hope that lead him and his family out to Oklahoma, and into the mouth of poverty and despair. Obadiah pondered so many, many things as he sauntered to the north, body tucked in tightly into his jacket to retain as much body heat as he could, the bitter wind bit and snapped at his exposed face, the breeze was relentless and blew constantly across the plains, gathering speed and abrasive soot along the way.

The sun rose overhead and began to fall towards the left of the weary Obadiah, whom had been walking since breakfast, there was no need to stop nor time to waste, the inner hope and desperation of Obadiah had given him the gusto to walk in a hurried pace in hopes of reaching his destination rather promptly. The trains were one of the last remaining arteries in the area, fuel had stop coming to town and half of the roads had blown over with sand, but the trains still ran coast to coast, and thousands of people that took on a transient lifestyles hitched up on cars and rode the railways with the hope of work or new life near the coasts, where there was still hope.

The sky grew dark, the gray had given up its last bits of illumination and there was very little ability to see any more than shadows off in the northern distance. It was abrasively cold, the wind bit and stung the uncovered portions of his body as he trudged on. He had decided that once he could no longer see further than ten feet in front of him, even after his pace had slowed and his tired dragging feet had begun to trip along the ground, he needed to continue to march on. His body fought exhaustion as much as it fought the urges to trip and fall every few steps; it was of no use to stop as the goal wasn't to walk all day, but to reach a destination. It grew dark and finally convincing enough to lie down for the night.

Mary Sue spent the day with her children and struggled with the notion that her husband was walking so far and away, her thoughts always returned to him and what he possibly may have been up to. Mary Sue hardly went without wondering what he may have been thinking or hoping, why had he been in such a hurry to head out, yet again? They had ample food to sustain them till the warm months but he had some deep seeded desire to head out and venture without his family. Mary Sue seemed bothered by her intuition that her husband was shucking his fatherly duties, it seemed as if he was driven to flee, it may have just been her insecurity about how hard things had become, it may have been the stories from the deli that set her uneasy some time ago.

Mary Sue often reflected back to her childhood, one of the girls in her grade school that she knew came to mind, a young dirty blonde haired girl named Dolly, she wore her hair in twin ponytails, her dresses were usually a bit dirty and she hardly smiled. Dolly once confided in Mary Sue that her father would beat her if she didn't pray, beat her if she was to loud during play or beat her if he had been angered whilst drinking. Mary Sue found herself further doubting the notion of religion, everyone grasped the ideology and held it dear to the their heart, it confounded Mary Sue because she had been raised in church but always questioned so very many things.

Mary Sue was labeled by her father as curious, hard pressed and with an unending need to make logic of things, she often questioned many attributes of the gospel, they were hard fables to swallow so she simply looked upon them as mere stories for entertainment, nothing was ever truly explained nor aligned with any real things in her life, just a long winded individual preaching from the pulpit about how everything can lead you to eternal damnation, the threats seemed empty and manipulative. It was often those beaten to follow biblical teachings, or those raised with the heavy hands since birth that wept and hollered the loudest when it came to tithing's, and yet when the nation dried up and prayers went unanswered by the millions, the church continued to expect more and more of its congregation, the leaders didn't seem to miss meals as the congregation members withered away and starved.

The charades of the priest in town made for exciting sermons, his arms flailing as if actually fighting demons, smiting as if he himself was the bringer of salvation, while he huffed and puffed and turned red in the face, robes flying in every which direction, it was a pretty entertaining show. Many parishioners back home attributed every good thing to the lord, not to say that there wasn't a grand scheme in the works, but when people began to see the lack of god, the excuse changed to it being part of the plan, how many people simply waited on their asses and starved to death, all while waiting on an answered prayer? Mary Sue began to suspect she found out how her husband felt, he brought the family out here on a prayer and it dried up faster than the fields.

Mary Sue felt an urgency deep inside of her, she found herself with anxiety as she could no longer hope to count on subtle blessings, she felt a dread hit her as she felt lost, there was no longer a god, there was no distant hope of anything that might swiftly deliver people from the demise that was taking lives all over the country. Mary Sue had a strange sensation to pray, it was sheer habit, but it was useless. Mary Sue still kept hope in her heart that her husband would return to her, he had come back from town when he had money in his pocket and a motor vehicle to get him anywhere else, and he came back to her. There was a relief in her heart but it was still tainted with fear and insecurity, it was conflicting and it left her dwelling. Mary Sue still felt blessed to have brought her two children into this world, maybe it wasn't a blessing but maybe what she was born to do, or designed for. So many thoughts and feelings left the tired woman emotionally torn, she felt the urge to cry overcome her many times as she played with her children late into the waning hours. Elizabeth sensed that her mother needed her affection, she held her closely as Isaac hit blocks together, the family listened to the radio program talk about more struggle around the country.

The news program that played each afternoon spoke on about New York money men taking their lives after they lost millions of dollars for normal hard working people, the price of cotton had fallen to less than a sixteenth of what it was three years ago, the times continued to prove trying, steel mills were faltering, textile companies in New York and in other area had slowly closed down and that was the way things were around the country.

Elizabeth wasn't sure of what she was hearing as she had no idea what stocks were, not certain of what hardships meant and only hardly noticed when food was scarce, but she knew the look in her mother's eyes when the news hit and watched the brows of her mother fall when they failed to mention rain time and time again. Each news program would report how arid and dry areas in the country were, each storm that may have come from the gulf was pushed up and along the east coast, bringing them snow and rain, neglecting the mid-west plains, leaving it further parched and baron of life. Mary Sue tucked in her young children, their ignorance towards the strain of the land was a blessing, she carried enough of a burden for all of them.

The home was quiet as Mary Sue fed a few logs to the wood stove in the kitchen, she brewed a small cup of chicory root, the strong steam rose from the cup and moistened the tip of her nose as she took deep panic laced breaths, the steam softened the inside of her nostrils, hardened from the dry cold, her eyes hung heavy and she struggled to hold her eyes open, the stresses and strains of life had worn on the mother, being able to hang her head over a steaming cup was almost an escape on its' own, even if only for twenty minutes. Mary Sue felt her nose tingle, her head began to bob, dinner was minimal but it was fortunate to have another meal to feed her children, she was able to feed herself but her twisted and knotted stomach prevented her from eating much, her husband had been gone all day, she still wasn't entirely sure what he was looking for but she knew he needed to find something, and soon.

Mary Sue sniffled as she felt her nose begin to run a little, opening her eyes and looking down, blood dripped from the tip of her nose and into her coffee cup, the small splash made a *plop* as Mary Sue searched quickly for a paper napkin or rag to wipe up the splash as well as dam up the bleed. Mary Sue felt distraught, a nose bleed was minor but it was another defeating event that left the weary woman further defeated as she tilted her head back to let the blood run down the back of her throat while she waited for her nosebleed to clot.

The metallic taste of the blood pooled in the back of her throat, she needed a hearty sniffle, and Mary Sue sipped her chicory to wash back the bitter taste in her mouth, eyes clenched as she returned her head backwards against the chair back. The crackles of the fire shot pieces of wood embers against the metal sides leaving the occasional ping and pang, the loud bursts of wood were disruptive to the low roar of the flames and crackle of the wood drying as it burned. The heat radiated across the kitchen, it was the main source of heat and it was now solely Mary Sue's responsibility to keep it stoked and fired over the next few days and nights to keep her children and home warm in the absence of Obadiah. Mary Sue was hesitant in raising her tired body from her chair and carrying it off to bed, only to get up every few hours and keep the fire going to keep her kids from getting cold.

The missing of her husband had already hit Mary Sue, she severely hated the notion of being up over and over again, it was like feeding babies all over again. The worn woman rose to her feet, with a swig to finalize her cup of chicory and she stood up straight, her head spun a bit and she needed to clench her eyes tightly and waited for the spell to pass. Mary Sue looked adamantly at her children asleep on the couch as she stepped towards her bed for the next few hours, the wood stove task was usually Obadiah's job as the man of the home, the concerns about her husband made it hard to concentrate or relax enough to fall asleep.

The early morning woke Obadiah, it was freezing cold and the temperatures dropped into the upper teens, the curled up man was bound in his tarp, he had taken refuge in a small divot to hide under the path of the breeze as it ushered in the cold temperatures overnight, his shivering had kept him from a solid night's sleep in the pitch black darkness that had blanketed the land. The frosted land was hard to wake up to, the earth beneath the traveling man was soft as it had absorbed his body heat throughout the night. With the sun beginning to rise from the east, Obadiah used a trick that his father had shared with him to find his way around.

Drawing a straight line from the left side of the sun, and the line from the right side angled towards and meeting the line left an angle in the dirt, with two foot long lines, using one more line meeting the top straight line to make a right angle, gave a pretty good direction of what true north was. With a quick look around for some rocks and a handful of the bristly weeds, Obadiah had a small fire smoking and crackling within a few moments, the flames licked at the rocks, the smoke billowed in different directions as the breeze kicked up or died back down, over and over again. Obadiah wanted to knock off the cold before he returned back to his journey. He kept his tarp over his shoulders to keep the wind off of himself and the fire as well as cover the fire enough to absorb as much heat as possible; his body ached from the cold and having slept on the hard ground.

Obadiah used some of the paper that wrapped a sandwich to help start his fire, he also set half of the meal on the rocks in order to heat the morning meal for himself. The sun let streaks of light pierce the sky above, the bright orb broke through cracks of the sky, the cold stung on the skin but the fire warmed the legs and feet of Obadiah as he curled his arms around his knees awaiting for his food to be warm enough to pad his stomach with. Obadiah sipped his water and poured a bit of his chicory into the metal lid to heat by the fire as well. The rations were meager, slim and devoid of much flavor but it was food in his stomach nonetheless.

After his rear had frozen from sitting for almost twenty minutes, Obadiah slurped down a bit of his water and the urge to urinate encouraged him to rise to his feet and begin his day by capping his thermos. After arching backwards to stretch from hard sleep on the stiff ground. Obadiah used his full bladder to extinguish the small fire, the searing cold made it hard to grasp himself to urinate as the cold forced his penis to hurry and retract back in to his zippered fly almost instantly, like a snake racing into a hole to elude a predator.

Obadiah folded his small tarp back up and slung it over his satchel and headed north yet again. Based on educated estimates, the weary traveler roughly figured he should make his destination before sun down and camp there for the night. Obadiah turned his head over his right and left shoulders, the horizon wasn't without upset, there were no roads or cars, hardly many trees in the distance, just vast openness and very little hope, there didn't even seem to be streams or rivers in the view and much like the stream back near his home, Obadiah suspected that all of the other water reservoirs had been filled up and erased from the landscape by the blowing sands. The heading seemed extensive, the journey ahead was long and drawn out but it seemed that it may have already been unsuccessful.

Obadiah debated with himself as to why this journey was so important to him, it was a conversation that troubled him to the point he was almost arguing with himself out loud as to why he had left behind his home, family, wife, and food in order to wander the frozen tundra of north-west Oklahoma, searching for a railroad, two iron tracks that ran across a wood trail that headed east or west. Obadiah could feel his cold pant legs flap against his dry skin as he walked, he shoved his hands deep into his pockets and shrugged up his shoulders near his cheeks to try and keep warm as he walked on.

Mary Sue woke up cold, her body rolled into her blankets and she fought to keep warm as best as she could, she had a few moments of warmth and it caused her to fall deeply asleep, oversleeping when she was supposed to fuel the house warming fire. The air had become so cold in the home that she could see her breath when she opened her eyes causing worry set in. Mary Sue was hard to throw aside the warm covers, she desperately needed to fire up the stove and she hoped the children weren't frozen in the living room and she was certain they were going to wake up hungry. Mary Sue slipped into a sweater as she left her bed in order to perform her duties as a mother, breakfast and a hot fire were in order, and promptly.

Mary Sue crept into the living room, breathing softly to prevent waking up her sleeping angels, Elizabeth curled up on the far end of the green couch, at her feet, Isaac laid out while his right arm hung off the couch. Mary Sue worried that the exposed arm of her son would be cold but moving it may wake the little guy. Mary Sue scraped and shoveled out the ashes from the wood stove, she then began to load the stove with sticks for kindling, the stove had grown cold overnight and it needed to heat in a hurry. Mary Sue struck a match to ignite the twigs and bark, looking at the match as it burned down, Mary Sue thought back to the honeymoon with Obadiah, the two of them living off of a small wood stove and wandering around in the buff as they explored one another, nights spent staring into the fire as it crackled and popped the hours away. With a shiver, Mary Sue snapped back to reality, the match had all but burned down; she had drifted off and forgot to put the match to the kindling to start the fire. Mary Sue tossed the burned match stick into the fireplace and reached for another one from the strike anywhere box, this time she held the match to the sticks and once again, a fire began to take hold inside the stove.

Mary Sue remained huddled near the stove, it slowed to warm but the crackling was a welcomed distraction from the cold, she struggled to envision what she was about to fix for her children for breakfast. The salted goat wasn't the greatest way to start a day but perhaps thinly sliced in conjunction with some butter fried potatoes. Making large meals out of small helpings and the small children were often thankful just to eat. Mary Sue wondered how her husband fared the cold night, the frost on the window proved that the temperatures plummeted and she hoped that he had managed to survive.

Mary Sue knew Obadiah was a fighter and had the physical means to keep himself out of any trouble and to be able to protect himself if things got out of hand, she also knew that his conscience must have been clouded after having had to defend Elizabeth against the black monster at Basks farm, it must have been troublesome to have to bear the guilt of taking someone's life. Mary Sue often wondered how long before his guilt got to him, he stoically pushed aside the notion of what happened, both husband and wife were convinced it was necessary, Mary Sue would stand beside her husband no matter what, and Obadiah would forever do what was necessary to safeguard his family, against anyone.

Obadiah trudged along in the early hours, the frozen ground made each step painful in his heels and knees as the large stride he took carried him quickly along his uncertain path. Obadiah rubbed at his achy hips as he walked, the cold battered his body, the frigid weather made all of his injured or abused joints ache with each step, his knees took hard thuds with each step and they throbbed between steps, he tried to keep his eyes up and looking ahead but the cold also battered him to keep his chin tucked to his chest to duck some of the cold. Obadiah let his stomach growl as the chicory churned with his starch heavy morning meal, the mixed meal was a welcome relief but the lower abdominal pains weren't.

Nearing one distant tree, Obadiah looked for other distant trees, small goals were better markers along his path rather than aimlessly walking into the horizon, without guidance or direction. The endless desert was ominous, depressing, it spread out forever and there were no signs of life, no tracks along the way, no signs of rabbits or gophers, no birds making noise in the distance or in any of the few scattered trees around, everything was devoid of life, desolate, no grasses or critters, not even cars or people within sight or sound, the only sounds were of the wind skipping along the sands.

Mary Sue began to slice and pan fry some potatoes for her sleeping babies, with three small thin slices of goat meat ready to be warmed in the pan once the home-fries were finished cooking. Sprinkling a small amount of chicory in a cup and topping it up with boiling water, she made herself a southern morning cup of wake up juice as she continued on with her morning, the fries sizzled and sweet Elizabeth rounded the corner. The girl was rubbing her eyes and was awaken by the slicing and sizzling in the kitchen, her nose and stomach brought her to the kitchen where her mother was dutifully stationed. Elizabeth grabbed herself a stool and dragged it to the stove and with wooden spoon in hand, she began stirring the spuds in the cast iron skillet, she hardly spoke but picked up her share of duties in the household, she picked up what she could and let her caring mother spend a few moments to herself sipping her coffee. Mary Sue tilted her cup to the young assistant in a quasi-offer to share, having tried it once and also having found it too bitter for her liking, Elizabeth quickly shuttered away the offer and made a snarling face while plugging her little button nose with her free left hand.

Elizabeth dashed a bit of salt into the pan, she saw her mom cook a lot and infrequently got to get so hands on but Isaac was still dozing on the couch outstretched as his sister had given him more room. Mary Sue bent to look at her son, his odd sleeping position would leave his mother debilitated for several days to sleep in such a position. Mary Sue chuckled to herself at her sons' short, but out of sorts hair and dangling arm were completely oblivious to the almost hibernating young boy. Elizabeth corralled the items in the pan from left to right and back again, Mary Sue leaned back against the counter and watched her young homemaker work, the pride that filled her gave her the sense to well up a bit, after a hearty sniffle, the urge was quelled and she realigned her focus to her daughter and finished up for breakfast. The home-fries browned and the meat sizzled, Elizabeth bounced a bit on her stool and bopped her head along with the grizzle crackle from the pan, as Mary Sue finished her cup and started to assist the small cook with removing the hot pan from heat was the time Isaac came wobbling into the kitchen. The little guy was feeling left out of the cooking fun, his arms were crossed tightly, hugging himself to remain warm, the smell of food and sounds of sizzling meat grease in the pan brought him wandering in to join his sister and mother.

Isaac placed his hands on a chair and pulled with all of his might, with hardly enough room the small boy climbed up and readied himself to be fed, his hair still pointing in many directions and his eyes wandering about independently from the tired. Elizabeth stumbled down from her heightened perch on the stool, almost falling to the ground on her way to the breakfast table herself. Mary Sue scooped portions to the children, each plate didn't appear to have the grandest of servings, it certainly wasn't a feast but it was edible and warm.

Isaac didn't bother to cut his meat, he tore at it like a carnivore and heaped in mounds of potatoes into any open space in his mouth that was available while Elizabeth looked on with disgust. Mary Sue smiled as she watched her babies tussle and poke fun at each other, she didn't bother to correct them, and she just let them be children. Mary Sue knew it must have been tough on Elizabeth to spend a fair amount of her time being her brothers caretaker, as the youngest sister of three girls herself, Mary Sue knew she was a handful when she was younger and both of her older sisters had to help to keep her busy. With very little to do for the day but keep the stove warm and stay indoors awaiting the return of the mister of the home, the family decided to take up board games after learning sessions.

Obadiah had walked well past the midday sun, it rose high overhead as he hid his face down to keep it shielded from the breeze. The sky was still gray, small rays of sun pierced to the ground, it wasn't warming or even brightened the area in the distance much, but the rays that shone through had left brighter blotches in scattered areas, it was tempting to think that those areas were "X's" on a map that might pinpoint water or areas of fortune, like from a fantasy novel, but that was just lunatic thinking.

Obadiah only had his own breathing to keep him company, he spent the better part of yesterday adjusting to the silence, it was awkward, no voices or kids to interact with, no Mary Sue to hug or kiss on, or even to have doting on him, the old adage was that "silence was deafening," a strange quip but when the breeze was still and between footsteps, the only sound that could be heard was the hard thumping of his heart, the beating in his temples felt like a sledgehammer being swung at his ears. Norman used to sit close to Obadiah in a pine branch deer blind in the woods, they would sit quietly for hours, Obadiah would lose feeling in his butt and toes and slowly everything in between while sitting there for the long hours but it was never this silent.

Hunting in the winter was often tranquil but still strewn with branch snaps, leaf crunches or dirt settling, not here. Obadiah honed his skills at looking for the slightest changes in things, if a bedded buck rose its' head, you had to be able to see the antlers and recognize them deep into tall grasses. Obadiah often found himself aimlessly restless while hunting, it was usually freezing cold and boring for such a young kid but he enjoyed the time with his father and over the span of his childhood, he adapted and continued to learn small tricks to keeping his eyes wandering and his mind alert at all times.

As Obadiah walked he kept a keen eye on the trees, any signs of birds in the trees would mean food, or at least a source to find food over the coming summer, if they make it that long. The trees were bare sticks reaching up from the ground, no leaves and hardly any sign of life left, the trees were few and far between around the landscape. Obadiah could feel his face tighten when the winds swept across the land and surrounded his body, his scruffy facial hair brushed against the collar of his jacket as he huddled down for more protection, his eyelids wore heavy and when the winds blew hard enough, tears would stream down his cheeks but dry before reaching his jaw line in the breeze. Obadiah peered over his left and faced straight into the cold winds to judge how much sunlight he had left. Norman taught him the trick that if you hold your hand along the horizon, each finger width you have under the sun is approximately fifteen minutes, this time he had about forty five minutes, just enough to find a low laying area to camp in to be under the winds overnight again with his tarp. Obadiah found a small depression, a shallow portion in the ground that seemed made from the dirt drifts; they would serve his purpose ideally.

Mary Sue spent the day learning and playing games with her children, card games and reading games to help Isaac to learn the letters of the alphabet while Elizabeth practiced her penmanship on a slate board with chalk. Elizabeth practiced her name over and over as well as the rest of the letters of the alphabet, each screeching letter that swooped, gave Isaac a slight distraction as well as a sound to mimic to pester his sister. Mary Sue gathered a small meal for supper and the children were fed before an evening phonograph show just prior to bed.

Mary Sue fought her best to keep her focus on her children and keep her mind from drifting out the windows trying to imagine what her husband had been up to, did he last the first night? Was he making any progress or is he frozen to death somewhere out there never to return? Mary Sue wondered if he was going to return, she struggled enough two days prior when he went to town and when they got together intimately after he returned, it was most reassuring that they were in love still and that there was nothing to have to worry about. Mary Sue still wondered if maybe he might hop on the train and haul ass out of town and to a new life somewhere, letting her heart sink more and more each time she thought about him not returning to her.

Obadiah woke again in the early morning, it was once again cold and everything was frozen around him, it hadn't thawed in weeks but during the day some of the frost at least decreased. The chilly air made it difficult to emerge from the tarp turtle like shell he created to retain most of his own body heat, even while his body weight and ability to warm himself decreased. Obadiah was once again stiff and sore from his earthen bed, it was a hard ground and with his bony body made for an awful sleep, his shoulder ached from laying on it and his neck sore from no support, his lower back ached and shot pains upwards through his back and downwards through his legs, it was difficult to move and the tightly wrapped tarp hindered his ability to wriggle free and start his day. Obadiah slowly rubbed his sore knees together to create enough friction to start his blood circulating, all while looking around for some tinder to warm a bit of chicory and half of a sandwich, as well as himself. He gathered a few rocks and used his boot to dig a small divot in the ground to place his fire into, it was a small smoky fire but it was heat nonetheless and he could feel his fingers and toes begin to thaw while it crackled on.

In the distance Obadiah thought he could finally make out the railroad, the shapes and images were a bit tough to decipher as his eyes watered from the cold and smoke while he was still trying to shed off the intense chill that caused his whole body to jerk uncontrollably as he warmed up.

The small metal cup of chicory warmed on the side of a few small rocks, half a sandwich was going to make up his morning meal, his stomach was feeling like an abyss with no bottom, he had been hungry for years, starving was the most recent feeling and emotion he had anymore. The smoke swirled as it plumed from the small hole full of twigs and thistle that was turning ashen as small flames licked at the metal cup and half sandwich that were warming near the side. With his back to the wind in an attempt to blockade the fire, Obadiah fixed his sights on the train tracks, it appeared as if there were clusters in the distance, the curiosity had stirred in him, he wanted to pick himself up and run towards the distance but he was also wondering what he had come across and what he might find there, he also lacked the energy to run and was still too cold to stand. With elbows wrapped around his knees overtop of the fire, absorbing as much of the heat as possible, his inner thighs grew hot while the back of his neck was still rife with goose bumps from the cold, every other breath was filled with smoke, it was choking, gagging and thick as it billowed.

Obadiah ran low on sticks and tinder, signaling time to finish his chicory and drag himself to his feet yet again, it was difficult to rise, with achy joints and stiff muscles it was already a major task just to stand upright. Lightheadedness spelled the venture, with a swift kick of dirt over the fire, it was time to finish the two day journey and see what he set out to see. With tarp folded and laid over satchel, the weary traveler leaned forward to use momentum to convince the rest of his body to move in the same direction. It was hard to find the adequate rhythm to walk, his boots dragged a bit in the dirt as he walked, his body was exhausted and it made him clumsy, he almost tripped and fell to the ground a few times and each time, he was fortunate enough to stumble back up rather than to the ground. His feet ached, his knees ground together with each step and his hips took the brunt of the force and pain when he almost tripped each time, making it difficult to find the will to carry on. Nearing the railroad tracks, Obadiah could make out small shelters, and an upward standing post. There were a few more trees nearby than the previous portion of the journey, a few small clusters stood together near the tracks.

Coming upon the cluster of shelters, they were recognizable to be few large cardboard boxes with a tarp layered over top with sand and dirt strewn over top. The tall post at the end had a bunch of chalk markings up and down on a few of the sides, the markings were suspicious. "Hello" Obadiah shouted out to announce himself at his arrival, he didn't know what he was going to run into or startle and wanted to announce himself if there was anyone about that might object with his being there. Sure enough there was a faint voice coming from one of the boxes, four boxes made a semi-circle with the openings facing east around a small metal fire ring. "Whaddya want?" some meek voice asked from within the cardboard cave. "*Muh names Obadiah and I'm looking for information, I have a family to feed and was hoping to learn how I could do that?*" the weary traveler spoke aloud. The voice snapped back; "*We all do mister, train won't be by for a few hours, go back to sleep.*" Obadiah bent his sore back a bit to try and get an angle to possibly look into the dark box to place the voice, his lower back cracked and popped, his knees ached as he pushed against them to ease himself down and then back up.

"*Can you talk to me, I have a family that I just gotta fend for*" Obadiah repeated into the box, it then began to shake and rumble a bit, a pair of small dirty bare feet emerged from deep in the shadow, the heels dug into the bottom to drag the rest of a young body out. A frail girl scooted out of the darkness in the box, she remained seated in the edge of the box, a small insulate between her body and the frozen ground beneath. The girl was small, she had dirty blondish hair, it was really long and curly, her green eyes stood out through the layers of dirt on her face. The girl huddled tightly under a wool blanket, she held it tightly around her shoulders, her legs covered in tattered jeans that frayed near her ankles, her feet callused and caked in dried mud and blisters. Obadiah took a moment, along with a deep gasp, he thought back to the admirable Joe Martinez whom spoke about the young boy that was kicked from the train some time ago that had injured his arm. The box began to shimmy again, the young girl looked back over her shoulder and nodded a bit back into the darkness as it continued to shake and then moan a bit. Another small face broke from the darkness of the shadows, a young Asian face entered the dim light of the morning.

"Who are you girls?" Obadiah inquired; to see two kids maybe twice the age of Elizabeth was quite a surprise. The blonde haired girl spoke up; "*Names Wendy Connors, I'm from Virginia, family was hard up so I struck out to make my own living while tracking to San Francisco where my pops is a prison guard.*" the girl introduced the mute girl that was her partner. "I call the chink Suzy, she don't talk much when strangers' around but we met up near West Virginia, she and me been hiking the rails for a few weeks, we saw the post there (she motioned to the erected wood post) night before last and hopped off" the girl explained the series of chalk markings on the tall wood post that Obadiah was leaning on, each mark was made by hobos and train hoppers, it expressed that a mile up was a bypass and when the train slows, it meant to hop off to avoid a train guard that would check the cars for people riding the rails. Wendy spoke about being shot at in Georgia somewhere, the girls were trying to get down when a large man wearing a navy blue uniform began shouting and chasing the girls, as the girls fled to avoid trouble, he took a shot at them. "*I was scared for a minute but Suzy and me, we ducked under a car and gots away, that was the first time Suzy talked to me, was right after we got back on a car after bein chased.*" the girl lamented.

Wendy and Suzy had been out for a few weeks, Wendy had been sharecropping with her mother and siblings back in Virginia and finally when the end of the year came, the food thinned and Wendy set out to take care of herself so her mother could take care of her three other siblings. Wendy mentioned her father was harder and colder than a railroad spike but a loving father; "*he was a tough sumbitch*" but took care of his family from across the country, Wendy was a lot like him; "*tough and don't take no gruff*" so she figured she could hitch rides on freight trains as hobos, ducking "Bulls" which were the railroad patrol guards. Each set of train tracks had camps set up along here and there, smaller than the Hooverville's but a few boxes gave enough protection from some cold each night to make it habitable. Obadiah knew he had time before the girls hitched out on the next train so he stood up and headed down the way for a few steps. Obadiah gathered a handful of thistle and tinder sticks to build a small flame to thaw the girls out and keep them talking, he needed to know what they knew and the leader of the two; she was thick skinned and hard to share.

The struck match met the tinder taking flame, the little hitchhiker girl scooted further out of the box near the fire, she couldn't have weighed more than sixty pounds, she was itty-bitty and probably frozen stiff, she extended out her bare feet towards the small ring of rocks that circled the small handful of fire. The Asian girl huddled tightly into the tattered wool blanket also, she kept her slant eyes locked on the fire and refused to make eye contact when spoken too, and of course she remained silent. Wendy spoke up again; "*Suzy traveled with me almost a week before the shooting, she was silent the entire time, after a day of talking to her, she learned to nod, but didn't say nothing.*" the man sat quietly and listened to the dirty girl speak, her hair was tied in a rag above her head but her blonde curly hair flared out from underneath and also the blanket. Wendy began to tell what she knew about Suzy; "*I can't say her name, it's all chinesey and stuff but we keep each other warm and don't have to travel alone. She's from West Virginia, she has four older brothers and everyone picked tobacco during the season, it was her job as the youngest to keep the house clean during the day, and to lay with her brothers at night. She was pure till she was twelve but shortly after that, her older brother came in one night and lay with her.*" Obadiah was left speechless, he wasn't sure what he was hearing and closed his eyes a bit when he finally realized his eyes were wide open and affixed on the girl while listening to the tales.

The young girl said that she was thirteen; Suzy was twelve and had been sharing beds with her brothers for almost a year now, each time she cried when she redressed after they climbed off of her. Obadiah was appalled that brothers would do such things to sisters and then Wendy spoke up again; "*two days after that guard bout shot us, a grown man started rubbing on Suzy when I was takin a squat, when I came back his hands were up her shirt and he was kissin up on her.*" Suzy dropped her head as Wendy talked on about that encounter. The man had ridden almost all of the hundred-thousand miles of train tracks that crisscrossed the country and he was sharing news with the girls to be friendly and helped them, then expected a repayment of flesh. Wendy flipped out a folding knife, it was three times longer than her hand was wide, she said she was angry when she saw the grown man pushing around her friend and she attacked him, "*kickin an yellin an slashin*" at him as best as she could with the knife, leaving a few slash marks in his forearm as the man rose up and slapped the young girl back before taking off. Wendy said that the trains were often to full to try and sleep during the night on the cars so they hopped off at night, it took them longer to get to their destination but it seemed much safer.

Wendy had a solid head on her, her hardass father must have taught her pretty well as she took it upon herself to set out and has managed several weeks of independence, hopping from one train to another as she navigated around the country, such a large undertaking to go alone, and now to also look after the little Chinese girl that depended on her for protection and everything else, she was a tough little girl and will probably make it to wherever she wants and with piss to spare, this girl had a lot of inner strength for her size. Obadiah broke out his third sandwich, he had only one left and it would have to last him a two day trek back to his family but these girls needed to eat also. Obadiah placed two halves on the rocks near the fire to heat, Wendy looked at the food like it was a feast, Suzy lifted her head enough to look at the food and fixed her eyes on it, her posture straightened up and her upper body leaned forward a bit.

Wendy had a course attitude, she had become as hard as a ten penny screw over the last few weeks of her travels, and she had stood her ground against adult men, caught train cars while they were moving and had leaped from the same moving train cars to take to tumbling on the ground each time. "*When was the last time you ate?*" Obadiah asked the girls as he turned the potato stuffed bread over for even heating. "*We had us some mulligan two days ago*" Wendy explained that they caught two field mice and skinned them before adding them to a small cup of boiling water and added to some roots, anything edible that could have boiled down to a thick stew like substance, each girl had a small cup of the stew, it wasn't filling but it did settle their stomachs.

Wendy learned to make mulligan the second day riding the rails, a few bo's gathered simple supplies and diced what they could with pocket knives into a pot, while some water in it began to boil and it made for the stew, just added anything possible to make any sort of meal. Wendy reached forward to grab her half of the warming sandwich, she also grabbed the other and handed it to her pal, there wasn't much waiting. The little chink girl took small bites; she seemed unsure of the meal but chewed slowly and in cadence, her head bobbing with each bite. Suzy had dark black hair that was filled with dust and dirt; the souls of her feet were thick and seemed as if she hadn't worn shoes in years. Neither girl shed their blankets, Wendy said the next train should be by this evening and they planned to be on it to make more distance towards California.

Wendy was heading to find her father, a hard working prison guard that would find a way to help provide for her, there was no news of prosperous farms nearby, no sign of better things to come, no hope. Wendy said she knew that the sun rose in the east, and set in the west where she could find the ocean near where her father was, the old codger would care for her and raise her up to be a strong woman that would never have to fear nothing. Wendy came across as infinitely strong as a young girl, as an adult she would probably have the strength to do anything she set her mind to and should stand tall about all that she had accomplished and should let her strengths hold her up.

Obadiah wanted to heat his sandwich and chicory but also wanted to make it last, he had at least two more cold nights and mornings ahead and even feeling weak, he wanted to save some of his energy to make the last push to get back home. The little Asian girl climbed back into the box after she finished eating, Wendy seemed to want the company so she stood up and wandered a bit for more things to burn, she hadn't had a fire in a few days, this was such a relief to the stark cold that ate away the energy of the girls, the heat refilled their hope. Wendy came back with a fair amount of things to keep the fire warm for the remainder of the day, the fire brought such comfort, especially to the two girls traveling essentially from one coast to another. Obadiah thought about finishing out the last half of the day with the company, having started a second fire it was hard to have to leave but his family needed him and he wanted to get back to food and his adoring wife, and especially his bed. Obadiah wanted to hope that the two girls would make it safely, he recalled the dead priest, dried up and just dead in the dirt, no one is safe from the elements and there were no guarantees.

Obadiah stared down the tracks, they faded out into the horizon, the cold steel ran straight and true, unwavering, and un-wavered by the realities of life, the rails were oblivious to the starvation, the hunger, the stresses of life and the prayers of so many people fighting for any small morsel of food to hold off starvation, even if only for one last minute of life. When the energy in your body begins to dim, the strength has been gone and all that is left is the acceptance of what will be, the rails are laid for a purpose, they are cold, quiet and have an understanding of their purpose. people spend our lives in search of a purpose, every other creature on this round globe knew its' purpose except man, we search for meaning because we need one, we have to have a purpose to our existence, even if it is just simply how, or why we evolved and came to be.

Wendy said that Suzy ain't never been to school, the girl was raised up to clean and lay with her brothers in their beds, Suzy had heard her parents talk about promising her off for money when she was a few years older, her mother was a timid woman, she always took orders from the father. Her father was the first one to introduce her to the male body, he entered her room one night, reeking of smoke and began to touch on her. He un-buttoned her long dress and exposed her legs to him, he then rubbed his hands on her bare stomach and moved his hands in circles around her chest and neck. Wendy looked over her left as she explained to the silent man, the stories of the two girls were horrid and just awful to have to hear. Obadiah tried to comfort the girl and explain to her that everyone had their stories, their demons, and their baggage that they carry with them, including himself. Wendy dropped her chin onto her shoulder, avoiding looking at the visitor to the cardboard camp, she seemed to want to keep her tough attitude about her but everyone needed someone to talk to also as she spoke to Obadiah about her friend and what she had been told.

Obadiah continued talking with Wendy, he spoke of how he didn't want to tell everything to his wife and change her opinion or perception of him to her, he carried the burden upon his shoulders to ensure that his wife always looked at him lovingly and as the protector, he needed that of her as his wife, and because he needed such endearing regards from Mary Sue, he would never stray or cause her harm in her life.

Obadiah found himself exposing his soul to this young girl, he spoke about his children, how he wanted to retain status as head of household and father, he spoke about the anguish on the face of the priest he found, a man of god that had died in such a painful way, alone. Suzy sat up and asked who "god" was, the little girl was curious, she had never heard of such mythology and the stories sounded intriguing, Suzy was curious enough to speak, after listening to the man speak through the morning. Obadiah tried to explain in a nutshell what he could recall, the notion of a creator left the small girl looking more and more puzzled with each attempt at an explanation, he recited some of the bible school stories he had heard, even if he himself never believed.

Suzy asked for clarification, why she had to lay with her brothers if such a god protects the children, why her pain went without salvation because she didn't know of such god, why god punished the same people he created just because they didn't worship him enough, if such a god was so powerful than why does he need the praise, why give freewill to make decisions if only to punish people for exercising that same right. Suzy was very intelligent, even for not having been schooled; she could immediately see the hypocrisy in the notion of a loving invisible person that wants pure obedience for no return for such obedience. Obadiah tried to explain the story of Noah and the ark, Suzy almost found humor in the fable that god drowned every person on earth because he loved them. Obadiah had struggled with the same notions, all of the stories had been beaten and fed to children since birth, it was forced teachings and it was often beaten harder into those that wanted to think for themselves instead of being blind followers.

Suzy said that she was raised as a happy girl but a few years ago when the economy had caused her father to lose his farm, they had moved to become sharecroppers on a farm, her father's demeanor had changed. Suzy began to receive beatings, abuse, she was suddenly viewed for the flesh, her only worth seemed to be between her legs, she was no longer seen as an equal child along with her brothers, now as a rag doll for the physical pleasure of teen boys, to be kicked out of bed and made to sleep on the floor when they were done with her. Suzy turned angry, she hated the notion of such a god, some invisible nonexistent entity that watched everything happen, watched her wake up with blood streaming from between her legs after nights with her bigger brothers, and didn't change any of it, and she grew angrier and angrier.

Obadiah had struggled with many of the same concepts, the fabled notions of such things, he had the deep seeded need to make sense of things, he gave up his faith a long time ago and it was reinforced after hearing how these two girl had been dealt just terrible hands in the last few months alone. Wendy reached over and hugged her friend, the two of the were looking out for each other and been doing it almost a month now, Wendy hadn't heard some of the stories and was frightened hearing how much like a dog her new friend Suzy had been treated. The two girls embraced and shook while crying for a few minutes, Obadiah added a few more twigs to the fire and poked it a bit to keep it producing heat. The rocks steamed and were warm near the hands as he held his palms open facing the fire, giving the girls a bit of privacy to console one another. Wendy let her hair obscure the face of Suzy as the hugged; Suzy sniffled to clear her nose before the embrace broke. Wendy turned back to Obadiah, she began to thank him for the sandwich, he really didn't have to but he did. Wendy said that the two girls were going to go back to bed because they had a late train to catch and being girls, they had to stay awake through the night to keep from becoming victims of some sort, Wendy seemed to have a solid grasp on some of the things people were capable of.

Obadiah reassured the girls that they will be OK, they were tough and had each other and needed to keep calm and carry on hitching, they would make California in a few more days. Wendy reached out and shook hands with the man that offered up the warm meal, she wished him luck in providing for his family but she had to keep herself moving on. Obadiah watched the two girls climb back into the box; it jostled a few times and then fell silent. Obadiah let the fire crackle for a bit longer, judging by the angle of the sun, it had passed overhead while talking, it wasn't mid-afternoon but it couldn't have been much earlier.

If he left now to begin walking back, he should have a few well lit hours to make progress back towards his home and family. Obadiah stood and brushed off his dirty backside, his hips popped as he stretched a bit, he could hear his knees grinding as he transitioned to standing, his body was sore and hurt in many places. His back was tight and tense and his shoulders were very limited in their range of movement, he felt like he was falling apart and was physically in need of his soft bed. Obadiah twisted his lower back to look up and down the train tracks, there was no sign of a coming train or even of other people nearby, these two girls were simply alone with no one to look out for them or help them to move along to their destination,

Obadiah left his last sandwich near the feet of the girls inside the box, he decided that they needed it much more so than he and

257

he began his journey back to his home for the remainder of the winter. The walk was long and grueling, even worse on an empty stomach. Obadiah left his last piece of food in hopes that it would help feed the girls even if only for a little and get them to the girl's father. The return walk the first day was shortened by the darkness, but the next day was more progressive, his morning was an early one as hunger pains and the bitter cold had forced open his eyes in response to his ruthless shivering.

With no kindling for a small warming fire, Obadiah sipped at the icy chicory that he had left as he walked, it was ever more bitter when cold but it was liquid and helped to fight his parched mouth, he decided to walk long into the night, he planned to be close to home in the morning so he walked a bit further in the night for progress. The nights were dark and intensely cold, Obadiah walked the later portion of the day wrapped in his tarp around his upper body for the extra thermal layer, and protection from the chill. When it had finally gotten to dark to see, Obadiah simply fell down, he attempted to lay down rolled in his tarp but fumbled near the ground and just simply fell over and slept where he lay.

Spring broke, the days grew longer and warmer, Mary Sue had continued to encourage the children to play longer outdoors, the fresh air cleared out the stagnant smell inside the home and the fresh air always helped the children to sleep better each night. Mary Sue enjoyed an open cracked window each night; the air was warming and helped her to relax at night as she began to show. With times still being hard, there were a few sprinkles that had softened some of the sands and dirt, a few pitter patter spots had been found, the signs helped to bring hope that the grounds might hold seed, once plants grew and the roots tangled together, the dirt could be held in place and life could be restored to the area, it was looking hopeful to the mother.

The young Elizabeth was growing bigger every day and the language of Isaac had grown in articulation, Mary Sue couldn't be more proud of her two children, she also explained what a third child might mean to the family. Elizabeth already knew the ramifications of a younger sibling, she had Isaac already mimicking her every move as well as pestering her to no end, and they still argued several times per day and strained the nerves of their mother with their bickering.

Mary Sue started her spring garden in jars, again with a great hope that this year's garden could be more progressive than the last, with a little more rain to fluff up the soils, and ready the land to receive seeds and maybe even produce a crop this year and reverse the misfortune of previous years and help to support all three children. Mary Sue often took time for herself, handling so many things on her own sometimes broke her down to tears, she had so many questions for life and still had to answer to her children when they wondered why their clothes were often patched over and over again with fabric from the flour bags, why meal portions were growing small, and when there would be trips to town to shop or get groceries in plenty.

Mary Sue knew she was limited in fuel so if she was going to make any more drives to town, she had better be able to get more fuel while she was there, she might make it back home and truly be abandoned and remote. Mary Sue enjoyed watching her babies play in the yard, there were a few grasses that took root in the distance, few small green blades that pierced through the sand layer and reached for the warming sun, the green could be spotted from several yards out and it further supported a reason to hope.

Mary Sue was bearing another child, she was terrified that things might not improve and then she would have even harder times feeding children, she worried for so many things but it was out of her hands. The beans and rice sources ran thin as the season turned to summer, the jars with small sprouts had grown much like her children, she kept the garden covered with a sheet to prevent any blowing sands from taking away the precious dark soil or covering over with sand, the sheet made it simple to sweep away and protect her plants. Mary Sue planted more than twice as many plants as she had the previous year, she desperately needed additional crops, not just to survive the summer but to store for the winter as well.

Tomatoes, beans, corn, vine plants like cucumbers and squash as well as several hundred carrots were planted, most of her plants would further produce seeds as well as bountiful harvest over the summer to feed them all. It was tasking to continue to pull weeds from the garden, she paid close attention to her soil, churning over, burying weeds so that they would decompose and add richness back to the earth. Mary Sue staggered her plantings, there were several vegetables that would mature late in the summer, and would be easy to store. Some of the garden lasted into the winter and she had ample seeds she retained and stored in anticipation for a much larger garden this year.

Radio shows spoke about the government coming up with plans to buy cattle for slaughter before many the cattle starved to death, the meat from the cows were then fed to the residents of many of the Hooverville's, it was a relieving progress that might help to ease some of the strain on the country, farmers with remaining livestock could certainly use the money while people could use the meat. Other programs began to flood the living rooms, one such plan was to begin to hire farmers and workers around the mid-west to plant trees around the edges of their property for soil conservation, the trees would tap deeply into the earth for steady structure, as well as deep nutrients that the more shallow rooted crops couldn't reach, and then when their leaves fell to the earth, the rotted waste product would return nutrients to the soil for crops, it was an agricultural epiphany, it would just take time and government money to hire enough farmers to plant such trees, the other problem was a matter of getting enough rain to keep the trees alive, not a promising aspect based on the very little amounts of rain the area had received over the previous years.

Obadiah looked forward to the possibility of work, a man should be stand up and provide for his family, it was especially trying on the father, his children were often hungry and his wife spent half of her time patching clothing with other rags instead of trying on new dresses like she ought to be.

Obadiah found the hardest part of this depression was struggling to keep himself together for his family, his ego was detrimental to who he was, he was not a pompous man but being a solid and providing man was a large part of who he was. A man's ego is just as fragile as a woman's emotions, tell a girl she's fat and she'll cry, tell a man he is an awful provider and he might just be capable of murder. The nature of man is a sense of self and each man works his life to maintain or earn that sense of self, it mattered. Obadiah had seen the devastation to his land manifest into his wife wasting away, his children malnourished and his body aging ever so much faster than it rightfully should be. Every time he looked in the mirror, more of his hair grayed, his skin had leathered, his eyes bore the weight of all of these burdens, and for far too long, his hands shook and ached even without any activity.

Each morning brought a bright light in the mornings, with such light brought hours that Obadiah should be working, there wasn't enough soil to till or prepare for planting, there weren't many wheat seeds, no money for seed, there was also no hope or reason to bother working anymore. Obadiah felt lost, there was no need of him for much, the land didn't call to him, it didn't give him any reason to leave the home to work the land, he also figured he would acquire the Basks property and plant that as well, it was a large farm and with plenty of acreage, the work could prove trying but again, with no seed or ability to plant anything, there would be no harvest. Obadiah struggled with his neutral state of ambivalence; he had a purpose until the storms blew away his livelihood.

Elizabeth grew taller, her legs stuck out farther from under the bottom of her dresses, she outgrew her shoes and now she was building calluses and thick skin on the bottom of her feet. Isaac hadn't grown into any of the shoes in the home yet, all they had were a few pains outgrown by Elizabeth, his clothes were becoming more and more patched together from old clothes and the patterned flour bags that Mary Sue had sewn together. Obadiah was more and more impressed each day, his wife had continued to make due with so very little when it came to food or clothing, she would sometimes spend half a day stitching overalls or patching worn out portions of clothing to keep them holding together a little longer.

One night in late May, the winds blew in cool, there was possible rain in the forecast according to the weather fella, providing the area wet weather, and the hope eased some tension. The cool breezes sent the couple into a spring fever, they were young again, and prospect of rain had made them as eager as children the night before Christmas. Obadiah was excited at the possibilities that the rain may bring, his excitement was easily noticed by his mate, and she was as welcoming. Small tings had begun to pitter patter on the roof, the excitement of the couple had left them too overjoyed to contemplate sleeping so they turned to one another in loving embrace, they were both overwhelmed with glee.

Mary Sue was tender with her belly but it didn't stop her from writhing up and down on her husband, her chest hadn't become swollen from pregnancy yet but the loving husband paid her ample attention, she was enticing, she ran her fingertip along his chest and shoulders, leaned back and braced up her body on his raised thighs as they worked together. The noise of the rain on the roof grew louder, the moans of Mary Sue matched, his breathing raced, her rhythm increased, soon her body was trembling and shaking as her climaxing had peaked. The state of her pregnancy had left her desiring his touches very often and much easier to arouse and excite.

Mary Sue had convinced her husband to take her a few days prior, they were out past the barn looking for other areas to increase for a garden, they found themselves alone without the children, Obadiah stood close behind her, his left arm ran up her bare thigh beneath her dress while his right hand brushed her hair away from the back and side of her neck to kiss and suckle on it. Mary Sue reached back to her husband, his arm groped at her chest as she coerced him out of his clothing and into her.

Mary Sue thought about being taken out by the barn, her mind flashed to many of the areas the couple had made passionate love, replaying their sessions in her mind was titillating, she found herself very hot and excited thinking about the different scenarios while in the midst of another, she used to feel ashamed to be excited by such thoughts, she felt dirty, until an honest night with her husband in which he expressed finding her excitement, exciting himself. The couple remained in love with each other, passionate about each other's' bodies and they retained their ability to remain lustful to one another as best they could. When Mary Sue was near the end of her first pregnancy, her needs for her husband had peaked, her chest was more than full and the new breasts of his wife had become a new focus for Obadiah, he knew it was natural, but they were a turn on to him anyways when they had enlarged.

Mary Sue understood that men liked looking at female forms, she wasn't insecure that any bosom would attract the eyes of her husband momentarily, girls noticed other girls, sometimes out of jealousy while most men were simply admirable. Mary Sue enjoyed the wild attention of her husband, before having given birth to Elizabeth, the couple would lay around without their clothing and just admire each other's bodies, randomly kiss each other, massage each other, and touch each other. Something about being pregnant for a third time sent Mary Sues' hormones and urges bouncing off of every wall it seemed, she could change from stressed and worried about the upcoming child, to fighting back from ripping her husband's clothes off to take him in the most primal, albeit clumsy of ways.

The husband and wife found great solace in the embrace of each other, they sought comfort and pleasure in their intimate times, sometimes they would frolic in the sheets together to simply pass the time, to fill quiet time, or just because they could. The family was gaining ground in life again it felt; the government was speaking about making payments to farmers to plant trees for soil conservation, providing relief money to ease the vise that was gripping the country, the notion of payment checks would help breathe some form of life into the mid-west once again.

As the June heat baked the earth again, the sands wafted across the open parcels of fields and further snuffed out any potential life that may have grown, then dried. To watch the wind trace patterns across the tops of the sand as it swirled about was serene, Obadiah watched from different positions, either standing in the house and watching out a window or from the porch and risk being pelted with airborne sand as it flew in from the west. The dry air prohibited any plants from holding on to life, their roots dried and shriveled and failed to hold any dirt in place long enough to establish growth.

The land itself picked up and moved just as much as the people of the country, last winter the east coast had reported red snow, or red dirt mud falling from the sky, it was supposed to be an aggressive snow storm but so much of the dirt from the plains had taken flight and mixed with whatever moisture that had surpassed falling onto the desperately dry region and gathered enough fury to snow a red tinted muddy paste on the northeast. Stories had come about, reports of millions of cubic tons of nutrient rich topsoil had blown away and depleted the area of any ability to support life, and the area was already devoid of enough trees and deep rooted plants to hold the ground against such strong violent winds. The winds blew divots in the ground, deeper and deeper, they took on the nickname "Buffalo wallows" because they resembled the size and depth of the craters that buffalo would dig up and roll in to keep cool on the hottest summer days.

The winds gathered up again in July, the searing heat had parched everything, you couldn't even find cool or moist soil if you dug four feet down, everything was just dust, layer after layer of dust. News reports echoed across the radio about a congressmen beginning to make a speech about soil preservation as the skies over D.C. grew black, soil began to precipitate from the skies, every person in the crowd began to panic as dirt fell from the sky as the man on the podium bellowed about needing to plant trees and before he was able to finish his speech, the winds kicked up and chased off most of the attendees, his bill was passed without question. The governor had made a public announcement about looking into planting what was called "shelter belts" which were supposed to be miles upon miles of trees planted to hinder the blowing winds, mostly planted between fields, north and south to break up the east to west winds and prevent further erosion.

Subsidies had begun to trickle to country farmers, the checks were measly and depended on what type of farmer they were, most of the cattle farmers had been getting paychecks, wheat farmers were still a ways out from their paydays. Too many farmers had packed up and left, many western states such as California had been turning away Okie's for years, signs posted along route 66 stated that non-residents weren't welcome and to go back where they came from.

There were standing jokes that you could tell a rich Okie from a poor one because a rich one had a second mattress strapped to the top of their car. FDR had been reassuring voting citizens that help was on the way, first there had to be preventative measures established and he supported the shelter belts. Obadiah had found such great hope in the matter to come, the thought of relief checks for him and his family, with a third child on the way, would be a salvation as his concerns grew exponentially. After the last few years of barely squeaking by on crumbs, there was hope in the future and it left the whole family in a grand attitude, spirits were uplifted and it was contagious. The glee was resonant between Obadiah and Mary Sue, and with another joy on the cusp of joining the family, they found themselves embroiled in lustful passion often. Obadiah and Mary Sue still struggled to eat, the food supplies were scarce and hope doesn't fill the stomachs of his family.

One late July Friday the sun never rose, when the couple awoke, there was no light outside, the black of night had changed its' color to a dark brown sky, the winds had taken tons of dirt from the more western states and blown it high into the atmosphere eclipsing the sun before the wall of dirt and sand had begun to blanket the lands. The wall was thousands of feet tall, it slowly marched east and as it did, it tore down buildings, ripped boards from walls and stomped out and kicked around plant matter.

Obadiah and his pregnant wife fought to erect wind blocks for the garden, the house provided adequate shelter but sand that blew over the top still fell upon the garden and tried to choke out the mediocre plants. The sand filled their noses and eyes, it was abrasive and almost paralyzing, Obadiah stood in the storm, the brute force of the storm was broken by the home and provided him shelter from the assaulting winds, grains of sands and grit in various sizes found their way into every nook, pocket, ear hole and nostril of the man trying to shield any last remaining garden supplies to feed his family. Obadiah fought against the blowing and growling winds, they tried to knock him to the ground, Obadiah continued to fall to one knee or another but continued to fight back to his feet, Shortly after the winds bore down on Oklahoma again, Obadiah had shouted orders for his wife to return inside for shelter, free and clear from such aggressive storm winds. Obadiah braced burlap sheets on the outside of the garden border and reinforced them as best he could before fumbling and crawling back in the home, hacking and coughing out dark chunks of dirty mucus.

The storm raged on throughout the day, the family retreated to the inner room of the home, the outer rooms that faced the west were closed up but sand still blew in, around the windows that were shoved full of rags and even then, fine silt still puffed through cracks with each growling forceful wind. When Obadiah climbed back into the side door from the storm, Mary Sue had already been worried, she recalled how the first storm had grown so fierce that it took the life of the dear Rupert Basks as he fought to get back to his home but must have gotten disoriented in the storm and lost his life, she worried about the same situation happening to her husband, but the sky was to dark and bellowing to stand watch or call for him.

Elizabeth sat on the couch and huddled under a blanket awaiting the passing of the storm, the roaring was so loud and the vibrating of the roof joined in that no one could hear one another, even when shouting. Isaac clenched his mother ever so tightly, the noise muted his cries and there was no sign of the storm running out of energy anytime soon. The energy charged the home, there were small lightning discharges flashed just out of the windows, the radio crackled and filled with static. The home felt like it was buzzing, the finer hair began to stand up on Isaac and Elizabeths' heads, Mary Sue let go of Isaac and when she did, a small shock passed from her fingertips to the shoulder of her son, causing him to rub the area to relieve it of the pain. Each member of the home sat still, they were afraid to move because of the static energy building up.

The light bulbs flickered and grew bright, ones that were switched off still lit briefly as the electricity in the air caused the filaments within to flicker orange and yellow. As the lights flickered, they made shadows dance around the living room as the family sat still, frozen with fear and rife with the electric buzz that made their entire hairs stands tall. Mary Sue and Obadiah had a metallic taste in their mouths; they wiped their tongues trying to clear the bitter taste away. Mary Sue wanted to hold her children, her husband, she just wanted to be held herself but the small shock with Isaac was already painful, the potential now was a frightful level after having watched an unplugged light bulb flicker with the electricity in the air.

"*Prisoners*" Obadiah murmured to himself, he felt trapped, none of the family members were brave enough to move, each was afraid of touching anything metal and receiving such a shock that it might knock any of them from their feet from such strong muscle spasms, it was frightening to just endure and have to wait out. Isaac didn't understand what was happening, he understood the storm but not the feeling that was making his skin tingle and tighten, his hairs stood tall atop of his head and as he cried, he tried shaking the hairs back down, an irritant he couldn't fight nor win.

Elizabeth sat still, she was quiet and solemn, the unknown was heavy in the air. With a blanket draped over her head, she shivered, it was hot inside the home as the air grew heavy and still, the young girl held tightly to the blanket that protected her from whatever elements that were filling the air and trying to suffocate the family members. The roaring winds were deafening, the sight of Isaac crying was heartbreaking, there was no sound to accompany the poor weeping child, and he was inaudible in his cries.

The winds growled and the walls shook, the storm was intense with power, the wall of energy marched across the countryside and drowned most of it in blowing sands. Obadiah thought about whether or not the shelter belts would have withheld such storms, the arid land gave ample earth to blow away with the storm, hearty trees would merely absorb some of the impact of the storm, a million trees probably wouldn't be able to absorb such wild ferocity. The savage storm raged on, out the front windows displayed sideways blowing sand and was occasionally illuminated with static discharges that streaked and zigzagged through the air. The tin roof sang an eerie pitch as the grains caused the tin to vibrate much like a bow rubbing against violin strings. Looking up through the windows into the sky was ominous and spooky, the dark black sky showed illuminating spots of light as lightning flickered from different angles, the mouth of hell seemed to be swallowing the farm, and the family couldn't even hold each other's hands to wait out the storm.

The storm surged on for hours, each member awaited the end of the day, seated in corners around the couch, Obadiah had an idea that might hopefully offset so much of the static in the air that was imprisoning the Withers. Obadiah walked towards the kitchen, it was so dark through the windows that the concerned man couldn't even see the barn through the window, he hoped it was still standing, the contents weren't likely to blow away in the intense winds but the barn itself was subjected to the assault and destruction from Mother Nature, *"sumbitch"* he thought. The farm had taken such abuses, there couldn't be all that much more it could withstand, it had given up almost everything with the exception of the home and family members, Obadiah wondered how much longer it might be before any of them began to succumb to the destined fate of the lands. Obadiah grabbed one of the metal pans from the kitchen, he suspected that using the metal pan as a shock absorber, if the kids touched it before touching the adults then they wouldn't get such a shock from their parents, it eased some of the tension in the room, the thought of dragging a chain around, wrapped around the ankle, would ground them and keep the static from building up.

Obadiah thought for a moment that if he jammed a long pipe into the ground that maybe it might take some of the charge out of the storm and with hope, he might keep the static build up from reaching points of electrocution from megawatt discharge. The buzz in the air was unnerving, it felt as if the fillings in his teeth were ready to pop like popcorn or leap from his teeth like a bullet. Obadiah clenched his jaw and ground his teeth together, struggling to keep his fillings where they had been placed; it was distracting while he struggled to focus on the frightened children right behind him. Lights flashed outside of the window, the black skies sent lighter brown surges of light from the static discharges from deep within the storm, the black earth that blew past the window made the roof hum and the walls vibrate. Obadiah felt the floor boards move under his feet, the entire house twitched with energy, he felt like he was standing inside of a ticking bomb, the home seemed like a grenade with its' pin missing, all of the built up energy seemed to wait for the right spark to ignite the home like a pile of dynamite near a burn barrel.

The remainder of the day was a cautious one, each person carried a fork or spoon to touch door handles with, rather than get the zap by touching the metal. Mary Sue found humor in the whole situation, each family member having to carry around a spoon almost like a blind person using their walking sticks tapping each thing for safety before touching anything else, Isaac didn't understand, he just drummed on things with his small spoon like everyone else. The clock showed that it was late but the sky had been dark all day, the sun never rose that day, it remained dark, the storm had blocked out the sun and it was as if the day never even happened, the day that never came. The family ate while being cautious with their cutlery, each item they grasped let out a small spark and each time, it caused a wince with each bit of sting. It was after the supper meal when they finally decided to turn in, it had been a restless day and there were no radio programs on, nothing but static had fuzzed from the speakers each time Obadiah tried to tune in any form of information, the storm was creating the static and there was no news or information as to how long the storm might last or how the rest of the country might be affected, they were cut off, they were alone at the farm and there was no communication, no correspondence, no voices outside of stranded family at the farmhouse.

Elizabeth was hard to put to bed, she was antsy and still teeming with energy from a day trapped indoors, and she had so much pent up energy. Even with the dim light all day, her body still desired to run and play to vent all of the energy in the small body. Isaac was less of a challenge, his body fell more susceptible to the dark skies outside and kept him yawning most of the day so his body was ready to surrender to bed and as he neared his bed, his body began to stagger and fumble with exhaustion. Isaac had complained for months about his lips, the drier seasons had left everyone's lips chapped, parched from the lack of humidity. Everyone had noticed the darker yellow tinted urine and knew that it meant dehydration; Obadiah wasn't sure how long the well would hold out so it was used with caution. Mary Sue often watered the garden early in the morning from the spigot, Obadiah also leaked out in the garden during the summer to contribute any moisture he could when there were plants growing and producing food.

Mary Sue continued to try and keep everyone's lips adorned with a small dabs of petroleum jelly, except Isaac always ate his, she tried to protect his chapped lips while he was asleep, he still ate and gnawed at the scabs on his and then cried about the pain when they began to bleed over and over again, it was an uphill battle for Mary Sue to keep her young son in good health.

Elizabeth tossed and turned, it could be heard through her door in the living room where her parents sat, they laid back on the sofa and tried to focus on the howling of the wind and dirt that battered the home. It had been an all-day assault, the sheer power of this storm was impressive, all the couple could do was take a seat and await the end results, whether it be the demise of the home and occupants or it finally ease up and allow the sun to rise and show some relief. The weather had compounded against the region, severe sun, drought, winds that blew away all of the topsoil that could have held and produced a crop that could have salvaged the farm, and now even the blotting out of the sun with the days storm. No rain, no dirt, and now no sun, there really is nothing left now, the family had each other, but now nothing else. The couple held hands and wondered if this truly was the end, the Basks passed on a few years back now, there was no years of struggle and slow decay, while still suffering through it all, Rupert had succumbed in the storm and when he didn't return, Anita took her life and there was no more hardship for them. The house has since blown down and been swallowed up by the land by being covered over by the drifting dirt, other than a few memories, the existence of the Basks had almost been wiped away, returned to the earth.

The Basks may have had family, kids or maybe grandkids that would never hear from them, no exchange of post, no holidays or visits anymore, but no one had visited or come asking about them, for anyone's knowledge, they picked up and left years ago with the first storm, long before life dried up and blew away. Maybe the elderly couple trembled away in the cold one night somewhere else; there were no grave markers near the oak that sat behind the house that once stood.

There was no proof that Obadiah had buried three people in the yard. The husband and wife of umpteen years were buried side by side, as they had lived for so very long. The stranger that had wandered out to the farm wasn't buried to far from the couple, Obadiah still struggled with what he was forced to do, Mary Sue could tell that he was troubled, he could duck her suspicion when she confronted him, but he couldn't hide his tossing and turning at night when they slept. Mary Sue often tried to counsel her husband to unburden himself from his guilt, he knew she was right but he also knew she couldn't really understand what weight he held on his shoulders. Obadiah appreciated that his wife wanted to help, her ignorance to things made her unqualified to weigh in on many subjects, she was often just willing to listen, but sometimes she came off a bit of a know it all and rather snide and arrogant about how she delivered her knowledge.

Obadiah appreciated the care his wife often took when it came to the detailed care of the family, he was truly lucky to have her and he tried to express his gratitude often, she did the same to him as often as possible, when they were both expressive enough, they found themselves engaged in fiery passion. Mary Sue didn't have the overwhelming sensation that their lives were to end, the storm raged in fury and the let down and pick back up of the wind and lightning made for an impressive display, the flicker of lights that danced just out the window made for romantic ambiance, giving Mary Sue cause to instigate marital goings on.

Obadiah had more than adequate energy left from a day spent lounging about, Mary Sue rubbed her fingers up and down her husband's forearm, glancing out of the corner of her eyes to her left, awaiting Obadiah to catch her looking at him so she could shoot him a sultry lip biting smile, assuring him what was on her mind. Sure enough Obadiah looked slyly at his wife, she was becoming playful and enticing him to join her in her escapades, she extended her left leg so that it rested across his lap, he rubbed her leg around her knee as she hiked up her dress to expose more of herself to him, and his touch.

Obadiah rubbed his hands on the thighs of Mary Sue as she leaned back and joined him, as he rubbed her legs, she let her hands move further upward, in the flickers of lightning Obadiah was able to see in moments of good light, his wife was partaking in what he normally did, and he was finding himself intensely aroused and curious to continue to watch his wife enjoy herself for his viewing entertainment. Mary Sue leaned back on the arm of the couch, she unbuttoned her blouse and continued to caress her skin, and her eyes peeked to ensure his eyes were locked on her body. Mary Sue encircled herself, her fingers wandering in all the right places, her chest beginning to thrust up and down as her breaths became shorter and closer together. Obadiah watched in amazement, his firm and still gorgeous wife was beautiful, her body was thin and slender but remained taught and still enflamed his desires for her. The couple enjoyed their carnal relations when they could, when stresses arose it was often moved to the back burner, when there are children in the equation, husband and wife relations often grew farther and farther apart, as well as lost intensity, but not this night.

With her legs exposed and her husband nearest her most intimate of places, Mary Sue continued her business, Obadiah undressed himself slowly as not to interrupt his wife. Mary Sue continued to let her hands roam her own body, Obadiah also let his hands and fingers assist his wife as she pleasured herself, his eyes roamed her body more than her own hands, her head leaned back as her back arched and her breath was held tightly between gasps for breath. Her skin glistened with perspiration, the flickers of lightning caused her skin to sparkle, her breasts engorged with blood and excitement, her ringers pinched and groped, fingertips rubbed in circles, and her legs straightened as every muscle in her entire body flexed and tightened. Obadiah kissed the bare legs of his wife, his coarse facial hair caused the corners of her mouth to curl as the slight tickle caused her legs to quiver, her mouth dropped open, her moans matched the pitch of the storm, her fingers worked feverishly and steadfast as her climax intensified, her legs trembled and her hands shook.

Obadiah groped and rubbed inwards to3ards her thighs, her body was sensitive so he held his hands for a moment as she fought to regain control of her body, Obadiah was ready for his wife, her hunger for his flesh was at its peak and she needed to feel him. Mary Sue pulled on her husband so she could upright herself, positioning him appropriately she eased herself down onto him, his pulse could be felt through most of his body as blood surged through him. The pair took turns kissing and nibbling on each other's' necks, chins, cheeks, and lips, her nipples were hard and erect and Obadiah suckled on them, alternating to further entice his mate, giving her cause to thrust up and down faster and harder upon him. Obadiah's hand enveloped her rear, each small buttock fit in his hand, she was much smaller than when they had first gotten married, her belly wasn't small in comparison but Mary Sue was aware as she straddled her lover, their thighs gathered sweat as they rubbed together, the friction added heat between them, their chests rubbed together, and their lips alternated between kissing and gasping for breaths, her hands holding his face.

Mary Sue let her legs clamp down on the legs of her perch, her hands gripped tightly around the neck of her husband to keep him still as she reached climax again, her body jerked and seized, her legs trembled and her hands gripped tightly, she needed a minute for her composure before turning herself around, she wanted to feel her husband's body behind her. She sat back onto him, her right arm encouraged her husband's head to kiss on her neck and against her face, her left arm steadied herself against his left thigh, he held her hips and pulled her back towards him. The hot and sweaty wife hung her head forward to let a little air between their bodies, she guided his left hand down between her thighs, his touch sent vibrations through her body, she too reached down between her legs and rubbed against him from another angle, his body thrust with harder force in response to her caressing. The couple volleyed touches and titillation long into the late hours, there was no way to know the time, nor any care for they had each other and if their world ended, there was nothing that could be done about it anyway so they reveled in the moment.

The morning light broke through mounds of silt stacked against the windows, the haze lit up the room, Mary Sue and Obadiah stirred, the unclad bodies had fallen asleep tangled up together, he pawed at her bare breasts to wake her, her smile broke before her eyes had squinted open, preceding a long bodied stretch. Obadiah eased his wife's head up a bit, she rolled to give his privates a playful kiss to greet him for the day, she was still in the mood for playful loving, in her pregnant state she had more intimate urges than any other emotion throughout the day. Mary Sue nuzzled at her husband for a moment, he was slow to respond as he was still trying to shake off the tired and weary of the late night that lead to an early morning, not to mention a left arm that stung as circulation returned. Mary Sue took the clue from his gurgling stomach and buttoned up her blouse before she headed to the kitchen to prepare the early family meal

Obadiah pulled his Tuf-Nut overalls up, his body ached and his legs throbbed from the previous night's activities, it was a long walk to the window, it felt as long as the journey to the rail tracks, even though only a few feet. As Obadiah neared the window to take in what damage may have been done, the sight he surveyed was ghastly, sand had piled up against the porch, the barn, feet upon feet had taken hold and mounted up against the few standing structures around, on the west side of the barn there must have been a six foot drift, Obadiah was exasperated at the notion that he would have to shovel out his house, and his barn yet again. Over his left shoulder he could see his wife in the kitchen, she was standing on her toes looking out the side window that sat over the sink, on her tippy toes, her butt snuck out from under the back of her blouse, her thin thighs led all the way up, her calf muscles were tone and flexed to keep her propped up to better her view out the window as the stove heated up.

Obadiah quietly took up position behind his wife, he let his overalls fall to the floor and reached around her waist to pull himself close into her, she pulled his arms around the front of her tightly to ensure a close embrace, the couple enjoyed an early morning tryst as the kitchen warmed from the stove and the day broke from the previous dark days hold on the area. The couple looked out the window and let their hands tantalize one another, his body felt warm against her cold backside, they struggled to remain quiet enough to prevent waking either child, they didn't want any such interruption, and a woken child would definitely be an interruption. Obadiah reached his hand up the front of her shirt and pulled on her chest, she craved his touches; her deepest desires were being met, and so were his.

The couple wrapped up their early love making session before cleaning up and beginning to prepare breakfast, Obadiah was unhappy about having to spend the better part of his day shoveling out the farm. With a handful of softened navy beans crackling in with some shredded salted goat, Mary Sue whipped up a few biscuits to make some sort of breakfast sandwich with, Obadiah made a pot of chicory, he made this batch fairly strong as he knew he was in for a really long day, despite running low on the root.

The couple ate together quietly, the food would keep warm enough for the children when they woke so there was no hurry, Mary Sue discussed her teaching lesson plan with her husband, they had a quiet breakfast date together. Neither child had awaken and the couple was enjoying the solitude, it was reminiscent of when they would arise in their honeymoon cabin, lust for each other before even eating a morning meal, satisfy their urges for one another and then prepare food, just like this morning.

Obadiah thanked his wife for the meal and gave her along hug with thanks and a kiss on the cheek before finishing dressing himself while she quickly dressed as well. Obadiah spent the better part of two days digging out as much of the tall piled dirt mounds as his body would allow him. The dirt rose up to the midpoint of the west facing windows, the amount of moved dirt was staggering. The radio snapped on with the turn of the knob each time and reports of dirt falling all over the east-coast echoed hourly, dirt blew all of the way up to Vermont according to some reports. Wind drifted for hundreds of miles from the plains, carrying tons upon tons of dirt high into the atmosphere before dispersing it all over the rest of the country. The dirt that was removed with each blowing storm over the past few years had ripped away the entire nutrient bearing black topsoil and left the sterile sand in its place.

Mary Sue showed more and more as each summer day scorched on, the blistering sun continued to parch the lands. The family fought their best to keep the garden moist enough to support the plants that hadn't been stripped away by the winds, or sun. A handful of pepper plants held sturdy, veined plants and other assorted plants offered promise of canning food to store for the winter. Mary Sue stood vigilant over her family and garden, the garden was to help feed the family over the winter, the food sources were already thin, Obadiah was worrying more and more each day as his new coming child grew larger in the womb of his wife. The stresses of the upcoming winter were ever present, even if the summer wasn't half over yet. Squash plants grew hearty despite the conditions, the vines reached tall to the eaves of the home, heartier plants survived while the more water based plants like tomatoes failed.

Each day's radio broadcasts ended with an ominous sign off, the broadcaster would talk about the remaining ability to plant crops, even winter wheat... "If the rains break." the hope of rain had been long gone, for years the land continued to expel more water than it had taken in, there had been a few sprinkles over the previous few years, nothing ever more than a few centimeters, nothing enough to restore anything around to what it was in years past. The radio played a broadcast story about how the annual rainfall had fallen to less than four inches for the year, total. The numbers had only tumbled down, in every category, rain, crop production, even residents had fled the state in record numbers over the past few years, leaving a mass exodus of Okie's to head out in search of prosperous lands elsewhere around the country, and the radio reported how many thousands still filled the makeshift Hooverville camps.

The president signed an order that sent some much needed financial relief to cattle farmers, they had been buying up drought troubled cattle and slaughtering them, the money given to the farmers was lifesaving, the meat from the cattle slaughter went to feed many of the Hooverville residents and it eased much of the pent up aggression from the people that had been displaced and crammed into the cardboard camps near the bigger cities. One news report spoke about a camp near Washington in which a mob of angry starving people rose up in protest against the government in strike, many police pushed back and a fight broke out, many people were hurt and three people lost their lives. Some of the people incarcerated from protests or strikes were fed, which gave reason to become incarcerated to many people.

The summer heat peaked long after the length of the days had, each day dragged on, when the winds blew, plants wilted, skin chapped and peeled, it was so dry that sweat instantly evaporated and failed to offer any form of relief from the heat. The family wore the least amount of clothing around the home for some sense of relief, open windows let in more sand than breeze when cooling the home, Mary Sue resisted as best as possible the need to feed her family from the stove when having to cook, the added heat from the stove would be too much to bear. The children wore thin shirts and short shorts that helped to keep their bodies cool, Obadiah went without his shirt under his overalls, and Mary Sue wore the shortest, flowing dresses she had but loose clothing only offered minimal relief.

The wood of the home seemed to swell and crackle in the heat; the walls seemed to expand inwards in the rooms. The sun sweltered, at its highest the land sizzled, the horizon skewed as the heat rose from the ground, creating a mirage of a lake out in the distance. Obadiah knew that there was no such lake, no hope of water, no hope for life anywhere, Obadiah hoped with all of his being that the stream that he dragged a catfish from, hadn't filled with sand or had been erased from the countryside, having passed it, it appeared as if it never existed.

Trees in the distance didn't offer any shade, any fruit, or even much in the way of a break in the dull scenery, everything was covered in dirt, few shadows to offer some depth in the distance but not much else, in a few more weeks some of the vegetables in the garden would ripen, offer sustenance and begin to provide for the family, the replanting of the dead plant matter from the previous years, the goats blood, every biodegradable item that could be sacrificed to the ground, kept vitality in the dirt and even with the heat, the dirt remained much darker than the sand and silt that scattered the land, Mary Sue watered every few mornings, she was cautious to be sparing with water, there was no telling how long the well would last but water wouldn't do them any good if the food finally ran out either.

Life was a difficult balance, the farm needed so many days of rain, the land was like a dry sponge, but if it rained too much, the loose sand risked flooding and landslides would further decimate the area, the main road that lead to the farm was hardly a trail now, drifts had slowly gobbled at the roadsides, grasses that once lined the roadsides and offered a screen for the blowing sands and dirt, now the grasses had been long gone and there was no distinguishable marks of the roadsides anymore.

Obadiah sat on the front stoop, elbows on knees and head on hands, there was nothing that could be done, no work, no crops to tend to, there was no use for him, there was no way to make any money, there was nothing for him anymore. Obadiah pondered about simply walking away, he could walk to the train tracks, hop onto a train and be gone, no more family depending on him, no more mouths that he couldn't feed, no more empty stomachs that were a result of his failings. He was a struggling father, every time the sun rose and his wife struggled to figure out something that resembled a bit of a meal, he failed more.

For months now Mary Sue had been brining the thick Russian thistle that had been the lone growing weed in the area, soaking the tough plant over warming water softened it up enough to give teeth an edge when chewing it, even boiled with a bit of salt, it was like plant jerky. The plant took a lot of work, and no one in the family could stomach much of it. Obadiah's diet had only consisted of the thistle for several weeks, he refused any other food subsidy because his wife and children needed it, his own grumbling stomach was overshadowed by the needs of his family. Even sitting on the porch seemed to exhaust him.

Long hot days passed, each day was a replicate of the day before, the children stuck to lessen plans designed by Mary Sue, and she often had them working in the sand as there was no paper or other writing media. Obadiah enjoyed watching over the shoulders of his children as they toiled away with their schooling, his sense of self was devoid of anything possible, but watching his children learn gave him just enough pride each day to retain a small sense of worth, that worth is also the only thing that had kept him anchored to his family.

Mary Sue was mentally strong, she hardly wavered when it came to rearing the children, she remained steadfast in her attitude that things would improve one day while Obadiah struggled with all of his might to find any reason to live anymore. The children were more of a reason to leave in search of a way to provide for them, with a third child so close to arriving, it was even more pressure to be the man of the house; it was also more feelings of failure. If Obadiah left, this new child wouldn't remember him at all, it would be one less person to remember his failures.

Obadiah fought off his feelings, the dark thoughts were always at the edge of most of his thoughts, like a pack of circling wolves, each thought he had he had to worry about the most was the one he turned his back on for it was the thought that snuck up on him the quickest. Mary Sue remained beautiful, she had true beauty, the kind that didn't need makeup to fake, he was fortunate to have her and the thought about abandoning her especially, was troubling. Mary Sue stuck by Obadiah, she stood beside him and helped pack and move away from her family when he made the decision to move his family to Oklahoma, he owed it to her to stick by her side in return, no matter what. The confliction ate away at Obadiah, his unraveled nerves caused tossing and turning while failing to sleep, Mary Sue had enough on her shoulders and the stress of her husband wore her down, causing silent weeping most nights. Mary Sue would wait for her husband to slow his breathing, sincere proof that her husband had fallen asleep, then she would let herself weep, tears would well up and begin to run back towards her ears from her closed eyes, she spent as much energy to cry silently as she did to cry, the exhaustion helped to ease her to sleep, but it didn't ease her burdens.

Mary Sue felt trapped, she had two children, and one on the verge of joining them to depend on her too, Obadiah struggled as best as he could to forage for anything edible for his family, it often came to boiled thistle. The parents added a bit of chicory root to their soggy thistle in the mornings and pretended that it was akin to oatmeal, the bitter root hadn't masked the earthy weedy taste of the thistle, but it was a substance that could at least fill a stomach for a short while. Mary Sue was on the verge of birth, she had been contending with contractions for a few days and they would peak and subside, until they finally didn't subside any longer.

Obadiah took control much as he did when he delivered Isaac, except this time he was a lot less nervous. Isaac remained on the couch but Elizabeth offered her small helping hands, she performed running tasks such as fetching water, and ensuring that Isaac remain on the couch as ordered. Elizabeth cried through Isaac's birth when it happened, she was too young to understand what was going on, this time she took stock of what she could see and what she could do.

Elizabeth was wide eyed and had concern for her mom as Mary Sue grunted and cried through the pains of labor. She grimaced at the blood as she watched a small head emerge from the birthing canal, she had a grasp of what was going on but how the baby got inside and why it had to come out through this particular place had eluded her. Obadiah shouted to his daughter on what to do and how to do it, Mary Sue held her knees towards her chest so she could bear down and push as her husband spoke sternly in command to her, the couple grunted through the process. Mary Sue had awoken early in bed with strong enough contractions that she reached and grasped her husband's neck in her sleep, thus waking him up startled and quick to release her vice grip on him.

Obadiah helped his kids with their morning routines, dressed, fed, and the like before her grunting had raised his concern enough for her to call him by her side. Elizabeth did her best to console her brother, his mother being upset him, he was in the same position his sister what in when he arrive at the farm, he sobbed and was scared as his mother let out random screams as her contractions caused every muscle in her body to squeeze and her teeth to grind.

Obadiah missed the good doctor Joe something fierce, he could have used the well-dressed intellect in the delivery of his third child. Martinez had long moved away from Indian Gulch, his medical expertise was very much needed everywhere he went, but it was sorely missed out at the Withers farm. Mary Sue sweat and labored in the early fall, the day was still hot out but the sun was setting earlier and earlier each night. The task of birthing took the better part of the morning, the sheets were soaked with fluids and blood, Obadiah knew he had a long day of laundering the linens as well as jetting between the three, scratch that, four other family members that now needed him, never mind what he needed of himself. Cradling the head from the loins of his wife, the shoulders squeezed out as he helped to wriggle the baby from its confines. Elizabeth stood close at hand as her father helped to bring her new sibling onto the bed, her eyes were locked as her mouth hung open, watching her father ease a slimy bloody pinked tiny body from between the legs of her mother, she was silent but her dismay shone from her face.

Obadiah used the little bit of momentum to pull the baby from his wife, it was a boy, Obadiah could feel the sweat bead and then streak down his face, the baby began to wail out as it hit the cooler air and the bed top. Elizabeth removed the towel that she held slung over her shoulders and her father used it to wrap up the tiny body, Mary Sue cried uncontrollably, a majority of the work was over with, Obadiah instructed Elizabeth on how to cut the umbilical cord before handing the child to its' mother. With an empty pan, Obadiah cleaned up the after birth, it was a difficult task to change the linens with Mary Sue right after giving birth but this way she could remain in bed and things could still get cleaned.

Elizabeth ran to gather her younger brother, he was teary eyed and confused where this baby had come from, as well as what the newborn was all about, he looked at it with hesitation, it was a small face wrapped in a towel, but every other member of his family was staring at it, and him. The children hunkered down around their mother, they climbed up near her as she welled up and yawned uncontrollably, she was utterly exhausted, every ounce of energy had fled her body while birthing the newest Withers baby had left Mary Sue with a wobbling head, unable to keep her eyelids open and beginning to slur her speech as her strong will finally let go.

Obadiah convinced his children to let their mother be to nap for a time while they headed outdoors so as she could have quiet. Obadiah gathered the large laundering tub, the sheets would need to soak to loosen the proteins in the blood and amniotic fluid, the smell was unpleasant to have to handle. Obadiah thought about soaking overnight and then dumping the water in the garden and hoping that the same fluid that supported the baby would help to add nutrients to the dirt that was growing food for the family. "Food for the family," thought Obadiah, while beginning to fill the wash tub, Obadiah thought further about the cleanup, his children played outside as Isaac ran his little legs around keeping up with Elizabeth.

Obadiah instructed his children to run off and gather some thistle; he intended to boil some down and with it, the afterbirth. Obadiah added water and some pepper to the pot that contained the bloody chunky mess that came from his wife, with suspicion, a slow low heat the glob would soften and cook down. Obadiah gagged for a moment as he used a knife to shred the chunks of placenta, the brown tissue was tough, had bloody parcels and a fleshy like texture to it that required some muscle to rip apart. Obadiah felt guilty that he was about to feed his family some of the usually discarded bodily waste, but he suspected that it held enough nutrients to suffice for one meal, after all; animals ate it. He planned to cook down and mix the tough slop with the thistle to disguise the stock and origin of the strange odor, and maybe taste. Obadiah tried to season the bisque with salt and pepper, the liquid in the pan churned slowly, it changed colors slightly as it cooked and the proteins denatured.

The argumentative children were returning, Isaac was dragging his feet and kicking at dirt while lagging far behind Elizabeth as she dragged a medium branch of thistle, he was tired and complaining about the walk and the heat to Elizabeth, whom was short tempered with her brother because she too was miserable with the heat, and also dragging more barely edible thistle. Obadiah hurried to finish what he was doing; he hoped to shred the thistle enough to make it mushy, hoping the gruel like consistence would make the concoction palatable.

The smell of the amniotic fluid that soaked the sheets was enough to gag a raccoon, the brown and yellowing of the water as it soaked the linens seemed unending, each rise and dumping of the basin continued to release the birthing liquid from the fibers, emptying the basin into the garden offered plenty of water and added nutrients to the remaining topsoil and garden plants growing from below the surface. The children were almost to the side door as Obadiah trounced between the wash basin outside and the simmering pot of afterbirth and placenta beginning to stew on the stove, it was hot in the sun but it was broiling within the kitchen.

Obadiah could feel the ever present exhaustion in his body, it was hard to wake up each morning, a struggle to transition from one position to the next, even in mid task, he found himself lightheaded and dizzy, in the heat he often saw spots in his vision and sometimes he needed an extended moment to attempt to increase his blood pressure and stave off passing out. Obadiah had begun to think more and more about how long before he had nothing left to give, he heard a saying once, something to the effect of " a candle can light a candle and in doing so, it doesn't shorten the life of the original candle," Obadiah used to think the proverb was intelligently quipped but at the same time, if the beginning candle spent it's entire flame life igniting other candles, it wouldn't be able to shine its brightest or even know anything else but to give and give, it wasn't long before there would be nothing left. With heat spells and waves of dizzying nausea, Obadiah was finding himself bracing against countertops and doorways to remain upright in these days, even the weight of his own torn clothing that had worn thin after years of wear and tear, seemed to try to pull him to the ground like an anchor and chains around his neck.

The children wanted to lounge around the couch; it was out of the sun, even as the air hung still and failed to offer any form of breeze for heat relief, being out of the sun gave the illusion of relief, even if it was only an illusion. Obadiah searched for any form of sugar in the kitchen, maybe a little would alleviate some of the lightheadedness that plagued him. Obadiah found himself concerned with the wellbeing of his family as well, if he was so ill with the heat then they couldn't be far behind, he fretted about his little children possibly falling sick also, such heat stroke could prove fatal for such little bodies. Obadiah fought to remind himself and them to keep them drinking fluids, they were able to scavenge small morsels of food for their growing bodies while Obadiah had only survived on the bland Russian thistle for weeks now, it probably had zero nutritious value, but eating something at least gave some form of momentary relief to the pains of hunger, brief moments. His muscles ached, his joints ground together when they moved, he found himself forcing his jaw open because the muscles tightened and caused his jaw to clench without purpose.

The tension from the clenched jaw caused headaches and coupled with the heat, headaches quickly turned to migraines that were debilitating. Mary Sue had given birth and was attempting to recuperate, her attention for the last two weeks or so had been solely on her and the kids, Obadiah had become a ghost to her and luckily she hadn't noticed his spells. Obadiah snapped back to consciousness, the children were sprawled out on the cooler wood floor in the main room, the radio crackled a bit as it spoke about the surrounding areas and their struggle to grow any form of sustenance, the garden was stunted from the raging sun, Obadiah and Mary Sue took special care to water lightly early in the morning as well as some nights, there had hardly been but misting once or twice over the course of the summer, each news broadcast that crackled across the radio that spoke of storms, only mentioned winds, never rain, each news report ended with the fading and empty hope: "if the rains break."

The drying years had ravaged the land, the remaining sands held no viability for plants, there was nothing that could support plant life and it would take some time to restore sustainability, it couldn't be fixed with some rain storms, at this point, it was an open ended question as to what could really fix anything anymore. The stench that originated in the simmering pot had filled the kitchen with moist heat that exuded a noxious smell, Obadiah had given in to a blank stare and not noticed the smell until he heard the yelping cries of his newest child, his two oldest children had leaped to their feet and were pushing and shoving to get in to see the newest family member. Obadiah kept an arm raised towards the near walls to help brace himself against possibly falling to the floor as he followed up the rear to join them, the urgency to feed his family was still the most forethought in his mind.

Mary Sue looked like she had been ripped apart by dogs, her hair was still sweaty and a tangled mess as she was semi propped up feeding her newborn. As the newborn suckled Mary Sue fought to keep her head upright, she hadn't eaten all day and as the child nursed, she could feel her energy flee from her body. Mary Sue forced a smile to her children as they stood bedside and volleyed for turns to see the small swaddled younger brother, as she smiled her eyebrows forced her eyes closed, she wearily asked each of Elizabeth and Isaac what they had been up to during the day as she slept. They explained having to wander to find the thistle for their father and as they began to tattle on one another, Obadiah made it to the doorway. Mary Sue caught a whiff of whatever was cooking in the kitchen, the smell caused her eyes to pop open and shoot a look of bewilderment to her husband as he jostled in the doorway attempting to find a way to lean and not against some sore part of his bony frame. Mary Sue wasn't sure what she was smelling but the newborn was sucking all of her energy from her and she was not only hungry, she was aware that she would require much more to eat to continue to feed the newborn, Obadiah just murmured "thistle" hoping to elude her and she knew enough to be satisfied.

Mary Sue sent the older children back out and nodded for her husband to come close, she wanted to debate names with him as well as suggest an idea to add with dinner, she informed him that there were still some canned peaches in the top of the pantry, away from where either child might see and selfishly indulge. The notion of the sugary fruit from Georgia brought a smile to Obadiah's face; the small amount of sugar in a slice of a peach might help to improve the heat sickened husband. The small child suckled and seemed to exert some form of a moan while doing so, it was comical for both parents, and they understood such hunger. The parents both struggled to keep their eyes open, Mary Sue had an extremely long day while her husband had an exhausting long few weeks, both needed some time together in a bath after a large meal and a good nights' sleep while rain tapped them both to sleep all night long, except absolutely none if it would possibly happen. The couple still hadn't pinned down a name for the fifth Wither, they narrowed down a few names such as "James, Michael, Alert," for the boys names and "Ellis, Sylvia, or Gloria" for girls names.

Obadiah offered up "John" for another potential name, Mary Sue countered with "Morris" and as Obadiah shuttered off such a suggestion, he rebutted with "Jacob," Mary Sue thought it was an adequate compromise and agreed to it, *Jacob* it was. Obadiah looked pale, his wife was worried about him, he had been pushing himself to much providing for his family and Mary Sue was just now realizing just how much he had been over doing things, she was bed ridden for a few days at least and having to chase around the two children meant further neglecting himself. Obadiah shuffled his feet towards his wife in the bed, Jacob still nursing, she was sweaty and fatigued still. Obadiah eased himself onto the surface of the bed, his body felt weak; his legs trembled as he lowered himself to the mattress. Mary Sue felt for her husband, her right free hand extended to pat his right thigh as he faced his wife, his head hung heavy and his eyes searched for a soft place on her shoulders to rest his head, she raised her hand to reach behind his head and attempt a hug.

The children were sprawled out on the cooler wooden floor in the living room as Obadiah returned back to his position in the kitchen, slowly simmering the bouillon like liquid in the pot on the stove, slowly shredding pieces of the greenish brown weed into the pot, the harsh texture ripped at his fingertips, it was dry and fibrous, it caused a lot of pinpoint sized holes in his fingers that bled as he worked. The smell of the stock was still putrid, vile, and reeked of iron and blood. Obadiah began feeling lightheaded again, the heat in the kitchen was trying to do him in, he pulled on the pantry shelf to help himself onto his tip toes to reach for the peaches, as he wrapped his hand around the glass jar, his vision began to waver, cloud, and turn white starting at the edges of his view and enclosing in. Everything turned white, the sound of the simmering pot still filled the background sounds for a brief moment before a body jarring "*THUD*" shook his whole body when he hit the floor. The sound faded from his ears within a moment of hitting the floor, everything went silent.

Obadiah fluttered his eyes, his chest was heavy and the pain was immense when trying to inhale, landing flat on his back knocked the wind from him. His head throbbed and everything was still muted as Elizabeth brought her head into view, she was mouthing something as her hair fell from her head down around her daddy as she attempted to shake him awake. The children had been alerted to the fall after the walls rattled, Isaac was too hot to bother rising but Elizabeth shot to her feet and speared to the kitchen to investigate the origin of the thunderous boom.

Fighting heavy eyelids, Obadiah continued to flutter his lids open and closed, sound became a slow murmur, Elizabeth's voice still sounded like an underwater muffle and still made no sense for the moment, the look of concern on her face helped to bring Obadiah to conscience faster, his head ached, his body felt stiff, now refusing to move as it had before his fall. Obadiah painfully rolled to one side and flexed his leg muscles a few times to force blood back into his head to fend off the spins. Elizabeth was still berating her father with questions, "*What happened pah? Are you OK? Get up we're hungry*" and the stammering went on. Her concern was more of curiosity but it was appreciated nonetheless.

Obadiah knew deep down he couldn't fail, his family needed him to be strong and this weakness needed to subside, and quickly. He slowly pulled on the counter to rise back to his feet, his head still woozy but he retrieved the jar from the floor and got back to his task of making supper. The porridge like slop was stewed together in an equal consistency, Obadiah minced a peach slice and added it to the pot, the goal was to add a little sweetness to the mix, and snuck a small bit of the fruit himself, his body had responded with a slight spike of energy; the spins reduced and nearly went away. Obadiah served out bowls of the makeshift stew, he felt a pit in his stomach at what it consisted of, but the nutrients would serve his family and that was his intent. The children poked at their bowls with spoons, Isaac had a look of dread on his face after the first bite but the small bits of peach kept him digging back in.

Elizabeth didn't complain or say a word as she spooned the mixture to her mouth and swallowed, the texture was less than appealing as the boiled thistle was not only bland, it was lumpy with some of the fibrous clumps making chewing a difficult task. Neither child was willing to complain or risk more hunger pains if they didn't eat, Obadiah joined his wife in eating in bed as Jacob slept. The children behaved in the other room, Obadiah felt guilty as he and his wife ate, he suspected she knew what she was eating but she also knew she needed as many calories as possible to continue nursing her baby.

The night closed out, the children slept, the sun turned to moon and all Withers were sleeping, except the father. Obadiah laid wide awake, the new baby would whimper now and then and Mary Sue would return to gently rocking, a habit she could do without even having to wake up. Obadiah couldn't find peace, there was no hope, there was no thought of relief anymore, his family had been abandoned and he felt alone. There was no higher power and prayers had long gone unanswered, a majority of the country had been wilting, drying out and millions of people had been uprooted and migrated to other parts of the country in hopes for food, work, or some sense of security. There wasn't a house

286

within eyesight and most of Indian Gulch had closed up, the stores struggled to remain open for their patrons but gave in to the burdens just like everything else, hope had fleeted long ago, it blew away with the planted seeds in the first sandstorm years ago.

The night lasted forever, the dim light remained through the window, the moon was almost full and the silence outside was eerie, no chirping bugs, no hooting owls, no crickets playing a chorus of racket, the only life left in the area was within the household, they had been deserted and now were a lone standing home in the midst of a wasteland, there was nothing left anymore. The angst that riddled Obadiah left him unable to sleep, his mind wandered, first the room, then the home, the farm and then the countryside, he thought about his walk to the train tracks, he hoped that the garden would suddenly triple in production, it was childish to have such fantasies, but it was all his mind could do. His family counted on him, his wife needed him more than ever and it was his sole responsibility to ensure that they survive, the burdens and worries were all that he could think of, he laid wide awake all night and no matter how hard he tried to erase his mind, his family remained at the forefront of his mind.

The morning lead to another long and unsuccessful day, no food in sight and bare minimal supplies to feed his family with, there was a little of the previous nights' mixture left in which Obadiah mixed in with some light flour and water to make a hardtack like biscuits. The children ate quickly and poured out through the side door to play before the heat forced them back inside, Obadiah tried his best to make sure they remained hydrated and he also doted on his wife hand and foot, he checked on her and to ensure she sleep he would cradle Jacob in his arms and walk him around outside in the fresh air, the sunlight was always good for kids, when Isaac was born, Dr. Martinez suggested some sunlight when possible to boost liver functions, the sunlight was a prevention of jaundice so Jacob was now being carried outside. The infant was docile, at this size he simply rested along the forearm of his father, face in hand. Mary Sue was displeased when her husband carried their children like footballs, she teased him about being ready to break her tackle at any moment, he always threw her a raised eyebrow and crooked sly smile implying that he was ready for her tackle at all times.

The children played in the barn this morning, Isaac ran amok in thin shorts, his feet were caked in dirt and his small feet left small impressions in the sand. Elizabeth chased her brother, her light dress flowed behind her, her hair was loosely braided by her mother and the tail bounced off of her shoulders as she ran, Obadiah just sat near the garden and watched his offspring play. The green tomatoes in the garden let out a strong odor, the smell of the plants filled Obadiah's nostrils, his mood lightened, the smell of potential food was great, the smell of the plants and the sense of fresh vegetables to come sent him in a staring trance, he just let his eyes wander into the garden while his mind, finally found silence. The day moseyed on slowly, with little to do and even less to eat, the children played until they grew tired from lack of energy and nutrition, Mary Sue regained her strength as the second day moved along since having given birth, she also became more ambulatory, she eased herself through the home and leaned against the kitchen counter to stare outside, she wasn't confident enough to attempt the stairs as her legs were still shaky and her hips needed a few more days to get back to working order.

Mary Sue leaned against the counter to keep some of her weight off of her pelvis, she wished to join her family outside but she was still tired, her energy wasn't returning as quickly as it should, her breasts ached from the arrival of her milk, her stomach still ached and her lady parts still felt ripped apart and turned inside out, her entire body seemed to revolt against her and the pain further exhausted her. She stood vigilant over her family, she glanced around and took stock of what little was left in her kitchen supplies, few beans and potatoes, few bags of flours left to thicken up anything, a hand full of spices and whatever might still grow from the garden, there wasn't enough to get them through the month, let alone through the winter, her heart sank and she was lost without any ideas, hope or way to improve their situation. Mary Sue still prayed for things to improve, she wasn't sure why, she assumed it was just out of lifelong habit, it was empty and meaningless. Obadiah sat on a splintered wooden seat, his body hunched over his newborn son, shielding its' body with his, Mary Sue struggled to remain standing as long as possible but in her weak condition, she retired back to her bed for another bit of rest before her newborn joined her for feeding.

The children grew weary towards the middle of the day as the sun sat high above; making shadows their smallest in the day. Jacob fussed and was taken back to his mother, the family retreated out of the sun and warmth and into the home, Obadiah was glad to open some windows but with how often sand blew in, he didn't want to open windows on the western side of the home so there was much less of a cross draft, but open windows still brought a pleasant breeze in, it seemed to attempt to usher in the fall. With a handful of cut pinto beans and a cup of flour added to peppered water, the stewed meal was meager but fed the family anyways. Mary Sue was doing her best to recover as well as feed their baby, it was all a challenge and even more so when food was as scarce as it was scarce.

Each time Jacob latched to feed, Mary Sue felt herself grow more tired, she sometimes struggled to remain awake enough ensure he was suckling appropriately, she fought her closing eyes most of the time, she would often lay propped up enough to minimize her energy use, as well as time awake. Mary Sue spent most of her day dozing off, her husband waited on her hand and foot as best he could while wrestling the older two children. The day ended like so many had, tranquil and defeated. The following morning was unlike any yet, as Obadiah stepped outside to water the garden and it had been decimated, tomato plants were bent and picked, the squash plants had been ripped, the other vines were missing their food and sustenance that was almost ready to be harvested for the family. Rage filled Obadiah's chest, his pulse ran like fire in his veins, his forehead began to perspire immediately and he wanted to know what soon to be dead creature had done such a thing. He felt like a failure once again for not having heard the commotion that must have taken place in the garden next to the home.

Boot marks in the softer soil of the garden had plainly given away that it was a man. Obadiah felt sick, he burned with fury and his hands shook with anger as he fumbled back into his home to inform his wife as to what happened and that he was leaving. Obadiah gathered his canvass shoulder pack, a thermos filled with water and a handful of beans to cheek and chew on. Mary Sue was distraught over what had happened, her face looked like as if she wanted to cry but nothing came out, no tears, and hardly any sound, this was yet another hard blow to the parents that simply wanted to grow their children and raise a farm. If there was a god, he was pinned against the Withers and refused to lighten up for he was a cruel bastard and let people suffer for pleasure. Obadiah figured to hell with god, he was going to take his food back and find who slighted his home. Obadiah instructed Elizabeth to take watch over her mother, as well as watch out the windows and keep everyone inside, she didn't fully understand but she heeded her father's instructions anyways.

Obadiah laced up his boots and headed out, he didn't even bother to put on a shirt under his overalls or grab a hat to keep the sun from his eyes. Obadiah made a quick stop at the barn, he had an ax handle just inside the opening from an old broken tool, he shouldered the wood handle and he began to track the son of a bitch that stole from his family. Rage and anger kept the vengeful man at a fast pace, the imprints in the sand tracked to the northeast of the home, similar to the path that he took towards the train tracks, he had a destination to catch up with the person, and reclaim his garden items. Obadiah legged out large strides over the sand, it was early and the lack of breeze helped to preserve the path that some bastard had walked, just hours before. Obadiah tried to span the distance trying to spot anyone that may have stood up from the ground and was also making their way north. The horizon was flat, there was no sign the person and Obadiah walked faster, his anger grew as each step didn't bring him any closer to revenge.

There was no telling how long had passed, it had been hours and Obadiah was still pressing to keep up his pace, his weak body had been struggling to keep up the gate that his enraged body had started, the soft dirt below his feet made him unsteady and some of his steps had tripped him up. His un-coordination coupled with a weak body from minimal nutrition for months, maybe even longer, had made him trip and fall to the ground many times as he trudged on. It was shear will covered in hatred that drove the man, he hated himself, he hated the fact that as a father he failed, he hated Oklahoma, he hated god for abandoning him and his family. Each time Obadiah had to stumble back to his feet, his anger grew more and more, he felt like a wildfire as he stormed northward. Obadiah cheeked a few hard beans, he used his tongue to move them back and forth in his mouth like a cud of chaw, he missed tobacco once in a while but this helped to pass the time, as they softened he would squish them and bite at them with his teeth before swallowing the pieces.

Mary Sue was trying her best to fake well for the sake of her children, her worry for her husband concerned her, he wasn't at his strongest like when they first moved out to Indian Gulch when he took her on the front porch while their daughter slept inside. Her husband had lost a lot of his muscle tone, his ribs shone through his skin now, he must have lost seventy five pounds since moving out here, he wasn't much over one thirty now, his shoulders no longer had the cannon ball size to them they did in years past, his chest muscles didn't ripple when he flexed, his skin just thinned and hung on his bones now, she worried more so now that he might not return than ever before. Elizabeth had locked all of the doors as instructed; she paced between the front and side door windows and watched for her father, her mother also tasked her with keeping an ear open to the parents' bedroom for the cries of Jacob as their mother prepped their meals. Mary Sue sat down often as she cooked, the meal was going to be scraps again but it was all she could do to feed her family.

Obadiah marched in into the late afternoon, his rage carried him across the sand, he thought he might have seen someone in the distance, near a small patch of trees as the horizon grew dark. The possibility of having caught up with some scoundrel that snuck in and not only picked his garden of its' bounty, but also thrashed the plants to prevent them from growing more food for the family, elated him, he wanted to smash in the skull of whomever it was that would put his family even closer to starvation. Sure enough there was a small sparkle near the tree, it looked like a small fire near the base, Obadiah fought the urge to charge straight over, he arced a bit as he still trudged on, he wanted to put the tree between himself and whomever the person was, to add surprise to his side as he slowed his steps and quieted himself while drawing near. Obadiah slunk as he walked, he knew with the setting sun to his left and the tree to his right that his silhouette would stand up and he didn't want to risk giving away his intentions. Obadiah needed all of his food back, he knew that family would still be doomed for the winter but reclaiming this much food and salvaging even portions of the bounty could mean holding back starvation just a little longer.

Mary Sue grew worried about her husband, was there a chance that he might not live through his mission? Might he have confronted more than one person and taken such a beating, or even worse? What were the odds that he lived through any skirmish or maybe even had some debilitating injury as he stormed through the land on his way? Last time it took longer than three days for her husband to make it to the train tracks last time, how long should she wait before she finally packed up anything she could and begin to move her family back home, as she had thought about for years now.

Mary Sue missed her home but hadn't had the courage to bring the idea back to her husband and undermine his ego in bringing them out to Oklahoma, a move that had already been haunting him and sabotaging his sense of self-worth. Mary Sue knew what it took to be a good wife: endless support for her husband in addition to being open minded to him and his thoughts, he was just as committed to her but she knew that he regretted his fateful decision to move and by the time it was time to pack up and go back, they hand long been blown in and trapped to any form of transportation except walking.

Obadiah had crouched down as he neared the tree with the small fire near it, he couldn't see anyone near the tree as he closed in. The sky was growing a dark maroon and it made things hard to make out but he stepped lightly closer and closer to the fire, as he stepped to one side he finally locked eyes on the person sitting against the tree, roasting a large acorn squash over the fire, one such squash that the bastard pillaged from the Withers' garden. Obadiah's heart began to pound, he tucked his satchel behind him a bit better and wrung his hands tightly on the ax handle, his teeth bit down in anger, his adrenaline made his heart pump in his ears. Obadiah neared the tree, keeping it between him and a man sitting at the base, he cocked his arms back to swing a mighty blow to the dark silhouette to disable the man before beginning to ask the "why" questions. As Obadiah begun to drag his arms around the front of him while stepping closer to the tree, a pair of bright white eyes turned to him,

A dark skinned man leaned back away from the club being swung by Obadiah, he raised his right arm up to block the hit and the long hard ax handle connected with the up righted forearm of the offender, a loud "*CRACK*" echoed out into the silence, the forearm snapped, near the elbow, causing the stranger to let out an intense howl from the pain. The stranger fell backwards and his left arm swiped into the fire, sending embers and sparks into the arm and speckling both men in fire. Obadiah stood tall and filled with rage over the man, he held up his wooden club towards the man and began to scorn the man for having slighted his family so. The man shoved his feet into the dirt and used his shoulder blades to crawl backwards away from Obadiah; his assaulter.

The aggression in Obadiah caused his hands to shake, his hands sweated and made for a hard grip on the handle as he stepped closer to the man trying to scurry away. The man was wearing tattered overalls, a yellowish buttoned shirt and a dark Bowler hat; he scrambled to apologize to the man as Obadiah shouted for him to shut his mouth. The man clambered for any way out of his predicament, the man spewed every excuse possible to avoid having to be responsible for his own actions, a cowards' mentality.

The man said his hat was from Detroit, it was custom order and Obadiah could have it if he let him go. Obadiah could only find enough coherence to ask "*WHY*" over and over as he continued to stand dominantly over the fallen man. Suddenly he recognized the man as the fire continued to illuminate the area, it was the vacuum salesman from in town a while back, son of a bitch was Willie Bennett, the fast talking swindling low life. Obadiah felt a slight tinge in his stomach, he already killed some man named Mickey with his own hands. Obadiah often fought the ghost of what he had done for years now and he couldn't be sure he could handle any of it again. Obadiah looked around for any remaining food that Willie had stolen, there was a small bag with edible contents in it laid up against the tree, Willie had instructed Obadiah to take it and let him be, he failed to apologize for his actions, the man refused to accept responsibility. The man's life hung in the air as the firelight hung on the shirtless body and his shadows hung on the tree behind him. Obadiah felt his chest swell, his arms felt lit steel and his eyes as sharp as a hawks as he tried to peer into the soul of the man whom he was standing over, eyeing where to bury his ax handle into his head to cave it in.

Obadiah questioned the man repetitively. He asked him what he had been doing and how he made it to his home, and after all these years, why was he still around the area, especially so far from town. Willie had explained he wandered for a while and found the farm so he hid out until after dark before peeking in the windows and then taking everything from the garden. Obadiah felt his chest well up further, his eyes began to tear, this man had been outside of his house and peeked in the windows, putting his children at risk.

Obadiah felt jealous of his children for a minute, his children were so ignorant to so many things and it was mighty fortunate. Obadiah shook; his legs trembled as he stood wide legged over Willie. Willie continued to confess about having swindled old ladies out of money, robbed from anyone possible because they had food or money that he wanted, he had spent his whole life taking advantage of others and he wasn't about to begin to feel bad for it. Obadiah grew more and more enraged as the pinned man spoke, Willie was named after his father, whom also scammed and fought anyone that got in his way. Willie had panhandled and rode the rails from coast to coast, he always found places where people were working for money, and then helped them from their money, without actually having to have worked him.

Obadiah had begun to feel bad for the man that was trying to nurse his shattered broken arm; he had stopped trying to wriggle free from the pinned position of Obadiah, whom stood firmly over the man. Willie had given up struggling, he spat as he grunted and spoke but he barely fought for anything in his life, he laid still with a cocky smirk on his face as he was convinced that he had never done anything wrong and lacked the ability to see himself as anything less than a god. The man remained unruffled about what he had done, oblivious to what his arrogance caused, ignorant to how his actions affected others, and for this Obadiah wanted to crush his skull in with his ax handle.

Willie calmed and stared up at the man that stood over him, he tried to ignore his subordinate position and attempted to intimidate Obadiah into backing down. Willie spoke tight lipped, his mouth puckered as he told Obadiah about looking in his windows, seeing two young kids asleep on the floor a pretty wife asleep in the room as her husband slept next to her, he tried to get a peek at her gams as she slept in a small night gown. He spoke about how his flesh reacted as he stared at Mary Sue while they slept. Willie maintained a dead eye lock on Obadiah; he still thought he was invincible. He spat upwards at Obadiah, called him an "ugly motha" as Obadiah swung high upward and then brought his dented and worn ax handle down and plunged the oak into the skull of the man who was cussing at him from the ground. Obadiah had choked Mickey do death out of a subconscious action, this was completely conscious.

The oak handle connected with Willie. His yelling and spitting turned to gurgling after the thick crack split his head. In the flickering shadows of the firelight blood splattered on the ground, reflecting the lights making the ground look like it was covered with shattered mirror pieces. Willies body went limp; his hands clenched at Obadiah's pant legs, his face looked like a Picasso painting. After the first hit, Willie still tried to kick and claw as Obadiah, raised up one more time and baseball swung across his body. The ax handle connected to the left side of Willies head, just near the ear sending blood into the air and skull and brain matter across the ground away from the fire, the wet squishy sound was enough to make Obadiah feel ill but he wasn't going to let some parasite steal from his family and put them at risk of starving to death, he certainly wasn't going to let this putrid bastard go on infecting the world he was raising his children in.

Obadiah could no longer raise his arms after the second *whomp*, the handle felt like a building in his hands, it fell to the ground as he could no long hold onto it and the blood splatter made it slippery as well. It was dark out and the day had been spent tracking the dirt bag rather than keeping track of where he came from. There was no energy left in his body to function, as his adrenaline was fleeting, so was his ability to control himself. The fire was warm and Obadiah was wet with sweat and blood his body began to shiver as his adrenaline wore out and let his body to actually feel the chill in the air. His skin tightened with goose bumps as he fell backwards crudely to his backside to sit near the fire. The body to his right was leaking blood pools onto the sand around the body. Obadiah had barely eaten, hardly had anything to drink and his body was paying for the exertion of the day. He not only felt ill after what he just had just done to Willie, but he also felt as if his body no longer had anything left. He could fall over and die and currently, he didn't feel like there was any more he could give, or even care about right now.

Looking down into the fire, the small bits of timber crackled and sent sparks into the air, the sounds of the crackling was relaxing, the body a foot from him was still, it was eerie and unsettling as Obadiah kept waiting for his chest to rise to gasp for a breath, the rise in the man's chest never came. As Obadiah sat and tried to take in the warmth of the fire. He watched the glimmer of the firelight reflect off of the pools of blood, the shimmering was all around him, one such sparkle caught Obadiah's' eye, it was the acorn squash that Willie was cooking as Obadiah came up on him.

The gourd was already picked and half cooked, it was a shame to waste if it sat so Obadiah grabbed the stick that pierced through the gourd and resumed cooking his meal. Obadiah felt guilty that he was eating something that was meant for his family. He shouldn't have been eating the gourd but he desperately needed to eat. His body had been failing him and all he could do anymore was want to cry. That sounded like a good idea, with only the mere thought of crying his eyes already began to well up, his body was so tired, his emotional state was well past unstable, he wanted to lay down in the dirt and let out his final breath into the night air.

Obadiah tugged the leg of the man he had just beaten to death; Obadiah laid down onto his side and bit at parts of the acorn squash he roasted over the fire with the leg of a dead man as his pillow. The meal was simply a roasted squash, eating so much of one thing became monotonous but it was an amazing euphoria to feel full, a nirvana had hit him as his entire body gave up and fell numb. Obadiah bid Willie a goodnight and apologized for what he had to do, the fire snapped a few more times as Obadiah curled up and fell asleep. Mary Sue worried about her husband, it was nightfall and he had not come back home, she worried that the absolute worst had happened and that he wouldn't be coming back, his rage that exuded from his body as he stormed out had worried her something fierce, she had three children that depended on her, and her husband that left her behind, there was nothing that she could do for him. Mary Sue fought to keep up with her two children while nursing Jacob, Elizabeth was curious how nursing worked and it boggled her while Isaac made no never mind.

The sunlight broke, it was a welcome relief as Obadiah had been curled up fighting to keep warm, the body of Willie was as cold as the ground he was covered in, his head resembled a busted pumpkin, with innards strewn about near the body with a caved in head. The body lay still, Obadiah stared at the results of a blood rage, his ax handle was covered with blood and brain matter and all was covered in sand where it had fallen. Obadiah had a sliver of clarity as he awoke, a moment of peace before the previous evening had flooded back to the front his memory, he had half of a second to feel like a young man again before the reality of his past few years had come back to him in the form of aches and pains. Obadiah looked out over the distance from which he came, he was a day's walk from home and had a long way to go so he wanted to get to it he reckoned as he stretched out some of the stiffness that resided throughout his body.

Obadiah had bent down to pick up the small green bag of his garden veggies that the criminal had taken from his garden, as he leaned forward and grabbed hold of the bag he heard a small snap just as he took a "*whomp*" hit to the back of the head. The blow had knocked Obadiah to the ground, he fell forward and the snap had sent his heart beating in such a force that his chest wanted to explode as he landed face down. Obadiah filled with panic as he flipped himself over and readied for another blow.

The back of his head behind his left ear throbbed as he tried to focus on what in the hell was about to happen. His eyes raced in every direction from his position on his left side to defend against another blow with his right arm. Obadiah sat for a moment, bewildered and surprised, his head temples beating from his rapid heartbeat, Obadiah couldn't find the origin of the attack, the body was still lying on the ground, there was no one standing near him and things didn't register as to what in damn hell hit him before scanning the ground around him. Obadiah searched then slowed his scanning of the ground around him, his eyes fixed on a thick pear that had rolled several feet from him, he located the source of what had knotted the back of his head now and he turned his focus on controlling his breathing. The surprise left him in aw, he let his chest pound as he fumbled back to his hands and knees, heavy with exasperation.

Obadiah arched his back to look above him, sure as anything else he was underneath a pear tree, oh what a welcome site. The tree was grand in size but thin in number of leaves or fruits, each pear were much smaller than they normally should be, but they were edible just the same. Obadiah sat in amazement for a moment at the fruit from this tree, the abundance was astounding and the overwhelming excitement kept Obadiah's blood rushing, the bounty brought elation to the worn out and renounced man.

The morning was chilly and having curled up next to the man he had killed, another one, and he didn't know how to feel anymore. Obadiah didn't ever want to take a life like he did last night, when he fought hand to hand with Mickey and felt the man's life leave his body at the grip of his hand to Mickey's throat, he felt himself change after that interaction. Obadiah let his head hang again; his excitement had left him lightheaded again, weak from the lack of good meals for months now. The squash sat in his stomach had pained his bowels, nature was calling for him and if he were to make the walk home, he needed to get moving so his wife wouldn't worry much longer.

As Obadiah sat back over a fallen branch and a shallow hole that he had dug, the partial solids raced through him and out, the gut twisting pains left the already weak man grunting and straining to evacuate his stomach contents. Obadiah spent his time staring at the ground as he bore down clenching most of the muscles in his body; the strain caused him to sweat. Obadiah tried to keep watch over the distance because of his inability to fully function given his circumstances; putting off what he had to take care of. Only a few feet away was the still corpse of Willie Bennett, the wretched bastard that though he could steal from the Withers' home and get away with it.

Obadiah shed the notion of an almighty power despite trying to bargain with one to stop the painful bowl discharge, he neglected the idea that some invisible entity would put his family through everything that they had gone through, only to keep track of all of the man's sins and eternally judge him for it upon death. Obadiah refused to spend the rest of his life tiptoeing to please some nonexistent master, refused to suffer during the rest of his life here on earth for some fantasy conjured up by clergy that wanted money in exchange for the mirage of salvation, maybe if he returned back to praying that maybe his lower intestine problems would go away, he chuckled a bit between having to bear down and keep his boots outstretched to keep them clean.

The small canvas shoulder bag that Obadiah brought with him wasn't nearly large enough to carry back any real score from the tree, most of the fruits were small and meager, the dry summers had wilted most of the leaves and stunted the fruit growth but the deep rooted tree had reached down far enough to feed some fruit growth, the edible fruits were spaced far enough apart to make harvesting them a task, but welcomed work that would result in an ability to feed his family, work that Obadiah would be glad to perform.

Obadiah had finally rid his stomach of whatever bug had plagued him, along with any contents he might have eaten in the last week. The relief from no longer having to grit down and strain his stomach muscles was ever so welcomed, more so than having found the tree that he had slept unknowingly underneath. Obadiah rubbed his backside with handfuls of sand to clean himself up before kicking dirt over the shallow hole.

Obadiah grabbed his ax handle and dragged some long strokes into the sand a few feet from the base of the tree; it took some time but a large enough hole was slowly forming in which Obadiah could drag the lifeless and no longer burdensome body into.

Obadiah grabbed the pant legs of the body, there was a large pile of clotted sandy blood that remained where the deformed head laid overnight, pieces of bone flecked in the coagulated puddle, the slush sound made Obadiah look twice. Obadiah had to lean forward in order to get some sturdy momentum in order to pull the heft from its indent in the dirt.

Obadiah dug his feet into the sand to give himself improved traction to drag the body he created, his mind was rife with things going on, his thoughts reverted back to his family, to times he made love to his wife, his children and even when nothing in the area grew, his family did. Obadiah dug in the rigid shadow the tree cast on the ground. The body fit into the shoddy grave. It was as makeshift as possible but it was something to get the body out of sight. As Obadiah finished dragging the dead weight into the hole, by a hand full of pant leg, it struck him, Obadiah stood up straight as his ingenuity enlightened him and he quickly got to work. The work to cover up the body was fairly brief; the sand was light and airy, easy to kick from the edges of the hole over the body.

Obadiah shook and picked as many pears as possible; he climbed many of the branches that would support his weight as he outstretched the bloodied ax handle to knock some of the deformed fruits from their stems and to the ground. Obadiah hit as many of the fruits as he could find, he crudely held on to the tree with his left hand, as well as fed himself the green juicy fruit, it was refilling his body, the sugars raced through him like his adrenaline had earlier, his body craved such a treat, each bite was tough and fibrous but each tasted like a feast, he began to feel suffocated+ as he gorged on pears while swinging his ax handle at pears as he freed them from upper branches, letting them bounce off of obstacle branches on their way to the ground. Slowly more and more pears hit the ground, this was a bounty that Obadiah finally felt proud of, his work was paying off, food was mounding up on the ground and relief washed over the treed man.

There were barely any other trees in the distance, the horizon stretched out in every direction, the sun was snaking its way up from the ground and into the sky, the clouds were thick but scattered about, the fall was setting in and it was getting closer to winter, it risked getting cold and hopefully this hoard of pears would make a significant difference in surviving the coming cold. Obadiah rung out the tree as best as he could, jostling fruits from their stems, shaking the branches to free them of green pears, the sand below the tree was speckled with green fruits, the harvest was an amassed relief that couldn't have come any later. Obadiah let himself down from the tree, he was cautious to avoid squishing any of the food, he now had to pack up everything he could and high tail it home.

Mary Sue awoke without her husband again, it was disheartening and she worried deeply about his safety and when he might return, she convinced herself that he would be home anytime and that he wouldn't rest until he brought back their garden stuffs, he had family to feed and provide for and he couldn't not come back, she tried to focus on feeding her newborn Jacob all while still keeping tabs on the two jittery and rambling children. The cooler morning began to keep them indoors longer and longer, when indoors they wanted to snack out of boredom, which was a hard strain when food supplies were already at their most scarce. Mary Sue picked many of the leaves from the trashed garden plants, she often tore, crushed, or shredded the plants into flour for terrible tasting crackers, the tastes were just horrid but the plant matter was edible and a hungry enough stomach hardly rejected food long enough, the children often grimaced through the slow chewing of their mediocre meals, the cucumber leaves had a pleasant smell as they boiled down in a small sauce pan, the tomato leaves on the other hand, let out a putrid smell that needed an opened window to vent the stench, the children held their noses the entire time, and thoroughly debated refusing the meal.

Mary Sue fought to feed her children, her body was being sucked dry by her nursing child, she nibbled on as much as she possibly had but subsisting off of plant leaves and flour, there wasn't enough sugars in her foods to assist in milk production, her body felt depleted each time Jacob latched, he seemed to hang on longer each feeding, she was struggling to keep up on her food intake, she felt guilty eating when her other children needed to eat also, but she also knew that Jacob was growing faster and faster and he needed her milk in order to do so.

The balancing act made Mary Sue want to cry, and some nights she just did, there wasn't much to go around. According to the news reports, some of the farmers were getting financial relief but not enough, not soon enough, and probably not for the Withers' family. Mary Sue had three precious children to raise up, she always dreamed about having large family holidays like Thanksgiving, a house full of warm mood lifting smells, pies and pans full of sides and kids and their families and their children all up to visit. Mary Sue dreamed so very often of a large family and being able is present in all of their lives as she and her husband aged slowly together, these last few years have caused them to age faster than the world spun.

Since Moving to Oklahoma Mary Sue has watched her husband lose near eighty pounds, she herself has watched her own face sink in, her cheekbones jut out, her eyes subsided into their sockets and her once full lips, thinned and lost their youthful color and appeal, even her exuberant blue eyes have seemed to glaze over and lose their glossiness, her skin has since become leathery, her breasts have succumbed to gravity and the rest of her body had begun to wrinkle and let go a bit, she couldn't see the daily changes in her body but all of the sudden one day she saw an older, less firm version of herself short years later.

Mary Sue thought forward to a day when she stood up from washing her face to see a silver haired version of herself, she still vividly remembered being a little girl playing in the crick with her sisters, it was so fresh a memory like it had just happened, she still felt the water on her skin as she and her sisters splashed and let their small bodies float in the stream. Mary Sue thought about having lost her sister Gertie, how she could still hear her voice. Early mornings she would awake and still think she was a little girl, her sisters already awake and calling for her, then her life fast forwards to her daughter calling for her instead. Time plays on everyone's mind, it rushes by each time you close your eyes and then one day you never open your eyes again.

The intricacies of life were overwhelming, as a young girl Mary Sue enjoyed the naivety of youth, days were spent helping around the parents farm, often helping to pick cotton or harvest around the gardens, but she and her sisters would race through everything, who could pick the most cotton, who could run the fastest through the rows of plants or jump the farthest from the creek banks for the biggest splash. Mary Sue felt her heart sink as she recalled how much fun she had as a young girl and how her own daughter wasn't getting to experience the same childhood joys, she wasn't being the greatest mother and encouraging such fun and games, she was spending most of her time struggling to survive, she felt she owed so much her poor daughter, who had to give up so much of her childhood to help her family instead of have young girl fun. Mary Sue began to weep as she sat upon the seat outside watching her children play inside the barn. Elizabeth still smiled, she didn't know much of the world outside of what she knew of the farm, she didn't really remember having to live with Norman, but she did remember "Pappy Man" her nickname for him.

Mary Sue kept a wary eye on the horizon for her mate. He had been absent for a long while, she longed for him right now, she wanted his companionship, he was the one person she wanted to grow old with and the man she wanted beside her as they both grayed, aged, and then slipped into forever together. Mary Sue hung her head, her heart sank and she finally stopped fighting the feeling she has had that sat quietly in the background. She had a feeling that she was failing in her duties as a mother. She needed Obadiah with her, on her weakest of days, the days when she became full of doubt, when fear overtook her, or insecurities plagued her emotions he would reassure her that she was doing her best and that as a couple, they were doing as best as they could with the given circumstances of their environment. Mary Sue sat with her elbows on her knees, her body was still trying to recover from the assault of childbirth, she still found herself tired very frequently, she wanted to trust her children to be safe playing but after what had happened to her garden, in such a remote homestead, she didn't feel like they could be safe until Obadiah returned.

Elizabeth helped to hoist her brother up the tractor tire treads to take a seat behind the steering wheel, he made "vroom vroom" noises and bounced up and down as he pretended to drive, Elizabeth instructed on how to till the fields and she spoke confidently about how plentiful the harvest would be after their make believe reaping, Mary Sue couldn't help but to admire the little girls steadfast trust and positive outlook, despite there being no reason to think the sand filled fields could ever produce crop again. Maybe it was time to truly begin packing or readying to find a way back to South Carolina, back to her home

Obadiah trudged back across the grassland turned desert back to his family, he slung his heavily bloodied ax handle over his left shoulder while he carried the trousers he removed from Willie, tied the bottoms of the pant legs and then filled them with pairs, the crotch of the legs straddled over his right shoulder to better balance the weight, the pants full of pears must have weighed seventy to eighty pounds, the pants were lumpy like a fat ladies legs and bulged at the seams too. The walk back to the farm was a struggle, Obadiah carried the pants that almost rivaled his own body weight as he walked across the unsteady landscape on his route back home to join his family, he munched a few pears as he walked and he stepped onto the eaten pear cores to push them into the dirt, thinking about the ways Johnny Appleseed must have when he traversed the young country however long ago.

Obadiah saved some of the cores waiting to plant multiple along the field edges of his property, he had enough pears to surround his property and if his family could last the next several years, then his property will have much more hearty food bearing trees as well as sturdy enough living plants to help act as a windbreak to further protect his fields, he thought he was doing his part to add to the shelter-belt that he had heard about on the radio news programs.

Eight pears and a day's worth of walking had left Obadiah feeling physically tired but fairly enlivened after being able to eat, except gastro-intestinally, he was still struggling. Obadiah scanned the horizon for any signs of people or anyone that might cause him any grief before he propped up the pants with the walking stick ax handle and squatted down over a hole he had to dig with his heels in the sand again. Obadiah doodled in the sand as he squatted down, he drew another line from the setting sun across the sand, drew his circle around it and numbered out the numbers of a clock where eight was where the sun was setting, four was where it rose and he continued to head towards the seven, where the six was due south, a trick Norman taught him when they used to head out for days of deer hunting, they would go out into the snowy woods, seeing the sun's orb could help you determine how many hours of light you have and when it rises or falls can help to determine where compass points are and how to get around to where you need to go, skills that have served the country folks for generations.

Obadiah resumed his march back home, heaving the trousers back up onto his shoulders, his ax handle clenched tightly in his right hand, there were small pops of the seam stitches as he walked, Obadiah fought his best to ease the bouncing of the pants to ease the abuse on the seams in hopes that they would hold up until he made it home with his fortunate find. He walked with as fast a pace as his body could muster to get back to his family, he missed them all and even though it wasn't two whole days without them, he felt a great sense of pride that he could finally provide for his family; it wasn't just chopping warming wood now but bring them food. He smiled under the crushing weight of the pear filled pants because he could treat his family, the pears were simple, menial, but each one meant more days of life for him and his family. Obadiah recalled having prayed so many times that his children's pains be his pain instead, every time he pained alongside with them, every parent hurts when their children hurt, they hunger when their children starve and when their children go without, the parents feel at fault

Obadiah could see his home off to the right far off in the distance, his body ached from two solid days of exertion, his shoulders felt torn and bruised, his lower back felt stiff and ached with each step and his hands were still stiff and swollen from swinging the ax handle into the skull of Willie Bennett, the first crack vibrated up the handle and through his forearms, the second swing to the left side of the already bleeding head just sank in deeply, sending pieces of skull and brain spewing over the sand next to him.

The exertion he put into beating Willie to death almost did him in. It was about all the mans body could do to fight for life as his body tried to collapse right afterwards, and his body may have shut down if the offending man hadn't already been cooking the squash that made for Obadiah's supper. Obadiah could feel his body slow down with relief from seeing his end destination, he was once again fighting to remain upright while trudging through the sandy soils of the fields that encapsulated his home.

Mary Sue paced as the sun set, she fixed thistle and flour tack yet again, she tried to spice what she could but the blandness of the food staples seemed to resist any attempt at seasoning, it was almost impermeable to flavoring. The children tussled, Elizabeth usually fought for control over her younger brother, he was rather defiant to his sister but listened respectfully to his mother when she instructed him to pipe down and behave himself when he acted up, especially later in the evening before bedtime. Mary Sue put her children to their beds shortly after sundown, she was without company, the newborn had left her exhausted and struggling to remain vigilant for her husband, she did her best to fend off passing out as she leaned against the counter in the kitchen and stared out awaiting the return arrival of her husband.

The minutes seemed like hours, the clock in the kitchen ticked the seconds, except each tick left an eternity to wait before the next tick. In her tired state Mary Sue would come close to falling asleep and then become startled awake with each tick that echoed within the kitchen, each jolt awake would cause her head to spasm back up and her eyes to fight to refocus out the window. Mary Sue kept the doors locked as her husband instructed and didn't want him to come home to find himself locked out, and if he needed medical attention she wanted to be able to assist as quickly as possible.

Obadiah neared his home, most of the home was dark as the he inched slower and closer, his bed had been beckoning him for the latter half of the day, his body ached in every conceivable way and even as the home grew larger as he neared but he failed to make any large strides to cover the distance, his progress seemed nill as each step he made failed to bring him closer to getting home. Obadiah labored on, his steps grew more tired, once he entered the area near the barn as he labored harder with each step and his bloodied walking stick, it took a moment to muster enough strength to pull the lagging leg from behind to the front in order to step closer, his hip joints ground together as he stepped closer. It was too tempting to lean against the barn to rest, to lean for a moment would have been the end of his travels, but he hated the notion of waking up on the ground again. Obadiah needed better sustenance for his body; he needed meat of some form to re-strengthen his muscles. For a moment he thought he should have maybe carved up the leg muscles of the man he beat to death, it would have been cannibalism but the form of meat may have sustained his growing children longer.

Hate is the biggest source of internal energy, you can love yourself and when you do, you stop fighting to improve, if you hate doing something than you'll dig deep down and grab the pissed off by the balls and push on. Obadiah hated the notion of being weak, he hated how sickly he had become, he hated that he had failed to support his family over and over, not this night, this night he hated the sand and that it had taken almost all the life from the area and how it took his pride from him. Obadiah hated the feeling of failure; he almost successfully moved his family out to Oklahoma and became wheat farmers, almost.

Obadiah hiked his makeshift pack back up onto his shoulders and stepped up towards the side door, he could see the shadow of his wife just in the window, he was so excited to share his find with his wife, he had watched her body deteriorate over the duration of the drought and he hoped to help revive her spirit with his edible fortune. He wanted so badly to see the excitement on her face as she laid her eyes on what he had brought, it wasn't a deer or hog but it was still food.

Mary Sue had blinked for a brief moment until she heard the door handle jiggle, the noise seemed amplified within the kitchen, startling her to the point that she almost leaped off of the counter or perhaps fallen. The failed attempt at opening the door gave Mary Sue a moment to hurry to the door and quick check whom was awaiting just outside the door before she unlatched the lock, depending on whom was waiting on the other side. Obadiah turned the door handle, it refused to open the door and he worried for a moment that he might be locked out, until he remembered that he had instructed his young daughter to secure everything to ensure the safety of his family in his absence. He made one more attempt at turning the handle before he reached his middle knuckle towards the glass to knock and hopefully awaken his wife so she could let him in.

As Mary Sue neared the side door, a loud knock rang through and it startled her, causing her to leap from her feet for a moment as she was turning the corner of the countertop readying to identify the person standing on the other side of the door. Obadiah was standing at the door, Mary Sue could see him through the window and she was ever glad to get her husband back, and whatever dirty rag whatever it was he had heaved up over his shoulder. Obadiah made his final step up and into the house, he was so relieved to be home, his eyes began to tear up from finally

306

getting to be home, his exhaustion had taken everything from him, except his ability to weep. Mary Sue took a longing gander at the state of her husband, he was wearing a shirt he hadn't left with and was covered in blood, his hands were stained as was the sack on his shoulder, the ax handle, his chest and face, and there was blood everywhere. Mary Sue reached out to her husband; he needn't say a word because she already knew the story.

Obadiah felt ever so apologetic for his actions, he feared and hated the idea that now how his wife viewed him might have changed again, he killed a man to protect their daughter and his wife and she fought put if from her mind, this day he had beaten a man to death, ever so much more violently and it stained his body, his clothes, his soul. Mary Sue just laid her eyes on her bloodied husband, his shoulders slouched, he shied his eyes to the pair of trousers on the floor, spilling pears out from over the waist, his aversion was of shame, his inability to face his wife was an ill-fated attempt to protect her from the monster that resided deep within him, the monster that fought free from his moral binds and collided the oak ax handle with the skull of the man whom stole from his family. Mary Sue reached out for her husband, his return meant no longer having to be alone, there was nothing certain in life, not even seed you yourself promised to the land, it could just as simply rise up with the wind and blow away.

Obadiah felt his tired body give in, his will could fight on but his body surrendered, his wife helped to ease him to their bed as the walk of only a few yards felt like more miles on the legs of the weary man, every inch of him hurt and as he laid back into his bed, he didn't even remember his head hitting the pillow. Mary Sue left her husband behind, Jacob was surprisingly still asleep in the bassinet and she headed back to the kitchen.

Mary Sue dined on a few pears to refuel her own body as she warmed a small pot of water to sponge off his dirty body, she carried a washcloth with the pan of water and sat down beside him, she wondered what he had put himself through, what had her once gentle and loving husband done in the name of feeding his family? Where did the bloodied trousers come from and how had he collected all of the hundreds of pears, did he pick them or take them from someone? Mary Sue washed her husband, she didn't scrub to hard so as not to wake him but she also didn't want to lay next to him while he was still covered in blood, regardless of who's it was.

Obadiah slept and through the night, his body slowly recovered, he was slow to rise in the morning, his body failed to comply with the wishes of his mind, his nose helped to encourage his migration to the kitchen, his children were dinning on pear biscuits as Mary Sue was topping off many cans to store them through the winter, Obadiah set himself down on the chair to finally join his family, the radio cackled on, the news report continued talking on about FDR's "New Deal" as well as soil conservation efforts that were still slowly making their way through congress, farmers were still being paid to plant trees to add to the shelter-belt lines, from southern Texas all the way to Canada, with trees put in place the reduction in storms and blowing sands should slowly give way to growing grasses, grasses should give way to fertile lands again, all of these hopes were slow to put in place but should offer long lasting results. Obadiah had already been planning to save and then plant as many of the pear seeds as possible, he thought about Mary Sue starting them in jars with good soil over the winter to establish a hearty root system and then planting them around the field edges, fruiting trees might take ten years before they produce but if they make it that long, the food sources would be plentiful.

Mary Sue served her husband and then the family sat down together to eat a morning meal, that included Jacob cradled in her arms. Elizabeth gorged on half a pear, the juice ran down her chin and her smile was as large as the room, Isaac too was feasting on half of a pear, his mother sliced his for him and he held a slice in each hand to prevent his older sister from snatching one away. The trousers were half empty and ferreted away in the pantry, most of the top shelf was stocked with jars of freshly packed pear chunks, Mary Sue had been busy all morning. The stock pile wouldn't be enough to sustain them through the winter alone but it certainly was a good start. Mary Sue and Obadiah used the endless energy of their children to gather more thistle each day there was enough light, the plant was crude and offered very little in the form of nutrition but after brining, it was edible and would cook with different mixtures and was a large staple in their diets already, it would subsist them for as long as it still grew from below the sands.

Obadiah filled jars with the small inedible tips, with a little dirt the plant would break down and offer life support to the pear seeds. With a little potential coming back, even the fleeting notion of potential, Obadiah held his head up a little higher, the garden still held fertile black dirt, the pear seeds as well as hundreds of other seeds were planted in various cartons and containers, the coming years crop planting was to be grand, each plant was started early to give each plant a head start as well as sturdy leaves to help grow the plants in which the plants would secure more dirt as well, it was all an investment and a gamble, but one that must be weighed in order to continue to propagate the family.

The radio crackled on through the remainder of the fall, rumors of different laws being moved in different judiciary steps being taken, there was slow progress being made in order to offer up relief to some of the hardest hit areas, the citizens of the dust bowl. Obadiah hoped that with the news coming through the dusty speaker, that if they could make it through the winter, then there might be relief come spring, maybe the state could find a way to breathe life back into the cities, clear the roads and reestablish a community.

The fall passed on, it had been tempting for Obadiah to head back out to the pear tree, except he knew he had harvested all of its' offerings, and he wasn't sure he could emotionally face the grave of the man he brutally beat to death, he also often stood on the front porch and stared out to the distance, where he also buried three people at the Basks' farm, the sand storms had caused thousands of deaths, thousands that were accounted for that is, but like the priest, how many fell during a storm only never to be recovered, or documented? The skies grew dark earlier and earlier, few flakes fell towards the end of the year, the wood supply wasn't as it should have been and the Withers had to lighten up on their wood burning so the house ran cooler than previous years and the family spent more and more time huddled together for warmth, as well as layered in whatever clothing or blankets they could find for warmth. Jacob remained nestled against his mother for most of December, Obadiah scoured the lands in as many directions as possible to search for wood to help warm the home, the months grew colder and colder, the winds whipped harder and the ground became firm.

Mary Sue often sat with her children, her body and theirs retained warmth for them when they all slept in the parents large bed together, her body still supported the small but growing Jacob. The infant spent most of its' time eating or sleeping but that was fine by his mother, she kept him swaddled and strapped to her body so they could keep one another warm. Elizabeth and Isaac played in the kitchen most of their time as close to the warming stove as possible, Obadiah had piled bricks atop the stove to elongate their warming properties once they were hot, Obadiah kept himself warm by keeping himself moving with chores and tasks during the day, by staying moving you don't slow down long enough to get real cold.

Mary Sue helped to stitch and sew clothing for her children as well as patch clothing for her and her husband, thin summer dresses failed to offer any warmth in the depth of winter, she layered as best as possible, nylons stitched with crude pants helped to retain body warmth under dresses and Elizabeth found it fun to wear pants rather than dresses all of the time, especially with as often as she was kneeling up and down on the hard floors, the family fought on as hard as they could through the coldest the winter had to offer, it bit at them near the corners of the home, frost gathered on many of the windows as January tried to freeze the family to death.

Obadiah spent his days accumulating anything that might constitute firewood to heat his family, it was hard to refrain from burning large fires to thaw the home but the wood pile dwindled and the fear of running out grew ever present. Everything was running out, the food had been meager for years now, the wood pile was nearing the ground, heat didn't seem to have any effect on the cold and numb body parts, the family had shivered since November, it was a long ways till the relief of the spring warmth. Elizabeth continued to practice her reading to Isaac, and when Mary Sue and Jacob were close, she read to them as well. The cold made the children rather docile, it was an unfortunate use of body energy to remain warm and there wasn't enough energy to get to play very much. The radio crackled on most days, it was the only change in the tedium.

As February fell upon the isolated homestead, the youngest Withers child developed a cough, the infant spent most of its' time bundled up near the warm body of his mother, it wasn't a concern for the cough but the issue was, there wasn't a doctor around nor any way to travel to one either. If only there was a way to contact doctor Martinez and make an appointment for young Jacob, with as young as he was, it was difficult to find a way to cure the young child, especially without any medical means, or even herbs anymore. Mary Sue remembers her mother having spread honey on her tongue and when a sore throat got real bad, she got to suck on a marshmallow, she was without any means of quelling the infants cough, there was nothing that could be done but wait and hope.

Obadiah began removing side boards from the barn in order to continue to warm the home, his sick son added urgency to his work and his desperation to warm his family. The barn wood was dry and weathered, it wasn't a sustaining heat but it flamed well and increased the warmth output from the stove in the kitchen. Obadiah moved the heated bricks around the home to help in the heating, moving the bricks from the stove towards the cold helped to heat the living room for the comfort of the family, each board he stripped from the eastern side of the barn brought him closer to having less and less, his tractor and his motor vehicle were enclosed within the safety of the barn, protected from the elements.

Each board that was pried from the wall meant more minutes of warmth for the family, but one step closer to the sands swallowing up the farm, a dread that interrupted the sleep of Obadiah, Mary Sue took notice as he tossed and turned at night while failing to sleep. Jacob continued to cough each day, his small nose ran and Mary Sue had to suck the mucus from his nose and spit it out to assist in the breathing of the infant, the poor child took on a blue tint to his skin and his parents grew more and more worried.

The family moved their bed closest to the wall that separated them from the stove that warmed the kitchen, Obadiah had forgone decent sleep each night to continue rotating bricks from the hot stove into the bedroom to warm the room where his family slept, the tedious task was daunting and each time Obadiah rested between stove stockings and brick moving. His nights were spent walking in circles with short rests in between, each time he sat down between having to add firewood to the stove; his body would barely begin to relax when his senses would hit him with a need to work again and he would rise back to his feet and make the rounds again.

Obadiah went sound asleep frequently; Mary Sue often massaged him in the midday to encourage a deep nap during the day as she would pick up the additional chore in warming the home. Obadiah sawed the barn boards most of the day, the work was further exhausting but the needs of his family must never go unanswered, he fought off lightheadedness on a regular basis, hiding his ills was easier than showing that he was having them, his time outdoors dragging a coarse saw back and forth across wood planks only further exhausted the husband. Obadiah could hardly function most of the time, it seemed to take an eternity to cut through boards, his strength was almost nonexistent as he knelt on the boards to brace them still as his weak arms struggled to hold the saw still as he cut, he had to squeeze his eyes often shut to refocus his strength and attention.

Mary Sue worried about her husband but her children took precedence and the cough of Jacob hadn't improved, even with the warmer temperatures in the home. Elizabeth and Isaac still shivered, they would often sit near the stove to absorb its' radiating heat most of the day, they would sort through the few books she had read and gone through over and over, but hardly leave the proximity of the stove.

Mary Sue sat at the kitchen table most of the day and she kept her children quiet for the sake of her husband, so he could sleep in the next room. His exhaustion overtook him quickly when near a bed and prompted him to remain deeply asleep. When in his slumber, his deeply ingrained fatherly duties would often jolt him awake, fearing he overslept and neglected a chore. Or, the even larger fear, that he left the stove unattended and that his family might get cold. Obadiah was heavily tortured with what he had to do for his family, the insurmountable needs were many and his ability to provide grew less and less. His feeling of failure grew larger and larger and it ate at him.

Obadiah often had headaches, his temples throbbed and the beating of his heart made his eyes feels like they were going to bulge and fall out. Mary Sue found herself in argument with her husband more and more as he refused to eat food that could have fed his family, or even mere water that could have cured him of his headaches.

Obadiah didn't want to be a reason any of his children went hungry, felt cold, or had to need for anything, he had already struggled enough over the past few years. His family had already had to forgo much because he made a poor decision in moving them to Oklahoma, away from their extended family and he felt everything that had happened was his fault. The hours of light outdoors were minuscule, they should have been growing longer but they never seemed to come. Each day only changed from black to gray and then dark gray and back to black again. The days were bleak, there was no hope in sight and the empty promise of a

312

government relief was still months out, if it would even make it to their solitary farm.

Jacob continued to cough, his little body was restless in the chilly home, Elizabeth and Isaac took turns telling him stories, Elizabeth would read to him and explain that grass is green and feels soft under your feet. When he was old enough to run with them, the three of them would run together in the grass when it came back or maybe this summer she would teach him to crawl just like she did for Isaac. Isaac made up stories, he would tell his brother about how owls hooted, dogs barked and chickens clucked, each story was full of made up noises and sounds, Mary Sue sat and chuckled at his attempts to become a great story teller. Isaac's hair was getting long, he kept twitching his head to keep it from his eyes but he refused to let his mother cut it, she tried to reason with him, but you can't with such a young boy, he would take off running and climb under the couch cushions, his head would be buried deep while his lower half would dangle on the floor, if he couldn't see you then he must have been invisible to everyone else.

February ran extremely cold, it had actually snowed and enough to drift high against the northwest corner of the home, as well as the barn. The distance turned from dark brown to the blanketed white, there were no discernible tracks anywhere, no sign that there was any life to hunt or trap to feed the family, Obadiah watched helplessly as his family drew weary each and every day, even as the days seemed to inch longer each day, the energy levels of the family members resembled the negligible food sources, each family member was slowly wasting away, independently together.

The radio spoke more and more about different levels of aid for residents, Obadiah knew that he had to register and secure his name and address on the ballot and then he would be eligible to receive government assistance to plant trees in the Shelter-belt, and that would be the means to a future for the family, things had been desperate for far too long. Obadiah had some deep seeded feeling that the rain was finally going to break free from the skies and once again bring life to the land around him.

The heavy heart had begun to lift within the chest of the dutiful man of the home, his wife had watched his hair thin, his skin weather, and his eyebrows take on a lowered clenched exasperated expression, when he did actually smile, it was so forced due to the heavy burdens he carried and his demeanor exuded how much

313

pain he really bore. Mary Sue wished she could take so much of her husband's pain when the radio would announce the programs coming up to put residents to work. The possibility to put in an honest day's work and to earn a real paycheck, to get the opportunity to put hearty food on the table for his family, it was those thoughts that gave Obadiah the hope to carry on each day. The three children whose lives depended on him to survive were his concern as their lives were ever so much more fickle than the lives he took to continue providing for his family.

Micky's life extinguished rather seamlessly, Obadiah crushed his throat and snuffed out his life light with his bare hands. He wrapped his hands around the stranger's neck and squeezed until it was half the size it started out. Smashing in the skull of Willie Bennett offered a small enjoyment. A day spent tracking the animal, much like a deer back home with Norman, only to finally come to the moment where the fatal blow is delivered, it was an adrenaline releasing moment/ The oak handle driving into the skull as it lay on the ground, shattering and crushing the sturdy brain encapsulating skull. When Willie spat blood and teeth into the air, Obadiah truly felt another life in his hands/His grip on the oak handle tightened, his vice like grip seemed to indent the sanded handle and his shear might have squeezed the solid chunk of refined tree branch into splinters.

Obadiah wanted to plunge the bar so deep into the strangers head that he struck oil. He wanted to muster all of the strength from the heavens and the earth and deliver such an almighty blow to the fallen man that he shook the mountains back to rubble. The anger and fury he had been building had collected in his chest and finally exploded into the mighty rage that left the bastard Willie damn near decapitated, he now rotted away in a shallow grave, despite the fact that he should have earned a cruel public display of his criminal body, like the days of ancient Rome when thieves had their hands chopped off and then they were hung in the public square as an example for all the others.

Obadiah carried guilt with him about Mickey, sure a low life but a life, like so many others, he lacked the intelligence to fight his most basic sexual urges, and he didn't deserve to live anyways. Stalking and then beating down that real scumbag was the last thing Obadiah imagined he was capable of, he worried so deeply that his wife would change her perception of him, the vision she held of him meant so much to him, he sometimes felt paralyzed at the mere thought that his adoring wife might ever see him as anything less than the best mate she could ever have, he needed that to be a big part of him, it was hard to explain but it meant a lot.

The snow that held on tightly within the shadows had finally faded, the temperatures had inched just above freezing during the high points of the day, relief to many whom were ill housed and poorly clad living in the makeshift homes in the Hooverville's. Obadiah and Mary Sue spoke often about their fortune of having been able to remain in their home rather than flee and take to a migrant life with their children. News reports spoke frequently of families that had uprooted and as they wandered the country, they slowly shed off things they once held dear, many families had been reduced to one another, vehicles left behind when there was no longer enough fuel to run them, heavy burdensome clothing dropped as the temperatures rose and unnecessary weight could be shed from roaming families. The Hooverville's were full of displaced people, families that struggled to remain together often wound up in these camps, they dotted the country and the larger the city, the larger the transient camps that sprang up within the city limits. Many older children as well as thousands of single individuals took on the hobo lifestyle as well, most boarded trains to search for work.

Men left families behind, children their parents and siblings, like the little boy with the broken arm that Martinez spoke about, people fought one another, like rabid dogs fighting for the last meager scraps in a back alley way. It had been some time since Obadiah had crossed paths with the bullock little girl named Wendy back at the train tracks, Mary Sue felt a sadness for both of the girls her husband had met while out. Obadiah told his wife about some of the stories they shared with him over cooked bean sandwiches, the two girls, Wendy and who she called Suzy the Jap, had stayed close to one another and fought off train security personnel. They had rode the rails together from the Virginias and weren't sure of their route, but they knew they were going to attempt the arduous work of finding her father in San Francisco, both Obadiah and Mary Sue wondered if they two young girls had made it to their destination.

Mary Sue gazed at parts of her body in the mirror over the duration of the years, she sometimes wondered what her husband still found attractive about her, her body was no longer as it was in her teen years, not everything had remained where it had originated, gravity and age had both weathered her, having three children had also changed her body in many ways. Mary Sue had also observed many changed in her husband, long cold nights had left her husband so exhausted that he slept whole days at a time.

When the young and in love couple had reached Indian Gulch with the toddler Elizabeth, Obadiah could spend all day plowing his fields and still return home to play with his daughter until her bedtime and still make love to Mary Sue late into the night, now the tedious tasks of bringing in firewood had tired him to the point of laying down for a nap. Mary Sue watched the youthful face of her husband wrinkle and age, so much faster from stress than of the time that went by. Obadiah kept his hair short, which had grayed and lightened from the dark black it had once been, his hair had almost whitened near the temples while the rest of his hair had more salt than pepper to it.

Obadiah had olive drab skin tones, but his skin had lightened over the last few years, it coupled with having lost over seventy pounds over the several few years. Mary Sue felt and saw a significant difference in the physical features of her husband, his skin thinned where his shoulders bulged and flexed, Mary Sue could see a lot of the tendons and muscles through the thin skin, his chest shone more ribs than muscle now as his thighs had thinned ever so much more and his face had worn thin as well.

Obadiah had watched his wife transform over the years, she produced two more children for him, her body filled and engorged when pregnant, then deflated again after. Mary Sue had lost weight, her legs were thin, her arms bony and her breasts grew smaller as the years passed, as did her backside. The husband and wife stood closer together as they fought through the struggles, there was only a whisper of hope, there was still a long way between the beginning of March and when hope may arrive, the Withers held onto each other, and to their children even tighter. It was all they could do anymore as there was nothing left.

Rain began to break from the skies and fall to the earth below, the saturation of the ground brought more than a spark of hope, it was a medium rain storm, one of the few the news had broad casted that actually came, the rain settled the sand and packed in the dirt, a new stream cut a path into the dirt that resembled the crick that dried up some years ago, rain carved at the landscape bringing texture and dimension to the view on the other sides of the windows. The day of gentle rain uncovered small sprouts of thriving grass, small pockets of retained soil, hidden under the sand, had become unearthed. Buried grass had decayed, seeds that had fallen into the same pockets were vaulted in the arid land until the rain set the seeds free to take root and reach for life. The rain lasted well into the evening, the warm humid air wafted over the land, filling the home and energizing the lives of the family.

With the children sleeping soundly in their beds, Jacob in his basket, Mary Sue turned to Obadiah, hardly able to contain her excitement about the rain finally falling down, it had been too long since she had enjoyed his company, and even longer since such a rain had blessed the land. The trickle of the rain dancing on the roof had created an erotic and sensual atmosphere, Obadiah had longed for his wife but often felt guilty that he lacked the confidence in his body to perform for his wife. Food sources had still been meager and Obadiah often went days with nothing to eat so that his family could. Mary Sue nursed Jacob as often as she could but she could often feel her milk drying up, she feared her breasts were shriveling up and that her infant son may soon starve. Mary Sue tried to balance her needs to provide for Jacob with the needs of her two other children's' requirements. The physical debts of everyone in the home were wilting and wasting away.

Obadiah felt his bones hit his wife's bones when they hugged, their embraces once brought such comfort but now due to their statures, the embraces they both sought for comfort were now borderline painful. Obadiah wasn't going to let his ego take a back seat to his physical setbacks, he and his wife hadn't made love since before Jacob had arrived and this was an opportunity, as well as the chance to enjoy her while it was raining. The rain was cool and the temperature dropped at little as the couple ducked away to their bed, the window slightly cracked for fresh air, the subtle breeze blew over their skin as they undressed one another. The couple was cautious when they kissed and touched, Obadiah felt his fingers ripple over her rib bones gliding up her sides. Mary Sue grasped her husband's shoulders as she lay with him, a few short years ago her hands couldn't palm them but now she could grasp his entire shoulder with one hand, further supporting the notion that he had lost very much weight.

Obadiah kissed his wife along the collar bones, his coarse facial hair stung on her skin when he kisses the softer parts of her, her nipples stood erect for him to kiss to further entice her. Mary Sue pulled herself closer to his body, his warmth wasn't as it was in the years prior but it still felt pleasurable against hers. Obadiah ran his hands down the sides of his wife, her hip bones jut from her side like a mountain protruding from the horizon, her hips were still soft, her skin felt like silk to his callused fingertips and her kisses were moist. The rain in the air added to the warmth moisture of her body, his fingertips were wet and her breathing held short pauses as Obadiah explored his wife like it was the first time. His touch made her quiver; his gentle motions of his fingers gave her goose bumps that he could feel with his lips on her neck. She raised her head up as her back arched and her top leg slung over his body forcing him even closer to her. Obadiah kept himself propped up with his left arm and ran his fingers through his wife's short dark hair, kissing on her neck and jaw line.

Mary Sue held Obadiah close with her right arm while her left arm helped to guide his right arm, his forearm muscles twitched and flexed while his hand worked. Obadiah fought off his lightheadedness as he worked; his wife deserved every ounce of energy he could give to her although he fatigued quickly. As he ran slim on his energy, Mary Sue gyrated her pelvis while holding his hand captive between her thighs, she had longed for his touch, his hands, his lips. Mary Sue let the world and all of its' damned problems disappear, the world had gone to hell and taken everyone with it, this moment she shared with her husband was the tiniest sliver of heaven imaginable, and this was her moment. Mary Sue felt her heart beat, her ears blurred out any sounds as the rain became a muffled sound behind her own breathing, her muscles tightened and spasmed as she wriggled on her husband's hand. He was dialed in on all the right places and she was nearing climax and her entire body was a slave to it.

Obadiah focused on his work, his precise movements were to further inch his wife to bliss, he enjoyed her as much as she did, her heavy breathing paused as she tried to control herself was a sure sign he making the right movements for her. Mary Sue laid back for a moment to regain her sight and to control her breathing. She let her hands roam the body of her husband as he ran his hands along her hips, stomach and chest, his touches made her skin dance, her muscle twitches and spasms made her body appear to seize and Obadiah smiled largely at his ability to still pleasure his wife. Mary Sue turned her focus on her husband now, his body responded to her touches, he became turgid in her hands and she further craved him. Their bodies rubbed and writhed together, the cool humidity laden air filled their lungs as they both gasped deeply for breathes while their activity increased.

Obadiah struggled to keep his focus on Mary Sue; her body felt incredible to him, the time without had been long. The desire to be with each other had been dormant, but it still grew deep within. Obadiah suffered quick flashes within his mind of so many things, when aroused while with his wife he thought of many of the ways he had taken his her, from areas in fields back home in South Carolina, their porch at their fresh new home here in Oklahoma, many, many of the times they had intimately shared their bodies, it all further excited him. Once or twice the vision of the attractive dancing Shanae had flashed in his mind; he often felt a tinge of guilt that another woman had entered his mind when he was being intimate with his partner. A few quick flashes in the mind of Obadiah sometimes lead way to other memories and it plagued Obadiah. Last time the couple had a love making session he was plagued with images of the fella, Mickey, and his life leaving his body as he choked the stranger to death. The images haunted Obadiah, troubling him even in the midst of love.

Obadiah couldn't tell his wife that his attraction to her couldn't overcome the haunting images of the murder he committed, this session he feared the images of bashing Willies head in, the head exploding with the second strike as Obadiah felt the raw power surge through him, not the worldly power of taking a man's life, but the harnessing of his inner most animalistic being surfacing, overcoming the tired and exhausted person he was, the small part of his oldest lineage from his caveman days had brought forth a rage to obliterate the skull of the man that attempted to take food from the mouths of his family. Had the drought and hardships changed the person he was or scratch the surface to expose what he had underneath?

Obadiah enjoyed the pleasures of Mary Sue, their passionate expressions of lust to one another was almost an offering to the gods of rain, like the Native Americans used to in the same area, before the settlers brutally killed them off and ran them out. As the couple found the shared rhythm of their heart beats, their bodies entwined and their breathing matched, they felt in unison with not only each other, but also with the land. The rain drowned out many of Obadiah's concerns, it washed away so many of his hard thoughts, it wiped the ghosts away from his mind, he let that moment with his adoring wife be the moment that would either be their truest and final embrace, or one that signaled a new beginning for the family.

The sounds of the drizzle muffled some of their bodily noises and they slid together, Obadiah deep within his wife, heart, soul and body. The couple grew weak and weary together, they remained in tight embrace as the rain continued to cleanse the world of many of its' problems, the rain also washed the soul of the depleted father and husband, he fell asleep in a way that he never had before. Obadiah finally fell asleep, his cleansed soul was finally light enough to restfully sleep, a sleep that had eluded him for years as the burdens he had amounted wore heavily on him.

Mary Sue felt her husband go limp, he held on for so long awaiting such a good rain, the rain had washed away the worries of a longer drought as the water fell from the sky and replenished the land. Mary Sue felt herself relax also, her body eased as peace overcame her, her children slept peacefully in their beds, the promise of fruitful gardens and government assistance cleared away uncertainty and reserve each and every day.

Mary Sue no longer had to feel guilty when she ate/She no longer had to wish with all of her might, with each meal that there was more. Her children hadn't eaten meat in months and her husband hadn't had more than a handful of food over the course of in months either/ He wasted away right before her eyes. There was no telling how much longer the family might have held on and there hadn't been anything but hope that each family member would wake up each morning, it was a waiting game each morning, one that Mary Sue no longer had to take part in. Each night as the family would tuck in there was the looming dread that someone might not wake up and it caused hair to fall from Mary Sue's head when she would brush her hair.

The two oldest children slept like any other night, oblivious to the world around them, their parents provided safety, their bellies hadn't been full in a long time but there was hardly days when they dealt with empty bellies either. They had a baby brother to join them and as they all grew, he would be right there with them. The family had peace finally come to them in the form of rain as it rumbled in with thousands of gallons to sprinkle in the drought plagued area that so desperately needed it. The rain initiated the beginnings of many more storms, rain that would support the life and restore buffalo grass and the trees of the Shelter-belts, birds, rabbits, ground hogs and the chirping crickets slowly returned to the prairies. As the rains broke free from the clouds in which imprisoned them, life had no longer been held captive within the sky and slowly found its' way to the ground.

Jacob passed away a week after the rain first returned, his pneumonia had too tight a grip on the tiny body, he was nursing in the morning and his breathing had simply stopped. By the time the tired Mary Sue caught on that his breathing had ceased it was already too late and the infant had already begun to turn blue and there was nothing that could be done. Mary Sue wept for days, losing her baby after all of the struggles it took to bring him into the world, losing a child, there is nothing to terrible in life and Mary Sue took it real hard.

Obadiah blamed himself for what happened to his youngest son, the sins of the father had caught up with him and his son paid the ultimate price. Obadiah took on work planting more of the Shelterbelt trees. The long days spent walking and planting brought him to a place that he could hide from what he had done. His burdens hadn't been washed away, nor could they ever be, even as the rains broke

Uncle Isaac and Aunt Elizabeth both farmed all of the family property with their father over the years, working diligently and then moving to different areas of the country when they became adults. Isaac joined the military and lost his life in the Korean War. His service to the great country was an honorable one. But it was another lost son that Obadiah felt responsible for, as if the costs of his sins were paid for by his sons.

Elizabeth had a hard time staying with her parents during the holidays, but she did visit. She made the drive over from South Carolina occasionally. My mother Ingrid was the fourth Withers' child to arrive; the third on the farm,. She followed the birth of Jacob by almost three years. It had taken some time for the Withers to reconnect after the loss of Jacob and Obadiah working to rebuild the family farm and livelihood that he owed his family.

I spent the last month of Obadiah's life with him; I was bedside right beside hospice as he recalled his life to me. Obadiah had held on just long enough to tell his story; he carried most of this for decades and finally wanted to unburden his heavy heart with the hope of eternal peace. Mary Sue preceded her husband in death by thirty three days. She passed peacefully in her sleep and that is an ultimate blessing. Obadiah knew that with all that he had done to save his family, he hadn't earned the privilege to die peacefully.

Obadiah lost both sons, a price he felt he had to pay for the two lives he himself had taken, ghosts that attached to his soul for eternity. As he aged Obadiah saw the faces of the men he had killed. Rarely did he feel haunted unless he drank, but they were present to him nonetheless. Obadiah never drank that I knew of. He told me he drank once after the drought had subsided and after drinking with his wife, the two souls growled and called at him. The voices vibrated in his ears and made his soul tremble.

I hardly knew my grandfather because his physical deterioration as he aged made it hard for him to get around during the holidays. When I did get to visit, he often sat quietly in a recliner and watched westerns. He usually snored through most things anyway. Obadiah had finished telling me his life story, given his full confession and hardly five minutes had passed before he did. Obadiah joined his wife in the afterlife. The only reason he waited so long was due to the need to lighten his heart. Without the great love the Withers shared, I would not be here, but without the deep seeded need to protect and provide for his family, there is no telling who would be.

Obadiah felt that the loss of his two sons were a debt he owed for taking the lives of two others' sons. He carried a heavy grief and his wife had to suffer alongside him for actions that he had committed. His family had suffered for his actions and he carried that with him his entire life; Self-inflicted shackles. Obadiah had finally lost his wife, and other than needing to confess, he had no reason to hold on, thirty three days he had lived without his Mary Sue, that was all he could do; thirty three days. When the rains broke from the sky in Oklahoma and ended the drought, the grasses slowly returned and Obadiah slowly fought less to provide, his demons still plagued him but his driven sense of duty had kept him on through the remainder of his days, and the love he had for his wife, gave him purpose.

Obadiah felt the guiltiest at the thought of ever having considered leaving behind his wife. He never admitted it until after her passing, but he suspected she could sense the black mark on his soul. Obadiah had kept his family alive, mostly; he provided for them and even at risk of self-sacrifice, he still carried on as a father should. Obadiah had hoped to join his wife and two sons in the afterlife if he truly confessed and finally unburdened himself. I was out of work and selected to sit with my grandfather whom was a stranger to me my entire life and listen to his story. I learned so many things about the man and his family who struggled to survive, even past the moment that the rains broke from the skies above Oklahoma. The man made every sacrifice imaginable but his lifelong guilt was a chain from which he was never free.

www.ingramcontent.com/pod-product-compliance
Lightning Source LLC
Chambersburg PA
CBHW071241170626
46809CB00001B/33